"An actress, sometime book reviewer and Phi Beta Kappa from Smith College, (Joanna Barnes) tells the story of a child star growing up alienated in Hollywood.... Miss Barnes is an excellent guide for tourists in the land of the plastic cactus. She is surprisingly generous. She is witty.... Her book is an absorbing look at one of the circles of hell Dante didn't anticipate."

—*The New York Times*

"**THE DECEIVERS** seems at first glance the same territory we've explored with Harold Robbins and Jacqueline Susann, the film world, the tinsel people with more tinsel inside, the wheeling and dealing, the narcissism, the decadence. Yet, astonishingly, the book works. We have indeed been here before, in Hollywood columns and fan magazines, in word-of-mouth scandal, and in the contemporary legends of the gods and goddesses who live out the subterranean sex fantasies of puritan America. What is different is the intelligence and skill displayed by Miss Barnes. She is a gifted storyteller and a compelling writer. The ultimate test is that we turn each page with curiosity and anticipation."

—*Los Angeles Times*

THE DECEIVERS
was originally published by
Arbor House.

Dedication

"I get by with a little help from my friends . . ."

—JOHN LENNON–PAUL MCCARTNEY

"Happiness depends upon two things: good health and a poor memory."

—INGRID BERGMAN

"There's no deodorant like success."

—ELIZABETH TAYLOR

The POCKET BOOK edition is published by arrangement with
Arbor House Publishing Co., Inc.
Printed in the U.S.A.

Contents

THE
DECEIVERS

1

Laura

9:55 A.M.

I wish there weren't so many people. It will be so crowded in the church. Maybe not. They can't all be here for the service, only the ones dressed for it. I wonder how the others found out. Did it give the name of the church in the paper? Did it say, "Coming Attractions at the Community Presbyterian Church on Rodeo Drive . . ." Now how in hell would I know, I haven't seen a paper in days. Maybe the country's at war and I don't know it. That would be a laugh.

Look at them. Sport shirts and muumuus all over the church lawn. The Presbyterians aren't going to be thrilled with the reseeding bills. They're probably used to it by now, though. I wonder if they just forward the bills to the studio. I'd like to see Jack's face if they did. But I will see Jack's face. Jack and Lisa will be inside. Oh God, why couldn't I have stuck with thinking about the reseeding bills. If all the Japanese gardeners in Beverly Hills worked one hour each . . .

"We're here. Do you want me to go first?"

I'm afraid. I don't want to leave the car. I'm afraid of the crowd. No, that's not it. It's not the gawkers I'm afraid of. I don't want to see the people inside. I don't want them looking at me the way they will.

"I'm afraid, Obie."

"Don't be. Ruth and I will be on either side of you."

Terrific. That ought to please Ruth, making an entrance with the star of the show. I wonder how much her basic black outfit set Obie back. Pity they don't give screen credits for costuming at funerals.

"Are you ready? We have to go in, Laura. It's ten o'clock already."

"Don't let go of me, Obie. The crowd makes me nervous."

1

"*I won't. Driver, you can open the door now. Come on, Ruth.*"

Do they have to come toward me like that? Jesus, talk about your lynch mob. Damn. That was stupid of me. Why do I always look when they yell "Look this way, Miss Curtis." The flashbulb. I can't see. Why can't they let us through? My God, they're not human, they're animals. I can't see. I should have worn my dark glasses. I thought they'd look too Hollywood. That's dumb, with me in studio makeup anyway. I wonder if Obie explained to the reporters about the makup. What will they think of me, false eyelashes and lip gloss? He said he'd tell them I had to go right to work after the services. Thank heavens for that. Where else would I go? Back home? No. Anyplace, but not back home. How long do you suppose I can go on staying with Obie and Ruth? Is there some way they can move me out of the house without my having to go back there? Obie can do it. Agents can always think of something. That's what they're paid for. But I'll bet Obie never bargained for this. What the hell, it won't hurt him to sweat a little for the money. He can move me out, and Ruth can shop for an apartment for me. Obie will love that. It'll keep her out of Saks Fifth Avenue for five minutes.

"*Let her through, please. Let her through.*"

I know that man. I've seen his face before. Did he come to the house? Is he the one who asked me all those questions until the doctor made him stop? Yes, I remember him now. Good God, he's a cop. What's he doing here and out of uniform? I don't want to see him. I don't want to see anybody from before. Get me away from this.

"*That's a stupid question. No, she won't give you an autograph. Get out of the way.*"

That's telling them, Obie. Oh, Lord, we're in. It's cool after the sun outside. The organ music. I wonder who told them what to play. I didn't have any idea when they asked me. "What were his favorite melodies, Mrs. Stanton?" What was I supposed to tell them? I don't even know. I couldn't tell them "Yesterday," but that's the only one I remember. Jesus, wouldn't that have been a hoot? All these people sitting so solemn in the pews, and the organist comes out with "Yesterday."

I will not look at them. I will walk straight down to the

front and not look at them. I'll sit where they put me and I won't look at anyone. Not anyone.

The air smells so sweet. How many different kinds of flowers, I wonder. Carnations. I can smell roses, too. And another one, so sweet, maybe orange blossoms. No, those are for weddings. Freesia maybe. There are so many. How many, do you suppose, were actually sent for Mike? I wonder if any of them were. I wonder if there is a single, solitary bunch of flowers here that was sent for Mike. I can hear them all telling their secretaries to call the florist and have some flowers sent to the church for Laura Curtis' husband. And not one of them sending anything for Mike. His mother, maybe, if they told her. I wonder if she even understood. I hope I never get so old I don't know what's happening. Not true. Today I don't want to know. How convenient to be old and senile today, in a nursing home like his mother, and none of it getting through to me.

"Laura. Here. This is for you."

"Obie? I don't want a flower."

"It's for you to put on the casket, afterward."

Oh my God, oh my sweet Jesus Christ.

"We thought it would be a nice thing for you to do."

Don't let me laugh. Please Lord, don't let me laugh. Obie is choreographing this whole show. Leave it to him. A nice thing for me to do. Whatever happened to nice things? Real nice things. Real things. Were there ever any? Is it like that riddle about the man who dreamed last night he was a butterfly, and this morning he doesn't know if he is a man who last night dreamed he was a butterfly or a butterfly who now dreams he is a man? Was any of it ever real? Or if it was, when did it stop? Or was it all real and I just don't want to believe any of it? Maybe it doesn't even matter. I can just go on doing my thing, saying my lines, standing on my marks, finding my key light, and it will be enough to keep making pictures and playing different parts, and I won't have to be me at all. I can go out at night and play at being Laura Curtis for the photographers and the gossip writers and the people who just stare. I won't ever have to be me. I won't think of anything except just what I'm doing at the exact moment I'm doing it. I won't ever think back. I won't ever have to go back to that house.

I did it. Damn. That's just what I said I wouldn't do. I

*thought back to the house and I wasn't going to think of any-
thing but the moment.*

*But I can't do it now. I can't think of what's happening
now. I don't want to listen to what that minister is saying.*

*No. It's him. It's that same one who married us. This isn't
even his church. He has that little chapel in Pacific Palisades
where you can see the sunset on the ocean through the altar
windows. Who thought to get him here? Whoever is directing
this whole scene, that's who. I'll kill Obie if it was him. It
damn well was him, you know it. Probably he thought the
other church wasn't big enough or maybe he thought a Beverly Hills church had more status. And he went and dug up
the minister who came out to the boat and married us because it would look good in the papers. Obie thinks of everything.*

*Not everything. Some things it doesn't pay for him to
think about. He doesn't think of those things. It never enters
his mind to question, not with this being Jack's picture and
Jack a client. And me a client. And Marty a client. No
wonder he threw himself into planning the service. Those are
a lot of things not to think about.*

*And I will not, I will not, I will not think about anything. I
could go over my lines for the scene this afternoon. I could
think of things to say to the people who are thinking of
things to say to me on the way out of the church. I could
recite a poem.*

> *There once was a man from Bengal*
> *Who went to a fancy dress ball.*
> *He went just for fun,*
> *Dressed up as a bun,*
> *And a dog ate him up in the hall.*

"LEWIS? What are you teaching that child?"

"It's just a harmless limerick, Flo." He winked in Laura's
direction.

"Well, she needs a real poem for public-speaking class, not
some jingle. Laura-Louise, how long does the poem have to
be?" Her grandmother held out the dish towel for Laura to
come into the kitchen and help dry.

"I like this poem. It's silly," she giggled.

"Don't sass. How long does the poem have to be?"

"At least twelve lines. Mrs. Abrams said anything shorter, and it can't be in the contest." She slid off the sofa and loped resignedly into the kitchen.

"We have to think of something. Did you ever read 'Kubla Khan'? No, that's too old for you. Get me a chair, Laura-Louise, you know what the doctor said about me standing too long. Now, let's us just think. What's a good poem for a twelve-year-old girl?"

"Thirteen. I'll be thirteen by the time of the contest. It's two weeks from yesterday." She separated the knives and forks and spoons into neat piles on the oilcloth of the kitchen table.

"So you will." Had they really had Laura-Louise for seven years? Yes, that was right because Lewis had retired that year, and now he was seventy-two. She remembered what Lucy had said, "You and Dad will both be here all the time. She'll have two parents instead of one. And I'm hardly one, what with having to be at work all day." And Lucy had gone to Fall River to get a factory job and send them money to take care of Laura-Louise. Or maybe that's not why she went at all. Devon was a small town where people knew your mother's and your grandmother's maiden names and never forgot anything about where you came from. Fall River was a bigger place and there, guessed Florence, people didn't know and didn't care.

Lucy had been good to her word. She did send the money. For a while at least. Florence wondered what the postmark would be on Laura-Louise's birthday card this year. Or if there would be one. Cards had come from Boston for a while, then two from Newark and one from Miami. Last year there had been none at all. The child semed not to notice.

Perhaps it was true that they had spoiled Lucy, given her too much because she had come into their lives so late, when they had just about given up hope. But Lucy was all they had. After they were gone, there would be only Lucy to show they had ever existed at all. You could hardly blame them for having ambitions for her, for wanting her to have the best. Now Lucy was somewhere far away from small-town Devon, pursuing the best. She hoped she found it. Lucy was

still their daughter, wherever her travels took her, and
Florence bore her no malice. Besides, they had Laura-Louise,
didn't they?

The time would come, she knew, when they might have to
give up the child. Last winter Lewis had had a mild stroke,
and her own heart was giving her trouble these days. She had
tried, in an oblique way, to prepare Laura-Louise for what
might happen.

Children were funny little things. When the subject came
up Laura-Louise would appear to listen and understand; then
always she did the same thing. She shrugged her shoulders,
accepting wordlessly the fact that people, for whatever reason, moved on, leaving others alone behind them.

"What?"

"I'm sorry, child, what did you say?"

"You made a sound. I thought you said something."

"No," Florence replied. "I was still trying to think of a
poem. Lewis? Lewis Curtis?" she called in the direction of
the sitting room. "Bring Laura-Louise's poetry book in here."

He came into the kitchen, shuffling in that odd gait he had
had since he was ill. He placed the book on the yellow-and-
white checked oilcloth and the three of them began turning
pages, looking for a suitable poem.

Laura always remembered that night. The sun had just
gone down. Outside the kitchen window, the purple grape hy-
acinths that were coming up where the same color as the evening sky. By the time they had settled on Wordsworth's
"Daffodils" it was dark, and a soft fog had come in from the
harbor. Out beyond the breakwater, the fog-horn mooed like
a drowsy cow, and it was time for her to go to bed.

She slid between the cool sheets. Tomorrow, in class, Mrs.
Abrams would coach her for the contest. More than anything
Laura wanted to be like Mrs. Abrams, to speak in that beautiful soft way without the flat New England sounds that her
grandmother and grandfather used, and everyone else around
here, for that matter. Her mother, she knew, didn't speak
that way anymore, not now that she lived far away from this
place. In time, Laura promised herself, she would speak as
beautifully as Mrs. Abrams and her mother. She would make
them all proud of her. Even the kids in school who teased
her about her name would have to sit up and take notice.

If, and she crossed her fingers on the blanket, she won this contest, she could then compete in the big contest for kids from all over Cape Cod. If she was very good, she might even make it to the finals for the whole state.

The school in Boston was enormous. How on earth, Laura wondered, did any of the kids find their way to classes? The only reassuring thing about it was that the long, hollow halls smelled exactly like her school in Devon, a stale mixture of disinfectant and books.

Looking back later, she realized that she recalled nothing about reciting her poem. She heard her name and school called out and went to the center of the auditorium stage. She was not the least bit afraid. The people in the dimness out front were strangers. Unlike the people in Devon, they knew nothing about her. They didn't care that she had her grand-parent's name and none of her own. For the first time in her life, she liked the sound of the name Laura-Louise Curtis. Miss Laura-Louise Curtis of the Miles Standish School looked at the rows of faces waiting just for her to speak, waiting for nothing else in the world except what she was about to do, and she realized that not only was she not afraid, but she had never felt so wanted in all her life. She began to recite.

"Mrs. Curtis. Are you Mrs. Curtis?" The woman's thick heels clacked on the granite floor of the school hallway.

"No. I am Mrs. Abrams."

"I'm sorry. I . . . is the child's mother here?"

"No, she is not. I am Laura-Louise's teacher," Mrs. Abrams replied guardedly.

"Oh." The woman looked down at Laura with a brisk thrust of her head. "What nice green eyes. You were very good, dear. I think you should have won. The girl who won isn't nearly as pretty as you." She looked up sharply to Mrs. Abrams. "Do you live nearby?"

"No."

"May I speak with you a moment?" She ran one hand through her close-cropped, graying hair. "I'm a little pressed for time. We have a situation here . . ." Her voice trailed off as she drew them to one side of the corridor. She opened a classroom door and, relieved to find the place empty, pushed them in ahead of her. "Do you mind?" she asked, not waiting for an answer. She seated herself on top of a desk, crossed her legs, and pushed her glasses up into her hair. "We are simply up the creek, if you know what I mean," she told Mrs. Abrams. "We must have this child. We need her. Desperately." She fished frantically in the pocket of her tweed suit. "Here," she said, pulling a card out of a little black leather wallet and handing it to Mrs. Abrams. "I'm sorry. You must think I'm nuts." She brought a package of cigarets out of the other pocket and lit one with her lighter. "I'm Drucilla Lang," she said to both of them.

"What is it you want, Miss Lang?" Mrs. Abrams asked coolly.

"What happened is . . . Is it Mrs. Abrams you said?"

She nodded.

"Well, what happened, Mrs. Abrams, is that I came up to Boston with a little girl named Jennifer Cauley, not that that means anything to you. I'm her agent, and the child's mother has four other kids to look after. I volunteered to come up with Jennifer to do this soap commercial that we're shooting on the swanboats in the Public Garden for two days, starting tomorrow. Jennifer got sick on the train from New York. It turns out the child's mother never told me she'd been exposed to measles. They do that, you know. Anything for the job. So there's Jennifer, propped up in bed at the Copley, ordering from room service and breaking out all over the place. Meanwhile, the whole crew is in town, and the director and the agency man and I are all going out of our skulls looking for a pretty little girl who can speak well enough to say a few lines on camera. We called the superintendent of schools to see if he had any leads. He suggested we dolly over here to take a look at the speech finalists." She coughed and stubbed out the cigaret on the sole of her shoe. "You see what I mean about being desperate. The agency is having apoplexy at the thought of footing the bill for a whole crew until we find a child. We already have a bunch of extras on the payroll. Background people," she explained for Laura's benefit.

Laura was trying to make sense out of her words. The woman was certainly wound up about the whole thing.

"You do see what I mean, don't you? There's a lot involved here. It all rests on finding the right child. We're up the creek," she repeated. "Screen Actors' Guild has nothing."

"I'm sorry——" began Mrs. Abrams, moving toward the door.

"Don't go!" Miss Lang almost shouted. She lowered her tone. "Please, don't be hasty. Just let me introduce you to the others, the director and the agency man. We're all perfectly reputable, I assure you, in spite of the fact that I may sound a little frantic. Besides, there's money in this. It's really quite a nice piece of change for you," she smiled fleetingly at Laura-Louise. "Come with me." She darted past them into the hall.

"Here we are. Here we are." She was waving at two men coming toward them.

"This is Laura-Louise Curtis, and this is Mrs. Abrams, her teacher. Mr. Doug Coleman and Mr. Ivan Lester. Boys," she said to the two men, "why don't you explain this thing? I may have scared them to death." She lit another cigaret as Mr. Coleman began to speak.

They were in the principal's office. Mr. Coleman had placed a phone call and now he was talking to the Curtises.

"The child will be in good hands. Mrs. Abrams has consented to stay in Boston at our expense for the two extra days, if the idea meets with your approval. She would be with Laura-Louise all the time the child is working. There are stringent rules about a parent or guardian being present on the set. We're also talking about a very short time here. There are equally strict rules about the number of hours youngsters are allowed to work. Are you still with me, Mr. Curtis?" He drew invisible circles on the glass-topped desk with his finger. "As for the other details, Social Security and so forth, we'll take care of all that. If you have any questions, please don't hesitate to call me." He smiled at Drucilla Lang and nodded affirmatively. As an afterthought, he smiled at Laura-Louise. "Here," he handed the phone to Mrs. Abrams, "he wants to talk to you."

"That was not so easy," he said to Ivan Lester. "Those people aren't used to these things. Seems they live in a rather isolated area. They don't even own a television set. Laura-Louise," he took her hand and shook it, "you're going to be on TV. Maybe your grandparents will let you buy a set with your earnings so you can watch yourself."

Finally someone had spoken to her. "My grandfather says television isn't good for your eyes," she told him.

"There are days when it doesn't do my heart any good, either," remarked Drucilla. "Next year I am but definitely going to retire and go into something quieter, like maybe spot-welding."

"What do I have to do?"

"All you have to do, honey," said Ivan, "is enjoy yourself riding the swanboats and say a few words the way I tell you. What could be easier?"

He was right. Nothing could have been easier. For the next two days Laura was fussed over and attended as she had never been before, and all just for riding the swanboats in the warm June sunshine and saying "So soft and smooth, swan-white and pure." For this she was given a new dress, two in fact, both alike, so that one could be pressed while she wore the other. The wardrobe lady smoothed Laura's skirt continually, flicking off imaginary specks of dirt. The hairdresser stroked her light brown hair with his brush and pinned it into soft curls. A makeup man reddened her cheeks with rouge of which Laura knew her grandmother disapproved, thereby doubling her pleasure. Strollers in the Public Garden stopped to watch her. Ivan, as Mr. Lester had insisted she call him, spoke to her gently before each take and gave her a hug if the shot was printed. Mrs. Abrams sat under a nearby elm, reading. Laura smiled to herself. Usually teachers made you come to them, but this time the teacher had come to her. She loved every minute of it. Too bad, she thought, that it's only two days.

In retelling the episode over and over to her grandparents, each time she remembered some small detail she had left out, like the way movie men made "fog" by spraying the lens with dulling spray and puffing bee smoke all around with funny little cans that had bellows on them. She watched her grandparents' faces, wanting them to share her excitement, but the events were all too distant and meaningless to them. They were bored. It hurt her that they could not understand. After a while, she gave up speaking about it.

Summer in Devon was a heavy time. It hung as still and unmoving as the motionless green leaves drooping over the quiet country roads. An occasional thunderstorm only weighted the air more, rained darkly, and made the stillness afterward all the more noticeable.

Laura took short walks with her grandfather. She picked raspberries and sold them to the store at the crossroads. She read her way through the adventures of Nancy Drew and Cherry Ames, Student Nurse. When the tide was in, she went to the stony beach below the house where she would swim to one of the large rocks that dotted out into the water from a spit of land. Here she sat on her haunches, her arms clasped around her tanned knees, idly watching the small waves rise and ebb around her.

Months later, she could only remember that summertime as a drowsy, dreamy void from which she was so suddenly awakened.

"Lewis," her grandmother called, "you'll have to take this." Laura heard them whispering together before he took the telephone from her hand.

"Yes? Yes, I recall." He was speaking cautiously, his back to the room. He listened for a long time to the person on the other end.

"I don't know," he said. "I don't know what to think. You'll have to give us some time." He paused. "An hour? I don't see how——" He raised a hand as if to stop the speaker. "This is a big decision for us." He turned and looked directly at Laura who found herself suddenly uncomfortable that whatever was going on was aimed at her. "In an hour. All right, I suppose so, if that's what you have to do. Goodbye." He hung up the phone and shook his head. "She's going to call back."

Laura sat perfectly still on the sofa.

"That was Miss Lang."

For a moment she had no idea who he meant.

"The lady you met in Boston last spring. She has asked your grandmother and me," he cleared his throat, "to let you go to New York with her to act in a television play."

Laura drew in her breath.

"It would be for three weeks. You would be back Labor Day weekend, a week before school starts." He waited, looking at Laura, but she couldn't think of what to say.

"It seems the people who are making this program saw the

commercial you did, and Miss Lang says they will pay you one thousand dollars. One thousand dollars," he repeated slowly. Her grandmother pursed her lips at the mention of the sum.

"You might want to think about it, Laura-Louise. It's a fact that your grandmother and I have tried to set aside some money for your future, in case you decide to go to secretarial school or college or some such, but this amount of money might be very helpful someday." He smiled sympathetically, interpreting her silence as timidity. "And you'll be back in plenty of time for shool. Miss Lang says you can stay with her. Well? How do you feel about it?"

"Yes," she said simply.

Paul Callum bypassed his director's chair and walked over to where Laura and Drucilla sat in the shade of a large umbrella. It was getting late in the day. Seagulls mewed overhead, and the ocean off Montauk was turning the color of brass. For a week they had rehearsed *The Wild Geese* in the soot and grime of a stifling rehearsal hall in the city. Now, instead of toeing chalk marks on the floor, meant to show where the sets would be, they were outdoors among the boats, the beaches, and the lighthouse that the studio had built for them.

"I have to hand it to you, Dru," Paul said, lighting up his pipe. "Face it. We bought a blind item. The others never would have gone for it if we hadn't been in such a time jam. I want you to know I stuck up for you. I told them I'd worked with your agency for almost ten years on and off and you'd never stiffed me yet." He shot Laura an appraising glance, then grinned.

"The others were yelling about a pig in a poke, but I said Dru Lang's word was as good as they come. If you said the kid was perfect and could hack it, then the kid was perfect and could hack it, as far as I was concerned. But it did take a little railroading to ram it through." He shifted his pipe in his mouth. "After all, to say you want an unknown is one thing, but somebody this inexperienced is something else again. I sure would like to see their faces when we get this show cut together."

"Hear that, Laura?" smiled Drucilla. "So far, so good. Let's try not to disappoint Paul."

"I'll try," Laura replied dutifully.

"That's enough for me," said Paul. "Stick out your arm. Here comes Maury with the fuller's earth."

"I hate being so dirty," she said, extending her arms as the makeup man daubed her with smudges from his little cloth bag. "My hair won't come untangled, and it blows into my mouth when the wind machines are on."

"You're playing a ragamuffin, aren't you?" retorted Paul. "Some other time you can do the fairy princess bit." He smiled and strode off toward the set.

"One thing, Laura," cautioned Dru as soon as the makeup man had moved out of earshot. "You must learn never to complain when you are on salary. You may request, but you may never complain. You took the job, and even if it had turned out to be hell on earth, it was your decision, and you're stuck with it until the show is over."

"I didn't mean to complain. It's just that I couldn't think of anything else to say, and he was being so nice that I thought I ought to say something."

"That's all right. Come on, they're calling you to rehearse."

They walked down the path to the salt marsh where the men were tilting their reflectors to catch the last rays of the afternoon sun.

"Light is getting yellow, boys," someone yelled. "Let's move our asses. I've got a hot shower and a cold beer waiting for me back at the motel."

"Is that all?" yelled somebody else, and they laughed.

Drucilla frowned and went over to whisper to Paul. He nodded and took the bullhorn from his assistant director.

"Now hear this. This is your captain speaking. I see no reason why we should be treating Miss Curtis to a liberal education before she's even out of school. Am I making myself clear? Let's watch the language from here on in. I'd hate to lose any of you because the child welfare people got a complaint. Now let's get on with this thing before it strikes midnight."

Laura took her place next to Harris Bolding for their scene. She liked Harris. He had told her to call him by his first name, but Dru forbade it. He was, after all, the most famous Shakespearean actor in both England and America. Laura had seen pictures of him, dressed in elegant velvet and gold costumes with capes and swords. It was strange to see him now with a scraggly beard, a humped back, and dressed in old, paint-smeared clothes.

"Hello, there, pussycat," he greeted her. "Ready for a go at this?"

She nodded up at him.

"That was a nice little speech Paul just made. Rather comforting to know that, for as long as one is a star, one is always protected. Shall we run through the words?"

Harris Bolding said she was a star. If he said so, it must be true. She didn't feel like a star. She looked at Harris in his wrinkled trousers and torn sweater and wondered if he felt like a star.

When they had finished the outdoor shooting, the company moved back to Manhattan to film the interior scenes. Workdays, an air-conditioned limousine called for Laura and Dru at seven in the morning. Drucilla said she had insisted on that in the contract.

They went directly to the studio, to a windowless makeup room with glaring fluorescent lights that gave everyone a sickly, greenish cast. A delivery boy brought their breakfasts in paper bags; grapefruit juice and cornflakes with milk and sugar for Laura, black coffee for Dru. Most of the time everything leaked and made a mess. Laura could never figure out how she was expected to eat the breakfast while she was lying back in a chair with Maury making up her face. She wolfed down what she could before the wardrobe lady became impatient for her to dress. Rosie would stand in the doorway of the makeup room, shifting her immense weight from one swollen leg to the other, waiting to swoop down on Laura like a huge motherly eagle and deposit her in the dressing room. Laura knew Rosie was afraid of being blamed if they were late on the set. Jobs were scarce, she had told Laura, because things were slow in New York. So Rosie was never kept waiting.

The studio was nothing like what Laura had imagined. Someone said that it had once been a warehouse. It was enormous, a city block long, and smelled of old wood, drying paint, and dust. The windows had been blacked out, and except for the little island of light where the camera was set up, it was dark and gloomy. It was also dirty, and no matter how careful you were, your hands were filthy in half an hour. The floor was crisscrossed with cables that lay coiled underfoot like large black snakes. You had to watch your step in the darkness. When they were not shooting, the men would turn on giant fans to stir up the hot, stuffy air. They didn't seem to do much good, and they had to be turned off whenever the camera was rolling because the noise would interfere. "Kill the blowers," the assistant director would yell, and always a couple of people laughed or made some sort of a joke up in the catwalks overhead where they were setting lights.

The crew brought their lunches from home and spent mealtime playing poker on the set. The others—Paul Callum, his assistant, the cameraman, the script girl, and some whose function Laura didn't quite know—took their sandwiches and ambled next door to a projection room in an adjoining building. Paul and Drucilla had decided to let Laura go to the dailies. Harris Bolding never attended. "Dear girl, there's nothing worse than having yesterday's mistakes reviewed in front of you today. It's rather like belching up a bad dinner. Besides, it's too late to do anything about them."

Paul and Dru felt differently. At first they had been a little hesitant, but they finally agreed that Laura could get a better idea of why Paul asked for certain things by watching the film they had shot each previous day.

"As an actress," Paul instructed her, "you can learn what your mistakes are when you see the rushes. That's where all the faults show. When the film has been cut together by a good editor and the music track is laid in, even a rotten actor can be made to look adequate."

Laura and Dru always sat in the second row from the back in dailies. Behind them, at a large console with the intercom and telephones, sat the producer and associate producer, the director, the editor, and some people from the network.

"Okay," Paul pressed the intercom to the projecting room, "let"s roll." They settled back and opened their lunch bags, fumbling in the darkness.

At first, Laura had been shocked to see herself. She knew she was the girl on the screen, but somehow she could not identify with the image up there. It was she, yes, but it was somebody else, too. For one thing, the girl was prettier than she believed herself to be. Laura, who was a slim girl, thought the girl on the screen looked a little fuller, not so thin. She did have a bad habit of slumping, especially during the scenes shot late in the day when she was tired. Dru called her attention to it several times.

Harris' closeup was on the screen now. He had a beautiful voice, thick and rich, like clotted cream. Laura loved to watch his scenes.

"Shit," his film image said, looking into the camera at them. "I blew the bloody line." The screen went black and the lights came on.

"Well, there's a piece of film for the Christmas party," chuckled Paul. "What's the verdict?" he asked his producer.

"Don't we have any more footage on that first scene?"

"That's the stuff the lab printed up wrong. It'll be here tomorrow."

"Right. Laura, will you come here?"

"Yes, sir."

"Laura, this is Chick Feldman from network publicity," he introduced the man next to him. "He wants to get some material on you for a biography."

"Marvelous performance, Miss Curtis." He shook her hand. "Mind if I walk back to the set with you?"

"Devon?" he was asking, "what's that near?" He had carefully avoided sitting in either of the two chairs marked "Laura Curtis" and "Director" as protocol demanded. Laura called to the prop man to bring a chair for Mr. Feldman.

"And you honestly never acted before?" He seated himself, scribbling her answers into a notebook.

"She did one commercial. That's where I found her." Drucilla was sitting next to him, balanced uncomfortably on a case of film. "I knew the minute I saw her that she had something special. It's my business to spot those things."

"What about your parents, Miss Curtis? How do they feel about having a television star for a daughter?"

"I live with my grandparents."

"I see. And where are your parents?"

Laura glanced at Dru.

"She hasn't got any."

"An orphan?"

"That's right," replied Dru quickly, not looking at her.

"An orphan," he wrote in his book. "That's great for our purposes. Makes a terrific angle. Laura Curtis. Is that your real name? Can't be. It's too good to be true."

"We're on a bell, folks," called the assistant, "let's have a little quiet over there. Sorry, Laura."

"All right, roll it," commanded Paul.

"Roll it!" echoed the assistant.

"Rolling. Speed."

"Scene thirty-eight Baker, take one."

"Action!" said Paul.

"That's Harris Bolding's entrance," whispered Laura. They waited silently through several takes until they heard, "Cut. Print."

"What's next for you, after this?" Feldman asked her.

"I have to go back to school." She shrugged.

"But you'll be established." He seemed surprised. "The word of mouth on this show is already fantastic."

"She's just an average child," interrupted Drucilla. "Of course, under special circumstances and for the right vehicle, perhaps some arrangements could be made. The quality that makes Laura a valuable property, Mr. Feldman, is the very fact that she is not some forty-five-year-old midget but an average and very beguiling young girl."

Laura listened to them talking about her. She felt the same way she did when she saw herself on the screen, almost as if it were someone else they were discussing, yet knowing it was she.

When they arrived at the apartment each evening, Dru would take off her shoes in the elevator and pad down the hall in her stockinged feet. Laura did the same. Her feet always hurt after standing under the hot lights for so many hours. It was seven-thirty when they got home. Dru unlocked the door and scooped up a telegram from the floor.

"Laura, do me a favor and turn on the oven. Four hundred degrees." She sank down on the sofa and tore at the envelope.

When Laura came back into the room, Drucilla was standing. Her face was pale and motionless, as if to move it might break it.

"Laura," her voice was strained, "I have to go downstairs to make a telephone call. Don't open the door for anyone." She made her way to the door as if she were trying hard to keep her balance.

Laura removed her makeup and put the frozen chicken

pies in the oven. She set the table and broke up the lettuce and watercress for the salad. Drucilla was staying away a long time. Why hadn't she used her own phone? It was almost an hour before she heard her key in the lock.

"Laura." She looked drained and upset. "Please come here." She motioned toward the sofa.

"There is—not possibly——" her voice caught in her throat, and she put an arm around Laura as if to protect her. "Oh God." She hugged her closer and took a deep breath. "Laura, I have just spoken to your grandfather."

Suddenly Laura knew.

"Your grandmother—passed away this morning. It happened very quickly. Laura," she took her face in her hands, "she had no pain. These things just—happen. She was not a young woman. Her heart just stopped beating. It happened very quickly," she repeated.

Laura was silent.

"You mustn't be afraid to cry."

"I'm not."

Drucilla looked at her. "There's something else." She paused. "Your grandfather has had a terrible wrench. He isn't feeling well. He is very concerned that he might not be able to take care of you right now. He has asked if you could stay here with me for the time being, perhaps start school here in a few weeks, until . . . " Her voice trailed off, not knowing how to end the sentence. "It's not that he doesn't want you there. He wants what's best for you. He isn't well. He just—can't handle the situation right now. I've asked him to have your school clothes sent." She waited for a reaction. "You know I'm happy to have you stay."

That was when Laura began to cry. It was the thought of anyone taking the things from her closet, her own things from her own room, and sending them away, as if she could be so easily erased. The tears, although Drucilla did not know it, were tears of rage.

Laura held an ice bag over her swollen eyes while Dru cued her from the script.

"You are going to have to be a pro about this. You must do your very best tomorrow. Your grandmother wouldn't want any less than that, would she?"

Laura shook her head.

"I know it's hard. Sometimes things happen that force us to grow up very fast. We have to be realistic. Schedules don't wait for anything. Besides, working helps you keep your mind off things. Let's try it again from the top, shall we?"

"Good Lord, kid," Maury examined her face under the fluorescent lights, "how did you get those circles under your eyes? You look like a goddam raccoon."

"Family problems," Dru cut him off brusquely. "Let's drop it."

But somehow everybody knew. Laura sensed they were being especially thoughtful. Paul spoke to her very softly, and the assistant director, Fred, instead of yelling for her as he usually did, came to her dressing room, put an arm around her shoulders, and led her to the set when she was needed. In spite of everything, Laura felt warm and comforted to know so many people cared about her. Dru had been right. She was glad she was working.

It was the last day of shooting. There were the usual jokes and laughter, but Laura found it hard to join in. Leaving the studio at the end of the day meant not seeing these friends again. In three weeks they had grown close, joined by the long hours spent with each other and the fact that they had, together, created something that hadn't existed before. It was going to be lonely to wake up tomorrow and not come to the studio.

"A little more teeth, Miss Curtis, and cheat your look to Mr. Bolding a bit."

She obeyed the still photographer and focused on Harris' ear instead of his eyes. She had finished all of her scenes before they had broken for lunch, but there were publicity photographs to be taken, and she was needed to feed Harris offstage lines from behind camera in his few remaining closeups.

Harris smelled terrible. She wondered if he had been drinking at lunchtime. He kept hugging her and whispering into her ear between pictures. She tried to turn her face away from his breath without his noticing.

"Now, if you would sit on the stool, Mr. Bolding, and Miss Curtis, you stand close beside him. Closer. This is a tight two shot."

"What a moment," Harris said, reaching to spread her hair

more evenly over her shoulders. "That looks better." His fingers slid down her arm, and he slipped his arm around her waist. "Smile, little pussycat," he whispered.

Posing for stills was boring. Laura found the positions awkward and she felt silly. The photographer kept asking for "just one more," and after you did that, he asked for "just one more" again.

"You can rest a minute." The photographer went to move one of his lights.

"I'm going to miss you, pussycat," Harris whispered, his mouth tickling her ear.

"Okay, let's have a nice smile from both of you."

The camera kept clicking. Harris' fingers straightened the belt in back of her skirt and smoothed it. His hand patted her backside lightly.

"Hold it. Don't move, please. This is very close."

Harris was stroking her. She tried not to move.

"Reloading," said the still man, turning to get a new roll of film from his case.

Harris whispered close in her ear again, something she didn't hear clearly. His hand left her, and when she felt it again, it was against her bare skin. He had somehow undone the zipper of her skirt and slid his hand inside her panties at the waist. He was cupping her buttocks, squeezing gently with his fingers. Laura didn't know what to do. The photographer was threading his camera. He wasn't looking at them. Laura felt the warm hand kneading her flesh. The still man was fixing the focus, peering through his camera. He said nothing, just looked at them.

"Makeup!" he finally called, not taking his eyes off them.

"Here I am," Maury said. The man murmured something to him, and he went away.

Laura felt Harris withdraw his hand slowly, his fingers lingering over her.

"Laura, they want you in the production office." It was Fred. "Come with me."

She followed him, not daring to look back.

"Skip the production office," he said, as soon as they were out of hearing. "Go to your dressing room until we're ready for you. And let's not mention this to anyone. I mean anyone. It wouldn't be good for you, and it wouldn't be good for the show. Understood?"

She nooded.

"The back of your skirt is undone. Zip it."

"My shoulders hurt," Polly was complaining. She complained a lot. Laura pretended not to have heard. Dru was always patient with Polly's complaints, perhaps because they were best friends. Every weekend Polly came in from her job in New Jersey to stay with them. The three would go to a movie or a museum or for a bike ride in Central Park. Polly rarely acknowledged Laura's presence on these occasions, except for necessities like "Please pass the salt." She persisted in talking to Dru as if they were the only people in the room.

Polly, Laura observed, was cream-colored, from her faded blonde hair and pale skin to the color of the clothes she chose to wear. There was a softness about her, a roundness that led Laura to imagine that if she poked Polly, she might make a dent, like sticking a finger into a piece of soft cake.

"Right here, between my shoulder blades," she was telling Dru in that little voice that was halfway between a whisper and a whimper.

"I'll rub it," Dru volunteered. "That will help. With me, it's my legs. I should either ride a bicycle more often or not at all. What about you, Laura? Got any aches or pains?"

"In my legs," she said, rubbing them.

"Tell you what, Laura. You go run yourself a big, hot tub. A long soak in the bathtub will help. Polly and I are going to take a nap. Did you know," she asked Polly as they walked toward the bedroom, "Laura made six hundred on that Atlas commercial last week? Her potential is fantastic."

Polly didn't reply.

Dru came through the door with the scent of winter on her coat.

"Boy, it's getting damn cold out there. Here's a letter from your grandfather."

Laura took the envelope stamped "The Groves Nursing Home, Wareham, Massachusetts." He had lived there almost a month now, since he had sold the house in Devon. His letters were short, a comment about the weather, a reassurance that he watched a quiz program every afternoon to see the commercial she had made in Boston, and he sent her his love. He wrote in an unsteady, spidery hand. In each letter he enclosed a dollar for her to spend. Once a month his friend Mr. Wortham, a lawyer, sent a check to Drucilla.

"Did you get your homework assignment to take to work tomorrow?" Dru asked.

"I got it."

"Answer the phone, will you, Laura? I'm up to my elbows in groceries." She went into the kitchen.

"It was Polly," Laura told her. "She'll be here Friday afternoon."

"Good. We can all watch *The Wild Geese* on TV together."

"I know. She said she hoped it wouldn't be a disappointment after you'd talked about it so much."

The show was anything but disappointing. Even Laura, who had lived it, found herself completely engrossed in the story. It played so smoothly, not at all like the lumpy bits and pieces of scenes she had seen out of sequence in the daily rushes.

When it was over, Drucilla gave her a big hug and told her how proud she was.

"You were good," said Polly and went to do the dishes.

Paul Callum called and asked her if she had been pleased. Dru whispered for her to thank him for all his help.

Maury called. "A beautiful job, kid. You had my wife crying a couple of times. Say, I spoke to one of the network guys today. He said the show's a cinch to win at least one Emmy, come May."

Western Union phoned with a telegram for her. A woman with a singsong voice rattled it off quickly. "Congratulations to a fine little actress, love, your proud Grandpa."

The next day's *New York Times* called her "an extraordinarily sensitive young actress." The reviewer in the *Post* said she was "the brightest new find in many a season."

Several strangers stopped her on the street and a few of them asked for her autograph. "Laura Curtis," she wrote. She didn't use her full name anymore.

Dru was waiting for her outside school. She left the office early every Tuesday to take Laura to her singing lesson. "It will help your voice projection," she had said.

"I have a surprise for you." Drucilla was smiling. "How would you like to spend Thanksgiving in an airplane?"

"You're kidding. How come?"

"Nope. Not kidding. I've been on this deal for a few days now, but I didn't want to say anything until it was firmed. You know Victory Studios?"

Laura remembered the silhouette of the Winged Victory that flashed on the screen in some of the movies she had seen. "An S. M. Victor Production," it had said at the bottom.

"They've been testing a slew of kids for a series of movies they're planning to make, sort of like those Nancy Drew stories of yours," she explained. "The girl is called Nikki. So far they haven't signed anyone. They saw you in *The Wild Geese* and got in touch with my office. We've been haggling back and forth for a while, and now they're pretty interested. We go to California Thanksgiving Day. You test the following day, a week from Friday. Then we fly back here and sweat out the verdict. Well? Aren't you going to say anything?"

A flock of feeding pigeons took flight from the sidewalk ahead of them, noisily flapping their wings.

"They're clapping!" Laura shrieked delightedly. "They're applauding!"

"Oh brother," Dru smiled.

They had taken a one o'clock plane, flying into an afternoon sun that still had not set when they arrived in Los Angeles. The limousine that met them drove through palm-lined streets dotted with used car lots, shopping centers, and rows of ranch houses that all looked much the same. They sped along the freeway, watching the cars twine above them on the cloverleaves overhead. The driver pulled off under a sign that said "Sunset Boulevard."

"Look," Laura pointed out the window. "How funny. The houses are all fixed up in front, but the sides are bare."

Dru took in the elaborate front elevations of the houses, embellished with abundant landscaping. Behind them, the sides of the houses stretched back into their lots, uniformly plain, devoid of architectural efforts.

"That's show biz," she acknowledged with a short laugh.

Beverly Hills spread out like a Monopoly board, its symmetrical streets neatly divided into precise plots. The houses stood side by side, rich and imposing. Most had their curtains drawn against the sun and the street, although the sidewalks were empty of anyone to look inside. It was all very clean and well kept. Even the overgrowing greenery which threatened to envelop everything had been restrained to its proper place. Every kind and color of flowers seemed to thrive here in these sleepy gardens, where only a passing car broke the stillness.

"Laura," said Dru, as the driver slowed for a left turn into the driveway of the Beverly Hills Hotel.

Laura followed her gaze. Beyond them, far away and above Sunset Boulevard, a snow-capped mountain caught the last pink rays of the sun. Next to them at the stoplight, a red Volkswagen with a surfboard on the luggage rack gunned its motor.

"It may not be paradise," Dru commented, "but it's a great advertisement for it."

The fog descended early in the evening, spilling over the hills like thick batter. It obscured the tops of the pine trees, swirling mistily among the branches until the landscape around the hotel looked like a Japanese print. The fog and the chill all but emptied the streets of cars. Once the temperature made its usual evening plunge of twenty degrees, people headed for home and hearth. The night here had a special scent, a bittersweet aroma of damp wood and the freshness of green and growing things. There was something wholesome and welcoming about it, yet at the same time it brought with it a certain melancholy. Perhaps it was the quiet.

Dru stood in the doorway to the patio, looking out at the street lights glowing fuzzily in the fog.

"What are you thinking?" Laura asked.

"I was thinking," she turned into the warmth of the room, "what I would have given at one time to have had the chance you're getting."

"Dru?" Laura was surprised. "Did you want to be an actress?"

"Don't look so shocked. Behind every agent and every dialogue coach and, in Los Angeles, every realtor, is a disappointed actor. It's the old story. Those who can, do. Those who can't become agents." She paused. "That was a long time ago. Do you want to run your scene again?"

"Okay."

"You aren't nervous, are you?"

"I don't think so."

"Good. Nerves are a luxury in this business."

"Dru, what will happen if I get the part? I mean, where will you be, and where will I live?"

"We'll live here. Both of us. If this thing comes through, you'll owe Victory three pictures a year. They may even want you for four, depending on the box-office response. You'll have a picture deal, Laura, not the seven-year contract bit."

"But what's the difference?"

"Contract players say a line or two, bit players really, and do a lot of publicity stuff until they get a little name for themselves. If they haven't washed out by then, the studio gives them bigger parts and builds them for bigger things. They work for peanuts, but the pay is steady, and they get a lot of chances. If they last the whole term without getting dropped, they're probably stars already."

"And my contract is different. How?"

"If they sign you. You got co-star billing on *Wild Geese*, Laura. It was serendipity. There were really only two parts in the show, you and Harris. Then along comes Victory with the Nikki pictures, and all they know is that you get near-top billing. For this they're willing to go for more money and a guaranteed three pictures a year."

Laura loved the business words, the terms. They were a language of their own, like passwords to a private club.

"If we live here, where will you work?" she asked Dru.

"I'll work for us. If this pans out, you're going to need a full-time manager. It's not just the pictures; there'll be TV appearances, publicity junkets, merchandising tie-ins—the whole enchilada. Come on, it's getting late, and you have an early call." She picked up the mimeographed pages of the test scene and began to read. "Nikki! We were waiting. What kept you?"

The morning, misted over, was diffused and damp. When they left the hotel there was little traffic. At seven A.M. only a bakery truck and a man tossing newspapers from his convertible onto the manicured lawns disturbed the silent streets. A few domestics, coats thrown over their white uniforms, walked from the bus stops along Sunset Boulevard. Here and there an Oriental gardener, squatting on his haunches, scooted errant leaves from a lawn with an expertly aimed jet from his hose.

They stopped at the studio gate, under the emblem of the Winged Victory. The driver announced Laura to the guard and they were waved inside. A knot of men and women in black tie and evening dresses straggled past in the early morning gloom. "Dress extras," explained Dru. They passed through a Western street onto a New York street where men were rigging pipes and sprinklers overhead for rain. As they turned into an alley between two stages, the driver had to stop for a reluctant camel which was being tugged onto one of the stages by its handler. Finally they drew up in front of a low gray building with a small sign that read "Makeup Dept."

Laura's hair was washed and set in a large room full of sinks and dryers. She ventured an occasional look at the other women drying their hair, wondering if any of them were famous stars. In curlers and hairnets, without makeup, none of them looked familiar.

She was made up in one of the many cubicles that lined both sides of a long hall. In the corridor she heard people greeting each other, swapping jokes, being hurried along by assistant directors. She followed the makeup man to another little room where a woman was sponging body makeup onto a pretty girl. Laura waited her turn.

"How far down does this neckline go, sweetie?" the woman asked.

"Here." The pretty girl pointed between her breasts. "Throw a little Dark Egyptian in the cleavage, will you, and hand me the Vaseline." She squeezed the tube and rubbed some on top of each breast. "You know our dear director. He likes a good show. The bigger the better." She wrapped her terry cloth robe around her and left. Laura stuck out her arms for the sponge.

"Are you Laura Curtis?" A blue-gray haired woman poked her head around the door.

Laura nodded.

"Good luck today. On your test. I'm Indigo. I'll be on wardrobe." It was easy to see where she got her name. From her rinsed hair to her stockings and shoes, Indigo was dressed in blue. "When you're ready, I'll take you down to the stage."

It was a long walk, past barracks-like buildings of offices

and dressing rooms, row upon row of warehouses and stages with their sound trucks parked outside.

"Here, lovey." Indigo grunted as she heaved open the heavy door into the airlock. She opened the inner door to the stage and gestured Laura inside.

Here, at last, it was all familiar. There was the same musty smell, the vast darkness and, at the far end, the reassuring island of light where the camera was set up.

"Where did I take off my sweater in the long shot?" Laura was asking the script girl.

"On the line 'I couldn't find him and I'm afraid to go on by myself.' You started with the right sleeve on 'find' and you had it all off by the end of the speech."

"Thanks." She approached Milt Gibson in his director's chair. "How tired do you want Nikki to be by the end of the scene?"

"Just a little," he explained. "Your eyes are itching, and your voice is becoming scratchy, okay?" He watched her walk over to the makeup table to be touched up.

"Dru Lang?" he called and looked up smiling when she appeared beside him. "Off the record, I can't tell you how pleased I am with this kid. You never know what they'll think upstairs, but for my money she's a natural for Nikki. Kurt Vogler is on his way down to see her. I think he'll be impressed with the easy way she works. The last thing a producer wants is to be saddled with one of those gloriously talented little bitches who's a baby prima donna."

"Close the barn doors on that one," the gaffer called and put his light meter in front of Laura's face. "All set here."

"Right. Now Laura," instructed Milt, bending down to whisper, "I want the tears to come very slowly in this take. Do you think you can manage that, or do you want makeup to blow some camphor into your eyes?"

"Let me try," she said.

It was easy to cry. She had only to use those thoughts that were otherwise forbidden, thoughts of her mother and grandmother, even her grandfather, all of whom had left her so carelessly. Two big tears rolled slowly down her cheeks, followed by a gush of weeping until she felt her blouse getting wet and Milt called, "Cut. Print it."

The makeup man passed her a Kleenex and began to repair the damage. She glanced over his shoulder into the
gloom beyond the lights where a heavy-set bald man stood
sizing her up. That must be Kurt Vogler. He watched her for
a while, talked to Milt and Drucilla, and left without a word
to her. She wondered what that meant. Was she doing something wrong? Had he stood there and decided she wasn't
right for the part? What was the matter with her? If he had
only said something, she could change whatever she was
doing wrong to please him. Didn't he know that? Did he dis-
like her so much he didn't even want to meet her? Why
didn't he like her? Was she really that bad?

"Oh, Indigo," Laura heaved a tired sigh and leaned against
the dressing room wall.

"What's the matter, sweetheart? You made a wonderful
test. You just listen to your Indigo. I've seen them all, the
biggest, and you did just fine." She smiled sympathetically.
"It's just the letdown afterward, honey, that's all. Sorry." She
disentangled her gold ring from Laura's sleeve. "Marilyn
Monroe gave me that ring. Even Marilyn Monroe was nervous sometimes. And Linda Darnell," she pointed to a ruby
medal around her neck, "why on the first day of a picture,
she was so shy she could hardly speak."

"Laura." Dru let herself in the door. "Kurt Vogler wants
us to stop by his office before we leave."

"He hates me."

"Don't be silly."

"He does. I know it."

"You know nothing of the kind. What a ridiculous attitude. When you're going into a producer's office you have to
show some self-confidence. You're going to have to learn
how to sell yourself, young lady. Walk in there as if you've
really got some special merchandise and just keep thinking
that if he doesn't sign you, it's his loss. Come on, now, let's
see some spirit."

"She's right, little doll," agreed Indigo. "Here." She handed
Laura her sweater. "Got all your things?"

"Yes. Thanks, Indigo."

She hugged Laura. "You remember, darling, when you
sign on that dotted line, you ask for your Indigo on your first
picture. Don't forget, you hear?"

"May I have your names, please?"

"Miss Lang and Miss Curtis to see Mr. Vogler," Dru told the secretary.

"Have a seat, please. Mr. Vogler is on a long-distance call and cannot be disturbed at the moment."

They waited. The office was undistinguished. Its green walls and carpet reminded Laura of a school principal's office. On the walls were a lot of autographed photos and some posters advertising Vogler movies. A table was neatly stacked with issues of the *Hollywood Reporter* and *Variety*. Laura looked at one of them and wondered what the headline meant. " 'Golden Egg' Hatches Boffo B. O. In Hard Ticket."

"Mr. Vogler will see you now." The secretary gestured toward a door, her face without expression.

"This is important. For both of us," whispered Dru. "Spirit. Remember?"

"Sit there," he commanded without a greeting.

They sat on a leather sofa, hard and cold under Laura's legs.

"Let's have a look at you." He raised the venetian blinds in back of his desk. The sun streamed in on them. Against the brightness it was hard to see him.

"Don't you know how to smile?" he demanded.

Laura tried to smile at the voice.

"Do that again."

She managed another.

"You're going to have to have that lower tooth capped. It looks lousy."

"What can we do for you, Mr. Vogler?" asked Drucilla.

"I want to get a good look at the kid. I got some stills here." He shuffled through the papers on his desk. "They were taken on that, whatchacallit, *Geese* thing. I had the network send them over."

"Yes?"

"I've been looking them over. Her hair's too dark. And her eyebrows are too thick. They look like John L. Lewis. I see Nikki with blonde hair. Delicate."

"That's not a problem," Dru said smoothly. "Is there anything else?"

"Stand up, kid. Turn around."

Laura tried to stand straight.

"You always been that thin?"

"She's slim," Dru answered.

"You understand," he said, sitting behind his desk and lighting a cigaret, "we can't sign some kid who establishes a following and then overnight turns into one of those fat, adolescent pigs. I mean, nobody comes with a cast-iron guarantee, but we can't wind up trying to peddle some dumpy little number to a youth audience. Those kids like to think good-looking. They all got pimples of their own; you read me?"

"If Laura should sign with Victory Studios," Dru responded coolly, "you may be sure we'd see to it that you were in no way disappointed any time. As for the cosmetic changes," she stood up, taking Laura with her, "I'm sure the studio will be delighted to take care of them when they've seen the results of her test. We can discuss it then. Good-bye, Mr. Vogler." She cued Laura with a squeeze of her hand.

Laura found her voice. "Good-bye, Mr. Vogler."

"So long, kid. I hear you're a hell of an actress," he called after them. "Call me Kurt."

Dru muttered, "There are a few other things I'd rather call him. What a crude s.o.b."

Laura followed her to the car, saying nothing. It had been a mess, and she felt as if it was all her fault somehow.

They left the warm sunshine of California and flew into darkness almost immediately. After her meal, Laura dozed, lulled to sleep by the drone of the engines. When she awoke, Drucilla was tucking a blanket around her.

"I didn't mean to wake you. I thought you might get cold." She smiled as Laura snuggled deeper into her seat. The smile faded as quickly as it had come.

"Laura, you know, don't you, that I'm very fond of you?"

She nodded.

"I'd like to have a daughter like you, but——" she paused, "that will never happen. You are happy living with me, aren't you?"

"Yes. Yes, Dru." Why was she asking her all these questions?

"I promise you that I will always take very good care of you, Laura, just as if you were my own daughter."

She waited.

"I didn't want to tell you before. You had the test ahead of you, and then that jackass Vogler upset you——"

Laura started to protest.

"Never mind. I'm not crazy about him either, but you don't have to like someone to work with him. Especially when it's something this big. What I have to tell you—" She halted. "There was a message waiting when we checked into the hotel Thursday, for me to get in touch with Mr. Wortham in Devon. Your grandfather died the day before yesterday. A second stroke. He was never really in good health after your grandmother died. You know that." She looked at Laura who looked back in silence. Laura looked small and pale in the dim night lights of the plane.

"I didn't want you upset when you made your test. It was too important to us both. With so much at stake, I couldn't risk having you disturbed. I decided to wait to tell you. There is never any right time or good time to say these things. I thought at first of waiting until we got home, but that wouldn't have helped either, would it?"

"I guess not."

"The funeral was today." She took Laura's hand in hers. "When we get back to New York, I'm supposed to call Mr. Wortham. He'll make the arrangements for me to become your legal guardian. Whatever money there is will be put in trust for you until you are twenty-one or married. Do you understand? It's like the regular percentage of your earnings that the court makes us put in trust."

It all seemed so businesslike, as if it were just another contract they were discussing. Laura tried to remember how her grandfather looked. So much had happened since August. It was difficult for her to remember his face clearly. She shut her eyes and slept.

They left New York on Laura's Christmas vacation from school. Polly had come to spend the holiday and drove with them to the airport, wiping her red eyes with a tattered Kleenex. There had been an argument, Laura knew, over their moving to California. Late at night Polly had cried and raged at Dru in their bedroom. Dru had answered something about "a valuable property" and "a chance like this." Then she had dropped her voice so that Laura could not hear any more.

Now Polly stood in the soot-encrusted snow, watching as the skycap checked their bags. The taxi driver waited to take her back to the city. Wordlessly, she flung her arms around

Dru and buried her white face in her neck. Dru made a move as if to stroke the pale hair but stopped herself.

"Not here," she said stiffly.

Polly's head reared back. For a moment she stared at Dru. Then she turned, very deliberately, toward the waiting cab, and her eyes caught Laura's. Laura had never known such a look. Instinctively, she retreated a step. Without speaking, Polly got into the taxi and turned her face from them.

Drucilla watched it pull away. "Let's go," she said unsteadily. "It's freezing out here."

Laura was sitting in the commissary's Redwood Room where the minor executives and stars ate their lunch. Upstairs in the executive dining room sat the higher echelons: vice-presidents, important producers and an occasional member of the Victory board of directors. The main part of the commissary was a barnlike cafeteria filled with the noisy clank of china and silverware on its Formica tables. Here the lesser actors, day players, and extras ate with crew members and laborers. From the arched doorway of the Redwood Room, Laura saw Kurt Vogler making his way through a gaggle of cowboys and roaring twenties flappers in the main room.

"Hey, kid," he heaved his bulk into the chair next to hers, "that was a nice crust of bread Harris Bolding threw you at the Emmys last night. That kind of stuff is money in the bank for us."

"At least half of this," Harris had said, holding up the golden statuette, "belongs to a very talented young lady named Laura Curtis." Drucilla had been all smiles, but Laura, her eyes on the television set, was impassive.

"I'll have the Jerry Lewis Salad," Vogler told the waitress without bothering to look at the menu. "Brought you a present," he said to Laura, reaching in the pocket of his golf sweater. "The tear sheets for the ads on *Now Nikki*. We get your name in big enough type for you?"

"Now Nikki," it read, "for all of us who were ever young. Starring Richard Battle and Marie Simms and introducing Laura Curtis." There was a picture of Laura, her arm draped around the neck of the sadfaced St. Bernard that was Nikki's dog.

"It's nice," she smiled. Kurt Vogler really wasn't half bad. Under that rude, rough hide he wanted very much to be liked. She almost felt sorry for him because he remained essentially an unlikable man. They ate most of their lunch in silence.

"I suppose you know Drucilla phoned me this morning. That's why I called this lunch. Listen, kid," he leaned over the table, "you got to level with me. Why the hell didn't you call me yourself and tell me this little bimbo we hired can't hack it?"

"Because that's Drucilla's job. She's always reminding me to be Miss Sweetness-and-Light and to let her do the dirty work. It keeps things from getting personal." She took a sip of her Coke. "Dru says that's part of a manager's job."

"Okay, okay. Now tell me what's wrong with Peggy Whatshername."

"Mr. Vogler," she had never quite gotten around to calling him Kurt, "I just don't think Nikki would choose that girl for her best friend. She looks—well—she swings her behind a lot around the set and flirts with some of the guys on the crew. I know she says she's only sixteen, but . . . Maybe I shouldn't say anything. It's only my second picture. Still, I think I know Nikki as well as anyone. This girl just isn't her type of friend."

"Anything else?"

Laura shook her head. It wasn't fair to downgrade another actress' acting ability. Besides, they'd all see Peggy's first day's work in the rushes tonight after shooting.

"Milt Gibson says she can't act." He waited for her reply.

"He's right," she said apologetically.

"So we struck out. It happens. She gave a good reading in the office. We should've tested her, but there wasn't time." He wiped his mouth with the back of his hand. "Let's see how she looks in the dailies. If she saves her keester on film, we got to keep her. If not, we'll recast the part and do two day's retakes. Dessert?"

"No, thank you."

"You going over to meet the Major?"

She nodded.

"Come on, I'll walk you."

S. M. Victor was never called anything but "the Major," which had been his rank in the Second World War. In spite of his advancing years, his posture kept its military bearing. He stood out among other men half his age, partly because of his stance and partly because of the power his presence conveyed. He was isolated from the rest. He lived in the baronial surroundings befitting a charter member of Hollywood nobility, his home sprawling over an entire Bel Air hilltop, peopled only by himself, his butler, and a staff of maids, cooks, gardeners, and gatekeepers. He had never married for the simple reason that women were always available to him, while his only real passion was the acquisition of corporate power. Each winter he would take his butler, his secretary, and whatever starlet currently caught his fancy and spend four months on his yacht in the Florida Keys. Occasionally the young lady evidently underwent some kind of sea change and was shipped back and replaced by another. In May the entourage returned to California.

It struck Laura that he was slightly shorter than she had imagined. She had pictured him a giant literally as well as figuratively. He stood in the middle of an office almost the size of a sound stage, his arms outstretched like a scarecrow, while a tailor kneeled on the floor beside him, measuring.

"Hello, my dear," he broke away and greeted her, his hand as smooth and cool as a calling card. "I'll be through in a moment. Please sit down." He showed her to one of the only two chairs in the immense room. The Major's life was based on the subtleties of power. Because there were only two chairs, one his own, most visitors were forced to stand for their audience while he surveyed them from the massive brown wing chair behind his desk.

Laura looked at the desk, empty of anything except for an oversized intercom and two silver-framed, autographed pictures of the President of the United States and Winston Churchill. On the wall in back, a series of pedestals, each holding an Oscar, formed an arch above the altar of his desk.

The level of noise in the room was curious. There was a great deal of steady conversation from many voices, all in a tinny tone. She peered at the intercom which seemed to be its source. It bore labeled switches for each stage, each cutting room, the wardrobe departments and the gates, as well as just about every other building on the lot. It was true, what they said. Everyone talked about "the Major's network." They said S. M. Victor made it a practice to eavesdrop on the doings of his several thousand employees at Victory Studios. She was fascinated.

"Now, my dear," he turned away from the tailor who rose and left, "I'm sorry we didn't meet before, but I've been out of town for a few months." He flicked off the intercom with a motion of one well-manicured hand and smiled at her from behind the desk. His hair was white, thinning, and he wore several strands slicked over his pink pate in the fashion of General MacArthur. There was a pleasant, citrus scent about him.

"We ran the answer print of your first Nikki film last night," he told her. "There are a few more changes to be made, of course, but I think you'll be pleased. Two of the members of our board of directors are in town, and they'll be seeing it tonight. We don't usually do that with an answer print," he explained, letting her know she was being complimented.

"I hope they like it."

"I wouldn't worry about that."

Laura smiled.

"Now, Miss. We hope we're going to have you around here for a long time. Are you happy here? Do you like your dressing room? Is there anything we can do to make you feel more at home?"

"No, sir. Everything is very nice. I like all the people I'm working with."

"And we're going to try to keep it that way. If you run into any problems, you come to me."

They both knew that was out of the question, but she thanked him for his kindness.

"I hear you had a papal audience," said Dru, settling into her seat in the projection room. "How did it go?"

"He was very pleasant."

"You can go home now, Mrs. Ruddy," Dru dismissed the woman who substituted for her as Laura's guardian on the set. Dru came nightly from her office at the house to see dailies and take Laura home. "Remind me to speak to you later about the contracts for the Nikki comic books," she told Laura as the lights dimmed.

"Christ!" Vogler exploded when the lights came on again. "She stinks! We must have had our heads in the wastebasket when we hired that one." He turned to his casting director.

"Get rid of Peggy Whatsherface and start scrounging around for a replacement. She comes off like the whore of Babylon."

"Wrong," said Milt Gibson, "the whore of Babylon could act."

"Indigo," Laura leaned toward the wardrobe woman several seats in front of her, "that pink coat looks pretty on the screen. Is it back from the cleaners?"

"Yes, sweetheart. It's in the wardrobe truck."

"Then let's wear it again in the last scene. Over the checked dress."

"Whatever you say, lovey." She held the door for Laura as they filed out.

The studio was quiet at night. Here and there a door was open, showing only a single bulb illuminating the vast and hollow darkness of an empty stage. In the administration building a few lights burned. At a distance, on the back lot, the sky glowed where a crew was shooting night for night. Laura wrapped her jacket around her shoulders and followed Dru to the parking lot.

"The Major is coming down off his mountain," Dru announced as she walked into the dressing room. "Publicity wants some stills of him presenting you with the car."

"Nice. It ought to get a good space. A lot of heartwarming garbage about the generous big daddy giving the sweet sixteen star a convertible for her birthday." Laura leaned into the mirror, plucking her eyebrows.

"Don't be cynical. It makes you sound hard. It's not becoming."

"You're the one who said it was only the grosses of those last two Nikki pictures that saved him from being lynched by the stockholders." She winced.

"That's all right for me to say. You have an image—"

"—to protect. Okay, then, what about the studio tie-in with the car manufacturer? Every kid in America is going to be bugging her parents for a red sportscar like Nikki's. You can't tell me they didn't think of that in Detroit. And besides," she opened the witch hazel bottle and daubed at her brows, "he knows I went on that Australian p.a. tour with a strep throat and a fever of a hundred and two. We could have canceled out. Even you said that."

"Just do me a favor and keep your thoughts to yourself

when you see him. Miss American Teenager is not a cynic. And I'm not sure I like to think Laura Curtis is, either." She lit a cigaret. "Leah told me she noticed you were wearing nail polish when she put on your body makeup this morning. Is this something new?"

"She's a fink. It's colorless, anyhow."

"Take it off."

"Oh, Dru, don't be silly." Laura examined her nails.

"I'm not being silly. It will show in the close shots."

"Do you want me to go back to biting my nails? That didn't look so hot, did it?"

"I told you to take it off, Laura."

"Dru, please," she begged, "all the girls my age wear a little clear polish." She spoke plaintively to Drucilla's reflection in the mirror.

"You are not 'all the girls' your age. You are Laura Curtis, alias Nikki. It comes off. Is that understood?"

She stood her ground for a moment. "Damn. All right, hand me the remover. It's on the closet shelf behind you. There are times I wouldn't mind being like the rest of the kids."

"And cut out the profanity. Here." She handed her the bottle. "There are times when you sound downright ungrateful, you know that?"

"I'm tired. I had six straight pages of dialogue today, and that idiot teacher gave me an algebra test on top of everything. I hate algebra. I know I'll never use it, so I don't see why I have to learn it."

"It all comes in handy. Laura, I looked at three more houses today."

"Hey, where?"

"One's in Bel Air—"

"Old or new Bel Air?" New Bel Air, she knew, was not as prestigious as the older section.

"New. The other two are in Beverly Hills. One is on Peck between Olympic and Wilshire, and the other is in the hills. It's L. A. County but Beverly Hills address."

"That's what counts. We can forget the one on Peck. Nobody lives below Wilshire. Where's the one in the hills?"

One of the internal snobberies of the film colony insisted that success was measured by where you lived and what car you drove. Dru had a Lincoln and Laura's convertible was the latest rage.

"It's on Beverly Drive. It's a Spanish stucco. Lots of trees."

"Does it have a pool?" That was another thing.

"We'd have to put one in, but there's room."

"Maybe we could make a deal with one of the pool companies in exchange for a little publicity," Laura suggested.

"You're learning," smiled Dru. "Want to take a run up to the house after work? I have a key."

"Let's. Will you hand me those blue jeans? I'd better get into my next change. They'll be yelling for me in a minute. One thing's for sure," she said, buttoning her shirt, "we have to get out of the Valley." The San Fernando Valley, unless one owned a ranch, was relegated to the lower echelons of the industry. Hollywood itself, though on the "right" side of the Santa Monica Mountains, was full of out-of-work beginners and retired character players. They had not considered looking there for a house.

"What time is the Major coming down?" Laura wanted to know.

"Any time now. Think of a couple of cute things to say. Some of the wire service reporters will be there."

"That boy called," Dru told her when she came out of the kitchen.

"What boy?" Laura asked through a mouthful of brownies.

"Jeff Wayne."

Laura made a face. She had felt like a piece of merchandise when the studio came up with the idea of the contest. "Win a date with Nikki. An evening in Hollywood, all expenses paid, with Laura Curtis." A blond freshman from UCLA named Jeff Wayne had been the winner.

"Don't eat any more brownies, Laura. You know chocolate makes your face break out. How would that look on film? Are you going to call him back?" she wanted to know.

She would not return the call. It had been a disaster. He had talked about basketball. Laura had never seen a game. When he realized she was bored, he had asked a lot of questions about movie stars. What was so-and-so really like? Then he talked about a Broadway show he had seen on his spring vacation in New York. "But I guess that stuff is old hat to you," he had apologized weakly.

They went to a preview where he stood by like a dumb ox while she was practically trampled by a crowd of autograph seekers. She had actually felt sorry for him when someone said, "Who's that with Laura Curtis? Oh. It's not anybody."

"I like that house, Dru." Laura stretched out on the sofa with her script. "It smells so good up there. Those pines. The jasmine."

"And the 'No Smoking. Fire Area.' signs," Dru countered. "The fire insurance is going to cost a bundle."

"So what? It's my money. That's the house I want." She wiggled her tired shoulders into a cushion.

"It's up to me to see that you take care of your money. Don't get up," she said, as the phone rang. "I'll get it."

"That was Mac Herman from publicity," announced Dru. "They want you to go to the *Windfall* premiere with Marty Tabor."

"Marty Tabor? Are they crazy? He's at least ten years older than I am!"

Laura had met the star of the *Caravan* series at a few of the studio functions. They nodded when they passed each other in the commissary. She didn't know too many of the television people. They came and went as their shows were canceled and replaced by new ones. Marty Tabor was tall and good-looking, with a shock of prematurely gray hair that saved his features from being too perfect. He had a shy smile that set most women to daydreaming that all he really needed to make him happy was a good wife. His piercing blue eyes, inevitably called "sexy," made Laura uncomfortable.

"Mac says the suggestion came from the Major's office."

"That's a switch. All I've heard for three years is that nice little girls like Nikki aren't seen at Hollywood parties."

"You know very well why. Nikki is the girl next door, not some teenage jet-setter. Anyway, this time I think you should go. Mac was pretty firm about the Major's request."

"He's really going to make me pay for that car, isn't he? Marty Tabor, for pete's sake. Isn't he too old for Nikki?"

"It's a last-minute thing. Probably someone dropped out, and they thought of you. In one way, it's a good sign." She paused thoughtfully. "At last the Major isn't keeping Nikki in rompers forever. She has to make a transition sometime. She can't play at being fourteen for the next five years. Maybe he has plans for you," she mused.

"He has plans for Marty Tabor. One of the extras told me Marty's having an affair with a stunt girl and the studio is very upset because they have bigger things in mind. Lately he's started going everywhere with Helen Farmer."

"You get your ears full on that set, don't you," Dru laughed.

"Can't help it. Everybody talks. What else is there to do sitting around between takes?"

"You might try algebra," she offered.

"Anyhow, the Helen Farmer thing is a fake. She's one of the Major's girls. Dru," she asked again, "do I have to go?" She sat up, grimacing at the soreness in her shoulders.

"Definitely, considering the source of the request. It won't kill you, Laura. Lots of girls would give their left arms to go on a date with Marty Tabor. What's wrong with your back?"

"It's not my back. It's here, between my shoulder blades. It's been sore ever since I did that stuff in the lake on the back lot. The water was freezing, and they had me in there for four hours straight. Dru? If I get the Vicks ointment, will you rub my back?"

"I—" she hesitated. "I don't think so, Laura. Why don't you try a hot shower. Get it as hot as you can stand it."

"But why won't you rub my back?" she persisted.

"Take a hot shower, Laura."

"But you used to rub Polly's back, and you give Rose massages when she visits you."

"I said no. That's it!"

"Don't you love me?"

"Laura! Get out of this room at once!" She turned away, her shoulders sagging. "I'm sorry. I'm a little tired myself."

"I know." Laura left the room.

2

Marty

12:00 Noon

"Lisa? Marty."

"We didn't see you at the church. Jack kept wondering where you were."

"I didn't go."

"Won't people think that was odd?"

"I understand there was a big crowd. I could have been there without being noticed."

Funny thing how death in Hollywood produces a herd effect. Whatever they think of someone, just let the poor bastard die and they regroup in closed ranks to bury him. Never an unkind word, even for a full-out son of a bitch. And Lisa, of all people.

"I still think you should have been there. You could have sat with us. Everyone knows you've known Laura for years."

"You make me laugh. I seem to remember a scene at Saint John's Hospital when I said something to the effect that Mike Stanton would eventually get what he deserved. Do you remember what you said then?"

Silence.

"You said, 'If Mike Stanton ever gets what he deserves, a lot of people might pay to watch.' Don't be a goddam hypocrite, Sis."

"Marty, for Laura's sake, don't you think you should have——"

For Laura's sake. For Laura's sake, the best thing that could happen would be for us never to come face-to-face again. After all we went through together, to have it turn out this way . . .

She was so alone. Frantic. Confused. Then, for a while, we both made sense out of things. And where is she now? Go directly to jail; do not pass GO; do not collect two hundred

41

dollars. Back to where she was when it started. For Laura's sake. Jesus. None of it would have happened if I hadn't opened my mouth for Laura's sake.

And now. She has to hate the sight of me. Whatever we had together was blown to bits.

How long does it take to recover from loving? A guarantee would help. "In a year's time you'll be fit as a fiddle." Something like that. A year maybe? No such luck. Some things can't be forgotten. That quote of Ingrid Bergman's, "Happiness depends upon a poor memory." Some of us aren't that fortunate. Every time Laura sees my face, she'll see what happened in that bedroom. And I'll see what could have been. Finishing this picture is going to be hell for both of us.

I remember her in New York, standing in the snow, chilled and angry. And the thaw that came after. The warmth, the woman. Laura.

"—at work."

"What? I'm sorry, Lisa."

"I said I thought you'd be at the studio."

"I'm not in any of today's stuff. Tomorrow."

"What do you want me to tell Jack? I mean, about why you weren't at the funeral."

"Tell him any damn thing you please. Tell him I've contacted bubonic plague. No, skip that. He'd have a heart attack thinking I couldn't finish the picture. Did he ask any other questions?"

"What kind?"

"You know. About—the party."

"Jack has a lot riding on this picture. It's all he can handle right now. You understand. It's this jam he's been in. If anything happens to this, I don't know . . . I just don't know if he could take it. Have you thought where he'll be if this one doesn't work?"

"Yes. I have."

"Well, so has he. Sometimes I wake up at night, and he's lying beside me, staring up at the ceiling. He doesn't sleep at all some nights, just lies there. It scares me. The worst part is seeing what's happening to him and not being able to do anything to help. I get so frustrated I want to scream and cry, but I know I mustn't. I try so hard to help him relax when he comes home."

"Sis. Take it easy. Please."

"*Damn. I'm sorry. This—this thing has been upsetting for all of us. Oh Lord, Marty. I love him so much.*"

"*I know you do. What the hell, take the cynical point of view. This whole mess has given the picture a million bucks worth of publicity.*"

"*That's a pretty repulsive thing to hear you say.*"

She's right.

"*Have you spoken to her, Marty?*"

"*I'm about the last person she'd want to talk to.*"

"*What's going to happen with you two?*"

"*I don't know.*"

But I do know.

"*I hear Jack's car. I have to hang up.*"

"*What's he doing home at noon?*"

"*We're doing a photo layout for* Look. *Jack thought it would be good advance publicity for the picture. He'll do anything to promote this one.*"

"*It's not exactly the best day for it.*"

"*I know. I have to go now. Marty?*"

"*Yes?*"

"*Take care.*"

Care. That's what families are for, right? Thanks, Lisa. What the devil is Obie's phone number? . . .

"*We missed you.*"

"*Did Laura say anything, Obie?*"

"*About not seeing you there? No.*"

"*How is she? Is she all right?*"

"*I guess she's as all right as can be expected. She went to work afterward, if that's what you mean. It was her idea. Ruth wanted her to spend the day at home, but Laura said she'd rather go straight to the studio, it would keep her mind off things.*"

"*I was concerned.*"

"*I expect you are.*"

What does that mean? How much does he know?

"*What's she going to do now?*"

"*Stay with us for the time being. We're not pressing her for decisions. Let's let everything take its course. She can decide later what she wants to do.*"

"*Has she said anything, asked anything, about me?*"

"*Not to me.*"

"*Obie. Please, if I can help——*"

"I know. Don't worry."

"Thanks."

That's a nice thing about Obie. He never asks, and you never have to tell him. His instincts are always tuned in. All those years of servicing clients have given him a feeling for situations. When to push and when to lay off. If there ever was a time to lay off, it's now.

Take care of her, Obie.

AT least the kid was pro enough not to complain that he had been late picking her up. What did you talk about with a Laura Curtis? He had entertained her, he hoped, with the ridiculous scene in the looping room that had delayed him. She had managed a grin at the silly picture of a fleet of technicians scurrying all over the Victory lot, looking for the lost sound loops while he waited, attired in black tie, to dub a sound track nobody could find.

He looked across the table at her. "What did you think of the picture?"

"It was okay, I guess."

Now what?

"I suppose we should feel honored, sitting at the Major's table." He saw her glance at Victor, making sure he had not overheard.

"Yes," she whispered.

Well, what the hell, why not jump in with both feet? "You're very quiet. Does that mean you're not having a good time, or are you just shy?"

"Maybe I'm shy. This is my first big Hollywood party. They would never let me go before."

"Never mind. All actors are shy. If they were so confident in their own skins, why would they have to put on somebody else's face to express themselves?"

"I never thought of it like that."

"Miss Curtis?" It was one of the waiters. "Could I have your autograph for my little girl? Her name is Carolyn."

He watched her sign. Jesus, but the kid drew the fans. They had been mobbed at the theater, she more than he.

"Marty?"

"Sis." He rose and kissed Lisa on the cheek. What a

knockout she was. She moved like a cat, black chiffon flowing softly from a neckline that showed just enough of those terrific breasts. He introduced her around the table. "This is my sister, Lisa Taylor."

"Please sit down, gentlemen. I just stopped by to say hello to Marty on the way back to my table. Have a pleasant evening. Mr. Victor, I enjoyed *Windfall* very much." She left at the Major's acknowledgement.

"I didn't know Lisa Taylor was your sister," Laura said, impressed.

"No? Our family name is Tabori," he explained. "By the time I decided to go to New York to study acting, Lisa Taylor was already a name. I decided to use Tabor. Independence, I guess."

"Who is she with?" Laura craned her neck to see across the ballroom.

"Hans Deitrick."

"He's handsome."

"Blond and blue-eyed. The perfect Kraut."

"He's Swiss. I read his bio in the publicity department."

"Laura. In this town all Germans are Swiss, and all the Swiss call themselves French." He hoped he didn't sound patronizing.

Laura thought he did. She changed the subject.

"Helen Farmer is beautiful, isn't she?" She watched Helen's fair hair brush the Major's cheek as she whispered something to him. They both smiled, and Helen placed her hand over his on the table. She had flawless skin, with a full rosebud mouth and big blue eyes. The effect was that of a china doll with spun sugar for hair. She looked as if she belonged on a Christmas tree with the rest of the angels.

"No!" The Major detached himself from Helen and waved away the waiter standing at Laura's elbow. "No champagne for Nikki. And take the glass with you. We don't want her photographed with a wine glass."

Laura wanted to sink under the table.

"Smile," Marty whispered. "If you weren't a star nobody would care. Just think, you could be the world's youngest alcoholic if it weren't for the loving care of Victory Films."

She smiled up at him. "Thanks."

"Look, there's Vic Strong. Add him to your list of names at your first Hollywood party."

"He's enormous!" she said in wonder. "People don't usually look as tall as they are on the screen, but he's huge!"

"Not exactly the kind of guy you'd want for an enemy."

"Isn't he the one who was supposed to have beaten up his girl friend, and then she changed her story and said she slipped in the bathtub?" Laura stared in fascination.

"That's the guy."

"I wonder if he did."

"I only know what I read in the papers. The release said she fell in the bathtub. So . . . she fell in the bathtub. No questions asked."

"Couldn't that be a phony story?" Vic Strong looked surly enough to take a punch at anyone who displeased him.

"Doesn't matter if it is. The result's the same: No questions asked. Does anyone inquire when the studio announces that so-and-so has been released from his contract due to the pressures of other commitments? Even if we all know he got fired, we don't say it. In Hollywood, all the emperors have clothes. Of course," Marty continued drily, "the girl in question did end up with a term contract at Vic's studio, and he suddenly agreed to do a picture he'd been avoiding like the pox for two years. One can always assume, but one never actually questions. Those are the rules."

Across the table, Helen Farmer laughed softly at some joke of the Major's. Laura envied her smooth, effortless charm.

"He usually goes to these things alone, doesn't he?" she whispered.

"Yes. With all the photographers and press here, this amounts to a top-level endorsement of her career." He nodded at Helen who was never unaware when she was the subject of conversation. Usually Marty would be escorting her. Something must have changed the Major's mind at the last minute. Was he casting Helen in a new picture? That might account for the switch. Marty had raised hell with Mac Herman at the idea of taking a kid to the premiere, but it was that old story about crossing an alligator with a parrot. When the Major spoke, you listened. Actually, he wasn't having such a bad time. The kid was all eyes and ears, which at least made conversation possible.

"Martin." It was the Major. "I have an overseas call to make, and Miss Farmer would like to dance."

Marty excused himself from the kid and led Helen to the floor. She was a beauty, no question about it. She looked as delicate and pastel as a Botticelli nymph.

"Pretty dress."

"Not on my salary. I borrowed it from the wardrobe department."

"Having a good time?"

"It's always the same, isn't it? Fruit cocktail, roast beef, potatoes, string beans, and that same old baked Alaska. They just change the names. Glace a la *Windfall*. It's still a drag, if you ask me." She shrugged resignedly.

"Maybe. But this is a coup for you." He nodded in the direction of the Major's empty chair.

She smiled, pleased with herself.

"How'd you swing it?"

"Really want to know?"

"Sure."

"It was easy. All I had to do was tell him I wouldn't suck him anymore unless he escorted me personally. Simple."

"Simple!"

"But that's all he likes, see? With him there's nothing else going. And me, I once got hooked up with a faggot who taught me some nifty tricks."

"Lucky Major." He didn't doubt for a moment that Helen knew some nifty tricks. He wouldn't mind her practicing on him. Then he remembered Kathy . . .

"I figure that this way the old guy gets his jollies and he doesn't have to bother with bed talk or even looking at the girl. Sometimes I wonder if he knows who's down there. He's probably thinking about his latest grosses or how to dump his theater chain at a profit before the SEC jumps him. Things like that."

Marty acknowledged Hans Deitrick's nod as he and Lisa danced by. "What do you get out of it?"

"Baby," she grinned, her hand making a wide arc of the ballroom, "this, baby. All this and more. That's what I get out of it. Hell, I'd go down on Jack the Ripper twice a day to get where I'm going." She tilted her head up to his for a passing photographer.

"I believe it," he said.

"A beautiful pair," commented Aces Norton, rising to give Marty back his chair. "You and Miss Farmer."

"What was Norton selling?" he asked Laura.

"Himself. Imagine. He moved in the minute you left the table. He asked me if they had cast the role of Nikki's uncle in the new picture. He wants to do it. Aces Norton!"

"I wonder why all nightclub comics want to be actors. I never heard of an actor who wanted to be a stand-up comic."

"Do you think they'll get married? Did she say anything?"

"Who?"

"Helen and the Major."

He shook with laughter. "Spoken like a true sixteen-year-old girl. No, Laura I don't think so. Neither one of them is what you could call a homebody."

"Then why is he taking her out in public when he never does that? And why is she making such a fuss over him, acting like they're so close?"

"Laura. We're in Movieland. Tinseltown. Those two," he gestured covertly in their direction, "are engaged in the famous Hollywood game of using each other."

"For what?"

"For the express purpose of making Helen Farmer a salable commodity. The more S. M. Victor builds her up, the more he can collect when he loans her out for pictures at other studios."

"And what does Helen get?"

He took in the room with a sweep of his arm. "This. All this and more."

"Well," she persisted, "why is that so funny? Isn't that what you want too?"

He fingered the stem of his champagne glass. "Men pursue professions, careers. That's their number. For women it's different. When a woman pushes her way to the top, she leaves some of her femininity behind on the way. It's part of the bargain. I prefer the less ambitious type."

"What about your sister? She has a career."

"I don't think she's found the man she wants to share a life with, that's all."

"I wonder," Laura confided, "if I could marry a civilian, someone outside the business. This is all I know now and all I probably will know. I haven't been to a school for four years. I have no idea what people my age think or what they do with their time. We don't have anything in common when I do meet them. Mostly they treat me like a freak."

"It's a cinch they don't have Aces Norton scrounging around them for jobs."

The Major caught Marty's eye and tapped at the dial of his wristwatch with an index finger. He tipped his head in Laura's direction.

"I think you were just turned into a pumpkin. The Major probably doesn't want to start a scandal by having Nikki seen out after midnight." He rose and pulled out her chair.

She felt humiliated, he knew. Why shouldn't she, getting sent to bed like a naughty child. She was making more money than half the people in the room and had five times the box-office draw of most of them. He felt sorry for the kid.

They posed for more photographs on their way to the door. Was it a romance, asked a reporter, smiling.

"We're just friends," he tossed the old chestnut. Helen was right. These things were a chore. You felt like a racehorse being walked around the paddock on display. It was all part of the job, yet somehow it seemed much more phony than acting in front of a camera. He wanted to get out of there, away from the noise and the music and the stale, smoke-hazy air.

"Just one more."

They smiled at the camera.

It was still early. He wondered if Kathy would be home. He didn't like the idea that she might not be. "Okay," she had told him, "if you're going to make yourself an item with Helen Farmer, I'll do as I damn please." She had been angry as hell, but she never let the tears go beyond the corners of her eyes. She stood her ground, that one. Had she gone out with another guy? With whom? The picture of Kathy with anyone else was unthinkable. She knew the ropes. She knew he saw only her when he wasn't doing publicity with Helen. It wasn't that she didn't trust him. After almost a year together, she knew better than that. But was she home?

"I have to make a phone call," he said to Laura. "I'll meet you outside the ladies' room."

"What's the matter, Marty? Did you and Helen have a fight? Only for publicity, of course." She sounded sleepy.

"Don't be a bitch, Kath."

w did you expect me to act? I'm not some chick who dates for a quick bang after the party."

'Jesus! I'm calling because I want to see you. So far that's not a felony."

"It's still a misdemeanor. So fuck you."

"Promise?"

"No promises. I'm still furious." She yawned and sounded less furious.

"Are you in bed?" He pictured the room in darkness and the sweet fresh smell of her body in the sheets.

"Mmm . . ."

"Think if I got there in half an hour you'd scramble me an egg?"

"Give me one good reason why I should."

"I'll tell you what a great party you didn't go to."

"Sweet. Then I won't have to read about you and Helen in tomorrow's paper. You really are a prick, you know?"

"How about if I tell you I wasn't out with Helen?" He waited. "Tonight I was out with jailbait. Miss Teentime herself. Laura Curtis."

"You nut," she chided.

"No joke. Very sexy. Like a mink. Wait'll I tell you the wild time we had." He knew he'd won.

"Mart?"

"Yes?"

"I think this may be worth two scrambled eggs."

She wore only a bathrobe. Marty kissed her gently, running his hands over her body through the silk of the robe, as if to reassert his rights of possession.

"You don't smell of sleep," he accused.

"I took a shower."

Her face was bare of makeup, tanned, and her hair light from the sun. In the dimness of the doorway, her eyes looked not brown but black. His fingers touched her neck, and his mouth went to her ear. Kathy pressed against him, fitting her body to his.

Kathy's body was pure pleasure. Perhaps it was her perfect physical condition. Perhaps it was her wholesomeness, her healthy love of the outdoors. Perhaps, because of her work, she had a greater awareness of her body than women whose occupations were less physical. Whatever it was, he had never known a woman as vibrant or exciting as Kathy. He looked into the dark eyes and saw her smile.

"Come into the kitchen and tell me about The Great Cradle Robbery." She slipped an arm around his waist, and they walked close together through the unlit hall.

"Are you working tomorrow?" Her back was to him as she rinsed the dishes.

"Only some looping in the afternoon. You?"

"No. They put off my crash scene until the end of the week."

"Good Lord, what crash scene?" Marty could never get used to the idea that stunt work seemed routine to her.

"You know." She turned off the tap and faced him. "It's that job doubling Barbara Wilde. There's a car chase in Griffith Park, and the car goes over the cliff with me in it."

"Just like that."

"Let's hope so." She knew he was concerned. He always was when they discussed her work, but he rarely commented.

"Sometimes I wish to God you were in another line of work."

"Like what? Besides, this is all I know and it pays well. I'm spoiled. I could never go back to shining shoes," she laughed.

"Since when did you shine shoes, you kook?"

"When I was a kid. Didn't I ever tell you? My brother had a stand, and when he couldn't be there I took over. It was fun. I was fifteen, and you should have seen the tips I got."

"Not to mention the propositions."

She laughed. "Never mind. I gave a hell of a good spit shine."

"I'm trying to picture you as a shoeshine boy."

"I was adorable."

"I'll bet."

"Pull up your trouser leg." She reached in the hardware drawer next to the sink and fished out a tube of polish and a cloth.

"You're going to put brown polish on my black shoes, I feel it."

"It's colorless. What do you think, you're dealing with an amateur?" She knelt in front of him and squeezed the cream into her hands. Her fingers traveled over his foot, massaging the polish into the leather. She stroked it in, her hands working deliberately, slowly. Her hair fell in front of her face. She made no move to brush it away, absorbed in the manipulations of her hands.

She looked up at him, her mouth slightly parted. As she straightened, her robe fell away from her shoulders, exposing her full, hard-nippled breasts.

Marty reached down, cupping a hand under each breast, and brought her to her feet.

The light from the bathroom streaked across her legs as she lay waiting for him on the bed. She watched him undress, enjoying the anticipation.

He covered her body with his. Their mouths and tongues met. His hands went to her nipples and, after a while, to her thighs. She made no sound. His mouth traveled between her breasts to the flatness of her belly, his tongue exploring her navel. He parted her legs and lifted them to his shoulders, burying his mouth in the softness between. Gently, teasingly, he pulled at her flesh with his lips, until he heard her begging him for more, and then his tongue plunged into her, hard and searching. She began to moan. Marty held her thighs tighter on his shoulders. He felt her body tense. Her hands gripped the brass posts of the headboard, and he heard her harsh cry.

As he stretched beside her on the bed, she moved to him, her hair brushing his chest. She kissed his closed eyelids and covered his mouth with her own. Her smooth hands traveled over his body until she found his hand and brought it to her. Softly, she kissed the palm, tracing the indistinct lines with the tip of her tongue. She moved her lips along his fingers to the tips and suddenly, swiftly, slid the length of his finger into her mouth, sucking and biting it lightly. She moved the hand to her breast, and his fingertips played at her nipple.

In the dimness, her blonde head moved to his belly. She nipped gently at his flesh and moved lower. He was in her mouth. She used her tongue and her fingers on him, until he forced her to stop. Marty hurled her to the bed and mounted her. Their bodies moved together, slowly at first, until the rhythm overcame them. Kathy's head tossed from side to side as she moaned. Her legs locked around him as she felt his speed increase. He moved mindlessly, feverishly, driving into her like a jackhammer until there was no control, and they screamed together, over and over, before lapsing into exhausted murmurs and sleep.

Mac Herman waved him to a table in the Redwood Room. "Nu? How was your date with Curtis? I saw you at the theater but I didn't stay for the film. Already seen it twice." He ordered a diet plate. Marty signaled the waitress for the same.

"It went all right. She's a nice enough kid."

"We got a helluva turnout, plenty of coverage."

"Good. I saw Lisa there with Hans Deitrick."

"The body beautiful?"

"Which one?"

"Somebody ought to tell Deitrick to stop holding his interviews in the buff." Mac bit into his hamburger without enthusiasm.

"In the nude?" Marty's fork stopped in midair.

"Displaying the goods, that's his shtick. Gives interviews in his sauna or while he's being massaged in that barn he calls his bathroom." He shrugged. "Shakes up the ladies, I'll tell you. Worse than that," he emphasized with a thrust of his knife, "someday some faggot reporter will make a pass at that schnitzel, and we'll have a first-class case of assault and battery to keep out of the paper."

"You've got to admit, Mac, you meet the most interesting people."

He grunted. "Want a word to the wise? Maybe the black beauty should watch her step with the *Wehrmacht*. She shouldn't get too hung up on him. There are rumors that his sex life is pretty varied."

Some fan magazine had coined Lisa's nickname, playing on her luxuriant brunette hair. Marty still thought it was corny. He made a mental note to relay Mac's message. She did not always take kindly to admonitions from her younger brother. Still, if Mac had made a point of mentioning it in the conversation, there must be a reason.

"Maybe I overdo my job." He wiped his mouth. "I shouldn't get ulcers from worrying about my people. Lisa Taylor isn't even under contract to us, but she is your sister." He lowered his eyes to his empty plate. "What the hell, I worry, like it or not."

"You got more?" asked Marty.

"It's—talk. Word of mouth." He hesitated.

"About what?"

"You. And Kathy Hayman." He shifted uncomfortably in his chair.

"Go on, Mac." He readied himself.

"Jesus, Marty! You know the score! Why in hell are you making trouble? You got a good show. You're getting a build-up this studio hasn't sprung for in ten years. You could never afford the kind of buildup you're getting. Nobody could. It takes a big organization, a five-figure budget. Where else are you going to find that? Why rock the boat?"

"I wasn't aware the boat was being rocked that much."

"You deny you're serious about her?"

"It's not that I'm denying it. I'm not discussing it."

"Be reasonable. For God's sake. The studio has an invest-ment to protect. You have a future to protect. You going to risk the whole mishegas for a quick shtup with some girl who does stunts?"

"You manage," he said, "to make it sound dirty."

"Do you think I like this? Some parts of this job are shit. Understand? Shit. I've got four kids to send through college on a lousy salary from Victory Studios. If the studio job goes, so does the salary and the pension. So I do my job, shit included. I'm an employee here, just like you. You got to play ball, Marty. One hand washes the other. Why in hell couldn't you have gotten your big hard-on for Helen Farmer?"

"Because I don't like Judas goats!"

"And I suppose you do like a dime-a-dozen stunt chick? This town is wall-to-wall with extras and stunt chicks. They're lined up ten deep at Unemployment. So how do they get hired with that kind of competition? They put out, that's how! You're going to sit here and tell me you'd risk blowing your big chance for some big-boobed semi-pro?"

Marty seemed to rise from the table in slow motion. He stood rigid. His lips were taut and white.

"You brown-nosing bastard." His voice was quiet. "Get your ass out of my sight. Tell your goddam publicity depart-ment to keep their filthy hands off my private life. And if S. M. Victor wants to drop my option, you can tell him for me that I'll walk out of this studio and straight to the top without any so-called help from Victory Studios." He strode out past a startled Kurt Vogler.

He put off calling Kathy in the afternoon. The taste of the

lunch was still with him. He didn't want it fouling their conversation.

"You're wound up like a tight spring," commented Sammy. "Hear anything about the show's ratings?"

"No." Marty's answer was terse.

"Trouble between you and Kathy?"

He shook his head.

"So I'm a brilliant assistant director and a lousy mindreader. There's a bottle of Scotch in the prop wagon. You look as if you could use a shot." He was gone and back in a moment.

"Next week's script came down from mimeo. I put it on your dressing table." Sammy nodded toward the green folder as he poured. "Another who stole what, with the standard red herrings before the fadeout." After two years, the scripts blended into each other from week to week, each, once shot, undistinguishable from the others.

"I had lunch with one of the secretaries from upstairs."

"And?" Marty let the warmth of the Scotch travel through him, cleansing the taste from his mouth.

"Not so good. They got the ratings this morning. A little too hairy for comfort. Those NBC movies are taking a big chunk of our audience. I could have waited for the brass to come down from upstairs and lay on the optimistic horseshit, but I thought you'd want to know." Sammy knew how he hated the professional bull artists.

"Thanks." He uncoiled himself from the chair. "At this point I wouldn't bat an eye if the *Caravan* series sank like a stone. I've had it up to here with Victory TV."

Sammy answered the knock on the dressing room door.

"Mr. Tabor?" She was stacked, but the face was a loser. Black roots belied the red hair. "I'm Eileen Locke, remember?"

He didn't but he said he did.

"I was one of the townspeople in the courtroom sequence last week." She patted the gold lamé swimsuit that was glued to her curves. "We're shooting a beauty contest scene on the next stage," she explained.

"Can I get you a cup of coffee?" Sammy asked.

"Oh, thanks, yes." She perched on the edge of the sofa, arranging her legs carefully.

"I wouldn't have asked in front of him," she said. "You could do me a big favor, Mr. Tabor."

"What favor is that?"

"I really need work. I've had a little run of bad luck. It's only temporary. Honest, it's not a big jam or anything. It's just that . . ." The girl was genuinely nervous. "Mr. Tabor. They're going to repossess my car." She paused, self-conscious. "I really need a job. Bad. This is only one day, the thing I'm doing. One of the grips told me he thought there might be a crowd scene in your next week's show. I don't know this assistant director. He wasn't on the one I did for you, but I thought since I had worked the show before, maybe a word from you . . . " She trailed off, chipping disconcertedly at the polish on a fingernail.

"It's not really my department———"

"Please, just this once." Her eyes stayed fixed to his while she uncrossed her legs very slowly and crossed them again. "If there's anything I can do as a favor in return . . . "

He took in the harsh red hair and the glossy mouth. Make-up had caked darkly in the lines of her neck.

Sammy stood in the doorway holding a steaming cup of coffee. His look asked Marty if he should intrude.

"I'll do what I can, Miss Locke. You have my word. Now why don't you take your coffee back with you to the other stage." He stood up.

"Thank you very much, Mr. Tabor," she said primly. "I sure appreciate this."

Marty turned away from them and began dialing the telephone. He could use a breath of fresh air. Talking to Kathy was a far cry from talking to Eileen Locke. A whole beautiful sweet world of difference.

"Mart. Come here."

Kathy stood in front of the large window in the living room of their suite.

"What are you looking at?"

"The sky. Look. That's what I like most about Palm Springs. When the sun sets, the sky turns iridescent, like a butterfly's wing."

Marty slipped an arm around her shoulders. Silently they watched the change of the sky from red to mauve to purple and then to blue. In the twilight, the brown camel-humps of

the hills disappeared into the inky evening. He turned Kathy
to him, and they kissed.

"Do I smell horsey?" she wanted to know.

"What of it? It never stopped Roy Rogers and Dale
Evans."

He held her, satisfied simply by her warmth. That afternoon they had gone riding on one of the dry desert trails so
full of surprises for those who cared to look. Passers-by on the
highway saw only the brown earth, sage, and tumbleweed. At
closer range, the desert bloomed with brilliant, tiny flowers.
Even the thick and hoary cacti grew delicate blossoms. Discoveries unrolled everywhere around them. They had ridden
slowly, talking little. The closeness of sharing made words
unnecessary. He liked to watch her ride ahead of him, her
body moving in effortless rhythm with the horse.

"Let's go to bed," he said.

"I'm going to take a shower first."

He followed her, the two of them shedding their clothes as
they went.

Marty held her to him under the spray of warm water,
gently sliding the soap over her shoulders and down her back
to her buttocks. His fingers ran over her smooth, soapy skin.
He reached the soap between her legs, lathering the soft hair,
and brought it lingeringly up to her breasts. Beads of water
fell from her taut nipples.

"My turn," she said, taking the soap from him. She knelt
on the wet tile and soaped him, working the slippery suds
with her fingers until he grew hard. She caught the water with
her cupped hands and rinsed him. Her mouth took him over.
He watched the rivulets that streamed down the curve of her
back from the silky wetness of her hair.

"Kath."

In a single motion they were onto the bathmat on the
floor.

She pulled the extra blanket over them. The desert night
had become chilly.

"Thanks," said Marty.

"I didn't mean to wake you."

"You didn't." He reached over and pulled her to his side
of the bed. "Kath. Do you love me?"

"Very much. I thought you knew that."

"You never said it. Most girls can't stop saying it, especially in bed. It struck me odd you never had."

"Most girls make asses of themselves, if you ask me. People know when they're loved. The words don't make a difference." She propped herself up on one elbow. "Didn't you know I love you?"

"Yes." He kissed her lightly on the shoulder.

"See? And I know you love me. We don't need all those statements of twenty-five words or less. Especially we don't need them in bed." She slid her leg under his.

"What would you like to do?"

"About what?"

"Eventually."

"Oh." She nestled her head into his pillow. "I suppose I'd like to marry a man I truly like and have his children. Any better suggestions?"

Marty lay silent.

"Are you falling asleep?"

"Kath, I don't know what's going to happen with *Caravan*. Our ratings have gotten chancy. It's the NBC competition. We may not be renewed for another season."

She waited for him to continue. Somewhere in the far distance a coyote wailed.

"I know we've been together nearly a year, but let's wait a while, until I know where I'm at."

She slid her head onto his chest. "Who's pushing?"

"Maybe I am." His arms went around her.

Marty propped his feet up on the dressing room sofa and reached for the phone. Kathy answered after two rings.

"Did you get your call for tomorrow?"

"Dammit, yes," she replied. "We're shooting off Santa Monica Pier someplace. It's that skin-diving thing I told you about."

"What do they want you to do this time, wrestle with a porpoise?"

"Nothing so complicated. Just a bunch of shots going under and coming up. Gloria French can't swim, so they need a double. Are you still going to be finished shooting before lunch?"

"Looks that way. All we have is a couple of pick-up shots

from last week's show. I was hoping you wouldn't have to work."

"I know." She paused. "Listen, why don't you drive down to the ocean? We'll have to come ashore for lunch. There are only two boats, the one I'll be on and the one for the camera crew. They're both fairly small. I'm sure they won't crowd them up with stacks of box lunches."

"Can you find out?"

"I'll call now. I'll let you know where to look for us."

"Okay, and I'll ask Sammy to double check if I'll be through before lunch."

He waited in his chair behind the camera while Sammy called upstairs.

"You that eager to get out of here?" Hal Denver was directing this week's episode.

"You would be too," Marty smiled.

"Oh, that's the way it is." Hal gave him a smile and walked toward the camera.

"Marty?"

He looked up.

"Mike Stanton. How are you?"

"Mike. Of course. Here, pull up a chair." He saw Sammy coming from the phone.

"All systems are go," he reported. "You should be out of here by eleven tomorrow, give or take half an hour."

"Thanks."

"I haven't seen you since New York," said Mike.

"Right."

Mike was a good-looking guy, wiry but strong as an ox. He was letting his dark hair grow longer than when Marty had last seen him.

"You going to be on next week's show?" Marty asked.

"I'm not acting. I'm observing. Just looking around. We're thinking of producing a couple of plays at a little theater on Melrose. Thought I'd look at the local talent."

Funny phrase from Mike. His father and mother had been in the makeup and hairdressing department at Warner Brothers. Mike had been brought up in the business, even to the point of having been a kid actor until his voice began to change.

"You living in New York still?" asked Marty.

"Just got here two weeks ago. Tell me," he leaned over the arm of his chair, "do you like your director on this show?"

"Hal? Sure. This is his first one with us, but he seems to be doing fine. Never blows his top, communicates well with the cast and crew. Why? You thinking of having him direct your plays?"

"Could be. He has a solid reputation."

Marty saw Sammy beckoning him to work. He stood up and gave Mike his hand. "Good luck. Let me know when you plan to open."

"Will do."

Marty and Hal were walking back from the commissary. They had spent lunch discussing the afternoon's shooting. Hal wanted to change his attack on the upcoming scene. Marty returned Laura Curtis' wave from across the street.

"What are the plays Mike Stanton is producing?" he asked Hal.

"I don't know. I don't think he knows."

"Did I misunderstand? I thought he wanted you to direct."

"Talk." Hal tossed away his cigaret.

"He's not producing?"

"He's got some Philadelphia society girl on the hook." He nodded at two secretaries who smiled in their direction. "The way I hear it, she's nuts about him and she has more millions than she knows what to do with. They rented a house here, and she's going to back him."

"Sounds like a good deal."

"Except for the order of things," he said wryly. "The guy I prefer finds a play he's burning to produce. Then he goes after the money to finance it. Stanton is going ass-backward."

"Now that he's fallen into a jam pot, he's looking for a toy to play with." Marty held the stage door open for Hal.

"You got it."

"Too bad. Mike Stanton was a fair actor. He has talent. I saw him do some damned good scenes when we were studying together in New York. I wonder why it never panned out for him. Maybe he wasn't ambitious."

"He's ambitious," Hal countered. "He's got all those millions on the string and he goes around calling himself a producer. The truth is, he's trying to do it the easy way. That gives you the answer to your question. He's lazy. Ambitious but lazy."

"I take it you're not going to direct the plays," he smiled.

Hal looked surprised. "Why not? If he comes up with two I like and there's plenty of bread to hire a good cast, why not? Hell, it might be fun to get off a sound stage and back into the theater. You all set for this next scene?"

"I'll go check makeup." He crossed toward his dressing room.

"Kathy just called," Sammy told him. "She said they'd probably break for lunch at twelve-thirty tomorrow and she'd meet you on the pier. That make sense to you?"

"Perfect."

There was plenty of time, so he took the long way to the ocean, along Sunset Boulevard and its canyons curving down to the sea. The top was down on the Jag, and the fresh air, with its first faint scent of the Pacific, invigorated him. He enjoyed taking the car around the turns, feeling the smooth, sure way it tracked on the road. The sun had burned off the morning fog. One last canyon, and before him lay the ocean, stretching as far as the eye could see, almost blinding in the noon glare.

Kathy waved him to the end of the pier. She sat on one of the weathered pilings, wrapped in a terry-cloth robe and munching a sandwich. Around her, several small children had gathered to bask in the company of "movie people." One of them recognized Marty and produced a battered notepad. He signed autographs for them.

"Most of the crew went to get drinks," she said. "It's cold out there."

"Are you warm enough?"

"Sure. I wear a wet suit. It's on the boat."

"Mr. Tabor," one of the kids cut in, "is she your wife?"

"Not yet." They caught each other's eyes and enjoyed the moment.

"Want some cookies?" invited Kathy. The kids scrambled around her. The littlest, a small boy of about five with a thatched head of flaxen hair, got shoved aside.

"Not fair," she said, retrieving him from the flock. She settled him on her lap with a cookie.

Marty liked to watch her with kids. They seemed to seek her out like a pied piper. Something in her manner let them know she was leveling with them. He smiled to himself, seeing her deep in conversation with the boy. There was something so right about the picture. Never before had he had the desire to have a child with anyone.

"Hey!" The crew was sauntering back from lunch. Craig Banner, the second-unit director, extended a hand to Marty. "Bring your fishing rod?"

Marty laughed and shook his head.

"Let's go. Come on, Esther Williams; time to suit up."

Kathy deposited the boy on the ground, and they headed for the boats.

"Afraid you'll have to come with us on the camera boat," Craig told him. "That thing Kathy's in doesn't have a cabin. Much as they might like to see you in this picture, I don't think that's what they planned."

The two boats headed out into the gently rolling ocean. The larger one pulled alongside Kathy's boat, waiting until the driver lowered an anchor and climbed out onto the camera boat. They anchored themselves about fifty yards away.

"Kathy," Craig was using the bullhorn. "This time go over the side near us and surface by the bow, if you can. Give us some time underwater so that there's room to cut. Got it?"

She waved an arm.

It took several takes to get the shot. Marty sat on the flying bridge, relaxing, watching her clamber in and out of the boat, slick and agile in her black wet suit. Even with the added weight of the oxygen tanks on her back, she managed to be graceful.

It was a lazy way to spend an afternoon. He was unconscious of the passing time. It was a welcome break from the pressures of the studio, pushing to grind out television shows for air dates which waited for no man.

"Now, Kathy, just two more cuts. This time I want you to stay under for quite some time. We're going to keep rolling. Don't come up for at least fifty seconds. Keep an eye on your watch. We'll use the footage to intercut for suspense."

She waved acknowledgment and, turning, gave an extra wave to Marty. He returned it.

"Coffee?" Someone produced a thermos.

"Yes. Thanks." He sipped slowly.

It took him a moment before he realized something had gone wrong. Below, in the cockpit, the sound of the men's voices had taken a different pitch. Craig was yelling. Marty, bolting from his seat, vaulted to the lower deck. Men were scrambling over each other. Two hauled frantically at the anchor line. One hurtled past him to start the motor.

"Jesus God," someone said.

Marty followed his gaze. A few feet off the stern of the other boat there was a disturbance in the water, a small churning in the otherwise calm ocean. He lunged toward Craig, questioning.

Craig's face was ashen. He stood frozen, face to face with Marty. Only from somewhere behind him did Marty hear the word "shark."

As they drew alongside, the men began to beat it off with anything they could get their hands on. Two men were using the sharp ends of the camera tripod. Marty seized an orange life jacket from a pair of hands and lurched to the side of the boat. He pushed through the men reaching furiously into the foaming spray, some with pocket knives, some with their bare hands. They were not close enough. He spun toward the stern, making his way to Craig who was in the likeliest place to pick her out of the water. Craig leaned halfway over the side, grasping, but two of the others a few feet down the line reached her first. Marty started for them.

"No!" Craig held his arm.

He jerked it away. Three men grabbed him from behind and pinned him against the side of the boat. They held him. It was Craig who stopped his struggling with a hard slap across the face.

"Don't go," he said. "I saw."

They would not let him go.

She was wrapped in a gray blanket soaked through with rusty stains. The ambulance they had radioed for waited on the pier. As they lifted her inside, Marty saw her hair cascading softly over the edge of the blanket. He moved toward her.

"Marty," Craig put a hand on his shoulder. "There's no sense in your going there."

It occurred to him then that they were not taking her to a hospital.

Lisa opened the door in her bathing suit. The doorbell had brought her in from the pool. She stared at them.

"What is it? What's wrong?" He shook his head.

She moved to let them in.

"I'm Craig Banner," he told her. "It's Kathy Hayman——"

"Lord, what——?"

"An accident."

Marty stood in the middle of the living-room floor, as if he did not know where he was.

"May I call my wife, Miss Taylor? I drove Marty's car, and she'll have to pick me up."

She showed him to the telephone.

"Here." She held the glass of brandy in front of Marty. He was hunched over in the chair, his face hidden in his hands.

"Please drink it," she persisted.

He forced it down, gagging.

"What happened, Marty?"

He turned away.

She read the story in the paper the next morning.

He woke with her shaking him. All weekend he had been in and out of sleep. The waking tore at him. The first few seconds were like any other awakening. Then he would remember, and the horror and the emptiness would come over him.

"What time is it?" He asked the question automatically.

"Six o'clock. Sunday night." Lisa held out a mug of coffee to him. He shook his head.

"Mart. Please. You have to drink it. Please. You've been drunk since Friday night. You have to go to work tomorrow. I called Sammy, and he brought over a script."

"Lisa," he rolled over, his back to her in the dark room, "I can't."

"You can." She reached for his shoulders and turned him toward her. "You know you can't stay like this forever. You've got to try." She flicked on the light. "Get up and take a shower and shave. I'll be in the kitchen."

"I loved her."

"I know, Marty."

She got some food down him and made him run his lines with her. His mind couldn't seem to retain the work.

"You'll be all right," she said finally. "I know you will. Sammy says you have a seven-thirty call in the morning. If you want to take a sleeping pill, I'll make sure you wake up in time."

He nodded numbly.

"Marty." She stopped him in the doorway. "I thought you'd want to know. Kathy's family came down from San Luis Obispo to take her back there."

It was the last time they mentioned it.

"You're doing fine," said Sammy quietly. They had the script spread out on the table in a corner of the Redwood Room. "Do you want to run that last part again? It's still not right." They went over the scene once more.

Sammy had nursed him through the morning's work, drilling the lines constantly between takes. So far, Marty had not cost them any shooting time. The morning had been a blur to him. He wondered if he would be able to remember this day at all or if the time would come when his mind would not be dulled with grief and he would remember all of it clearly

"Finished?" Sammy was taking their checks. "We'd better be heading back."

They stopped at the cashier's counter, waiting in line to pay. The queue moved slowly. Sammy, out of the corner of his eye, saw it happen.

Mac Herman must have just paid his bill and stepped aside when Marty lunged for him. He spun him around and, in front of people too puzzled and stunned to move, smashed his fist into Mac's face. Sammy leaped out of line and pulled Marty up from where the two men lay struggling on the floor. The huge room was hushed.

"Christ! Take it easy, Marty!" Sammy said. "What the hell are you doing?"

A couple of people were helping Mac up. He was trembling, holding a hand to his face. He brought his eyes up to Marty's.

"I'm sorry," Mac said.

Marty turned his back on him. "Let's get the fuck out of here."

Obie caught sight of Marty standing in the doorway and waved from his table without results. Marty squinted, adjusting his eyes from the brightness of the late July sun to the dim interior of the Brown Derby. He finally discerned George, the maître d', who led him to the table.

"Well?"

"What do you mean, 'well'? I hate it when clients say 'well.' Translated, it means 'what have you done for me lately?' "

"Well?" Marty smiled.

"So you're taping a week's shows of *Top the Odds,* aren't you? What's that, chopped liver?" Obie liked Marty. There was something decent and good-humored about the guy.

"You know as well as I do that it's not acting." He paused long enough for the waiter to take their orders.

"So it's a game show. It may not be great art, but it's money, and until we firm the deal to sell your *Caravan* residuals, you need the bread."

"I just get up to here with it sometimes. I haven't worked in four months. It seems nobody wants to touch me with a ten-foot pole. Come on, Obie. How do you think that makes me feel?"

"Lousy. Look, Marty," he leaned toward him over the table, "I warned you that if the show was dropped you might have to go into cold storage for a while. It happens. You know damned well it had nothing to do with you. That show made you a name. Hell, the network got more beefs from viewers for bouncing you than they've had for anything in five years. It was the concept of the show that failed. It was a one-gimmick premise, and it finally wore out its welcome."

"That doesn't help me." He set his martini on the table and ran his finger around the rim of the glass.

"The fact is, maybe you were a little too successful. You got yourself so identified with the character that none of the studios can see you as anything else. The networks think you're too closely linked with the sponsor's product. You did all those commercial lead-ins and endorsements, and they figure no other sponsor will go for you until people forget that previous identification. I warned you that those little extras paid well but they had their drawbacks. Now what are you doing," he grinned, "calling me a heavy because I told you the truth?"

Marty smiled ruefully. "Shut up and eat."

They ate in silence, if the din of the Brown Derby at lunchtime could be called that. Beneath the framed caricatures on the walls, tourists rubbernecked from their banquettes, chattering among themselves at the sight of each passing celebrity. The Derby regulars, all in the entertainment industry, table-hopped with abandon, swapping wise-cracks, hearty handshakes, and much backslapping. Above the clatter of dishes, silver, and conversation, the paging system announced telephone calls. When the name was famous, and most were, diners tracked the waiter with their eyes as he carried a phone to the waiting table, much as a cat watches a mouse to the cheese. Slowly the luncheon crowd began to thin out, and the noise lessened.

"I just wish to hell," Marty laid his napkin on the table, "that the Italian picture hadn't fallen through."

"So do I. You know I wouldn't have let you do it under those circumstances, though. When you ask those guys to put the salary in escrow in American dollars and they refuse, it only means one thing. They don't have the dough. If I'd let you go ahead with it, you'd have been stiffed but good."

"True. Thanks."

"Listen, Marty," Obie cleared his throat, "I have something here that I think you ought to read. I don't think you'll like it, but take a look at it anyhow."

"You don't sound very enthusiastic. What is it, a musical version of *Mein Kampf*?"

"In blackface. No, it's a play that was sent to me for Colin Kirkwood. He turned it down, of course. He's got more movie commitments than he can handle. Besides, he's so hot now that he'd be a jackass to junk it all for some Broadway show that could fold in one night. On the other hand, you have nothing to lose. I haven't mentioned your name to the producer, so I don't honestly know whether or not he'd be interested. If it turns out you like it, you might have to fly to New York and read for them, at your own expense, that is."

"Do you like it?"

"On the level, no, I don't. But you got to remember one thing. I'm strictly a *Gold Diggers of 1933* guy. My kind of stuff is the broads dancing on the wings of the plane and Dick Powell singing a love song in some rowboat. These days, the plays I read out of New York are all so goddam depressing. I can get the same results from reading the head-lines in the newspaper. What's more, I don't have to pay admission."

"Okay, hand it over." Marty took the thick manila envelope.

"Waiter!" Obie waved. "Bring me a telephone and the

check, please." He reached for his wallet. "What time are you due back at the taping?"

"A few minutes." Marty checked his watch and got up. "Walk you to the parking lot?"

"You go ahead. I have to check my office for calls and go on to an appointment."

3

Obie

12:15 P.M.

Actors. Children, all of them. Got to have that constant reassurance. Yes, you are still good-looking. You are still talented. Yes, the world is waiting to see you.

What the hell, writers are no better. They're all religious fanatics and paranoid. Every one of them thinks he's bringing the light of truth, the Holy Grail, to illuminate this dark world, and all the producers, directors, and actors are out to gun him down before he can complete the sacred mission. Nuts, all of them.

The directors make like goddam da Vincis. Always complaining about the inferior quality of the materials they have to work with. Inferior materials including their producers who never, but never, understand the Meaning of Art.

Sometimes I can't blame the poor bastards. Producers want it all yesterday but they still want it good. They commission the work of art and sit around sweating like pigs while the studio chews out their asses for running over budget. Nervous life.

Jesus, but Jack Haller better save his keester with this picture. He blows this number and he'll be a leper in this town. Lisa could always support him, but for Jack that would be like having his balls cut off and run up a flagpole for the world to see.

Laura's the unknown quantity. Either she's as controlled as she looks or she's going to blow sky high and take the picture with her. I don't want that kid out of my sight until I'm a hundred percent sure she's on her feet. That's a hell of a thing to have happened. She's a young girl yet, young to be a widow, anyhow. Hard to think of her being only twenty-two. Seems like she's been around forever. Damned rough, these last few years. She works too hard, one picture after another.

69

*No wonder her health has been lousy. She wouldn't have had
to break her ass if Mike hadn't had expensive tastes.*

*Who am I to talk? Between us, Ruthie and I hold the heavy
weight crown in that department. Eleven pairs of shoes.
Honest-to-God, Ruth, can't you buy anything except in job
lots? And since when is sable a fun fur? A sable poncho, for
chrissakes. And the eighteen pairs of gloves she hid at Rosemary's house last week so I wouldn't know. Rosemary talks
too much when she drinks. Poor Ruthie. That's what you get
for quitting high school and marrying a bum like me. You
get a husband who's never home because he's too busy making it big for you and the kids. You get two kids who go to
highbrow schools and colleges and learn so much they can't
even talk to us common people. Ruthie's got nothing to play
with but money. Christ, I can't even get her to read a book.
She doesn't like cards and she won't learn to play golf. Her
whole number is how she looks. Massages, exercise class, the
steam room, the manicures. And the clothes. The clothes.
Women in this town have it tough if they're not in the business. Can't go to the supermarket without first seeing the hairdresser for fear they'll find themselves standing next to Kim
Novak and losing the contest.*

*I'd give my ass if Ruthie could interest me. I like her, after
all. I'd lay off the broads, maybe even the track and the
poker at the club. But, God knows, a guy has to get kicks
someplace. What's life without some kicks? A desert, that's
what. I can't even get a thrill out of writing some dicey contract anymore. They're all just another deal. You cajole and
compromise and tell the expected lies until it pans out or
doesn't. Either way, life goes on.*

*Not quite. As long as I'm so far in hock at the club, there's
always that to keep me hustling. Except that I've been in the
red so long, even that gets to be routine. One of these days,
one of these fine days, a longshot will come in at the track,
and there'll be fuck-you money to spare. And as long as
Ruthie doesn't know, she can have her games.*

"Mr. Straus? Claire Poland is calling."

Shit

"I'll take it, Julie. Hello, Claire."

"Is this the Oscar Bernard Straus?"

"The same."

The withered old tarantula still thinks she's a flirt.

"Obie, darling, I missed you at the services. I did so want to express my sympathy to Laura."

"I'm sure she knows how you feel, Claire. She knew you were there. She just didn't feel like socializing. You understand."

"Of course. Poor Laura."

Hard to tell if she's dripping sympathy or sarcasm. Claire is such a full-on phony you never know what she's thinking until you read it in her column.

"Obie, what are Laura's plans now?"

"Just to finish the picture." We hope.

"No vacation? No remarriage?"

"She's in the middle of a picture, Claire, a picture the producer would prefer didn't go any further over budget. She has to go to work."

"Yes. We all understand about Jack getting himself out on a limb. There's been some talk of bankruptcy."

She's fishing, the bitch.

"I think that's overstating the case. Everyone in this town has a few enemies, Claire. I thought you were too smart to listen to malicious gossip."

"Checking, darling, just checking. Now tell me, off the record of course, do you think Laura will marry Marty Tabor?"

"Good God, Claire, isn't that a little premature? The flowers aren't wilted from the funeral!"

"You didn't answer my question."

"I don't think, at the moment, that Laura has anything of the sort on her mind. She's too busy working."

"Now? You mean she's working now? Today?"

"Yes. Call it occupational therapy, if you like. The girl's a real trouper. She couldn't let down all those people who are depending on her."

"She must have tremendous composure."

"She's an actress. She knows how to mask her own troubles."

She's still fishing, but what for?

"Is there anything else I can do for you, Claire? I have a couple of clients waiting in the outer office."

"Obie, dear, you're a great help. You could, if you would, tell me why Marty Tabor suddenly evaporated from the

*scene after the accident, when everyone knows he and
Laura——*"

"Marty? He hasn't evaporated to my knowledge. I spoke to
him on the phone fifteen minutes ago."

"But he wasn't at the funeral or the cemetery."

"Maybe you just missed him."

"Obie, never shit a shitter, sweetheart. He wasn't there,
and we both know it. Everybody involved in this unpleas-
antness has begun avoiding each other like the plague. I was
at the church. All of Laura's dear, dear friends found seats as
far away from each other as they possibly could without
being out on the sidewalk. I'd just like to know what's going
on here."

"Nothing. Nothing is going on here or anywhere else,
Claire. It's been a difficult time for all of us, not something
we want to discuss with each other. In fact, everyone might
be happier if it were forgotten."

"Is that why Laura won't return my calls? I've heard the
same story from a couple of other reporters. She won't talk
to anyone. She shouldn't forget that the press has been in her
corner for a long time. We've always been very fair with
her."

"Claire, once and for all, can't you understand that the girl
has had a terrible experience? She saw her husband die in
front of her. For Christ's sake, Claire, is that something you
think she'd like to chat about? The girl is very upset!"

"Not too upset to go to the studio and work."

"I've told you why she did that. As far as I'm concerned,
that's all there is to say. If you want to pursue it further,
you'll have to talk to Laura. If you ask me, your interest
borders on being ghoulish."

That may cost me, but it's worth it.

"Obie, dear, easy does it. You know I'm only doing my
job, and you know how fond I've always been of Laura. I
like Marty, too."

"Claire. What can I do? I don't know anything I haven't
told you. What the hell, weren't we together when it happened, you and Ruth and I? Weren't the three of us standing
outside on the terrace by the bar? You were talking about
what a good party it was."

"I said that Mike and Laura were giving a party that could

have held its own with any that Marian Davies gave in her heydey."

Writers. Writers and their sacred words.

"That was going to be my lead item until the accident happened."

"I have to sign off, Claire. I can't keep these people waiting any longer."

"All right, Obie. Talk to you soon again."

Not if I see you first, baby. Where did I put the extra package of cigarets? I smoke too much.

"Julie?"

"Yes, Mr. Straus?"

"Call Miss Curtis' dressing room on the set."

"Yes, Mr. Straus."

If I had any brains, I'd quit smoking. If I had any brains, I'd also quit gambling. If I had any brains, they'd be shot by now anyhow with all this aggravation.

"I have Miss Curtis' wardrobe lady on the line, Mr. Straus."

"Indigo? Where's Laura?"

"She's rehearsing. Is there anything I can do? Would you like me to call her?"

"That's not necessary. Just tell her for me that Claire Poland wants to talk to her in the worst way. If Laura's smart, she'll call Claire and have a very brief, very polite conversation with her. Got that? Very brief, very polite. Otherwise, I wouldn't put it past that barracuda to show up on the set this afternoon."

"I'll tell her. Is there anything else?"

"No, thanks. How is she? How's Laura bearing up?"

"She's doing pretty well, poor baby. She'll be all right. I think this is good for her."

"I'm glad to hear it. Good-bye Indigo."

Let's hope to God she is doing all right. At least we can keep that bitch Claire Poland from sniffing around and upsetting her.

Jack, your goddam picture better be a bigger hit than Ben-Hur after what I've done for you and the rest of my clients on this film. From the start, I've had my neck stuck out so far I feel like a turkey at Thanksgiving time. The last thing I need is to make an enemy of Claire Poland.

"Julie?"

"Yes, sir."

"Before you go to lunch, send Claire Poland two dozen red roses. Have them write on the card 'Thank you for being patient with an ulcerous old man' and sign my name." .. ..

"Mr. Straus? Do you have an ulcer?"

"Any minute, Julie, any minute."

☆

OBIE left the Brown Derby shortly after Marty. His appointment was with Christy. He called her more often than the others, not because she was better looking or had a wilder body. He called her because she neither asked questions nor favors. She didn't talk much, except for the words he wanted to hear. He enjoyed watching her. She seemed to really dig what he liked.

The motel on Sunset discreetly maintained its parking lot behind the building so that the cars were not visible from the street. Nevertheless, Obie parked a block away and walked to the rear entrance. Christy always had the same room.

She motioned toward the ice bucket and a half-empty bottle of vodka. "Want a drink?"

"You know what I want, Christy."

She smiled and tossed her dark hair back.

He sat down in one of the two plastic-covered chairs. The afternoon sun through the partially closed venetian blinds streaked across her body as she lifted the dress over her head. She wore no underclothes.

She reached into the ice bucket and brought out two cubes. Catlike, she walked to where he sat and stood above him, rotating the ice cubes over her nipples. He watched them grow hard.

He slipped a hand between her legs and fingered her lightly.

"The bed," he said.

Christy lay spread on the sheets, her legs apart, her hands between her thighs, manipulating herself.

"Talk," Obie commanded from the chair.

She moaned the words, exciting him with obscenities. She reached one hand to her breast and touched it lingeringly. He watched her body begin to move rhythmically as her hands did their work. Faster and faster she moved, gasping out the words that pleased him, until he saw her hands dive deep between her legs, digging furiously at her own body. Her pelvis vibrated back and forth as she whimpered a last tremulous phrase for him and was silent.

"Was it good?" he wanted to know.

"You saw," she said, catching her breath. "It was good."

"Come here, now." His fingers worked at his zipper.

She kneeled in front of the chair. "I'm so wet."

"Let me feel." He touched the warm wetness on her thighs.

Bending, she used her hands and her soft, dark hair to caress him. When he was ready, she opened her lips to receive him. He came into her, throbbing.

Christy came out of the bathroom and handed him a towel. "Want that drink now?"

"A short one. I have to be at the studio in half an hour."

He sipped the vodka and watched her dress. "I want you to do me a favor."

She turned to him, waiting.

"This one is English. A very important writer-director."

She gave no reaction. She had done favors for Obie before.

"You know these guys. Big egos, all of them. They want to think it's their own irresistible animal magnetism that gets the chicks."

"So I'm an actress friend of yours that you think he'd enjoy for a dinner companion. Is that it?"

Christy knew her job. She was good at it, well-spoken and well-dressed enough to put it over.

"He's at the Bel Air Hotel. I'll call you after I've spoken to him. Then you can ring him up. This one's important to me, Christy. I need him to owe me a favor. Make it a big favor he owes me." He took a fifty dollar bill from his money clip and reached for another bill. "This one's for today."

She slipped the money into her handbag. "I try to stay away from the English. They can be very freaky. Do you know anything about this guy?"

"Nothing to worry about. I met a girl in London who's been there. Says it's even a little dull. I'm going to trust you to see that it's anything but dull, okay?"

"Okay."

"I'll call you, Christy." He let himself out the door.

As he drove into the carport, he could see Rosita through the kitchen window. She padded around the stove in the slow, uneven shuffle that was as much a part of her as her Mexican accent.

Ruth, as usual, was on the telephone. She did not pause in her conversation which Obie guessed to be with Rosemary. She threw him a perfunctory kiss and handed him the message pad, nodding in agreement with whatever was being said on the other end of the line.

The only message was from Bob Mann. Since Obie had no need for a dentist, Bob must be calling to make a golf date. Either that or his wife, Vickie, had got after him again to ask Obie to read some of her work.

"Hello, dear." Ruth had finally hung up. "What's new?" she asked, as always.

"Not much." That was true. "I think Gordon Favor is going to leave the agency."

"You didn't ask me what's new with me," Ruth countered.

"What's new?" He glanced through the mail.

"I'll show you after dinner. What about Gordon Favor?" Ruth asked. Before he could reply, she stopped him with a motion of her hand. "Rosita!" she called in the direction of the dining room, "we'll eat whenever you're ready."

There came a "Si" from amid the clink of silverware as she set the table.

Obie lit a cigaret and dialed Bob Mann's number. It was busy. Ruth, curled up on the sofa, was leafing through *Vogue*. "You didn't tell me about Gordon Favor," she said, her eyes on the pages.

"I think he's going to dump us. Same old story. You break your balls for a kid, lend him money when he's starting out, send him to a decent tailor, send him to Bob Mann to get his crummy teeth capped, find him a good drama coach, and finally you get him the second lead in a TV series. Then he gets full of himself and dumps you for another agent. I guess," he said half to himself "that those who make it don't want to hang around people who knew them when they were down."

"Mmm," she nodded. "There's a great looking Galanos in this issue. Roz Russell wears a lot of his things."

"Good for Roz Russell." He tried Bob's number again, without success.

"I just want you to be proud of me when we go places."

"I am proud of you. With or without Galanos." In about

thirty seconds, he thought, the conversation will get around to Brentwood.

"Rosemary says she and Hal have seen a house in Trousdale they may buy."

Make that five seconds, revised Obie.

"How come? I thought they were happy in the Palisades."

"They want the kids in the Beverly Hills schools so they have a better chance for college. Besides, the taxes are lower in Beverly Hills. I like Trousdale. It's a pretty area."

"But our kids are grown up. Married. We don't have a school problem." Did Ruth feel as foolish as he did, going over the same old lines in the same old conversation like the actors in some yearly passion play but without the passion?

"We still have to pay taxes." She tossed aside the magazine.

"There's not that great a difference in the taxes. And Brentwood suits me fine."

"But what about me?"

"Ruth." He felt suddenly stifled with weariness. "You and that faggot decorator redid this place not eight months ago. Aren't you satisfied?"

"Of course I'm satisfied. We put a lot into this old house. We could make a good profit on it. Rosemary says it's a seller's market."

"So? If it's a seller's market, we'd lose the profit the minute we went looking for another place."

She fell silent. Evidently she hadn't considered that point. Rosita came to the doorway and asked them if they wanted to eat now.

"Marcy called today." Ruth stared into her coffee, watching the swirls as she stirred it.

"And?" Their daughter never wrote. Obie remembered when Marcy was a teenager, perpetually on the telephone. He used to tease her, "Where I come from, they'd say you have Brown Cord Fever." It was still the same.

"Regina has been invited to a coming-out party. One of the girls in the class ahead of her at boarding school is making her debut this year."

And so it went. Obie found himself wondering if Marcy would be buying his sixteen-year-old granddaughter a Galanos to wear to the party.

"I hope to God she's learning something at that fancy school with its fancy tuition."

"She won a red ribbon jumping her horse last Saturday."

"Yes? Good for Reggie." Marcy hated to hear her daughter called anything but Regina.

"They're thinking of sending her to school in France. The Sorbonne, I think she said."

How incongruous, Ruthie and he, of all people, sitting here talking about a grandchild going to debuts and being educated in Paris. He remembered Sophie, Ruth's mother, laying out her precious Passover plates on the tattered lace tablecloth she had brought from Austria. Sophie, smelling of good things from her kitchen, insisting they eat, eat. Sophie Rosensweig, who lost all three sisters in the Triangle Shirtwaist fire and her husband to pneumonia because they did not have enough heat in the apartment or money for a hospital. It was a long way from Brownsville to Brentwood.

He changed the subject. "I thought you were going with Rosemary to her painting class today."

"You know I can't paint," she shrugged.

"Neither can Rosemary, but that hasn't stopped her."

"We went to one of the galleries on La Cienega to look at some sculpture. An Italian sculptor has an exhibit there. A lot of good people are buying his things. They've already doubled in value since his last show. The gallery owner said Kirk Douglas and his wife have bought two pieces."

Obie pushed back his chair. The phone rang. "Tell Rosita I'll get it."

"Bad news," said Cal on the other end.

"How bad?"

"Aqueduct was n.g."

"Not even one race?"

"One. You recouped a little on the sixth with Comealong. Not enough to make a difference, though." Cal sounded apologetic.

"How much does that make?" Obie steeled himself.

"Sixty-two hundred this month. I told you, it's bad."

"I know. I'll go to the bank tomorrow."

"Sure. Don't like to see it get up that high."

"You'll get the money," Obie said tersely.

"Didn't mean that. I know I will. Hell, your credit is good with me. I meant your luck's due for a change."

"Damned right it is." He hung up the phone.

Ruth stood in the doorway, poking the tip of her shoe into the pile of the white carpet.

"Do you think we ought to dye it?" she asked.

Obie looked up.

"Do you think we ought to dye it? I'm beginning to think white looks too nineteen-thirties. I was talking to Rosemary's decorator, the one they'll use if they get the Trousedale house. He says royal blue is going to be the big color next year."

"Jesus, Ruth, dye it. Dye it black, for all I care."

"Black picks up too much lint. I thought maybe we could dye it and add a fur throw rug on top of it, under the coffee table."

He nodded absently and dialed the telephone. Bob did want a golf date, and Vickie did want him to look at one of her manuscripts. He set the time for Saturday and told Bob to bring along her work.

"I've been waiting all evening for you to notice," Ruth said as he replaced the receiver.

"Notice what?"

"My eyebrows. Eduardo gave me an eyebrow arch today and lightened them to match the streaks he put in my hair last week. You didn't notice?"

"I can see now. Looks okay."

"Just okay? Eduardo and I both think it takes off five years." She leaned toward him from the sofa to give him a better look.

"Very flattering," he said over the ring of the phone.

"Drucilla Lang, Mr. Straus," the voice announced brusquely. "Sorry to bother you at home, but I wonder if I might speak to you for a moment about Laura Curtis."

"Is that for me?" Ruth wanted to know. Obie shook his head.

"Of course, Miss Lang. What can I do for you?"

"I thought it might be Mr. Takemoto," Ruth went on, over his reply. "He told Rosita he wants to take out some of the camellias and plant tuberous begonias."

"May we keep this confidential?" requested Drucilla.

"Certainly."

"Laura's agency contracts with FAC expire next month. We're thinking seriously of not renewing."

"Haven't they been giving her good representation?"

"It's not a question of that. Laura and I have had a long talk about it this evening. We think it's time for a change."

"Why is that?" Laura Curtis was a plum. The kid had a great future if she were correctly handled. She could be a valuable asset on his client list.

"You heard, I suppose, that the Major has decided to put her in *The Texas Twelve*."

"I read that in the trades." *The Texas Twelve* was the Major's prestige picture for this year. It was a multimillion-dollar Western extravaganza about the opening of the South-west, complete with a cast of big names in virtually every part.

"This is a departure for Laura. It means she's out of the Nikki image and on to more adult roles."

"What sort of part is it?" He saw Ruth put down her magazine. Business talk bored her. She went upstairs.

"She plays Mary Foster, the young girl who is raped by the Indians and left for dead until Luke finds her. You've read the script?"

"I have. That's a hell of a part, plenty of chance for some good acting. You're right, it is quite a departure from Nikki."

"That's why we feel that maybe it's time for a change. The boys at FAC are used to thinking of Laura as a child. We think she might be better off with an agency that didn't have that image quite so firmly in mind."

"Have you spoken to anyone else?" There was no use thinking they weren't shopping around. They'd be fools not to and, from what he heard, Drucilla Lang was no fool but a very astute manager.

"We have spoken to one other agency, again, in strictest confidence."

"Right. Tell you what, Miss Lang, why don't you and Laura come to my office Monday morning, and we'll talk it over?" That would be wiser than a lunch meeting where the FAC boys might spot them and get their backs up. No sense making enemies at another agency. Better to let FAC know it was all Drucilla Lang's idea.

"Eleven o'clock good for you?"

"Fine. Look forward to seeing you."

Ruth stood at the top of the stairs, waiting for him. She

wore a soft, downy something. He saw it was a red net peignoir, covered all over with fluffy white maribou.

"Isn't it beautiful?" she asked.

"Beautiful," he acknowledged. The fullness of her breasts showed him she had nothing underneath it.

"I got it at Magnin's. Do you like it?" She reached her arms around his neck.

"I like it very much." He hoped Rosita did not walk by in the hallway below where she might see them.

"It's a Lucie Ann. It's very sexy."

"That it is." Obie felt the awkwardness and guilt of all their moments like this.

"Shall we?" She looked up at him, hesitantly.

He loathed himself for pitying her. "I'm very tired, Ruthie." The old words.

"But you said it was sexy."

He could see the hurt in her eyes. "It is, Ruthie. It's very sexy. But I put in a long day today . . ." These were the bad times, he thought, the sad times.

"Too long a day to behave like a husband?"

"Don't. Please, Ruth."

"I mean it. Don't I do my best to be a beautiful wife?" Her voice wavered.

Obie didn't answer, or couldn't.

"Please," she insisted.

He allowed her to lead him to her room where he managed to perform his duty, feigning enthusiasm for the joyless, remorseful act that passed for love. Only the shower afterward felt good to him, as if the hot jets of water might wash away the sorrowful scene.

Obie declined Julie's offer of coffee and strode into his office. Already a few phone messages lay on his desk. He directed Julie to return Marty Tabor's call, but he was not home. The next one was from Gloria French. He wanted to put it off, but he knew he'd have to get to it sometime. Clients like Gloria French constituted charity work.

"Gloria? How are things?" He readied himself.

"I should be asking you that question." Her voice was still the same sexy syrup that had spawned a dozen imitations.

"I know, beautiful. It's a long, dry spell." Perhaps the compliment would ease things. Gloria was one of that breed plucked from noplace and shoved to stardom before she knew what had slugged her. Like most of that lot, she never had learned how to act. The special magic of her own presence, which was what some astute still photographer had noticed in the first place, more than compensated for the lack. Up to a point. It's a tough time, thought Obie, when the looks begin to go and there's not enough talent there to start playing character parts. Not that Glorida had got that old yet.

Over the good years, she had established a fairly high standard of living. She was used to luxury. She had been well schooled by the studios in the value of appearances. The trouble was, when the youth and the money began to dwindle, the studios were not on hand.

"At least," she was saying, "it's a cut above that piece of junk you sent me last week."

He had known at the time that he probably shouldn't give her the script of *The Venus Fly-Trap*. It was a low-budget science fiction thriller, and she had to be insulted, but it had been so long since he had any request for Gloria's work that he had sent it over anyway.

"I'm sorry, dear," Obie broke in. "Go over that again."

"This Mike Stanton. I never heard of him, but he wrote me a lovely letter saying how much he'd always admired me and how much he'd like to have me do this Tennessee Williams play he's producing."

"Producing? Where?"

"Some new little theater here. I forget where he said."

"Do you want to do it?" He hoped he sounded encouraging.

"I can't. You know I can't," she protested. "Those awful, slatternly women? They're wrecks, all of them in those plays. Besides, I looked up Tennessee Williams' birthday, and his sun is in direct square to mine. It would never work."

"Some of our finest actresses have done Williams plays. They're a great showcase."

"But what would the public think? That I'd gone to rack and ruin? That I was some fall-apart old slut?"

He wondered if that was what she was really afraid of or whether she actually feared the live stage and the limitations of her own abilities. Better not press too hard, he decided.

"You know best," he assured her.

"He did write a beautiful letter. I'll save it for you to read."

"I'd like to see it."

"I think I'll write and thank him anyway. He was very flattering. I wonder if he's a Pisces. He writes like one."

When he had hung up the phone, Obie lit a cigaret and swiveled his chair around to look over the view of Wilshire Boulevard, grayed by a slight smog. How, he wondered, to secure the Laura Curtis business this morning. Those starfuckers at the other agencies were probably sucking up to Curtis and Lang till hell wouldn't have it. Honesty, maybe, was the key to this one. More than honesty, candor. He would try that tack. A good offense was the order of the day.

They were prompt. The Lang woman charged in briskly and shook his hand in a firm grip. Laura Curtis tagged behind. She had grown much taller than when he had last seen her. She hadn't yet filled out her new stature, but the promise was there. She would be one hell of a good-looking woman one of these years. He seated them and returned to the desk.

"First, Miss Lang, I want to ask Laura a few questions."

Laura looked at Drucilla.

"Laura," he began, "what exactly do you want out of your profession?"

"I beg your pardon?" She shifted in her chair.

Good. Her voice was good. Some of the kid stars never outgrew the Mickey Mouse voice.

"Take time to answer, if you like." Obie rephrased the question. "Do you want to be a movie star?"

"I am a movie star," she answered, looking squarely at him.

"You are a kid star. Regardless of the fact that you are becoming a very attractive young lady, up to now you have been merchandised as a kid actress. That is the way the public knows you, so that, to all intents and purposes, is what you are at present."

Laura glanced at Dru for support, but she only proceeded to light a cigaret, nodding at Obie to continue.

"Shirley Temple began phasing out of the business at about your age. Elizabeth Taylor, on the other hand, went on to become a major star. Is that what you want for yourself?" Obie knew, more than most, the waste of pouring time and energy into a Laura Curtis if she planned to junk it all and elope with some nobody in a fast two years.

"Of course that's what I want," she insisted. "I love my work."

Drucilla, Obie saw, was watching the two of them intently, weighing their effect on each other.

"I have no doubt that you love your work, Laura. Your acting shows that. You're very good. The question is, Are you prepared to take the consequences of your work?"

"I don't know," she stammered slightly, "I don't know what you mean."

"Every profession has its personal consequences. Miners get silicosis and emphysema. Stock brokers have heart attacks. Agency men get ulcers. With movie stars, it's a little more complicated."

They waited.

He took his time, lighting a cigaret.

"There is no way in which a successful movie star can avoid becoming, to some degree or another, his public image. The edges between the private image and the public image get blurred. It's an occupational hazard. Some people are ruined because of it. Others become pains in the ass. Others learn to live with it."

"Go on," said Drucilla.

He coughed and stubbed out the cigaret. "The female stars, the big ones, have to live with that image. Face it. Art is not truth. Acting is a lie. In part, anyway, they become the lie." He directed his gaze at Laura who sat motionless, listening. "We are, all of us, essentially dull people who do things like cleaning our fingernails, opening the mail, and worrying about our bowels. That's not the stuff glamour girls are made of. Their occupation," he pointed at Laura, "and, if they're successes, their preoccupation, is to appear bigger than life, above the petty details that pass for living with the rest of us. And because they are an exaggeration of life, they become, to some extent, a parody of it. They become a parody of femininity, of sexiness." He paused, letting the words sink in. "Do you think you can handle something like that if it happens to you?"

She started to speak, but Drucilla stopped her. "I want to hear what else Mr. Straus has to say."

Obie couldn't tell whether or not his attack was working.

This damned honesty thing might be backfiring. If it was, it was too late now to change the way he was playing it.

"I'm trying to point out that being a major star can be, for a woman, a rather unfeminine way of life. It's not anything for a chick who wants to diaper the kiddies and turn out home-cooked meals. Sometimes the glamour is exaggerated to the point of camp. It's as if the poor girl were some kind of drag queen." He glanced at Laura to see if she understood. Evidently she did. "What's more, any profession in which the merchandise you're peddling happens to be your own attraction is some form of prostitution, no matter how legitimate. Are you ready to give your life over to being a commodity? To being sold to the highest bidder?"

Laura cleared her throat. "I think I'm used to that by now," she said coolly. "Victory Studios has already spent a few years doing that."

"And do you like it?"

"It's not whether I like it or not. Sometimes it's embarrassing, but it's part of the job.

"I think," Drucilla put in, "that Laura is objective enough to view things in their proper perspective. At least, I've tried to see that she does."

He pushed his chair back from the desk. "I think you've done a good job. Both of you," he smiled. Laura's shoulders relaxed. He hadn't realized the kid had tensed up that much. "I'm sorry if I seemed harsh, but I have to know what you want before I can offer any suggestions as to how to help you get it."

"It seems we all understand each other," Dru said. "Now I'd like to hear what you have in mind for Laura."

"How old are you?" he asked Laura.

"Seventeen."

"Okay. The first thing we do is get you a smart hairdresser. That lanky bob is strictly kid stuff. You need something a little more glamorous, not old-looking, but pretty." He saw her self-consciously brush an invisible hair from her cheek. "And you need to wear makeup. Not caked-on stuff like at the studio. Eyeshadow, mascara, lipstick, maybe a little rouge for color." He turned to Drucilla. "Nothing inappropriate, but she has to have the look. Most kids her age have been wearing the stuff for a couple of years already." He went on. "The clothes have to change. No more of this Peter Pan collar crap. You have to look chic, swinging. Young and fashion-able at the same time. One of my wife's friends is a buyer at Saks. I'd like to put you in her hands. She has great taste, and she'd know exactly what to do with you."

Drucilla, at last, was beginning to look as if she approved of what she was hearing.

"You need a publicist," he told them.

"I have one," Laura protested. "The studio has a man as-signed to me."

"Forget the studio man. He's been publicizing a kid. You need someone with a fresh viewpoint. Someone who will take you to one of the glamour photographers and get a bunch of new stills. You need to do fashion layouts for the top maga-zines. Show them you're a big girl now. You need romantic items planted in the columns. You have to date, go out, be seen on the nighttime party circuit, preferably with names as big or bigger than your own. You need somebody to book you on the hot TV talk shows. That's the quickest way of reaching the largest audience with your new image. For my money, I think you should start overhauling yourself as soon as possible. Today."

"Obie," Dru smiled, "you make a lot of. sense. I think we've come to the right place."

Bingo, he told himself. With Curtis in his pocket, that sixty-two hundred he owed Cal seemed smaller every minute. It was a good day, so far. Maybe even Aqueduct would pay off.

In the afternoon Obie made the rounds of the studios, serv-icing those clients who merited his personal attention. Re-turning to the office, he hunched over his desk for the daily wrap-up of phone calls. The first one he returned was to Ian Driscoll at the Bel Air Hotel.

"Obie, dear chap," came the ebullient greeting.

"Ian. Everything going smoothly for you? Anything I can do to help make your stay more pleasant?"

"I should say you'd done rather enough already," Ian laughed. "That's a smashing young lady you introduced me to. Splendid."

Christy had been a success. He hoped Ian was the grateful type.

"Glad you two got along. I hope that means you'll trust

my judgment if I make a couple of casting suggestions for that picture of yours."

"Any time. No promises, you understand, but so far I'd say your taste is impeccable."

"Nice to hear we're on the same wave length. Any chance of our having a meeting this week?"

"Afraid this week's out of the question. I'm off to see northern California. Going to be scouting locations with a studio fellow. San Francisco, Lake Tahoe, some of the old gold towns, that sort of thing."

"Perhaps the first of next week, then? I'll call you at the hotel Saturday or Sunday to confirm."

"You'd best wait till Monday. I'm going to stay the weekend up there. Combining a little pleasure with my business. Your young lady, in fact. Hope I'm not trespassing."

"Not at all. She's just a friend." Christy must have been an even bigger hit than he anticipated. She was on her own now. He hoped she knew what she was doing. If this thing blew up, it could get plenty awkward.

"I'll call you Monday morning," he told Ian.

"Right-o. *Ciao.*"

As long as the idyll lasted through the casting of Driscoll's picture, he'd be satisfied. Obie couldn't help being amused that Ian, recently divorced from Lady Clarissa Burnham, was now touring California with a very cute but very professional hooker. He wished Christy luck and presumed she'd have enough sense at least to walk away with a fur coat or some little trinket from Gump's.

Two calls later he finally reached Marty Tabor.

"Sorry we've been missing each other all day," Obie apologized.

"I've been at the gym, working out."

"I spoke to the boys in New York this morning to break the news that Colin Kirkwood turned down the play. I told them you were reading it. After I hung up, they phoned back. They'd talked it over among themselves, and the reaction was very enthusiastic."

"Yes? That's good news. I like the play, like it a lot. I think you're wrong about its being downbeat." Marty's voice was eager. "If it's played right, played against the lines instead of into them, it can come off as a strong statement about——"

"Like the man said, if I want to send a message, I'll use Western Union."

"You watch Ruby Keeler on the late show. I want to do this play. Do they want me to go East and read for them?"

"I wouldn't be surprised if that wasn't necessary. They seemed to think you were an inspired idea. Jeffries, the director, said he wished he'd thought of it himself. I'll check it out, though."

"When does the project go?"

'They start rehearsals the end of August. They're scheduled for tryouts in Boston and Washington before they bring it into New York in the fall."

"Sounds good," Marty said. "How fast can you get on it?"

Obie glanced at his watch. "Too late now. The office in New York will be closed for the night. I'll call them sometime tomorrow. No sense appearing too hungry. You may have a bit of a shock coming. Broadway salaries are not famous for their largess."

"To hell with their largess. If this play is any kind of a success, I'll be able to come back to this town with a Broadway hit behind me. We can recoup the money then."

"You seem to have a lot of faith in this thing," Obie spoke cautiously. "I hope to God it's justified and you don't break your ass."

"I'll take care of my ass," Marty laughed. "You just get those guys to say yes."

"I'll talk to you tomorrow," Obie promised.

Julie buzzed him before he could make another call.

"Mr. Straus, Claire Poland is on line two."

"Yes, Claire?"

"I have an interesting report here." Claire liked to toss out a teaser before she got down to business.

"What is it?"

"It's about your client, Jack Haller. Does that tell you anything?"

"Not so far. He's in Europe, producing a film."

"I hope you're not being coy."

"I'm not. What's up, Claire?" He tried to conceal his impatience.

"You don't know anything about Jack and Astrid Swensen?"

"I don't even know who Astrid Swensen is."

"Of course you do," she insisted.

"The devil I do. I never heard of her." He wished Claire would come to the goddam point. At this rate he wouldn't get home until after seven.

"You'd know her if you saw her. The model. The leggy blonde who's been in all the magazines. She's the top model in Paris this season."

"I still don't know her."

"I trust you're not holding out on me."

"What's to hold out when I don't know what the hell you're talking about?"

"I have it on very good authority that they were secretly married in Paris last week and she's expecting a child." The note of pride in Claire's voice betrayed the fact that she was immensely pleased with herself.

"That's news to me, Claire," he said wearily. "I spoke to Jack over the weekend, and there was no mention made of any marriage."

"You better be giving this to me straight," she warned. Claire never liked the idea that she might be wrong.

"I am. I'm sure he would have said something about it."

"This comes from a very good source. It's worth a head-line. I have no intention of letting somebody else get the drop on me with this story."

"Claire, I don't care if it comes from the Pope. Have you tried to locate Jack or the Swensen girl?"

"Nobody's available for comment. I have a call in to the girl's family in Stockholm." She paused. "I'd hate to think you were deceiving me, Obie. I've never presented you un-favorably in my column. I wouldn't want to start now."

"What's that supposed to mean?"

"Girls talk. You know. The girls," she used the word point-edly, "when they go to the health club and sit around the steam room, get to exchanging trade talk. In my business we hear all those things."

He crushed an empty cigaret package and hurled it into the wastebasket. "I don't see what this has to do with Jack Haller's matrimonial status."

"I just wouldn't want you to deny the story if it happens to be true."

"If it's true, Claire, which I doubt, I know nothing about it. You'll have to check it out elsewhere."

"And I will. Now," she continued, "as long as I have you on the line, what have you got for me? Any news?"

"I may have something for you by the end of the week. There's some interest in Marty Tabor doing a very good play on Broadway this season. One of the top shows coming into New York."

"A musical?"

He knew she was running through the titles of the new musicals in her head.

"No, a straight play. Prestige operation. Big producer-writer-director team."

"And you can't tell me who."

"Not yet I can't. If you want to drop the hint, don't let on it came from me."

"I won't. On the condition that I get the story first when it's confirmed."

"You got it, Claire. Good-bye."

That took care of Claire and gave Marty some good coverage in the bargain. Christ, but this job had its idiot moments.

4

Lisa

2:30 P.M.

*How odd that I should feel cheated. It's as if Mike had
cheated me out of something by dying. When he was alive, I
could hate him. I think I even enjoyed it. But it becomes difficult to hate somebody who's no longer around. Strange that
it should make me feel so empty. I suppose you get used to
hating people the same way you get used to loving them.
When they're suddenly taken away, it leaves a void. What a
curious kind of mourner I am.*

*The best thing would be to have it all buried with him. I
think I could have managed that, even today, if that inquisitive Look reporter hadn't kept firing those questions at Jack
and me while we were posing.*

And what is your favorite style of furniture, Mrs. Haller?

*How secure we must have looked to her, standing in front
of our elegant hearth, surrounded by our elegant Queen
Anne pieces, being photographed in our elegant clothes.*

*Our favorite style of furniture, I'm afraid, is a good an-
tique that can be sold if the wolf makes it to our front door.
While I'm at it, I think you should know that this place is
mortgaged to its rooftop. My husband, here, is mortgaged to
his rooftop. So, in fact, am I. I have promised S. M. Victor
three pictures, partially paid for in advance, to help get my
husband off the hook. And I don't want to work. I want to
stay home with the baby. When we get the baby. Oh God,
you don't suppose the agency is checking too deep into our
finances and they won't okay the adoption. Please, no.*

And do you have a family, any children?

*No, Miss Look, we do not have any children. Yet. My
husband divorced his first wife because she was more interested in playing around than having a family. But there is a
child. Jack's son. He belongs to a Swedish girl who didn't*

want to get married. She was more interested in her career than having a family. I think you could say my husband has had rotten luck in that department. Not the least of which has been my doing. If I could give him a child, I'd give him as many as he wanted, half a dozen, if that's what he wanted. Unfortunately, that door was closed to me by, as my brother Marty succinctly put it, "a two-bit leech, a gigolo, for God's sake."

And are you involved in any charity work in the community, Mrs. Haller?

Yes, I work at Saint John's Hospital. Shall I tell you why? Because they were good to me. The nuns never said a word, never gave me a reproachful look. They just kept sticking those needles in my arm to stop the pain and holding my hand until the stuff worked and I fell asleep. I thought I owed them something for the way they handled it and kept it quiet.

Do you do much entertaining at home?

The usual amount, I guess. But I know what you want. You'd just love to ask me about the Stanton party you've been reading about in the papers, but you don't dare because that wouldn't be polite. After all, that's where it happened.

Was it only last weekend? Lord, it seems so much longer. I remember how beautiful their house looked. Jack said something on the way up the driveway about how pretty the lights were, set out like that between the trees. The music echoed all through the canyon. I remember he laughed and said he hoped they'd invited the neighbors or one of them would call the police for sure. If only that had been the reason they came.

Do you suppose that if it hadn't gotten chilly out on the terrace and I hadn't gone upstairs for my coat, none of it would have happened? Would it perhaps not have happened if we hadn't all been in that same room at that same time? I wonder how much Marty had been drinking. Is that why he let it all out? I just wanted to get my coat and get out of there, away from whatever was going on between the three of them. I remember the look on Mike's face when it happened. How blank he looked. Expressionless, as if he were already dead. And all of us frozen like statues, unable to move. Below, in the garden, the mariachis were playing "Arrivederci Roma." *That made it so unreal, the way the music just kept on going.*

Are your friends mostly in the film colony like yourselves?

I'm glad Jack answered that one. I'm not sure about our friends anymore. You see, there are some of us who have a hard time meeting each others' eyes now.

Tell me something about your picture, Mr. Haller.

Thank God she finally asked him. Today of all days we wouldn't be spending two hours making smiling faces, if it weren't for the picture. There are a lot of things we wouldn't be doing, if it weren't for the picture. Maybe we could even afford the luxury of honesty. If it were not for Laura's precious health and the fact that the studio can't get her insured, maybe someone might have been interested in telling the truth. Marty? No, not Marty, he loves her too much. She's the only one he's really cared for since Kathy.

Laura? Would she have said something, if Obie hadn't had a sixth sense about the whole thing and put her under wraps? Maybe she talked her head off at Obie's and Ruth's after the sedative wore off. If she did, we'll never hear about it. Not the way Obie protects his merchandise.

No, Laura wouldn't say anything. She's tougher than she looks. She knows how to protect herself. And who am I to blame her, feeling the way I do about Mike?

Well, what about me? Who am I trying to kid; I didn't keep silent only to save the picture. I shut up because I love my husband. I may not be able to undo what's been done in the past, but I can keep it from hurting him. What a small thing to do when I owe him so much. Such a small thing, to protect our life, our home, our chances of getting a baby.

You just keep thinking that. Never, for one moment, must you think anything else. That's the way things have to be, and that, by God, is the way they're going to be. In time, a long time perhaps, but in time, it will seem it really happened that way. Believing it is the important thing. And no reminders like the inquisitive woman from Look. *It will die down. There's nothing as old as yesterday's news.*

Will you tell me about each of those awards in the bookcase, Mr. Haller?

Jack was so patient with her. This is the Boxoffice Award. This is the Producers' Guild Award. This one was an Oscar nomination. Yes, all of them were for the same film.

*How solid they look, ranked on the shelf like that. How
sure and safe the room looks, even to the dog lying asleep in
the patch of afternoon sun on the carpet. It's so warm and so
quiet now that they've all left.*

*I should tell Teresa that Jack will be home at eight, so she
can plan dinner. I think I'll cut some anemones for the din-
ing-room table.*

LISA gasped with relief as Mae undid the lacings of her corset.

"I itch," she complained, scratching at the red welts left by
the stays. "I swear, I don't know how those antebellum ladies
stood it." She gave a contented little shimmy. "I feel as if I'd
lost ten pounds."

"You lost twenty-two," said Mae. "It's the beading on the
dress that gives it the weight. Burt was afraid to tell you
when you were being fitted. I think he was scared you'd belt
him." She grunted, hefting the dress over her arm. "I'll have
this freshened up in the department during lunch."

"Thanks, and tell Burt I just found out he's not a designer,
he's a sadist. Would you hand me those slacks?"

"Lisa?" Her hairdresser knocked at the dressing room
door. "Wear something over your head. It's pouring outside."

"Is there a car to take us to the commissary?"

"Yes, but at the rate it's coming down, you still need to be
covered. Try to get back to the set early, so if any of the
curls have fallen I can use the iron on them."

"Right." Lisa craned her head while Mae lined the neck of
her sweater with Kleenex to keep the body makeup from
staining it.

"Miss Taylor?"

"Yes, George?" She waited at the stage door until the dialogue coach caught up with her.

"Mr. Frost wants to run the words with all the principals
right after lunch."

"Okay. Want a lift to the commissary?" She stepped out
into the downpour as he held the door.

There surely wasn't anything, she thought, as dismal as a
rainy day in Los Angeles. Continuous sheets of water de-
luged the parched earth, carving muddy rivers in the hillsides
and driving the brown, swirling streams down onto the flat-

lands. Torn branches, leaves, and weeds choked the gutters, backing up the flow until streets and lawns were underwater. Cars, their engines flooded, were abandoned at random. Traffic became a nightmare.

Today the sound man had twice lost his temper because the heavy drumming of the rain was audible on his earphones. Curious, thought Lisa, how in places like New York or Chicago rain seemed to bring people together, scurrying into the same doorways for shelter, sharing taxies, joining with total strangers to rail against the elements. In Los Angeles the rain always had an isolating effect, an unsettling loneliness.

"Every man for himself!" she shouted at George as the driver drew up at the commissary. Half-crouched, she dashed across the sidewalk to the safety of the building.

"Nice weather for ducks," said the cashier as she entered. She said "Nice weather for ducks" every time it rained. When the Santa Ana blew in from the desert and filled the dry air with dust she said, "That's some wind out there."

"Lisa! Lisa Taylor!"

She looked for the source of the voice. A table of tourists gawked in her direction and exchanged elbow digs and whispers. Lisa spotted Obie Straus waving from his table.

"Will you join us?" He rose and pulled out a chair.

"I will if you promise not to try to steal me from my agent," she teased him. The man with Obie stood until she was seated.

"I won't promise anything, but I will buy you lunch."

"And I'll let you, but remember, I like the agent I've got." She smiled at Obie's companion, a tanned, slightly graying man with handsome features and large horn-rimmed glasses.

"Lisa, this is Jack Haller, producer, client of mine."

"I've heard of Mr. Haller," she said, turning toward him. "Are you going to be producing here at Victory?"

"It's possible. Are you under contract to the studio?"

"Not after this picture. It's just a one-shot. I've never worked here before, but it's been quite pleasant."

"Jack's in an enviable position," Obie said. "Universal and Paramount and Victory are all interested in him."

It was the usual lunch of small talk, business gossip, social notes, and the inevitable rumors. Lisa tried to steal an occasional unobtrusive look at Jack Haller. She decided his face had nice lines in it, the kind that, carved deeper by time, would make him look even more distinguished, rather like a mellowing Italian movie idol.

"So what do you hear from Marty?" Obie asked, attacking a piece of pecan pie.

"I spoke to him Sunday. He's very happy with the TV show. My brother," she explained, to Jack, "is doing one of those ninety-minute specials in New York."

"He doesn't miss the sound of that applause every night?" asked Obie.

"He said it was a bit sad, leaving the play. It had become a home and family. Still, after a year's run, I think he's glad to be onto something new."

"Do I know your brother?" Jack asked.

"Perhaps. Marty Tabor."

"Yes?" he smiled. "I saw his show when it first opened last year. He did a great job, especially in that business where he talked directly to the audience. Very few performers can manage that without seeming hokey. He was terrific."

Lisa responded with a proud smile. "I think so, but I'm prejudiced because I love him a lot."

"Nice guy," said Jack. "We have some mutual friends back East. I ran into him on several occasions. Your brother and I spent most of our time discussing the relative merits of the Packers, the Jets, and the Rams. It turns out we're both football junkies."

"Lisa, did Marty say when he's coming back? His picture starts wardrobe fittings the first week in December."

"Around Thanksgiving, he said."

"That's two more weeks. Does he have some girl back there?"

"Search me. He wouldn't tell me if he did. He's very discreet that way." She paused. "Marty's awfully loyal, Obie. I mean, I'm not sure he's ready again, after what happened. It's over a year, I know, but it hit him pretty hard, and I don't think it's been easy for him. He was very much in love with that girl."

"What happened?" Jack wanted to know.

"An accident." She was evasive, not wanting to remember it clearly herself. "My brother's girl was killed in an accident."

"I'm sorry. It can be difficult to wipe out memories, especially good ones." His sympathy was genuine.

"Hi!" Obie waved at a passing couple.

"Who's that?" asked Lisa, wanting to change the subject.

"A guy named Mike Stanton. The blonde is Fort Knox. She's bankrolling some little theater he runs. It's not doing too well, but she keeps siphoning money into it. I think she's more interested in keeping him than being a patron of the arts. I saw his production of *Antigone* a couple of months ago. It stank."

"The girl's name is Virginia Hopewell," Jack provided. "Her uncle is my attorney in New York. He's her guardian since her parents were killed in a plane crash in the Bahamas. Obie's right. She's worth millions."

"I keep seeing them all over town," Lisa said, "in all the restaurants and discotheques."

"They're everyplace," shrugged Obie, "Chasen's, Perino's, La Scala, Scandia. What the hell, if she can afford it."

"Will you excuse me? I have to get back to work." Lisa stood up.

"If you'll wait until I pay the cashier, I'll cadge a ride from you. Your director, Ben Frost, is a client of mine. Might as well drop by and see how things are going." Obie reached for the check.

"Well?" Jack grinned. "Shall we walk to the door together and give everyone something to talk about?"

"You washed your hands," the body makeup woman scolded her. "Hold them out." Lisa held them out for the sponge.

"Stay still," ordered Keith, brushing a new coating of eyeliner onto her lids. "Looks like you batted your eyes a lot at lunch."

"Just the usual amount," she laughed.

"Oh yes? I saw you smiling at Jack Haller."

"You're an old auntie, Keith, you know that? You're the Claire Poland of the makeup department."

"Got to keep myself amused." He handed her the lipstick. "Just gilding you lilies day in and day out is a bloody bore."

"Okay, then, you're fired." There was little chance of that. Keith was Lisa's favorite. He had been her makeup man for six years.

"Lisa?"

"What is it, Ben?"

Frost came into the dressing room with Obie following. "I want to remind you. When Marco begins to speak in the scene, you have to start your move. Your exit must time out to coincide with his breaking the glass. Another thing. I'm going to need more energy on your last speech. We have to keep up the tempo." He gave her a dismissing wave and left.

"Obie," she said. "Wait a second. Tell me about Jack Haller. And you," she warned Keith, "no smart cracks."

"What's to tell? He did some TV writing and was an associate producer on a couple of horror films for Allied. Then he went to Spain and produced two arty low-budget Westerns that did well at the box office. Now he's back here."

"Married?" She caught Keith's grin. "Drop dead, you," she called after him as he left the dressing room.

"Separated. From Valerie Normand."

"I heard she gets loaded and makes it with everyone from the delivery boys to the headwaiters around town."

"She flipped out. He took it pretty bad, says it's partly his fault. Say," he asked, "may I use your phone? Someone was on the one outside when I looked."

"Of course."

Obie checked his office for calls and hung up, shaking his head.

"Something the matter?"

"Laura Curtis."

He was interrupted by someone from the publicity office. "Miss Taylor? There are some doctors and their wives coming on the set this afternoon. There's a medical convention in town. Would you mind posing with them for a few pictures?"

"Not at all," she said. He disappeared from the doorway. "What's wrong with Laura Curtis, outside of the fact that she looks like death these days?"

"She wants Harris Bolding fired from her picture. Says if he's going to be in it, she's not. The studio, on the other hand, has a firm commitment with him. They don't want to have to pay him off and hire someone else. Laura's just overtired."

"Well, she looks terrible. I'm glad you're not my agent," she kidded, "you work your clients too hard."

"She had some sort of female trouble last year and went

back to work too soon. She was shooting a rough show, and it was too much for her. She came down with pneumonia and she still isn't as strong as she should be. She insists on working. Says she can't stand to be idle. She keeps thinking her fans will abandon her if she isn't in front of them all the time to remind them."

"We all have a little of that. Maybe the reason I don't try so hard is because I'm fundamentally lazy."

"Not a chance," smiled Obie.

George stuck his head through the doorway. "We're ready to go over that scene now."

"I'll be right there." She turned to Obie. "Thanks again for lunch. I liked your friend."

The rain stopped during the night. In the first minutes of waking, Lisa wondered why the house seemed so silent. Then she realized that the beating on the roof had stopped. She lingered in bed, enjoying the luxury of a day off. She reached between the clean-smelling sheets and ran her hands over her nude body. Damn, she thought, what's the fun of waking up alone on an idle day? What she needed, and wanted, was a man. God, but it was depressing to be between love affairs. That's what you get for being choosy, she reminded herself. It was all well and good to have high standards, but it meant you woke up alone sometimes.

This can be a bitch of a town, thought Lisa. Half the men wanted dates with actresses just to boost their own egos, to be able to name-drop the celebrities they'd slept with. A good man, as the saying went, was hard to find. She had heard the reverse complaint from many men. Girls who came to Hollywood usually came for one reason only, to advance themselves. Consequently, they were either hell-bent on getting to the top or on trapping a husband who could give them the status they wanted without their having to work for it.

Maybe Jack Haller would call her. But don't be disappointed if he doesn't, she cautioned herself. He's an attractive man. He probably has more women than he can handle. Still, she wondered what he would be like in bed.

There was always Hans Deitrick, if only he weren't so damn strange. It made her uncomfortable, the way he kept watching her when they were together. He would stare at her, his eyelids half-closed, like a drowsy reptile. Then, toward the end of the evening, in that perfunctory, Prussian way of his, he would invite her to have sex with him. Her refusal never seemed to faze him. He could wait, he said, he could wait.

What the hell, she told herself, why wait? It's there if I want it, and today I want it. She reached for the telephone.

Lisa pressed the button to put the top down on the car. The day was glorious. However bad the storms were in southern California, they brought their rewards. Los Angeles, washed clean by the rains, became a jewel. The sky was a dazzling clear blue. The jade-green hills were never richer or more lush. The colors of the houses and the flowers in the bright sunlight stung the eyes with their brilliance. The freshness of the air made all things seem newly possible.

Buoyed by the weather, Lisa hummed confidently to herself as she guided the car along Sunset Boulevard and up Benedict Canyon. This could quite possibly turn out to be one marvelous afternoon.

Hans lived in an old high-walled Spanish house with two fortlike turrets. The neighbors secretly referred to it as "the concentration camp" because of the big German Shepherd that guarded its iron gates.

The gates were open, and the dog was nowhere to be seen which relieved Lisa, since he had once knocked her over in his enthusiasm. She parked in the driveway and walked toward the house where the French doors were open, their curtains blowing in the light breeze.

"Hello?" She stood in the vacant living room amid its heavy, dark furniture. "Hans?"

"Here," he called from the direction of the pool.

He rose to greet her. "You know Helen Farmer, yes?"

"Sure we know each other," Helen said from under the shade of a giant umbrella. "Care for a glass of wine? We're planning to get quietly stoned. That short-cock Victor refused to give me a raise."

"Liebfraumilch," said Hans reaching into the shallow steps of the pool where the bottle lay cooling.

"Thanks." Well, Lisa told herself, there goes your sexy afternoon. She sat on the coping of the pool and took off her shoes, sliding her legs into the barely cool water. "That feels wonderful."

"I think I'm already a little tight," Helen giggled. "Hurry up, somebody, and join me."

The sun and wine did their job. Lisa lay back on the bricks of the patio and watched the clouds drifting overhead. She had a lazy, floating feeling.

"More?" offered Hans. "I opened another bottle." He stood over her, gazing down.

"More." She smiled.

"How many bottles is that?" Helen wanted to know.

"*Drei.*"

"God, no wonder I'm loaded," she laughed. "Lisa, are you loaded?"

"A little."

"It's getting hot as hell out here. I wonder what the temperature is. What's the temperature, Hans?"

"I don't know. I'll go see."

"Yes, go see. Find out how hot it is. Christ, I'm sweating like a stevedore." She took off her blouse and fanned at the beads of perspiration between her breasts. "Anybody mind if I take off my bra?"

"The temperature is eighty-two point five," Hans reported. "I myself am going to swim." He stripped off his shirt and slacks and dove into the water.

Lisa rolled toward the edge of the pool. She watched him swimming slowly, gracefully, underwater. The sun on the surface dappled his lean, tanned body. He came up beside her, shaking the wetness out of his hair.

"You splashed me when you dove in."

"Yes? Okay." He took a handful of water and allowed it to trickle over her neck, watching her face as he did.

"It feels good."

"So come swim."

Helen emerged from under her shade. "That," she said, stretching her naked body in the sun, "is the best idea anyone's had yet." She tested the water with her toes and stepped in.

"Venus rising from the waves," said Hans appreciatively, looking at her. "Lisa, come." He reached over the edge of the pool and began to undo her shirt.

The water caressed her skin, making her aware of every inch of her bare body. She stroked slowly, lazily, feeling the waves against her flesh. She swam to the shallows where Hans was pouring wine.

"This is the life," said Helen, raising her glass. The water lapped at her pale shoulders.

Lisa took her glass, smiling at Hans who lounged across the steps of the pool, his flawless body shimmering below its surface.

"You like what you see?"

"It's a fact, Hans," Helen took a swallow of wine, "you have got one of the great bodies of our time."

"But so have you, *liebe*." His hand sauntered over her, dark against the whiteness of her skin. "And Lisa," he embraced her with his other arm, his fingers playing at her nipple made hard by the water, "she is also exquisite. Imagine, three such beautiful people together, appreciating each others' charms. It is perfect, yes?"

"It is perfect, yes." Helen lolled on her side and put her hands on his tanned shoulders. She brought them slowly down over his chest. Her fingers explored his flat belly and his thighs.

"This will make me very spoiled," he smiled and turned to kiss Lisa. He teased her mouth with his tongue. He took Lisa's hand and placed it between his thighs. She felt the coolness of Helen's hand as they both fondled him. He pulled her closer to him, his mouth on hers. Her breasts grazed his chest.

Helen glided into the water. Her silver hair, glistening, streamed on the surface of the pool.

Lisa felt his breath quicken. He grasped her tighter. His tongue thrust into her mouth, hard and rhythmic, until his head reared back and he gasped with pleasure.

Helen brought herself up beside him. "That was kicky, baby." She stroked his hair. "Now I want some."

He took Lisa's hand and placed it on Helen's soft breast. Helen's fingers closed over it. She guided it to her nipple. Hans slipped his hand between her legs, and his finger probed her body. She moaned softly and reached a hand into Lisa's dark hair, bringing her mouth to hers.

"No," said Lisa, breaking away.

"Yes," demanded Helen. "Come. Kiss me. Kiss me. Don't worry, you'll get your turn." She touched Lisa's breast.

"No," she said, shaking her head. "No. I don't want to."

"But what is the matter?" Hans asked.

"I just don't want to."

"But you are being foolish, Lisa."

"It's not—what I like."

"Baby, you're spoiling the game," said Helen impatiently.

"Lisa," Hans stroked her skin, "is it not exciting to enjoy a beautiful body?"

"I think I'd better leave." She moved away from them.

"You are making a mistake," he told her. "You will be missing a great deal of pleasure."

"I don't want that. I'm going." She stood beside the pool, assembling her clothes.

"Stay," he commanded.

"No. I can't. It's not for me." She turned away and retreated quickly toward the house without looking back.

"Goddam you," Helen cried after her. "Goddam you, you bitch!"

"Mart? It's me, Lisa."

"I just walked in the door. It's one A.M. here."

"Are you alone?"

"Yes. Not my lucky night. Wait'll I take off my coat."

She waited. "Are you there?"

"Yes. What's up?"

"Nothing. I was just a little depressed and I felt like talking to you." Lisa was curled up in a corner of the sofa, her bathrobe tucked snugly around her feet.

"What's bothering you, Sis? Should I get worried?"

"No, nothing like that," she reassured him. "I guess I'm just lonely."

"And depressed."

"Yes. Listen, I ran into Obie yesterday. He wants to know when you're coming back."

"I spoke to him. I'll be there on the thirtieth."

"If I'm not working, I'll meet the plane."

"Don't have to. Twentieth-Century-Fox is sending a limousine."

She smiled to herself. Marty had been right to take the gamble. With a Broadway success to his credit, he was coming home to an important picture and more money than he had ever made in television. "Sam Star, that's you," she said. "I just thought . . . "

"What?"

". . . About meeting you."

"You really are down. What hit you?"

"Nothing's the matter with me, if that's what you mean. I guess I just have a slight case of moral hangover."

"You should know better than to set yourself up for that. You're just going to have to let whatever's bothering you wear off."

"I know. Mart, it'll be good to have you back here. Everyone's been asking me when you're coming."

When she hung up, she stared blankly around the living room, wondering whether she should read for a while. She had prolonged their conversation as long as she could, wanting an excuse not to go to bed. Finally she turned out the lights. She took her script into the bedroom and went over the next day's work, the pages propped up on her blanketed knees. She smoked three cigarets in swift succession, idly listening to the soft night noises outside. At last, she dialed her telephone service and left a wakeup call for six in the morning.

"You really do have a problem, you know?" Lisa came in from the kitchen and put Jack's sandwich down on the coffee table in front of him.

"I do?" he said absently, not looking in her direction.

"That, for pity's sake." She gestured toward the television set, raising her voice over the volume.

"I told you I was a football nut. You knew that up front. Never mind," he got up and turned down the sound. "It's half-time."

"Does that mean I have to learn the game?" she smiled.

"Not if you don't want to, but it does mean no conversation in the middle of a play."

She grinned as he slipped an arm around her. "You're making rules."

It had been a month between the time she met Jack Haller and the time he called her, apologizing for the wait, saying he had been in Europe on personal business. On their first evening together she had been surprised to find herself holding back slightly. When she wondered at the reason, her intuition told her that somehow it seemed very important to go slowly this time. And so they had. Jack made no move toward closeness. They attended the annual rash of Christmas parties, discovering each other's friends more readily than they seemed to want to discover each other. It was only last night, after seeing each other every evening for two weeks, that he had pulled up in front of the house, let her out of the car, and they had gone inside, shutting the door behind them and locking it for the night. There had been no conversation. They simply belonged there together.

Jack held her closer. "Why did we take all that time?" he asked.

"I was thinking about that. I don't know. A couple of times there I thought you weren't interested."

"I'd have to be crazy not to be interested. I got the feeling at the beginning that I had a lot of fences to get past before I reached you. Were you testing me?"

"Maybe. Why didn't you just jump over the fences and grab me?"

"Because I wanted you too much to scare you off. You would have been scared off, wouldn't you?"

She nodded, rubbing her cheek against the rough tweed of his jacket. "I think I wanted to know for sure what kind of man you were, what I might be getting into."

"It's funny," he said slowly, "how easy it is to have the meaningless affair. You jump into bed and out without anyone putting much thought to it."

"What are you saying?"

"I'm saying the same thing you are." He turned to look at her. "You and I met at a time when we were both tired of casual alliances. After a while, they all become a little sad. You go through the motions, getting as much pleasure as you can, knowing nothing will come of it. Just a way of not being lonely for a few hours. When you realize that," he smiled wryly, "it becomes even more depressing."

"Yes." She slipped her hand into his, and their fingers locked together. "I never liked that life, that business of going from man to man, looking." She squeezed his hand. "You know."

"Sure I know. Running from one scene to another for bigger and better thrills. If you had been one of those chicks on the kicks circuit, I wouldn't have come within a mile of you."

"I came close to it. A couple of times. It scared me." She

looked up at him. "I think you are a very special man. I think——" she stopped.

"What?"

"Never mind," she said over the ring of the telephone.

"Lisa." He stopped her hand as she reached for the phone and turned her to him. "I think I'm falling in love with you, too." He put his arms around her and held her close for a moment. "You'd better answer that thing," he said and walked to the television. "If it's your brother, tell him he's going to lose that ten bucks he bet me on this game."

Looking back, she would always marvel over the ease of it. The thing was so right, so natural for them both, that it became hard to remember any good reason for having loved anyone else before.

"Where are you going?" Jack demanded.

"I thought you were asleep." Lisa stopped in the bedroom doorway.

He rolled over, enjoying the sight of her body silhouetted by the light from the hallway. "I was lying here thinking."

She walked back to the bed and, turning aside the covers, stretched beside him. The sheets still held the heavy odor of their sex.

"We ironed out the last points of the Victory deal today," he told her.

"But why didn't you say anything?" Lisa propped herself up on one elbow. "Damn you for holding out! That's exciting news!"

"I suppose." He caressed her arm lightly with his index finger. "I guess I'm thinking of all it involves, getting five pictures made."

"Killjoy. What kind of a deal is it?"

"Do you really want to know?" He seemed surprised and pleased.

"I want to know everything that happens to you. What happens to you matters to me."

"Five pictures. Co-productions. Victory Studios and The Haller Company."

"The Haller Company." She savored the name.

"Simple and to the point."

"What about the details?"

"Nothing spectacular. I'm involved financially up to a

point. Victory handles most of the financing and does the releasing."

"Did you want to have your own money in it? I mean, I remember what my father used to say. He got wiped out in the crash when he was very young, and he used to din it into Marty and me always to use the other fellow's money."

"He was right." Jack stretched lazily. "In this case, though, I'm only modestly involved. It gives me a little more autonomy to start with and a better cut of the profits when the picture hits."

"I still think you're a louse for not telling me first thing."

"How could I?" he chided her. "I arrive here and before I can get my jacket off, some beautiful girl starts kissing me and running her hands all over my body. It went clear out of my mind."

"I wanted you very much tonight."

"The evening," he kissed her briefly, "has only just begun. Let's pull ourselves together and go out for dinner. Then we can come back to bed again."

"Practice makes perfect?" she laughed.

"It makes a hell of a lot of fun," he said from the hall.

She sat on the edge of the bathtub, watching him shave. "You make some pretty funny faces when you do that."

"Thanks," he said drily. "I only do it for your amusement. Oh. Lisa." He laid down the razor. "I also forgot to tell you I agreed to a p.a. tour of *Welcome's Army*. That'll be my final obligation under the European deal."

"That's the last one you did in Spain?"

"Yes. The trip won't be for a few weeks yet. It'll have to coincide with the release dates." He resumed his shaving.

"Do you want some company?"

"Doing what?"

"On the trip."

"No." He peered into the mirror. "That wouldn't be a good idea."

She was taken aback. She tried not to show it. "Jack, I want to be with you," she said cautiously.

"Not on this junket, you don't. I'm taking my writer-director for the next picture with me."

"Who's that?"

"Ian Driscoll. He's going to be working on the script days while I'm out touting the film. Nights we'll be working together in the hotel. The trip's going to be a ball-breaker. Fifteen cities in three weeks, plus a week afterward, scouting locations in New Mexico and Wyoming."

"Is his wife going along?" She hoped she didn't sound jealous.

"She's in England. Doesn't like to fly. Her name's Christine. Christy, I think he calls her. Seems she used to live here and hates Hollywood, anyhow." He filled the basin with water.

Damn, she thought, I wish I didn't feel so hurt. "I don't think I'm going to like our being apart." She ran her bare toes over the calf of his leg. "I may even hate it."

He said nothing, so she changed the subject. "Where do you want to have dinner?"

"If you don't stop that," he seized her foot and held it, "food is not going to be the issue."

"I love you," she smiled as he brought her up to him.

Lisa was glad to have another picture commitment to occupy her days. Evenings, after the assistant director had called "That's a wrap," she would drive out of the Universal Studios gate and over the hills to home and to Jack's voice on long distance. Sometimes when he called, she could hardly hear him. A day of radio, TV, and newspaper interviews had taken its toll on his voice.

She had been concerned for some time about the way he drove himself. He would push to the brink of exhaustion, far into the early morning, then collapse for two or three hours' sleep and start again. He attacked his work with a single-mindedness which excluded almost everything else, even, at times, her.

They had talked about it. He admitted that this had been the thing his wife, Valerie, never understood. She had needed the reassurance of a man in constant attendance, and Jack had more often than not been absent when she needed and wanted him. At the last, her affection had curdled into hostility. She despised him for being more attentive to his ambitions than to his wife.

Lisa knew the experience had tempered him, that he did make an effort not to exclude her completely from his affairs. She also knew that, whether she liked it or not, his work would always come first. She accepted the fact. It seemed so small a sacrifice to make for someone so worth loving.

She wondered if he would ask her to marry him, declining to think of the alternative. In fact, he was still married to Valerie.

"We discussed divorce at one time," he had told Lisa. "That was over a year ago. I thought I was going to get married, so I got in touch with Valerie to see how she felt about going to court."

"And?"

"It ended in an argument, just like always. As it turned out, I didn't need the divorce, so I let the whole thing drop. Lisa, I think you should know——" he paused, trying to find the words.

"Know what?"

"I think you should know that I have a child in Europe. An illegitimate child. A boy." He waited for her reaction.

"I see," she said quietly. "Do you want to tell me what happened?"

"It's not much of a story. His mother is a model, a Swedish girl. I began seeing her shortly after Valerie and I separated. Astrid Swensen is her name. I was willing to marry her for the child's sake, but she didn't want that. She had her mind made up. There wasn't anything I could do to change it."

"Have you ever seen the child?"

"Once. He's with her housekeeper in Paris. He was only a few months old then. To him I was just another strange face."

"I don't understand. Why does he live with a housekeeper? Where is his mother?"

"Working. Modeling. She travels a lot, all over the world." He shrugged.

"But doesn't she want him with her?" Lisa was surprised. "I would."

"She's a very ambitious girl. Dragging a child along might interfere with her career or her social life."

"Then why does she want the baby at all?"

"I don't think she really does want him. She doesn't love him. She just thinks she should look as if she loves him, so she won't give him up."

Lisa spoke softly. "Did you want the child?"

"I thought I did."

..

Lisa wondered occasionally how it must feel to have a child somewhere that could never be yours. Someday, perhaps, she would make it up to him, give him a son of his own. She smiled to herself. How good it was to be in love. It gave one the luxury of daydreams.

"Would one of you please tell me why we're going to this party?" Lisa glanced from Marty to Jack.

"Don't you know? Hollywood people will go to anything." Marty drove through the stone gateposts marking the entrance to Trousdale Estates.

"Be serious. I don't even know Mike Stanton and that girl he lives with. How come you were invited, Marty?"

"I met Mike about six years ago in New York when we were both studying there. After he washed out as a kid actor, he went East. We were in the same acting classes."

"I didn't know he'd been an actor," Jack said.

"I don't think he was any Roddy McDowall or Brandon de Wilde," Marty remarked. "He did the kind of movies where Daddy went off to war, and he said lines like 'But why does Daddy have to go away?' "

"And Phyllis Thaxter always played the mother," put in Jack. "She said 'To make the world a better place for little boys like you.' " They all three laughed, remembering.

"What's Mike Stanton doing now, since the theater folded?" Lisa wanted to know.

"He's made a documentary film. They're going to screen it tonight. Something he did down on Skid Row with hand-held cameras. He told me he thinks it's 'a poignant social commentary.' " Marty shrugged. "So why not take a look? Hell, we're all moths at heart. We'll watch anything that flickers."

"I think it sounds very dreary, not to mention a little pompous," said Lisa. "I think you guys have shanghaied me."

"If it's that bad," Jack assured her, "we can always duck out early."

Marty peered out the window, checking house numbers. "This must be it."

"Good Lord," exclaimed Lisa, eyeing the collonaded Grecian manse at the end of the cypress-lined drive. A fountain splashed into a lighted pool in front of the doorway. Parking attendants scrambled for their car as they stopped.

Jack took in the surroundings with a sweeping glance. "I

think the word is 'sumptuous.'" He nodded in the direction of the twin tan Bentleys in the garage. "I hope your friend is worth it," he remarked drily to Marty.

"He's managed to assemble a fairly impressive group," said Marty, surveying the guests as the butler relieved Lisa of her coat. "There's Claire Poland and Colin Kirkwood and Hans Deitrick."

Lisa turned away. "Obie and Ruth are in the corner over there, talking to Gloria French," she pointed out. "There must be fifty people here. God, what a gorgeous house."

"I'm glad you like it," said the smooth voice at her elbow. "I'm Virginia. We're delighted you could come." She was tall and fine-boned, with an abundance of natural blonde hair, tamed to a conservative style. Her speech, precise and polished, carried the ring of tradition and Eastern private schools.

"I was admiring your antiques," Lisa told the girl. "There are so many, and they're such beauties. Excuse me, I should have introduced myself. I'm Lisa Taylor."

"I know," she smiled warmly. She greeted Jack and Marty by name.

"I see you've met." Mike joined them, extending a hand to Lisa and giving his name as Virginia excused herself to meet some of the others.

"Quite an establishment you have here," acknowledged Marty.

"That's Virginia's doing. The furnishings are from her family's house in Palm Beach. She sold that and kept the duplex on Fifth Avenue."

"Nice."

"How's the picture going, Jack?" Mike asked amiably.

"So far so good. I'll know more Monday. I'm going back to location for a week, until they've finished the exteriors."

"Jackson Hole is a beautiful place," he commented, and then, to Lisa, "will you be going along?"

"I don't believe so."

When he had left them, she remarked, "He certainly keeps well-informed. And lets everyone know it," she added.

"The sure mark of someone on the outside wanting to be in," Jack said. "Damn. Here she comes."

Lisa followed his gaze and saw Claire Poland bearing down on them.

"Well, hello young lovers," she chirped cheerfully. "Any

news for me? You haven't gone and taken out a marriage license behind my back?"

"Hardly," Jack replied.

"Not so fast." She caught Marty's sleeve as he attempted to cross the room. "What's new with you, besides the fact that you're becoming one of the hottest actors in town? No secret romance you'd like to confide?"

"You're my only secret love, Claire, you know that," he parried. "Anyone want a drink?"

"She actually blushed," Lisa laughed later. "Be careful, she may make a pass at you yet."

"There's a dismal thought."

"It's been a pretty dismal evening all around," voiced Jack. "Mike Stanton is no picture-maker. That film was a piece of junk."

"I like the girl, though, Virginia," said Lisa. "She's very sweet."

"At least Mike's trying to do something different," Marty allowed.

"You're being too charitable," Jack argued. "I have a suspicion that Mike Stanton has never marched to the sound of any drum more distant than the next free lunch."

"That's a rotten thing to say when you're sitting here eating his buffet," countered Lisa.

He shrugged.

"He's awfully handsome," she observed. "I like his looks. No wonder she fell for him. Still, there's something . . ." She paused, searching out the words. "He does an odd thing, did you notice? He makes a great point of looking straight into your eyes and noplace else."

"What the devil are you talking about?" asked Marty.

"Men. When they first look at me, they give me the once-over, up and down. I watched Mike talking to Gloria French, and he never even looked at her body."

"Are you saying he's a fag?" asked Jack.

"He's not," Marty corrected. "That I know."

"No, he's not," she said, "but I think he's so preoccupied with looking sincere that he gives himself away. I'd give a lot to know," her eyes followed Mike, arm in arm with Gloria French, across the room, "what he's really thinking. There's something going on behind that facade."

"Does he interest you that much?" interrupted Jack.

She turned to him, sensing his impatience. "Darling, no. You know better than that. But I'll tell you one thing, it's the kind of puzzle that's catnip to any woman. And Mike Stanton knows that."

"Good evening." Hans Deitrick stopped in front of them, his greeting punctuated by the illusory click of his heels.

Lisa busied herself with her dinner plate while the men exchanged pleasantries.

"What was that all about?" demanded Jack.

"I don't know what you mean," she replied diffidently.

"Like hell you don't. You treated Deitrick as if he had measles."

"If you two will excuse me," Marty separated himself tactfully.

"I'm not crazy about him, that's all."

"Didn't you used to see him?"

"Not often."

"Were you lovers?"

"Jack. Since when do we ask each other questions like that?"

"I don't like the fact that he disturbs you. I don't like to see you that way." He looked at her intently. "What is it?"

"Whatever it is, it's not important now. I don't like him because he makes my flesh crawl."

"For any good reason?"

"Yes." She put aside her plate and held both his hands. "For a couple of years I used to see him now and then. When I wasn't going with someone special. You know there were some empty times before we met. I thought Hans was attractive. Then I," she halted, "I found out what he was like. I guess I'm a little sick at myself for ever having been remotely interested in him."

"You must have been more involved than you thought."

"It's possible. I was very bored with my life."

"Look, Lisa, past is past." He held her hands tightly. "Smile."

She smiled at him, glad of the strength she felt in his grasp.

"It's a small town we live in," he said. "No matter what we think of each other, we can't avoid the occasional confrontations. We have to learn to live with them on a social basis. We have to be, at the least, cordial, if not friendly. It may be that I'll consider using Deitrick in a picture at some point. I don't want to have to prohibit myself from hiring a fine actor just because he makes my wife uncomfortable."

She glanced up sharply.

"You heard me."

It was, of course, not that easy.

Jack's attorney met with Valerie's in the hope of convincing her to file for divorce. That was politely considered the wife's prerogative. She would have none of it. For three months the messages went back and forth, all, to Lisa, agonizingly secondhand.

"Anything new?" she asked Jack when he came home.

"Yes, damn it. We're having some trouble cutting the shooting-the-rapids scene together. We're going to have to send it over to the matte department at MGM and let their artists go to work on it." He mixed himself a drink at the bar.

"I wonder," she said, "if the house was burning, would you save me or your scripts?"

"That's easy. You. But only because I have copies of everything at the office."

"Bastard."

"You wanted to know if there's anything new with the Valerie situation?" He handed her a drink.

"Thanks."

"I've decided to file." He sat facing her on the sofa.

"Are you sure," she said cautiously, "that you want to? You were always so against that."

"I was trying to be the gentleman. I guess it only works if you're dealing with a lady." He stared into the glass.

"Jack." Lisa rested a hand on his knee. "Please don't do anything you'll regret later, not for me. I want it all to be good for us, no guilts."

"I know you do."

"Have you spoken to either lawyer?"

"I called mine today. He's going to draw up the papers and file as soon as possible. Mental cruelty. He said he'd inform her attorney as a matter of courtesy. Then," he set his glass on the table and took her face in both his hands, "then I am going to ask you to marry me, but not until then. Lisa, my God, don't cry, you idiot!"

They were interrupted by the telephone.

"That was Marty," he told her. "He wanted to know if I'd bought the rights to the spy book."

"Does he want to do the picture?"

"He's lukewarm about it. Anyway, I am going through with it. I'll have to go to New York next week on the deal. Want to come along?"

"Are you serious?"

"It'll only be for three or four days, but I thought we could get in some theater." He stood up, unbuttoning his shirt. "Well?"

"Do you really need an answer?"

"Start making up your mind what plays you want to see. I'm going to take a shower."

The telephone rang again over the noise of the running water. Lisa answered.

"Miss Taylor?" The woman's voice was unfamiliar.

"Speaking."

"You're an ass, you know that?" Her speech was husky.

"Who is this?"

"This is Valerie Haller, that's who this is. I'm the wife of the man you live with there." She stumbled slightly over the words.

For a moment Lisa couldn't think of anything to say. "What is it you want?"

"About thirty percent of his income for the next ten years. Will that do?" She gave a short laugh.

"Do you want to speak to Jack?"

"Fuck Jack. But not very often, right?"

"Look, Miss Normand——"

"Mrs. Haller."

"I don't want to talk to you." Lisa looked over her shoulder toward the sound of the shower.

"I'll bet you don't." She paused, and Lisa heard the clink of ice in a glass close to the mouthpiece. "But maybe you should know what you're getting into, dear."

"I'd rather not discuss it."

"The sonofabitch may be a professional producer, but he's

an amateur husband. I hope you enjoy neglect, because that's what you're going to get. Take my advice. Start looking around for some young stud. You'll need it."

"I'm going to hang up."

"Sure you are. Take my advice. Take a lover. And you tell that cocksucker for me," she gulped a breath, "that all I want from him is a big fat check every goddam month until the day he dies. And——"

The shower stopped. Lisa cut in. "I'm hanging up. Don't call me again." She replaced the receiver.

"Was that for me?" Jack stood in the hall, a towel wrapped around his waist.

"No." Her voice was unsteady.

"Anything wrong?" He frowned.

"Nothing. A crank call. I've had a couple of them today," she lied.

"Call the phone company and have the number changed." He disappeared into the bedroom.

"Lisa?"

She straightened up, brushing bits of newspaper off her slacks. "In here."

"You sure are a mess. What are you doing?" Jack gave her a brisk hug.

"Packing china. I thought if I packed as much as I could, we'd save some time and money with the movers."

"I just came from the escrow office. I signed the papers." He wore a pleased grin.

"Is that the last of it?"

"Everything. We move in next week."

Buying the house now had been Jack's idea. It would be another ten months before the divorce was final, but he was insistent that they wait no longer to start their life together.

"I did a wonderful, silly thing today," she told him.

"Like what?"

"I went to the stationers and ordered paper and envelopes with the new address. It gave me such a kick. Oh Jack, moving is a big pain in the neck, but I honestly think I've never been so happy to do anything." She circled her arms around him and nuzzled close to his neck. Up on the hill, just above Sunset Boulevard, the house was waiting. She saw the brick courtyard in front, the stone and timbers of the house covered here and there with glossy ivy and upstairs, in three family bedrooms, their floors dappled with sunlight, ready for them.

"Did you get the keys?" she asked. "Let's go up there tonight and go through it again."

"I can't. I have a meeting. Obie wants me to meet with one of his clients. He thinks he's the guy to do the script for *The Jonas File*. Seems he worked for the CIA at one time before he became a writer."

"Sounds interesting." She was disappointed, but Jack had set his sights ahead on the next film. With the Ian Driscoll picture already in a rough cut, he had plans to get a script from the spy book and start filming no later than the middle of next year.

"Obie said something about you turning down a picture. Said he heard it over at Paramount." Jack looked at her questioningly.

"I did. They were going to start shooting this month, and I wanted to get settled in the new house instead. Do you think I did the wrong thing?" She had been concerned about buying the house. She knew the divorce settlement had been hard on him.

"I told you. We can't let our lives revolve around paying for the past. That's no way to live. You did the right thing. Any phone messages for me?"

"Marty called."

"I know. I ran into him on the Victory lot. He doesn't want to do *The Jonas File*. Says it's not for him."

"What about the girl's part, the waif? Have you thought of anyone?"

"Laura Curtis, but she won't be available next summer. The Major bought some potboiler about young unwed mothers that he wants her to do. He says it'll get her an Academy Award. That means I have to find someone for the waif and someone to play the sexy female spy. I want to get a European name for that. It'll help our overseas grosses. God knows who we'll get for the leading man. I'm hoping for Colin Kirkwood." He brushed off the shreds of newspaper Lisa had left on his jacket. "I'm going to change. If you want me later, call me at Obie's office. Maybe we can meet for dinner if I get through early."

"Damn," she swore softly, surveying the mess of newspapers on the carpet. She knew that there was little chance he'd come home before midnight. She began packing the rest of the china.

How do your cigarette's tar and nicotine numbers compare with True?

20 CLASS A CIGARETTES

TRUE

MENTHOL FILTER

LATEST U.S. GOVERNMENT TESTS:
13 MGS. TAR, 0.7 MGS. NICOTINE

Place your pack here.

Compare
your cigarette's
tar and nicotine
numbers
with True.

20 CLASS A CIGARETTES

TRUE

FILTER CIGARETTES

LATEST U.S. GOVERNMENT TESTS:
12 MGS. TAR, 0.6 MGS. NICOTINE

No numbers on the front of your pack? True puts its numbers right out front. Because True, regular and menthol, is lower in both tar and nicotine than 99% of all other cigarettes sold. Think about it.

LATEST U.S. GOVERNMENT TESTS:
12 MGS. TAR, 0.6 MGS. NICOTINE

Warning: The Surgeon General Has Determined That Cigarette Smoking Is Dangerous to Your Health

Regular or menthol.
Doesn't it all add up to True?

Regular: 12 mg. "tar", 0.6 mg. nicotine.
Menthol: 13 mg. "tar", 0.7 mg. nicotine, av. per cigarette, FTC Report, Aug. '71.

5

Laura

2:45 P.M.

"*Are you all right?*"

"*Sure I'm all right. I always come straight from a funeral to work.*" Jesus Christ, if I could just stop my hands from shaking.

"*You didn't touch your lunch. I sent the tray away. Did you call Claire Poland?*"

"*Yes, Indigo, I called Claire Poland.*" It's true what they say. Life really does go on in spite of everything. You do call Claire and you do have a nice, polite, inane conversation, just the way you were told to. See what a good girl I am, Obie. I said all the right things about picking up the pieces of my life and how Mike would have wanted it that way. Such a good girl. Such a lying bitch. Lies. Thank God for lies.

"*Laura, there was a phone call while you were on the set just now. Drucilla called from New York. She said she'd been trying to reach you ever since she heard the news.*" .

"*What did she want?*"

"*She didn't want anything. Just asked me to tell you she's thinking of you and hopes you're all right.*"

I'm all right, all right. She's probably delighted. Smacking her lips over all the juicy details in the Daily News, thinking how it serves me right. To hell with her. If there's one thing I'm long on, it's grit. That grit made Drucilla a nice pile of cash for herself, and now it's going to save my skin. Don't count on being able to gloat over little Laura's misfortune, Drucilla.

"*Your hands are shaking.*"

"*So they are.*"

"*Can I get you something? A Librium from the dispensary?*"

"*Please. And see if there's any Scotch in the prop wagon.*"

119

Maybe that will do it. If I can just relax a little. Christ, my hands are vibrating like a pair of tuning forks.

Jack Haller, I hope you appreciate that I am doing you one big beautiful favor just by showing up here today. I may have a percentage of the picture, but this kind of devotion to duty is something else again. You're a lucky man to have an obedient little pro like me.

Lucky man. You with your beautiful wife. I wonder how much he knows about her. From the look on her face in that bedroom, I'd say he knows nothing. Sweet Lisa. So much in love with her husband. Such a good wife. Such a lying bitch. Never mind. Whatever she did, however much I hate her for it, it works for me now. Keep up the good work, Lisa. Keep those lies coming. That way we'll all be safe.

"That's better. It's nice to see you smiling."

"I didn't know I was. Is that Scotch in that paper cup?"

"Yes. Here's the pill."

Good. Warm. Oh God, let it stop my hands from shaking. They weren't very generous with the booze. Probably afraid to give me more than a sip, afraid I'll come apart at the seams. Like hell I will. Onward and upward. Don't look back, something may be gaining on you. Why should I, anyway? Why should I have to think of what's past? What happened was paid for. In advance. So no backward glances.

"Feel better?"

"A little."

"You know, sweetheart, it was a beautiful service."

"Was it? I've never been to a funeral before."

If that was beautiful, I'd hate like hell to see an ugly one. If you ask me, the whole thing is bizarre. Funeral ceremonies. Ceremonies. Man has managed to make dying almost as unattractive as he's made living.

"They want you on the set for a camera run-through when you're ready."

"I'm ready. Zip me up the back, will you?"

"Turn and face the mirror. I can see better that way."

There it is, folks, the face of your box-office favorite, a little puffy under the eyes, maybe, but the makeup will take care of that. Look at it. Don't frown, you'll get wrinkles.

Is it true that what people are shows up in their faces? Does any of it show, I wonder? No. I am what I see. A pretty girl, a little too thin, perhaps. All the better to hang clothes on. Nervous eyes. Got to look less highstrung. Relax. Think placid.

"All set."

"Thanks."

I will calmly say my words and make my moves for the camera. Everyone will comment on what a marvel I am. A great trouper, that's me. But what else would I do today?

"Let me have that magnifying glass, Mona." Laura squinted at the strip of photographs.

"Here. Take a close look at the second from the top."

"I agree with Mona," Dru said. "That one's the best of the lot."

"You two never disagree on anything, do you?" Laura moved the sheet of contact prints closer to the light. "Well, I guess you're right. There's still something about it I don't like, but it is the best shot of the bunch, so let's use it. How many are you going to have printed up, Mona?"

"A couple of thousand to start. Do you want to sign any of them yourself?"

"No. Let the secretaries do it. I've got enough to do without having to answer fan mail. What time is that interviewer due?" Without waiting for a reply, she moved toward the dressing room door. "If he comes while I'm gone, tell him I'll be back. I'm going to get some water to wash down this pill."

"What is it?" demanded Dru.

"What's what?"

"The pill."

"You'd think I was a dope addict. It's a Dexamyl, that's what."

"You took one yesterday morning and the day before, too."

Laura looked from one to the other. "What if I did? I don't notice either of you getting up at six thirty and knocking yourself out all day. One month on this picture and I've lost six pounds."

"I don't like it," Dru said. "Those things make you jumpy."

Mona nodded. "They do."

Laura shook her head slowly, looking at them. "Tweedle-dum and Tweedledee." She slammed the door behind her.

"I hate to see her this nervous," said Dru.

"You'd have thought the vacation would have helped." Mona began to collect the photographs from Laura's makeup table.

"You saw what happened. For the first week she was crowing about how glorious it was to have all that privacy and nobody fussing over her. The second week she kept looking around to see if anyone recognized her. The third week she was frantic to get back here before people forgot her name."

"She should know better. It's my job to see they don't. By the way, I have the copy on that last interview. She should read through it and give it her okay. I have to get it back to the magazine before Monday." Mona extracted the typewritten sheets from her attaché case.

" 'From Nikki to Nympho,' " Dru read. "Can't we get them to change the title?"

"It's not that bad. It'll grab the readers. The content isn't all that sensational. It says a lot of nice stuff about her versatility. Do you want to look over these pictures again before I take them?"

"No. I'm not really pleased with them. I guess we chose the best one."

"I know what's bothering you. Come here." Mona covered the bottom part of the photograph with her hand. "Look."

"The eyes."

"I don't know what to call it. Is it tension?"

"Whatever it is, it's not charm."

"It's a very intense look," Mona offered helpfully. "It makes for an interesting picture."

"Always looking at the bright side," Dru smiled at her. "I'm going back to the office. Have a good interview." She kissed Mona on the temple. "See if you can keep the conversation away from the nympho role and more on her acting ability."

Mona steered the interview subtly in the direction she had been told. Both the reporter and Laura were not unaware that they were being manipulated, but that was standard operating procedure for publicists, and Mona managed to be less obtrusive about it than most.

"What's Hans Deitrick like to work with?" the writer was asking her.

"He's very exciting. He commands your attention. It's hard to look away from him."

"I imagine he effects most women that way," he grinned.

"That's not what I meant," she snapped.

"I think," Mona put in, "that Laura was referring to the degree of his dramatic intensity. Am I right, Laura?"

"Yes, that's what I meant." But why had she bristled so quickly at his statement? She knew very well why. As long as neither the reporter nor Mona could read her thoughts, however, she was safe.

"Isn't it type casting, though? Deitrick as a psychiatrist, accent and all?"

"That's not my department." Laura closed the subject. She wished she were not being so short with this man. Mona should have known better than to schedule an interview on a day when she was in the middle of shooting such a difficult scene.

"I'm sorry I look so awful," she apologized to him. "I've been crying all morning, and it does dreadful things to my face."

"What's the hardest thing about shooting that kind of scene?"

She smiled. "Dehydration."

He laughed.

"No, I'm serious. You have to drink quarts of water to keep the tears coming."

"We're ready, Laura," someone said from outside the door.

"I'm coming."

"Would you like to watch?" Mona invited.

"I—— Never mind." Laura wished the reporter would leave. The scene was upsetting enough without having some outsider observing and taking notes all through it. Resignedly, she walked onto the set.

"It's too tight. Indigo, you're tying it too tight!" Laura heaved her shoulders in discomfort.

"That's the way it has to be. Look, sweetheart, a straitjacket is not supposed to be a comfortable garment." She gave Laura's hair a soothing pat.

"Damn." She jerked her head away. "I don't care. Undo it just a little. I feel as if I'm suffocating in here."

"I can't, dear. Jason said he wanted it very tight. I think he wants you to be uncomfortable in this scene."

"Jason! Jason!"

He left his director's chair and walked, unhurried, to where she stood.

"What's the idea?"

"The idea," he took a long, slow drag on his cigaret, "is to make this as realistic as possible."

"Why don't you leave that to the actors? I can do just as good a job with this thing looser."

"I figure," he said, "that we can always use every bit of help we have."

"What is that supposed to mean?" She glanced in the direction of Mona and the interviewer, huddled behind the camera, and lowered her voice. "Please, Jason, be reasonable. I'm extremely uncomfortable."

"Use it in the scene." He walked away. "Is Mr. Deitrick ready? I'd like to try this on film."

"Here." Hans stepped into the set and seated himself on the hospital bed.

Laura turned her head to the wall and began to weep. When she heard "Action" called, she spun around, screaming the words at Hans. He made the attempt to calm her. She wrenched away from his grasp, darting around the small room like a frenzied creature until, cornered, she collapsed into unintelligible moans.

"Cut."

Hans reached down and brushed a strand of hair out of her mouth.

"Do you think, Hans," Jason requested, "that you could be a little more careful on that move near the window? You threw a shadow across Laura's face. I know it's difficult with such quick moves, but give it a try. Now you," he stood over Laura, "you could give me a little more."

"I could what?"

"I need more from you. Our girl is quite insane here. This is the peak of a nervous breakdown. I want everything you have."

Her voice was shaking. "I've never dogged a scene in my life."

Hans stood impassively beside Jason, watching her.

"Then let's see you give me the scene I want."

"What the hell do you think I was just doing?" She writhed uncomfortably as Hans lifted her to her feet.

"If you are, as you say, such a professional, you will do what I tell you without any prima donna antics. You are just another actress as far as I am concerned. Just another piece of meat owned by S. M. Victor. Now, do as I say."

"Bastard!" Tears of rage choked her throat. She butted the wall with her shoulder, straining against the tightness of the jacket. She gasped for the breath to speak. Hans again reached to comfort her. With all her strength, she hurled herself toward him, beating at him with her body. He tried to grab her. She kicked him. She dashed, stumbling, out of reach and spun off the wall, hitting the bed. It was like watching a moth trapped in a jar, smashing mindlessly against its confines. His arms wide, Hans lunged at her, pinning her to the wall. She fought him, shrieking, until her voice broke and she weakened. Silently, the tears streaming down her cheeks, she slid down the wall and fell at his feet.

"Cut. Print."

Hans bent over her. "Are you all right?"

She turned to look up at him and started to speak, but no words came. The tears would not stop.

"Get her out of this thing," he said.

Indigo kneeled beside her, and the two of them began untying the restraints. Hans helped her up. He put his arms around her and steadied her against him. "You were beautiful," he told her. "I have never seen such passion."

"Perfect," commented Jason. "Do you smoke?" He offered her a cigaret, smiling. "Sorry I had to lean on you so, but I wanted something very special. And I got it."

She turned and walked to her dressing room.

Laura looked up from her chair as Hans came across the set and seated himself beside her in the shadows.

"You are fatigued," he said. "It shows here." He ran a finger lightly underneath her eye.

"I am fatigued," she agreed with a wan smile. She wanted to feel his fingers on her face again, perhaps even to touch his hand. Ridiculous. Hans Deitrick was as inaccessible to her as some bronzed and mythical god. She shook her head as if to empty it of the idea.

"After this film will you rest?" Hans inquired.

"Not for long. We'll be finished before Christmas, but I have to ride in the Rose Bowl parade New Year's and leave that night for a telethon in Chicago. Then I go to New York to tape a segment of a TV special, *The Major Mogul*. It's a tribute to S. M. Victor."

"You exhaust me. And then?"

"I have business in New York. New merchandising contracts. I'm lending my name to a dress line and I have to meet with the designer and the manufacturer. I'll do a week or two of fashion layouts and pictures for the magazines. After that, I'm off to Florida on one of those celebrity junkets. The Major is backing some kind of amusement park there, and he's importing a bunch of stars to dress it up. Then I go back to New York to make a record. That part is comical," she confided, "because I don't really sing well enough, but they're writing some special songs for me. I'm supposed to sing one of them on *The Ed Sullivan Show* in the beginning of March. That terrifies me."

"I doubt," said Hans, "that much of anything terrifies you."

Laura gave a nervous laugh. "Do me a favor and don't watch the show."

"I plan to watch with great anticipation." He leaned back in his camp chair. "When will you do another film?"

"I'll start wardrobe fittings in April. It's a picture about unwed mothers. The Major bought the property especially for me. That's one of the reasons I'm doing the appearances for him."

"Do you never do anything for yourself?"

"Like what?"

"Indulging yourself. Relaxing. Pleasure. Whatever pleases you."

"I enjoy my work," she protested.

"But surely there is more to life than working. Even the simplest pleasures. Reading, perhaps." He withdrew a book from the side pocket of his chair. "Do you know Strindberg?"

"Who?"

"Strindberg, the playwright."

"No," she said cautiously, "I don't." She hoped he wouldn't think she was stupid, but it was better to tell the truth than to have him catch her in a lie.

"Chekhov?"

"I've heard of him. I know he wrote *The Cherry Orchard* and *Uncle Vanya*." There, she was not so dumb after all.

"But have you read them?" He glanced at her. "No?"

"I can name all the Oscar winners for the past five years, even the winning songs."

"Tell me, you have worked always? No time off even to be a foolish adolescent, to have what they call the awkward stage?"

"I couldn't afford one." His gaze made her uncomfortable, as if it could penetrate her thoughts.

"How sad," he smiled.

"Not really. I don't think I've missed so much."

"But you have. Here you are, an intelligent, pretty girl with great drive and passion, and what has it all been used for? To make money for the Major."

"And me."

"Yes, and you. Do you know what Napoleon said of China?"

"No, I don't." Damn, but he made her feel foolish.

"He said that China was a sleeping giant, and if it ever awoke—watch out. I think," his fingers tapped on the cover of his book, "that Laura Curtis is also a sleeping giant. Whoever wakes her will make some extraordinary discoveries."

She felt her cheeks redden.

"How old are you?" His eyes had not moved from her face.

"Nineteen."

"You are a virgin, aren't you?"

She stared at him.

"Incredible. So sophisticated in so many ways, yet still a virgin. All that intensity spent on nothing but a strip of film. You have so much to learn." He took her hand and placed it on the book in his lap. "Here. Start with this. You may not like all of Strindberg, but you cannot help admiring the way he wrote."

Laura took the book and laid it beside her in her chair. Her hand trembled slightly.

"Take it to bed with you tonight. Read a little before you go to sleep."

She found her voice. "I will." She managed to meet his eyes. "You're right. There are so many things I don't know."

"But think of all the pleasures in store for you."

"Drucilla didn't want me to grow up too fast." The words sounded lame in her ears.

"Drucilla Lang? Your manager?"

"I live with Dru." It became an apology.

"You do?" He frowned slightly. "The publicity woman, Mona, she lives with you also?"

"No." Laura shook her head.

"And who are Drucilla's other clients?" he asked.

"That's all. Just me."

"I see. And you live with her."

Why did it all sound suddenly so strange? Laura felt awkward. She averted her eyes from his face and opened the book to the table of contents. She looked at the page without reading it.

"Not now," Hans said. "The light is not good here. Tonight. When you are comfortable in your bed."

"Tonight," she said, watching him walk away, wondering what it was that had been said, or unsaid, which he seemed to understand and she did not. She shivered. Something frightened her, what she didn't know, but it was a thrilling kind of fear, not at all unpleasant.

"What are you looking for?" Indigo asked.

"Me? Nothing," replied Laura, hastily returning to her script.

"I thought maybe the Major was planning to pay a visit, the way you keep looking out of the door."

"Not that I know of. I was just letting my mind wander, I guess." She exhaled slowly, trying to relax. It wouldn't do to be obvious.

"Sweetheart," Indigo began, "is it Deitrick you're watching for?"

"Why would I watch for him?"

"Just asking. I saw you two huddled in the corner yesterday." She continued folding the pile of sweaters beside her on the sofa.

"We weren't 'huddling,' whatever that means. We're working together, remember?"

Indigo seemed absorbed in the business of sorting the sweaters. She did not look up. "I've been on Deitrick pictures before."

Laura deliberately turned a page of her script before responding. "And?"

"He takes it all very personally."

"Indigo." Laura turned in her chair to face her. "Don't beat around the bush. If you have something to tell me, come right out and say it."

"Well," she searched out the words cautiously, "Hans Deitrick tends to become personally involved when he makes a film."

"Doesn't everybody?"

"Not that way. Baby, he does have a reputation for romancing his leading ladies."

"Jesus, Indigo! He loaned me a book, that's all!"

"I wouldn't like to see you get hurt."

"Don't be silly. How could I?"

"It happens. I've seen actresses get cases of leading-man-itis that broke up their marriages. Then, after the picture's over, the whole thing evaporates, and there the poor girl is with no husband and no boy friend, either." She opened the closet door and put the sweaters on a shelf.

"That's no problem of mine." Laura turned back to the dressing table. "And if it were, I don't have a husband to worry about."

"But you are young, honey. And Deitrick does like to get very thick with his leading ladies. It might be awfully flattering. He's a handsome man. Any young girl's head could be turned. There's always a first time."

"Will you, for heaven's sake, stop gassing about how young I am! I've seen a lot more and done a lot more than ninety percent of the girls my age. I'm not a child. I can take care of myself."

"That's what I hope, dear. Do you want to wear the brown hair ribbon or the rose one in this scene?" She held one in each hand.

"The rose. It's prettier."

"You're not supposed to be so pretty at this point in the

story. She's still a sick girl. Are you sure you wouldn't rather look like a drab little sparrow?"

"Yes, I'm sure. I want to wear the rose one. If a lousy hair ribbon makes me feel prettier, why shouldn't I?"

"No reason at all."

There he was. She watched his reflection in the mirror. His hands thrust into the pockets of his trench coat, he walked across the stage, apparently unaware of her. His blond hair was uncombed. The penetrating blue eyes were hidden behind a pair of sunglasses. She wondered how a man could move so gracefully and still be so masculine. She would not call out. That was too eager. She'd wait until he was almost by her door and say his name softly.

"Hans?" Laura saw Indigo turn in her direction.

"Good morning." He bowed his head briskly. "And how are you today? Well rested, I hope." He removed his glasses, and Laura looked up into the pale blue eyes set off by the deep tan of his face.

"I'll be outside if you need me," said Indigo.

Laura smiled. "Not so well rested, thanks to you. I read all of *Miss Julie* last night. I couldn't stand to put it down before I'd finished it. I lived every scene. Hans, it's so beautiful. Thank you so much."

"Thank August Strindberg," he laughed. "May I sit down? I'm not due in makeup for another ten minutes."

"Please. You know, someday I'd like to play *Miss Julie*."

"You'd be very good. It's an excellent part for you."

"May I keep the book awhile? I want to read the others." Laura looked into the mirror and pulled her hair back, looping the rose-colored ribbon around it.

"As long as you wish." He was watching her in the glass. "After Strindberg, perhaps we shall try a little Chekhov, if you like."

"Are you going to make an intellectual out of me?"

"Intellectuals are never as pretty as you."

Oh God, she wondered if he had seen her hands falter, tying the bow.

"It's only a little sample of what you call 'the liberal arts.' Do you want some help with that ribbon?"

"Would you? I'm afraid I didn't get it even." She tried not to react to the touch of his hands at the nape of her neck.

Her tongue felt dry and heavy. She attempted to sound off-hand. "I've never known exactly what 'the liberal arts' were."

"I believe," he seated himself again, "that it can mean almost anything. There is an art to everything. Acting, singing, cooking, lovemaking. Anything done with talent and skill becomes an art. Is it not so?"

"I—I don't know."

"Take the Renaissance, for example. Under the apprentice system raw novices, apprenticed to master artists, became great artists themselves. One must be exposed to art before one can fulfill his maximum potential." He reached in his pocket for a package of cigarets. "Do you smoke?"

"I'll try one of yours."

"They're English. Virginia tobacco. Very mild." He held out a match for her.

Laura drew in the smoke as lightly as she could. She didn't want to burst into coughing. The cigaret felt awkward between her fingers. She tried to hold it the way she had seen Drucilla do, effortlessly, as if it grew from her fingertips. "I was never a very good student," she warned apologetically. "My tutor made me read *Madame Bovary* and *A Tale of Two Cities,* but I only skimmed through them. I was too busy learning my lines for Nikki."

"That is too bad. Such things should be enjoyed at leisure. They should be savored."

"I'll try," she offered. "Anyway, I like reading plays."

"But you must not limit yourself to plays. As I say, everything can be an art. There are worlds of painting and sculpture. And the poetry, the novels. You must read Baudelaire, de Sade."

"You won't be impatient with me if I don't understand?"

"Never. I shall be a gentle teacher," Hans stood up, "with a young and beautiful pupil." He touched her hair lightly with his fingers. "I will see you on the set."

Laura parked her car in the driveway and let herself in by the front door. Dru was sitting on the living-room floor, rummaging through two large cardboard cartons.

"What are those?" Laura settled on the sofa, letting her script and her book slide to the floor.

"All the scripts from every picture you've done. I had copies of them stored in the closet."

"What for?"

"I thought they'd be nice to keep. I'm putting them in chronological order." She added one to the pile beside her on the carpet. "Did you happen to hear the news broadcast when you were driving home?"

"No. Why? What happened?" She sat up.

"Very sad. Harris Bolding committed suicide in New York. The radio said he was despondent about finances and had been drinking heavily."

"Oh." Laura dropped back into the comfort of the cushions.

"I think we should send flowers. After all, he helped get you started in the business."

"Do whatever you want."

"Is that all you have to say?" demanded Dru.

"What else is there?"

"If you ask me——"

"—Which I didn't."

"You've grown hard lately. I don't like it."

"You're not exactly Sweet Sue yourself, you know."

"What I am or am not isn't the point. We're talking about you. It's not attractive, this toughness."

"No? Well, where do you think you'd be without it?" Laura gave her a defiant look. "If I didn't have the stamina to turn out picture after picture from six A.M. to six P.M. daily, where would you be? Back in New York peddling snotty-nosed kids, that's where. It takes a damn hard head and the guts of a burglar to stay on top of this business. Are you going to deny that?" She propped herself up on one elbow to face Drucilla.

Dru's lips were taut. "I don't like bitchiness, Laura." She took a deep breath. "Look, I know your nerves are shot after six weeks in a part like this, but that's no excuse for your behavior. Plenty of stars make it big in this business without advertising how tough they are. Real strength doesn't have to be so noisy. Your attitude is unbecoming to a pretty young girl."

"I'm not a child anymore!"

"I'm not so sure. I think you're confusing hardness with maturity."

"I'm not confusing anything." Laura lay back on the sofa.

"Maybe you just don't like the idea that I might grow up and have a life of my own."

"Yes," she admitted, "that could be part of it, I suppose, but it's certainly not all of it. A lot of it is your doing. I wish you'd try to change your approach. Is it possible you're getting too involved with your part in this picture?" She lit a cigaret and dropped the pack onto the floor.

"Maybe. Let me have one of those, will you?"

"What?"

"Give me a cigaret, please." She stretched out her hand impatiently.

"Laura Curtis. Since when did you start smoking?"

"I do it now and then," she replied, reaching for the pack on the carpet.

"Well, don't." Dru seized the cigarets and put them in her skirt pocket. "It doesn't look right for you to smoke."

"Damn it!" Laura exploded. "When will you realize that I'm old enough to do as I please? I'm old enough to get married. I'm old enough to have a baby. And I damned well am old enough to smoke!"

Drucilla collected herself. "It will ruin your voice. Laura, what's happening? I thought we were close to each other."

"Oh hell." She sat up. "I just want to be my own person for a change. You know," she said pointedly, "it is something I've never done."

"Dear," Dru let a small sigh escape, "if you will only understand that any advice I give you is for your own good, and if you will just try to accept it in that light, I promise you I'll do my best not to interfere in your growing up. Is that fair?"

"I guess so." She bent down and collected her script and her book from the floor.

"What are you reading?" Dru asked amiably.

"*Les Fleurs du Mal.*" She pronounced the French with casual expertise.

"Very highbrow," smiled Dru.

"Would you put these things in my room? I have a voice lesson at eight."

"Tonight? I thought she was going to come to the studio at lunchtime."

"Something came up." Laura stood and stretched, shaking the tenseness out of her shoulders.

"What about dinner?" asked Drucilla from the floor.

"Don't worry about it. I'll grab a hamburger on the way."

"Take a coat," Dru called after her. "It's going to turn cold tonight." She heard the door shut. Slowly, she stubbed out her cigaret in the ashtray at her feet. She sat still for a moment, frowning. Then, with a sudden, nervous motion, she quickly lit another.

Dru was waiting for her in the darkened room. She could see her ash glowing in the dimness. Laura flicked the wall switch, and Dru looked up, blinking at the light. Her eyes darted to Laura's face.

"Where were you?" she demanded harshly.

"Where do you think I was?" She took off her coat.

"You weren't at a voice lesson. I want to know where you've been."

"It's only ten o'clock," said Laura.

"You didn't answer my question. You weren't with your voice coach." One hand gripped the arm of the chair.

"Are you saying you checked up on me? Are you?" Laura's voice grew loud.

"I didn't. She called to say you had forgotten your tape cartridges yesterday. She has them." Dru sounded suddenly weary. "Laura, please. I was worried. Please tell me where you were."

"I met a friend for dinner," she answered.

"What friend?"

"Is this a cross-examination? What business is it of yours?"

"Laura! I am concerned! Don't you understand?" She ran a hand distractedly over her forehead. "I thought I knew most of your friends."

"If you must know," she said lightly, "I was with Hans."

"Deitrick?" Dru stiffened. "Are you crazy?"

Laura answered coolly, folding her coat over her arm. "No. I like him."

"I think," Dru tried to control her voice, "that you're in danger of getting in over your head, young lady."

"How that?" Laura smiled confidently.

"Deitrick is out of your class. He's strictly heavyweight. You have no business being with him."

"I'm over eighteen. You can't decide who I can go out with."

"I'm trying to warn you."

"I like him," she repeated.

"You're too young," replied Dru flatly.

"He doesn't seem to think so."

"He's not your guardian, and I am! Laura," she persisted, "I don't want to have you get mixed up in something you can't handle."

Laura looked away. "I can take care of myself."

Druoilla walked to where she stood. "I'm not the least bit sure of that," she said, looking into her face. "You may have far more experience in some matters than most girls your age, but there are certain areas in which you are still quite inexperienced. You have to admit that's so. Isn't it?"

"My so-called virtue is still intact, if that's what you're after."

"I'm not 'after' anything! I'm trying to protect you."

"From Hans Deitrick?" she laughed.

"From getting hurt."

"Frankly," Laura challenged, "it would hurt me more not to see him. Do you want to do that to me? Is that your idea of making me happy? I have a right to choose my own friends," she said acidly. "Don't try to stop me." She turned abruptly and started for the stairs.

"Laura! I don't want you to see him outside of the studio!"

Laura stopped halfway up the stairs. Very deliberately she turned around to look down at Dru. "That's not very nice," she said slowly, smiling. "How would you like it if I said you couldn't see your friends? How would you like it if I said you couldn't see Mona anymore?" She whirled and ran upstairs, slamming her bedroom door.

The sound echoed through the silent house.

Laura halted in the doorway. She saw his reflection in the mirror first. Hans was lounging on her dressing-room sofa, leisurely smoking a cigaret.

"You were not in the commissary. I would have asked you to have lunch with me."

She stepped inside. "I had a voice lesson. I ate a sandwich on the way." It was becoming easier to respond as his equal. She was less unsure of herself each time she saw him. The knowledge that Hans found her attractive had given her a

new authority. There were times when she even believed in
her own nonchalance. That is, until he touched her.

She dropped her music tapes and book next to him. He
slid his fingers up her forearm and, holding her lightly,
brought her toward him and kissed her cheek. Laura straightened up hastily.

"Indigo might come in."

"Close the door."

For a brief moment, she started to obey him. "No," she
said, "that might make it worse."

Hans laughed. "She's spying on you for your keeper?"

"She could be." Laura seated herself in front of the mirror
and applied a fresh coat of lipstick.

"Dreadful stuff."

She looked up, questioning.

"That." He gestured toward the tube in her hand. "A de-
terrent to lovemaking second only to chastity belts and girdles.
What man likes to find his face smeared like an African war-
rior?"

"I don't usually wear it when I'm not working." What
would have been a lie had just become the truth. Scrutinizing
herself in the mirror, Laura wondered what else he did and
did not like in his women.

Hans idly traced a finger over the cover of her book. He
made smooth loops around and around the "O" of the title,
The Story of O. "Have you started the book? How do you
like it?"

"I've almost finished. It's very dirty."

"What?" Hans burst into incredulous laughter. "Don't tell
me you are one of the American puritans I've heard about."

She flushed. "No," she answered cautiously. More firmly
she added, "But I still think it's very dirty."

"Dear Laura." He was still smiling, amused at her. "You
must learn that nothing is dirty. Different people have different pleasures. It is as simple as that. Perhaps your tastes
are not those of the characters in the book. Isn't that possible?"

"It's possible," she replied airily, covering her loss of composure. Whenever he made her feel naïve, she was once again
the awkward adolescent, trying hard to appeal to a wordly
man with whom she had a mere fraction of a chance. The reality of the situation embarrassed and frustrated her. If only

she were given the opportunity, she could prove to him she was as much a woman as any of those creatures he escorted around. Besides, men were supposed to want virgins, weren't they? This last thought still scared her a little, but each time it floated to the surface of her mind, its terror seemed to have diminished slightly. After all, weren't half the girls her age either having affairs or married? She was sure of it. It was obvious she might be missing out on something that was an ordinary part of life for most people. She tried hard to keep thinking of it as that—ordinary.

"What is going on in that mind of yours?" asked Hans.

"I was considering what you said," she lied.

"That nothing is dirty?"

"Yes."

"The words 'dirty' and 'bad' have no place in one's sex life." He stated it like a physician advising a simple cure. "Surely you must agree."

"I see," she said quietly. This also now became the truth.

"But what was it that offended you?" he wanted to know.

"Well," she hesitated, not wanting to disappoint him, "for one thing, the way that girl did anything he said, anything at all. After a while, it seemed as though she wasn't even a person anymore. He kept on degrading her, and she sank lower and lower." It was not so much a positive statement as a questioning one.

"For a woman to please her man, this is to sink lower and lower? Where did you pick up such unpleasant ideas? From your keeper?"

"Why do you always call her that?"

"Because it appears that is what she is. Answer my question. What could be wrong with a woman wanting to please her man?"

" . . . Nothing," she said weakly.

"So," he smiled, "one less puritanical concept to confuse your mind."

"Hans," she objected, "the man in the book hurt her. I mean, he actually hurt her."

"The sadistic element. Yes. The poor girl chose unwisely, perhaps. But of course, not all men are such brutes."

"I wouldn't like that," she said firmly. "I wouldn't like that sort of thing at all."

"Naturally not."

Laura relaxed. Her confidence returned. It was not so difficult, after all, to discuss sex personally with a man. It was all quite casual. Ordinary, that was the word. She was pleased with herself.

"Shut the door."

She glanced up quickly. Hans met her eyes and inclined his head toward the open door of the dressing room. She hesitated, motionless in the chair.

"Do you think I am going to seduce you? Such things take time to enjoy. I merely suggested you close the door."

This time she did as he said.

"Come here. Beside me."

Tentatively, Laura sat next to him on the sofa. He took her hand in his and kissed it lightly.

"You see? I told you that not all men are such brutes." Hans cupped her face in his palms and softly kissed her mouth.

A sweet warmth seemed to envelop her, slowly at first, then urgently mounting in strength until it overcame her and she responded to his mouth and his tongue.

Hans broke away, looking at her. Laura stared back at him, hurt. She felt empty, robbed, as if something had been taken from her. He spoke softly. "Not now." One hand lingered in her hair. He withdrew it gradually. "There are better times and places," he smiled.

Laura moved to him, and he held her. She felt the hardness of his body under his clothing. It was hers. The realization excited her. Everything that had seemed so out of reach was going to be hers. Hans would belong to her, and she would belong to him, to Hans Deitrick.

"I must go now, before they start calling for us." He rose and opened the door.

"Whatever you say," she replied.

"Who was that you were talking to just now, Indigo?"

"Now? Outside the dressing room? He's the dialogue director on a picture that starts shooting next week."

"He's very handsome." Laura made an elaborate business of being preoccupied with pushing back her cuticle.

"Gloria French sent him over to find out if I was available. She doesn't like the wardrobe girl they gave her. I told him we wouldn't be finished here until a couple of weeks before Christmas."

"Who else is in the picture?" she inquired.

"I think they set Colin Kirkwood. I'm not sure. And they had a script out to Lisa Taylor, but she just moved into a new house. She said she's too busy right now."

"If I want to find out anything, I always know who to ask, don't I? What's his name?"

"Whose?" Indigo handed Laura a terry-cloth robe. "If you'll wear this to rehearse, I'll clean the makeup off the collar of your dress."

Laura tied the robe around her. "The tall, dark, and handsome dialogue coach."

"Well, really." Indigo smiled. "Mike Stanton is his name. I thought you were only interested in blonds with blue eyes."

"I know that's what you thought. Now maybe you won't take it quite so seriously. There are lots of attractive men, all kinds." She returned to the examination of her fingernails.

"I should hope there are, lovey." Her relief was apparent. "You certainly get to see your share."

That was true. With Obie and the studio attentively providing escorts for her every engagement, it seemed she must have worked her way through half the young men in the casting directory. All but a few made the routine passes, easily fended off. Laura had never been interested. They were boys, all of them. Hans was different. He was far beyond the others in his worldliness. She doubted that she had ever been out with anyone who had even heard of Baudelaire.

"They're ready to rehearse," Indigo reminded her.

Laura joined Hans under the lights. As she stood next to him, she could almost feel the warmth of their new intimacy reaching out to touch her. She glanced at the others on the set, all ignorant of the secret before their very noses. Laura couldn't suppress a smile.

"Lovely," Hans murmured.

She looked away as if she hadn't heard. Jason was giving her directions for the scene. He finished and stepped back into the shadows. They waited together for a light to be reset.

Quietly, Laura said, "I think I threw Indigo off our track."

"Clever girl. Perhaps your keeper will be less suspicious now."

"I intend," said Laura primly, "to be such a good little girl that all her worries just fly away." She gave a low, conspiratorial giggle.

"Perhaps then we will be able to see each other with no interference."

Laura looked up at him.

"Shall we say Saturday? Come in the afternoon so we can take a swim."

"I'll think of some excuse," she whispered.

Laura paused for one brief second before ringing the doorbell. The afternoon sun filtering through the tall eucalyptus trees made a mottled pattern on the front door. The sky was cloudless. High up, a lone hawk swooped in lazy circles over the canyon, scanning the terrain for careless young jackrabbits.

A slight apprehension held her back. Then she remembered how it had been with Hans in her dressing room. Apprehension became anticipation. She pressed the bell.

He stood looking at her for a moment, then drew her inside and shut the door. He took her into his arms, brushing back her hair, and kissed her softly on the neck. Sliding his hands down her back to her buttocks, he pressed her to him. His mouth moved lingeringly over her neck to her ear. Playfully, he pulled at the lobe with his lips.

Laura giggled nervously. "You act as if you were waiting for me."

Hans pulled back and looked at her. "But I was. Come." He led her into the living room. The German shepherd, asleep until now, bounded up from his place at the hearth and sniffed curiously at Laura.

"You didn't tell me you had a dog."

"No? You are not afraid of dogs, I hope."

She shook her head. "He's beautiful."

"A perfect specimen. He likes you. See how attentive he is."

The dog gave her a cursory lick on the leg and resumed his exploratory sniffing.

"What does he want?"

"He is a male. What do you think he wants? He likes the female scent. Go," he commanded the dog, "lie down."

Laura surveyed the living room. The furniture was massive and masculine. She felt a thrill of excitement at the overwhelming maleness around her.

"Do you like it?" asked Hans. Before she could reply, his mouth was on hers, his tongue probing inside. He rested a hand on her shoulder, allowing it to slip downward. He cupped her breast and squeezed it gently.

Laura made a small sound and broke away. Her lips were wet and her eyes bright. She glanced quickly around the room.

"We are alone," Hans assured her. "I gave the houseman the day off."

"Oh."

"Dear Laura," he smiled, "you have nothing to fear. That is, unless you fear pleasure."

She gave him a hesitant smile. "I told Drucilla I was going shopping."

"Will she be waiting for you to come home?"

"Not today. She and Mona are going to Pasadena for an early dinner and a sneak preview of some picture. I told them I'd rather stay home tonight and read." Laura laughed. "I've been a perfect darling all week. Dru hasn't had the least reason to be concerned."

Hans slid an arm around her shoulders. "She should be, you know." He traced the contour of her ear with his tongue.

Laura felt the familiar sweet flush of warmth take her over. She turned and pressed against him. Taking her face in his hands, Hans kissed her briefly.

"Would you like to go for a swim?" he asked.

"That would be nice." She looked around. "Where shall I change into my suit?" She reached into her bag to take it out, but his hand stayed her.

"You won't need that. I told you, we're quite alone. Come, I'll show you where we undress." He took her hand and led her through the hall and up the winding staircase to an enormous round room at the end of the upstairs hall.

Laura studied it with open curiosity. "What is this?" she asked.

"A bit of everything. See." He slid back a paneled door, exposing racks of neatly arranged suits. "Dressing room." Hans strode across the thick black fur rug and opened a second door. "Sauna. And here," he showed her still another door, "bath. And these," his hand swept the room, "massage table, sunlamps, vibrating lounge, exercise bars, and for guests," he opened a large armoire "the refreshments." Hans held up a glass from the bar. "Will you join me in a little drink?"

"A Scotch and soda. Not very strong, please," she added. She took in the expert ease with which he poured, extracted a few ice cubes from the small refrigerator, and handed her a glass.

"Cheers."

Laura smiled and took a sip. She looked around for a place to sit and settled on the foot of the lounge. Hans leaned back against the bar, watching her.

"You must tell me, Laura, are your menstrual periods regular?"

"What?" She spilled part of her drink.

He seemed not to have noticed. He repeated the question.

"Not always." She felt extremely uneasy that he should be asking her this.

"And when did you have your last one?"

She took a swallow of the drink. Her hand trembled slightly. "It was over day before yesterday."

"That is good. You will be in no danger. Laura? Is anything wrong?" He walked over and sat beside her. "I know. Such details are not so romantic." He laid his hand over hers. "But until you are equipped with the proper precautions, we must take great care."

She managed to look up at his face. He was only thinking of her, of course. She rested her head against his shoulder.

Hans put his glass between his knees and reached around her, his fingers at the top of her dress. Slowly, he unzipped it. She felt the cool air on her back. Lightly, his fingertips traced a pattern on her skin. With one smooth motion, he undid her brassiere and, together with her dress, slid it forward over her shoulders. It fell at her elbows. Hans bent his head and kissed her nipple. Gently, he pulled at it with his mouth. Laura buried her face in his hair. A moan of pleasure escaped her.

He brought himself up. "This is awkward. Let us be more comfortable." He rose and pulled his jersey over his head.

Laura watched as he undid his belt buckle. Then, realizing he wanted her to follow, she stood and stepped out of her dress. She slid her petticoat to the floor.

"Here," he moved to her, "let me." Hans bent on one knee

and lowered her panties down over her abdomen, her thighs and her bare legs until they lay at her feet. He kissed her thighs. Laura trembled and put her hands on his shoulders to steady herself. She bent to kiss him as he stood up. She saw that he was erect and tried not to stare. He was large, and the thought that he might hurt her suddenly frightened her.

"You have never seen a man before?" he asked quietly.

"No."

He sensed her thoughts. "Don't be afraid. Men and women have been designed well to accommodate each other." His hand touched her breast. "You have such fair skin. We must not let the sun burn you, or your keeper will ask embarrassing questions. Wait here." He went into the bathroom and came out with a plastic bottle of suntan oil. "Over there," he gestured toward the massage table.

Laura stepped out of her panties and lifting herself onto the table, stretched out for him. It had started, she thought. It was too late now.

Hans paused over her for a moment, assessing her body. His eyes took her in. "Perfect. You have not a blemish on you." He filled his cupped hand with oil and stroked it over her stomach.

Laura felt her flesh quiver under his touch. She shut her eyes as his hands traveled upward over her breasts and shoulders. Spreading, smoothing, he slid his fingers down her arms to her hands, massaging her palms lightly.

"Laura?"

She opened her eyes. Hans placed the bottle in her hand and, reaching both arms under her, lifted her up. She let her head fall back against his chest, trying only to think that whatever happened, it would be good.

Hans carried her across the room and kicked with his bare foot at a door which was partly open. They were in his bedroom, its curtains still drawn and the bed still unmade. He laid her gently on the rumpled sheets and resumed the motions of his hands. Taking the bottle from her, he poured the soothing, scented oil over her feet and stroked it between her toes. Laura let out a small sigh. She felt heady with the sensation of his hands on her body. Slowly, tantalizingly, he moved upward, his fingers barely touching the flesh of her thighs. She willingly parted her legs for him. His fingers played at her until she writhed with pleasure against the pillow behind her. Hans pulled a pillow from the head of the bed and placed it under her buttocks. Wordlessly, he held her hand and filled her palm with oil. He drew it between his legs and she began to caress him with his one hand guiding her movements, the other massaging, manipulating her. Her eyes closed, Laura felt her body responding to the mounting heat. She moved hungrily, rhythmically under the pressure of his fingers, and suddenly she realized that he was inside her, stroking inside her. She cried out her excitement, asking him for more. Parting her wide, he mounted her. In one fleeting moment of pain, she moaned hoarsely, then knew she was free. Her fingers dug into the flesh of his back, and she moved with him in a mounting frenzy. His speed increased until she thought her senses would not stand it. From her throat came a sound, soft at first, then increasing until, in an explosion, she screamed his name over and over. He came at her, thrusting deep inside with all the force of his body, and finally, with a deep sigh, he fell upon her, and they lay silent, out of breath and strength.

It seemed a long time until, groaning slightly, Hans withdrew and stretched beside her. Laura looked at him lying there disheveled and drained. "Hans?" she whispered.

He opened his eyes and smiled.

"Was I . . . Are you happy?"

He rested a hand on her leg. "But of course. Aren't you?"

"Oh yes," she breathed. "Yes."

"Then sleep. Rest."

She lay beside him as he dozed.

After he awoke, they went downstairs and outside to the pool. It was still early, and the sun had just begun to sink behind the tops of the trees behind the house. The water was warm and pleasant. From the edge of the pool, the dog watched them as they swam.

Hans laughed. "What are you doing, you foolish girl?"

"I can't help it," she held his waist with her hands, "I just want to touch you."

"We'll drown," he warned.

"I don't care."

"You have no discomfort?" he asked.

"Every part of me feels wonderful." She kissed his neck.

"That is good."

"I want . . ." she paused, "more."

"Be patient. There will be more." He ducked under the water and swam toward the end of the pool.

Laura followed him up the steps, shivering as the breeze touched her wet skin. She took the robe he handed her. The dog ambled toward her and licked the drops of water from her feet.

"Enough," said Hans, taking his collar. "Wait here. I will put him in his yard."

Laura lay down on one of the mats beside the pool. In a minute he rejoined her. "What were you thinking?" he asked.

Laura turned to him and covered his mouth with hers. She kissed him greedily. Hans broke away. Smiling, he shook his head.

"I have created a monster."

Laura loosened the tie on his robe and ran her hands over his body, kissing the rough hair on his chest. Reaching up, Hans parted the terrycloth that covered her and cupped her breasts. He watched her face as her nipples grew hard under the touch of his fingers. Slowly, he laid her back on the mat and bent his mouth to her breasts.

Laura felt his lips and tongue teasing her flesh. "Please," she begged and placed his hand on the moist hair between her thighs.

Hans lifted his eyes to her face. "It is not yet time for me." Seeing her look, he leaned down and kissed her mouth.

"Please, please," she said again.

For a moment, he gazed at her, and then she felt his fingers at her breasts once again. Lingeringly, deliberately, he aroused her, his eyes on her face. He was enjoying his effect on her. Her breath came faster now, and he bent to her body. His tongue traveled over her skin. He kissed the soft flesh of her stomach and, kneeling, raised her legs to his shoulders.

"You are an excellent cook," Hans said, rising from the kitchen table.

"I'm not. An omelet is the only thing I know how to make." Laura put the dishes in the sink.

"Leave them there. My man, Lim, will do them later." He glanced at the clock. "What time should you be home?"

Laura frowned. Reluctantly, she said, "About ten, I suppose, to be safe. In case they come home early." She wanted never to leave, never for the day to end. She wanted to stay with Hans.

"Come sit with me. We have yet a couple of hours."

Laura came to him and sat on his lap, laying her head against his cheek.

"You are happy, little virgin?"

She laughed and kissed his ear. Hans held her closer.

"You see?" he said. "I told you I would be a kind professor."

"Yes," she answered softly. "I love it. Teach me everything, Hans. I want it to be so wonderful."

"It will be."

She kissed him, enjoying his stubble against her face.

Hans put his hands on her shoulders and gently pushed her downward. She kneeled in front of his chair and watched as he drew his robe aside.

"Come here." He took her head in his hands and spread his legs. She let him guide her. Coaxing, commanding, he directed her attentions to him. When he had grown hard in her mouth, he pulled her to her feet. "Upstairs," he told her.

"Laura?"

"Here," she called, "upstairs. How was the movie?" she asked as Dru came into the bedroom.

"Long. If they don't cut half an hour out of that thing, they're going to have to give out air cushions with the tickets. What have you been doing?"

"This," she propped the book up on her knees, "reading."

"Well, you didn't miss much."

"No."

"You look very comfy and contented," Dru smiled, "all wrapped up in your blankets. What did you do to your hair?"

"I washed it. Did Mona go home?"

"I dropped her off. You were wise to skip the picture. I'm glad to see you getting some rest for a change. You've been so tired lately."

"I feel marvelous."

"Good. I'm going to bed. Don't stay up too late." She closed the door quietly behind her.

Laura buried her face in her pillow and laughed with secret delight. Then, sobering, she turned off the light and lay back in the darkness, wondering how she would get through tomorrow. She must find a way to call him, to hear Hans' voice. If she could just speak to him, it would not be so intolerable to wait until she saw him Monday at work. Somehow she'd find a way. Nothing was impossible anymore. Instinctively, her hand moved between her thighs. She felt him still. The slight tenderness of the raw flesh inside her warmed her now.

Laura had purposefully stationed herself at a table in the doorway of the Redwood Room so that she could see Hans when he entered the commissary. All morning long he had been in one of the dubbing rooms recording sound loops. They had no scenes together until after lunch. Still, she had spent the hours on the set anxiously hoping that he would appear. Both Indigo and Jason had remarked on the fact that she seemed unusually restless. She was. The salad on her plate lay untouched. Nervously, her eyes flicked over the crowd in the main room and settled on a cluster of people at the door. There he was. She saw the blond head bobbing in conversation with someone she did not know. He broke away, only to pause for Helen Farmer who said something to him that caused him to throw back his head and roar with laughter. He kissed Helen on the cheek. Laura felt her stomach constrict. She wanted to stand up and call out to him, but at last he was making his way in her direction.

She tried to sound casual. "I saved us a table."

"Laura," he apologized, "I cannot. Mac Herman is over there with an interviewer, waiting for me. I have a luncheon appointment with them." He patted her hand briefly. "I will see you on the set."

Laura did her best not to look at their table as they ate. Toying with her food, she tried to appear composed and careless while inside she felt wound so tightly that at any moment the sound of his voice overheard in conversation might cause her to break and shatter here in front of God and everybody. She had to get out.

"So," Hans sauntered onto the set and settled in the camp chair next to Laura's, "you had a pleasant lunch?"

She nodded, avoiding his face.

"Mine was quite dull. I should have preferred to be with you."

"I called you yesterday. Twice," she said. "You weren't home."

"I went to Laguna to see some friends for the day."

"What did Helen Farmer have to say that was so funny?"

"Helen? I don't remember."

"But it made you laugh so."

"I forget now. She's a charming girl. Very amusing."

Laura couldn't stand it any longer. "Hans." Her voice wavered. "When are we going to be able to see each other again?"

He shot her an appraising glance and drew his chair closer to hers. "Laura, there are certain things to be considered." He lowered his voice. "Have you seen a doctor?"

She shook her head.

"Do you have a women's doctor?"

"Yes. I have trouble sometimes, and I go to him."

"What kind of trouble?" He saw her hesitate. "Don't be embarrassed."

"Ovarian cysts. It's happened twice. He gives me some kind of pills, hormones, I think, and they go away. But Hans," she protested, "I can't go to him. He'd say something to Drucilla. I know he would."

"You are probably right. I will give you the name of a friend of mine. He has an office in the medical building in Westwood. Go to him. Laura?" He studied her face. "You're very quiet."

"Please," she whispered, "can't we go somewhere? Now? I want to be alone with you. Please."

He paused, his eyes on hers for a moment. Then he got up and walked to where Jason stood with the script girl.

"Come." He returned and extended a hand to her. "Jason says they won't need us for half an hour. I told him we would be going over the scene in my dressing room."

Laura pulled into the driveway just as Obie stepped out of his car. She collected her script and her handbag from the front seat and caught up with him at the door.

"What brings you here?"

"I'm on my way home from the office. I thought I'd drop these contracts by for you to sign. Seems we've been missing each other lately." He waited while she found her house key.

"I heard you'd dropped by the set. Sorry I didn't see you."

"They said you and Deitrick were rehearsing privately and were not to be disturbed."

"Oh, that." Laura inserted the key in the lock. "We find it works very well. The more we run the scenes together, the better they play. Come in and have a drink or something. Dru?" she called.

"Hello, Obie." Dru came into the hall with a sheaf of papers in her hand. "How was your trip to Vegas?"

He shrugged. "Ruth thinks I came away a winner."

"And?"

Obie smiled wryly.

"I see," said Dru, leading the way to the living room. "What can we offer you to repair the damage?"

"How about a beer?" He sat on the bench in front of the hearth. "That fire feels good. It's cold these evenings."

"What's new?" Laura reappeared from the bar with three beers on a tray.

"Is anything ever?" he asked morosely.

"Come on," Dru laughed. "Things can't be that bad. What's going on at your office?"

"Business as usual. Jack Haller's first picture for the Major is shaping up to be a winner."

"I heard they were rushing to get it out before the end of the year to qualify for the Academy Awards." Taking off her shoes, Laura stretched out on the sofa.

"I saw a print of it last week. Damn good. Ian Driscoll did one hell of a fine job for Jack. And," he brightened, "if it gets a nomination or two, that means Driscoll's writing and directing prices go up."

"That ought to make you happy," offered Dru.

"What else is going on in the outside world?" asked Laura. "I feel like I'm being held prisoner on stage twelve at Victory. I never see anyone."

He thought for a minute. "Claire Poland called today with a checklist of gossip to test on me."

"Oh good," Laura giggled. "Like what?"

Obie took a breath. "Let's see." He thought back. "She wanted to know," he began, "who is the redhead that's being seen with Marty Tabor; is it true Gloria French is having an affair with her dialogue coach; is Hans Deitrick secretly seeing Helen Farmer, or, and get this, is he secretly seeing Laura Curtis?" Obie exhaled in mock fatigue.

Laura had seen Dru stiffen almost imperceptibly in her chair.

"What did you say?" asked Drucilla sharply.

"I said," he paused to remember, "I don't know her name. Yes, I think so. Maybe. And I doubt it. In that order."

"Obie," said Dru, "I wish, as far as Laura's concerned, that you'd refer that kind of question to Mona. After all, she is handling Laura's publicity, and she's on good terms with Claire Poland. She knows how to squash these ridiculous rumors. We do have Laura's reputation to protect."

"Okay." He set his empty glass down on the hearth. "In the future I will."

Laura was silent. Hans and Helen. Was it possible? It couldn't be. She was the Major's girl. But Obie had said "maybe."

"I have to be going," announced Obie. "I have an appointment with my dentist's wife."

"What?" Drucilla raised her eyebrows.

"Nothing like that. I'm nursing her through her first novel. She's not bad. Already gotten a couple of short stories published. Name's Vickie Mann. It wouldn't shock me to find she could actually have herself a career as a writer. Dru," he told her, "give those contracts I brought the once-over. I think we have everything you wanted in there."

"I will," she assured him as she walked him to the door. "I want to talk to you," she said to Laura when she had returned to the living room.

"What about?"

"These." She fanned the papers in her hand.

"What are they?"

"Bills."

"That reminds me," interrupted Laura, "did you order the cases of champagne so that I can give each of the crew a bottle at the end of the picture?"

"I did. Now let me ask you about these. There are three bills here I don't understand. The ones from Saks, Magnin's, and Robinson's have items on them I want to clear up. Did you buy any nightgowns?"

"Nightgowns? No."

"But there are charges on these three bills for lingerie. They total over a hundred and fifty dollars in all."

"Oh, I know what they are. I bought some new underthings. Bras and panties, stuff like that." She shut her eyes and listened to the crackling of the burning logs in the fireplace.

"What did you do that for? I wasn't aware you'd worn out all the things you had. Why didn't you tell me? I could have picked them up for you."

"I didn't wear out everything. I just wanted some different styles," she answered, her eyes still closed. "I decided I didn't like the stuff you'd chosen last time."

"Why not?"

"They weren't frilly enough. I wanted to feel more feminine."

"I could have returned them, you know, if you'd just said something. It's pretty foolish to pay twice for the same articles."

"You couldn't have returned them. I'd already worn most of the stuff you got me."

"And with three drawers full of underthings upstairs, you suddenly decided you have to have an entire new wardrobe? Over one hundred and fifty dollars," repeated Dru. "Isn't that a bit much?"

Laura shrugged it off. "Call it a whim."

"Laura," she sighed, "I've tried to teach you to handle money sensibly, in spite of the fact that you have an uncommon lot of it for someone your age. People can't afford to indulge every whim that seizes them."

Laura rolled over on the sofa and, propping herself up on one elbow, looked at her. "Dru," she said flatly, "I've had it with this conversation. Let's drop it."

"You know it's up to both of us to handle your money wisely," she reminded her.

"Really? That's interesting. Do you know how much the average personal manager gets? Ten percent, that's how much."

Dru's voice was quiet. "I was aware of that, Laura."

"Yet you," Laura pointed out, "have collected twenty-five percent of the gross of every paycheck I've ever brought in. That's the gross we're talking about, remember?"

"I never said it wasn't."

"Don't you think it's a little out of character for you to be lecturing me on acquisitiveness?"

"I see." Dru stopped and took a breath. "Perhaps you've forgotten that very few personal managers live with their clients, run the household, hire and fire the help, and nurse their clients through various illnesses. You won't find many of them running upstairs and down with medicine, bringing the clothes to the cleaner, making out the menus, taking the car to be serviced—or doing your personal shopping, to mention only a few little chores."

Laura waited for a moment before she spoke. "That's funny," she said drily. "You told me once that you loved me and wanted to treat me like your own daughter."

"And mothers don't get paid, is that it?" Dru's tone was exasperated.

Laura flopped back into the sofa cushions. "It's a thought," she said sardonically. "Maybe if mine had been paid, she'd have stuck around longer."

Dru stood up. "I don't know what it is, Laura, that's gotten into you these past few weeks. It's as if you're determined to make an argument out of every single thing I say to you. But let me tell you one thing. I earn that money, and I intend to stick around in whatever capacity you want to call it. If you think I'm overpaid, I suggest you try running yourself and your house and your career for a while. You may get a different picture of things." She walked out of the room.

Laura closed her eyes again and listened to the sounds the fire made. She wondered how it would feel to be on her own.

They lay on adjoining chaise longues beside the pool. Hans broke the restful silence. "What did you tell her this time?"

"Dru? I told her I wanted to take a long drive, maybe go to the beach." Laura reached over and took his hand.

"When does she expect you home?"

"Dinner time. I can cheat a bit, though. There'll be hell to pay, but it's worth it," she added, "for you."

"No. It's just as well. I have to go to a screening at the Major's this evening."

She tried to cover her disappointment. "You didn't tell me that." She waited, but he said nothing. "Will Helen Farmer be there?"

"I would think so."

"Is that what she meant when she said she'd see you this weekend?" Laura persisted.

"When did she say that?" he frowned.

"When she came to see you on the set the other day. I heard her tell you that as she was leaving."

"Eavesdropping, were you?" His frown disappeared, and he laid his head back on the lounge.

"Not really. Is she a close friend?"

"Why do you ask?"

"I just wondered. Are you taking her to the screening tonight?" She tensed, waiting for the reply.

"She'll be with the Major, I suppose." Hans yawned lazily and stretched his body.

"Of course." Laura relaxed. Then she asked casually, "Do you see her often?"

He brought himself up on his elbows and looked at her. "What is this?" he demanded. "Why are you interested in Helen?"

Laura swallowed uneasily. "I heard that you were seeing her. There was some talk."

"From whom?"

"Claire Poland."

Hans laughed incredulously. "Claire Poland. And do you believe everything she says?"

"Not everything. But Helen did visit you on the set."

"What if she did? Laura, are you being jealous?"

She paused. "Yes," she admitted, "I am. But Hans, how could I not be? I mean, when——" Laura took a breath. "——When you know I love you so much."

He shook his head. "You are being very unwise. I have many friends. Some are beautiful women. I enjoy their company. They make life amusing, and," he went on, "that is how I want my life to be."

Laura blinked back the tears and nodded.

"Come now," he coaxed her, "your life is only beginning. You will have many men and enjoy each of them for certain reasons."

"But I don't want anyone else! I only want you!"

Hans smiled disparagingly. "You are being most unfair to the men of this world, depriving them of your company."

"Damn you! I love you! Why can't there just be the two of us? I want you, Hans. Why can't you want me?"

"I do want you. But not to the exclusion of the rest of my life."

"But why? Why aren't I enough? Don't I please you?"

"You know you please me, but life holds many pleasures. Surely you would not be happy restricting yourself to eating only potatoes for the rest of your life, not when there is such a variety of other foods. Laura, you are young. In time you will understand."

"I will not. Not ever. Why can't a man and a woman belong to each other?"

"Some do," shrugged Hans, "but I am not that kind. Is it so important for you to possess someone totally? In that case, you would do best to buy yourself a man. Is that what you want?"

She said nothing.

"You must get rid of these romantic ideas. They will only make your life difficult."

"I hate Helen Farmer," Laura said bitterly.

"Without reason."

"But you see her, don't you?" she demanded.

"On occasion. Helen is very sophisticated, very shrewd. She knows that a woman's body is the instrument of a man's pleasure, and she uses that to her own ends." Hans paused and smiled. "Let's go inside," he suggested. "I will show you something that will amuse you. Lim!" he called his houseman. Laura followed Hans to the open door of the living room.

The somber Chinese exited into the projection booth, leaving Laura and Hans alone in the sudden coolness of the darkened room. She wrapped her robe close around her. He drew her down beside him on the sofa.

"What is it?" she wanted to know. "What are we going to see?"

"Watch."

The heavy draperies along the wall in front of them parted, and the screen behind came alive with images. Hans rested his hand lightly on her thigh.

"My God." Laura took a sharp breath. There on the film was Helen Farmer, nude, examining her body in front of a full-length mirror. "Where did you get this?" Laura whispered to Hans.

"This, my dear, is Helen's screen test. Made after hours on the Victory lot. At the request of the Major. This is how she got her contract." He nodded in the direction of the screen.

"The Major has rather an extensive film library of such tests. A few famous ladies started this way."

Laura, intent on the picture, watched as Helen was joined by two swarthy men who dragged her, protesting, to an enormous round bed covered with red satin sheets. At first she fought their attentions, her body writhing and thrashing from one to the other. Gradually their caresses won her over, until she moved with them.

Hans reached inside Laura's robe and slid his hand under her bathing suit, resting his fingers between her thighs. She felt herself responding, whether to him or to what she was seeing, or both, she did not know.

The frenzy on the screen increased. Laura's breath quickened. Helen, her blond hair half obscuring her face, kneeled on the bed, satisfying one of the two men with her mouth, while the other mounted her from behind. Laura gasped with pleasure, feeling the increased pressure of Hans' touch.

The screen went dark. Rising, Hans called out to Lim, "We are not to be disturbed." Laura followed him out of the room.

They did not go to the bedroom. He stopped her halfway through the large dressing room and demanded that she undress. Laura did as she was told. Hans removed his robe and swimming trunks. He walked across the black fur rug and opened one of the several closet doors, exposing a full-length mirror. Grasping Laura's forearm, he forced her to her knees. Laura saw herself reflected in the gleaming mirror and watched as Hans, kneeling behind her, reached his hands around her and began to fondle her breasts. Her eyes closed.

"Watch," he commanded.

She looked into the mirror. It was like seeing the scene on film. His hands roamed her body, alternately caressing and demanding. There was no control now. Laura saw the girl in the reflection, her face and body twisted in passion. Forcefully, Hans pushed her to all fours and, gripping her buttocks, came at her from the rear. The figures in the glass jerked convulsively. Laura heard herself cry out and, falling, felt the weight of his body on top of her. She buried her face in the soft fur of the rug.

The Major smiled benignly. "I regret having kept you waiting, Miss Lang." He gestured her into the chair in front of his desk. "We're going into high gear with the Jack Haller-Ian Driscoll picture, and I've been tied up on long distance with our New York office." He seated himself at the desk. Crossing his legs, he folded his hands on his knees. The well-buffed nails glistened in a shaft of sunlight from the window. He took his time before speaking.

"Tell me," he said finally, "how is our girl?"

"She's working hard," Dru replied guardedly, adding, "I think she's tiring herself."

"A difficult role," he sympathized.

"Very." She waited.

"I asked you here because I am somewhat concerned for her."

"Of course." Dru sensed that he was choosing his words with care. "I'm sure Laura would be gratified by your concern.

"Are you?"

She glanced at him.

"This is a delicate matter, Miss Lang. Perhaps my concern would be better left unmentioned."

Dru hesitated. "Whatever you think best."

"It has come to my attention," he said smoothly, "that in the past three of four weeks the production reports show a marked slackening of pace in the filming of this picture. When this happens," he explained, "I become curious as to the reason. Especially so in this case, since the scenes involved have all been interiors with no inherent cause for delays. You understand," he continued, "this is strictly a matter of production time, of dollars and cents."

"Naturally," nodded Drucilla.

"Can you suggest any reason for the slowdown?" The Major studied her face.

She thought for a moment. "Laura is playing an unusually demanding part. She has a tendency to become deeply involved in her work. I think she's pushing herself to exhaustion."

He seemed satisfied with her reply. "Yes, that was my first thought also. I'm told that she has been extremely edgy of late."

"She has," admitted Dru.

"Still," he went on, expressionless, "It's unlikely that nervous tension alone would cause such delays."

Drucilla looked at him intently. "I am not sure I follow you, Mr. Victor."

"No. I believe that you don't. I'm convinced that you are quite in the dark." He leaned back in the chair. "When something like this puzzles me, I find it useful to monitor the shooting somewhat more closely." He tapped his fingers on the intercom beside him. "After all, we in this business have a notable tendency to protect each other. Admirable, but occasionally overzealous to the point of concealing the facts. Or perhaps," he amended, "we prefer to turn our backs on what we don't wish to see. That is the point at which I step in. I like to learn for myself what is going on." The Major flicked a switch on the intercom, listened briefly to the cacophony and turned it off again. He turned to face Drucilla.

"What have you learned?" she asked quietly.

"An inordinate amount of time," he stated firmly, "has been spent waiting for Laura and Hans Deitrick while they rehearse their scenes privately. It seems they both have insisted on closeting themselves in his dressing room to run their lines together. This happens several times a day, while the director and crew are kept waiting. Does this suggest anything to you?"

Dru's throat tightened. "Yes," she said hoarsely.

"Has there been any indication of——" he paused, "of this at home?"

She shook her head. "I was so sure I'd discouraged it. I never thought it had gone this far."

The Major appraised her. She was genuinely disturbed. "Now Miss Lang," he said comfortingly, "we are both concerned, you because you are her guardian and I because," he gestured modestly, "I am a businessman. Surely, between the two of us, we can arrive at some solution to this problem which will serve both Laura's welfare and Victory Studios'."

She nodded in agreement. "What do you recommend?" she asked him.

"First, I would suggest that anything said here today should be maintained in the strictest of confidence." He acknowledged her reply with a dismissing wave of his hand. "It is in the best interests of this company," he went on, "to protect its properties in every conceivable way. This applies also, of course, to our players under contract. Barring some front-page scandal which would force us to invoke the morals clause against a performer, we use every resource at our command to keep their reputations untarnished. And our resources," he added, not without a note of pride, "are considerable. In the case of Hans Deitrick, there was a sticky situation some years ago involving a young fan, a minor. It was exceptionally delicate because Deitrick's final citizenship papers had not yet come through. We stood to lose a valuable property if he were not allowed to work in this country. But with some effort and through certain channels, we were able to quiet the matter. It never went to court."

Drucilla reached for a cigaret. Her hand shook slightly as the Major held out his lighter to her.

"So you see," he pocketed the lighter, "Deitrick has a certain indebtedness to this organization. I am sure that he needs only to be reminded of the necessity of keeping production costs within the established budget. He is a reasonable man."

"I am sure you have excellent judgment in these matters."

"But naturally I wanted to apprise you of my intentions. There are bound to be some emotional repercussions."

"I'll handle that," she assured him.

"Then we understand each other." He rose. "I am sure you are as relieved as I am to solve this unfortunate situation." He walked the length of the office and, opening the door, waited for her. "Good-bye, Miss Lang. Thank you for coming." He shook her hand. To his secretary he said, "Would you bring me that file I asked for? Then please call Mr. Deitrick on stage twelve and ask him to drop by after they wrap for the day."

"Laura?" Indigo switched on the light in the darkened dressing room. Laura lay on the sofa, her back to her. "I got some ice cubes, sweetheart. They'll help a little."

Laura rolled over, looking dully at her through red and swollen eyes. Indigo handed her the paper cup.

"Put them on your eyes. It will help the swelling some. I'll call makeup. He's going to have to repaint you from scratch."

"Not yet," Laura stayed her. "I'm not ready yet." The melting ice trickled down her cheeks.

"Is there anything else I can do, dear?"

She shook her head.

"Can't you tell me what's wrong? I've felt this coming since the beginning of the week. You just haven't been yourself. Please tell me what the trouble is."

"No."

"But why not, lovey? Maybe there's some little thing I can do to make you happier."

"There's nothing you can do. There's nothing anyone can do." She began to shake, sobbing.

"Honey." Indigo put her arms around Laura's shoulders. "Don't do that. Whatever it is, it can't be that bad. If you'd only let me know what it is that's been making you so unhappy all week ..."

"I hate you!"

Indigo drew back. A hurt look shadowed her face. "But why?"

"Oh God, I don't hate you. I really don't."

"Is it something I said or did?"

"No."

Indigo shook her head, confused. "Then I don't understand."

There was silence. When Laura spoke, after a long wait, her voice was low. "It's him," she said resignedly.

Indigo, in spite of herself, nodded. "I was so afraid of this, baby."

"Well, it happened. And now something's gone wrong. I don't even know what it is. All of a sudden, he's acting so cool to me. He's shutting me out, and I don't know why."

Indigo handed her a tissue from the box on the dressing table. "Did you come right out and ask him?"

"Yes, but he only evaded me. Whatever it was he said, it was so vague that it didn't make sense to me."

"Perhaps you should try again. Maybe if you got hold of yourself and took him aside and asked him in a calm, collected way, he'd tell you. Upset as you've been, maybe he was afraid to say what's on his mind for fear of making things worse."

"Do you really think so?"

Indigo shrugged. "It can't do any harm. You couldn't be much worse off than you are."

"Indigo." She reached to touch her hand and held it tightly. "I'm so scared. I don't want to lose him."

"But those things do happen. Somehow, we all live through them." She paused, lost in some reminiscence of her own.

Laura released her hand. "I'll do it. I will."

"First you have to get yourself put together and under control. It wouldn't do to be on the verge of hysterics. Do you want me to get you a pill to calm you down?"

"Would you?" Laura's tone was brighter. She returned the dripping ice to her eyes. "Give me a few minutes with this on my face, and then we can call Frank to fix my makeup."

Drucilla stood riveted on the threshold of Laura's room. "What are you doing?" she repeated. Again, there was no answer. Laura, her back turned, continued stuffing clothes into the open suitcase on the bed.

"What is this?" demanded Dru, more sharply this time.

Laura shuffled frantically through one of the bureau drawers, pulling out random pieces of clothing. With an impatient motion, she swept a pile of empty coat hangers off the bed and onto the floor. Feverishly, she glanced around the room and, sighting two framed Boxoffice Awards on the wall, ripped them from their hooks and shoved them on top of a pile of hastily folded sweaters in an open suitcase.

Drucilla's efforts failed to conceal the note of panic in her tone. "Where do you think you're going?"

There was no reply. Seizing a pillow from the bed, Laura pulled off the pillowcase and began to fill it with pairs of shoes.

"Goddam it!" Dru grasped Laura's arm, spinning her around. "What in hell is happening here?"

"Bitch!"

"Laura——"

"You bitch!"

"Stop it!" Dru shook her roughly.

"Take your filthy hands off me!" Raising her free arm, Laura brought a shoe down with all her force on Drucilla's shoulder. Wincing, Dru pulled back.

"What did you do? How did you do it? What did you say to him?" The words collided with each other in her rage.

"I don't——" Drucilla stuttered.

"Like hell you don't! When I asked him what happened, he said, 'Ask your keeper.' That was what he said. So tell me, exactly how did you manage it?"

Drucilla leaned a hand against the wall to steady herself. "Laura," she said weakly, "let me explain."

"Damn right," she retorted savagely. "You do that."

"If we can only talk this over calmly."

"Bullshit! Don't give me any more of that mealy-mouthed crap about doing things for my own good. You wore out that one a long time ago." She slammed down the lid of the larger suitcase and snapped the locks shut.

"Where are you going?"

"None of your goddam business."

"Laura, please, let's talk this over. Don't do anything foolish."

"Foolish? That's a hell of a note after you've connived to make a damned fool of me. This is the smartest move I've ever made." She attacked the second suitcase, jamming the top down viciously to make it close.

"But I didn't——," began Drucilla. "It was the other way around. I didn't want him to make a fool of you."

"It wasn't your choice to make! It's my life. It's my risk. How dare you decide that I'm better off made a fool of by you than by him. Is it because he's a man?"

"What?"

"You heard me. I said, is it because he's a man?"

Drucilla's mouth went slack.

The flicker of a triumphant smile creased across Laura's face and hardened. Her words knifed coldly, aimed with precision. "How stupid do you think I am? Did you actually suppose that I could live with you all this time and not know what was going on? Those cozy mid-afternoon naps with your girl friends? The intimate little back-rubbing sessions? You and Mona trying bravely to keep your hands off each other when I'm in the room? Jesus, you must think I'm some sort of mental defective."

"Don't," she pleaded.

"Don't what? Don't fall in love with a man? Don't deprive you of your precious meal ticket? Don't live a life of my own? Well, which is it?"

Drucilla brushed a hand over her eyes. She shook her head back and forth.

"Forget it. It doesn't matter now." Laura yanked the two suitcases off the bed and started for the door.

Dru found her voice. "You can't! You can't leave, Laura!"

In the doorway, Laura stopped and turned. Her tone was ice. "But I am leaving."

"I am your guardian——"

"That," interrupted Laura, "is temporary. How long do you think it would take a court to decide you're an unfit guardian? With what I could tell them, you wouldn't last five minutes."

"Laura you're my whole life . . ."

"Wrong word. Try 'livelihood.' Christ, but I'm tired of being used. It's time I went where someone actually wants me. And not just for a damned percentage either!"

As she was halfway down the stairs, Dru ran after her. Laura turned her head to look at her. Drucilla gripped the banister unsteadily. For one defiant moment, Laura stared. "You pitiful bull dyke," she said softly, and left.

There was little traffic on Benedict Canyon at this time of the evening. Laura held the wheel tightly, maneuvering the car around the sharp curves. She had begun to tremble. Gulping deep breaths of the cool night air, she tried to hold back the collapse she knew would come. Later she could let go, later, when she was safe with Hans. She swerved to let another car pass her and shoot ahead into the darkness. Making a wide arc, she turned into his driveway, slowing to avoid the dog who usually bounded out to greet her. This time he did not come. Hans' two cars were in the garage, and the house was lighted. She turned off the ignition and opened the car door. Not stopping to close it, she ran across the damp lawn toward the French doors to the living room.

A single lamp cast its shadow over the heavy furniture. "Hans?" Laura called softly. The house was silent. She hesitated, then made her way to the hall and up the thickly carpeted stairs where a chandelier burned brightly. She heard a sound from the round room at the end of the corridor. A shaft of light came from the doorway. It was a second noise which stopped her. There, as she approached the room, she could see Hans. Through the hinged crack of the half-open door, she saw him standing over the lounge chair, naked, watching intently the two forms below him. Under his detached gaze, the German shepherd dog lay half-covering the paleness of Helen Farmer's body. "Beautiful," Hans was saying, "beautiful."

A slash of light from the venetian blinds struck Laura across her eyes. She attempted to raise her arm, but the effort was too much for her.

"Close those damned things." Her voice came in a hoarse croak. A renewed wave of nausea overtook her, and she gagged audibly. Someone adjusted the blinds. She looked up. The doctor stood over her. He was sandy-haired with pale, pockmarked skin above the white jacket.

"Are you aware, Miss Curtis," he asked in a nasal voice, "that it is against God's law to attempt to kill yourself?"

"Get out," she rasped.

"Being a movie star does not entitle you to rudeness," he continued. "Do you have any idea how you got here?"

She shut her eyes.

"You were found on a deserted fire road in the hills near the reservoir at six this morning by the Bel-Air patrol. Your car was filled with belongings from two open suitcases. You were bleeding profusely from lacerations on both wrists, inflicted by the razor blades found beside you in the front seat. You were unconscious, either from the loss of blood or a state of alcoholic intoxication. Which," he added, "is a breach of the law while operating a motor vehicle. There is a police officer outside, waiting to talk to you. Your agent and your manager are also here."

Laura opened her eyes. "No," she whispered. "Don't let them in. I don't want to see anyone."

"You are going to have to talk to the police." More kindly he asked her, "Would you rather see one of the others first?"

"Obie. My agent, Mr. Straus. Send him in. Nobody else."

"How is she?" Obie asked Ruth as she came into the lanai.

"She took one of those pills to make her sleep. I had Rosita put the pink flowered bedlinens and towels in her room. Don't you think they'll cheer her up?" Ruth bent down to scrutinize one of the rose bushes just outside the sliding glass doors. "Aphids," she pronounced. "Oscar," she straightened up, "did you read Claire Poland's column today?"

"Don't tell me. She gave me her word she wouldn't play it up. This is going to raise hell with getting Laura insured for pictures."

"It's not so bad," she soothed him, producing a crumpled

morning paper from the brass magazine bin. "She ran it as a blind item at the very end of the column."

Obie took the newspaper from her. She had circled the item in red ink.

HEADY STUFF: The hot young actress who has been combining pleasure with her business apparently found the combo too much. Taking her nympho role seriously, she was seen t'other nite cruising solo in several bars and discos. Next day found her victim of a suicide attempt. Watch your step, honey.

He sighed, "I suppose it could be worse. Might as well face it, the story is all over town anyway."

"But Oscar, Laura is well liked. You know the industry people will all cover for her."

"They'd better."

"Of course they will. Movie people are so nice and generous that way."

"Nice and generous, my ass. They're trying to earn points for the time when they may need the same favor of a closed mouth."

"Well, whatever." The telephone at her elbow jangled. Ruth answered it and, after a few words, placed her hand carefully over the mouthpiece. "Oscar," she said in a hushed tone, "it's S. M. Victor. He wants to speak to you."

"Yes, sir?"

Ruth watched closely. When Obie had hung up, she glanced at him expectantly.

"He wants me to bring Laura to his office Monday. Wants to have a chat with her, he said. God knows what's on his mind. At least he sounded sympathetic."

"Is he going to make her go back to work with Hans Deitrick?"

"She has a picture to finish. That's that. Fortunately, though, she's done with the scenes involving Deitrick. They're shooting around her for a few days, getting him finished. He'll be off the picture by the time she gets back. The Major said he'd see to it, but not to mention it to Laura." Obie lit a cigaret.

"Here." She handed him an ashtray. "That poor girl. What will she do?"

"What will *we* do," he corrected. "At the moment, she's our responsibility." He gazed toward the bedroom overhead. "I'll have to get her an apartment. She's dead set on not going back with Drucilla Lang. Can't say that I blame her after what she told us. That dame had one hell of a nerve, busting up Laura's love life just because she's a goddam lesbian herself. Laura wants me to settle her contracts with both Drucilla and Mona and hire her a new publicist. Let's hope it doesn't cost her a bundle to buy off those two harpies."

"Dreadful," shuddered Ruth.

"I'll have one of the secretaries at the office start scouting for a furnished place for her, until I can settle things with Drucilla and get some of the furniture out of the house. Some of it must belong to Laura."

"That poor girl," repeated Ruth, shaking her head.

"A most upsetting time," the Major said, "a most upsetting time for all of us. I realize that this picture has made exceptional demands on you." He fixed Laura with an attentive gaze. "I am also distressed to learn that you have had the extra burden of personal problems."

Laura said nothing.

"That's all over now," assured Obie. "She's going to have her own apartment, and my wife and I will be right there anytime she needs us."

"Is that what you want?" the Major inquired of Laura.

"Yes."

"Independence brings with it certain responsibilities," he cautioned. "Are you quite sure you feel up to handling any new obligations? To be specific, I would not like to see a repetition of the type of incidents which found their way into Claire Poland's column last week. I doubt that any of us in this room can afford to see you receive that kind of unfortunate exposure. Do you have anything to say, Laura?"

She chewed her lip nervously. "It was printed as a blind item," she answered weakly.

"But nonetheless readily identifiable."

"It shouldn't have been printed at all. I was paying Mona a lot of money to take care of publicity for me. Just when I really needed her, she didn't do her job."

"The accounts were settled over the weekend," Obie put

in. "Mona and Drucilla are no longer on salary. The contracts have been torn up."

The Major lifted his cigar from the ashtray and drew thoughtfully on it. "Does this mean you are looking for another personal manager?"

"No," she replied quickly. "I want to be on my own. Obie can take care of that sort of thing."

"Laura's been with me a couple of years now. I'm used to handling her business affairs. It's been a good agent-client relationship."

"You're very fortunate to be in such capable hands. Now to the second business of this meeting. Ideally, I would like to see you take some time off to rest after this picture. I realize, however, that you have a number of previous commitments to honor, not a few of which are on my behalf. I would like to think that, despite your schedule, life was being made as comfortable as possible for you now. There are not many ways to assure an easier time of things, but," he held his cigar out at length as if to examine it, "perhaps it will please you to know that I am having your contract with Victory renegotiated with a substantial increase in salary."

Laura was stunned. "Mr. Victor——"

"That's a very generous gesture, sir," Obie smiled.

"Call it a Christmas gift, if you like. Laura's films have always shown good returns. We have no reason to believe that the future holds anything but increased promise for her career." To Laura, he said pointedly, "You have a great deal to be proud of. You are an extremely valuable young lady. Take care of yourself accordingly."

"I will," she vowed. "I will."

He held up a hand to silence her. "I would deem it a favor if you would do just one thing for me. A gesture, if you will."

She agreed unhesitatingly, "Of course."

Obie echoed, "Whatever you say."

"Let's start the new year with a clean slate, no old cobwebs to clutter the mind and cause," he glanced at Laura, "disturbances."

She knotted her hands in her lap and, frowning slightly, returned his look.

"As an indication of your willingness to accept this new responsibility of being on your own, I would appreciate it if

you would drop by and have a chat with Doctor Seymour
Blazer. He's in Beverly Hills. My secretary will make the appointment for you. Doctor Blazer is a psychiatrist."

"A what?"

"A psychiatrist?" asked Obie.

"A gesture," the Major repeated, tapping his cigar ash on
the side of the ashtray. "It will be up to you, Laura, to decide
if you would like to pay regular visits. In the meantime, one
appointment can't hurt. Laura," he turned to Obie, "has not
had the ordinary life of most young girls, nor has she had the
ordinary companions. We're now in the last few weeks of the
old year, time to clear away the litter of the past, time for a
fresh start. We must insure ourselves against any repetition of
what happened."

"Yes," Obie acquiesced reluctantly, "but a psychiatrist?"

Laura stared sullenly at her hands.

"One visit." He had closed the subject. Placing the dead
cigar in his ashtray, he rose, dismissing them.

Laura said nothing all the way to the parking lot. Obie
opened the door of the Cadillac and held it for her. She did
not get in.

"I won't go!" she exploded, furious.

"Laura," he reasoned, "it's not——"

"I don't care what it is!" she blazed. "I'm not going."

"He's only interested in your welfare. A favor, that's all
he's asking."

"Damn him. First he makes the big, magnanimous offering
to get me on the hook, and then he springs this!"

"It can't be so bad," he reassured her. "It's only an hour of
your time."

"Do you think I want people saying I'm crazy? That secretary of his is probably on the phone now, spreading it all
over the lot."

"I doubt that. She's been his private secretary for a long
time. She knows better."

"Well, then, what's this damned psychiatrist supposed to
tell me about myself that I don't already know? Answer that
one, if you can."

Obie spread his palm upward in a gesture of futility.
"How should I know? I'm an agent, not a doctor. Laura,
throw the Major his crust of bread. What's it to you?"

"If I go—and I'm not saying I will—I don't promise to stay an hour."

"So don't stay an hour. Just put in an appearance so that your conscience is clear with the Major. Then you're off the hook. Now where can I drop you?"

"Never mind. I think I'll stay on the lot, maybe go up to hairdressing and get them to do my hair for me. That'll do my head a lot more good than Doctor Seymour Blazer."

"How will you get home?"

"I'll get someone to drop me off. I feel like playing it loose this afternoon. I'll just hang around here for a while and show everyone I'm still alive." She smiled grimly.

"Suit yourself." Obie closed the car door and let himself in on the driver's side.

Laura leaned against the green MG in the next stall and watched him drive away. She actually had no particular plans but neither did she want any more pressure from Obie. The thought of tomorrow's impending visit with Doctor Blazer galled her. It was enough that she'd been trapped into going; she didn't want to have to hear about it. Reaching into her bag, she fished out a cigaret. Her hands trembled as she rooted among her belongings for a match. There were none. She peered into the open window of the MG, thinking there might be a folder discarded on the seat.

"I'm sorry."

Laura shrank back. There had been someone inside. He had overheard her entire conversation with Obie.

He slid over to her side of the car and stuck his head out of the window. "I apologize," he said amiably. "I didn't mean to startle you."

"You didn't." She composed herself. "I was looking for a match."

"Come in," he invited, opening the door. "There's a lighter on the dash." He moved back behind the right-hand drive as she entered.

"Do I know you?" she asked, accepting the light.

"I don't think so. I know who you are, of course."

Laura brushed it off. "I've seen you. Do you work at the studio?"

"Sometimes."

"What do you do?"

"Dialogue coach. I'm working with Gloria French at the moment." He gave his name, "Mike Stanton."

"Oh, yes." Laura was relieved. At least he wasn't a member of some studio department who might spread the story among everyone in his division.

"Oh, yes what?" he asked, lighting a cigaret of his own.

"I meant I remembered who you are. I remember seeing you on the lot."

"That's a compliment."

She glanced at him to see if he was being sarcastic. In a quick appraisal, she took in the curly dark hair and the handsome profile. He was good-looking enough to be an actor.

"Well?" He turned to her.

She was flustered. "I thought you were putting me on with that 'compliment' business."

"Really? I wasn't." He smiled again, and this time she returned it.

"I——" Laura hesitated, "I guess you heard that whole conversation outside."

"Not intentionally."

"It was supposed to be private."

"The way I understand it," he said easily, "the Major is putting the squeeze on you to see a shrink."

Laura winced.

"It's not exactly fatal," he laughed.

"It's not funny, either."

"Why does he want you to go?"

"Do you read the papers?"

He tossed his cigaret out of the window. "I see."

"I guess he's afraid it might happen again."

Mike put the question to her blandly, "And will it?"

She shrugged uncommunicatively.

"What happened? Did Deitrick dump you?"

"Jesus!" snapped Laura. "Who the hell do you think you are? You've got some nerve to ask me that!" Her hand went to the door handle.

"It's part of my charm," he rejoined affably. "So. He dumped you. That doesn't make you unique. It happens to everyone some time or another. It's a pretty flimsy reason to go off the deep end."

"What would you know about it?"

"Oh, come off it, Laura." He turned toward her in his seat.

"Look. Last year I was riding high with one of the greatest looking chicks in the world." He draped his arm over the back of the seat. "Believe me, it was the perfect setup. Never the slightest trouble between us. Then," he drew a long breath, "she want to Paris for a family wedding. I guess the relatives ganged up on her and convinced her she was slumming out here. All I know is that I received a cable she'd gotten herself engaged to some Marquis. I prefer to think that with a title like that, he's a flaming faggot."

She was staring out the window.

"It's a slap in the face," he admitted, "but look around. You're not alone. There are plenty of broads in this town for me, and there are plenty of guys for you. No single one of them is worth killing yourself over. Hell," he grinned, "don't give 'em the satisfaction."

Laura felt a certain warmth from his understanding. "Do you think," she asked, "that I should go?"

"To the doctor?"

"Yes."

"Like the man said, it's no skin off your back. Why not?"

"You won't tell anyone."

"Why would I do that? Why should I make an enemy of you?"

She made a sudden decision. "What were you doing here?"

"In the parking lot? Killing time."

"Let's go get something to eat. I'm starved."

He didn't seem to be surprised. "You'll have to settle for a hamburger. I've only got a few bucks on me."

"I've got plenty of money. Let's go," she urged impatiently.

"At your service," Mike said pleasantly, turning the ignition.

Doctor Seymour Blazer was not at all what Laura had anticipated. Had she, she wondered, expected him to wear a white coat and have a long beard? Instead, he was youthful looking, despite a receding hairline, and attired in conservative tweeds. Laura took a seat where he indicated, in a large green leather chair. At least, she thought relieved, he doesn't have a couch. He seated himself across the desk from her. Who was supposed to say what? Did he expect her to open her mouth and let fly with all the most intimate details of her life?

"Suppose you tell me something about yourself," he suggested.

Like what? "Well," she began, "I'm an actress."

"I know that."

"Then what is it you want to know about me?"

"Whatever you feel you'd like to tell me."

Laura halted. His phrasing made it sound like some kind of clever psychological test.

He noticed the way she hung back and inquired, "What is it?"

"The fact is," she stated, "I don't really want to tell you anything. I came here to pay off a favor." Now that it was in the open, Laura felt somewhat less uneasy.

The doctor leaned back in his swivel chair and adjusted the window shade. "You see," he said, turning back to her, "you've already told me two things about yourself. One, that you resent coming here and, two, that you possess a certain sense of obligation. That wasn't too difficult to do, was it?"

"No," she admitted grudgingly.

"How do you feel, now that you're sitting here, paying off your debt with this appointment you resent?"

"Nervous."

"Why? What is it you think I'm going to do?"

"Pry. Poke around. Aren't I supposed to tell you all the deep dark secrets of my life?"

"Not all in one session. Surely your life has been more interesting than that. Where were you born?"

"In Massachusetts."

"Is your family still there?"

She shifted her position in the chair, wondering if it was too soon to get up and leave. It was, she decided. She'd stick it out for a while longer. "No," she answered, "there's no family there."

"Where are they?"

"They aren't."

"Would you explain that?"

"I lived with my grandparents, but they died, and I went to live with my manager."

"How old were you when you went to live with your manager?"

"Thirteen."

He reached into his jacket pocket and brought out a pipe

and a tobacco pouch. "And before that you always lived with your grandparents?"

Laura swallowed. "And my mother, until she went away."

"Why did she go away?"

She gave him a wry look. "I guess she didn't like it there."

"So it would seem. Any idea why she disliked it?"

"I think she went away to get a better job," answered Laura offhandedly.

"Did she?"

"Did she what?"

"Get a better job." He tamped the loose tobacco into the bowl of his pipe.

Laura tried to brush the question aside. "I don't know."

The doctor seemed absorbed in the business of lighting the pipe. "She didn't contact you?"

Laura realized that the palms of her hands were suddenly moist. She flattened them against her skirt as if to smooth away the wrinkles there and hoped he wouldn't notice. Summoning up a casual tone of voice, she replied, "No, I didn't hear from her."

"And how do you feel about that?"

"People leave people."

"Sometimes. What about your father?" He was still looking at her.

She attempted to match his gaze. "He left too."

"When did he do that?"

"I don't know. Before I was born." Her gaze faltered.

"Do you know why he left?"

"Is it all right with you if I smoke?" she demanded.

"Certainly." He pushed an ashtray toward her side of the desk and held out a light for her.

Laura made an effort to hold the cigaret steady. He was waiting for an answer. She took a deep drag of smoke and exhaled slowly. "I think," she looked him squarely in the eyes, "that he probably left because he wasn't married to my mother. Or maybe she didn't even know who he was."

"I see. Well, you had a point to make when you said that people leave people, didn't you? First the father, then the mother, then, by way of nature, the grandparents. Does it bother you greatly that these people seemed to have left you to make out on your own?"

In spite of the tight knot she felt at the back of her neck,

Laura managed to shake her head. "I've done all right for myself."

He smiled. "So you have, but does it ever occur to you to wish that things had been different?"

She paused, sorting out the thoughts in her mind. Cautiously, she responded. "Someday I'll get married and have my own family. Then I won't need anyone else."

"Why not?"

"Because I'll have someone of my own to belong to." The words escaped before she could edit them.

"Is it very important that you belong to someone?"

Laura tried to keep the surge of antagonism out of her voice. "It would be nice," she said.

"Nice?"

"It would be a luxury."

"And in the meantime, until you find this someone?"

"I have my work—and my fans," she added with a trace of irony.

"Tell me something about your work," he proposed, shifting his pipe in his mouth.

Laura unclasped her hands in her lap. She hadn't realized she had clenched them so tightly together. Flexing the stiffness out of her fingers, she pressed herself against the back of the chair. "What's to tell?" she said. "An actress is a commodity. The studio sells her to the public, and if they like her, they keep buying her."

"And if they don't?"

"The studio dumps her."

"Would that sort of thing happen to you if, say, you were not as successful as you are?" He seemed genuinely curious.

"Hell, yes," retorted Laura, "they'd dump me so fast it would make your head spin."

"In other words," he said slowly, "they too would leave you on your own."

It had been a trap. Infuriated, Laura grasped the arms of the chair and pushed herself to her feet. "That's it," she snapped, "time's up."

He got up and followed her to the door. "If you like," the doctor said smoothly, "I will check my schedule and try to arrange further visits at a time that will be convenient to you. Please telephone me tomorrow."

Laura brushed past him into the anteroom without stopping to answer him.

"May I speak to Miss Curtis, please?"

Laura reached for the clock on the bedside table. Fumbling in the unfamiliar surroundings, she found the light switch. It was nearly midnight. "This is Laura Curtis," she answered sleepily. "Who's calling?"

"Mike. Mike Stanton. I just got home from a basketball game, and my phone service gave me your message."

Laura stifled a yawn and tried to sound wide awake. "You said I could call after I saw him."

"How did it go?"

"It was awful. I hated him. He acts like a brain surgeon, only he doesn't even bother to give you an anesthetic. He just starts picking at your head."

"You went through with it, though. That's all that matters."

"I'm not going back."

"Who said you had to? How are you otherwise?"

Laura propped her pillows up on the headboard and raised herself to a sitting position. "I'm fine. I'm in my new apartment."

"You had a big day. Where is it?"

"Shoreham Drive, above the Strip."

"Do you like it?"

She smiled to herself, pleased that he took an interest. "It's okay. I'd like to get a house again sometime, though. This is only temporary."

"If you like it, that's the important thing." There was a sound of movement at his end of the line.

"Mike? What are you doing?"

"Lighting a cigaret, why?"

"I just wondered. I'm glad you called back. It's a little strange being alone in a place of my own."

"It won't be strange for long," he assured her.

"Will you come see it?" She held her breath for the reply.

"Sure," he agreed easily, "you just say when."

"Sometime after work," she put in quickly, "I'll drop by your set." Laura found herself grinning. "How was your basketball game?"

"Great. The Lakers won by fourteen points. Do you like the game?"

"Oh, yes," she averred. "The Lakers are the greatest."

"Do you have to work tomorrow?" Mike was asking.

"Not until the day after. I'm going to spend tomorrow getting this place in shape and putting my things away. I never knew I had so much stuff."

"That's what happens when you move. I'll see you at the studio later this week."

"Yes." She wished he wouldn't hang up, but it was late.

"Take care of yourself, Laura."

Somehow, she reflected as she lay again in darkness, the new place didn't seem all that strange, not when someone like Mike Stanton was only as far away as the telephone at her bedside, telling her to take care of herself.

"You didn't have to buy me a Christmas gift," Mike said, but he sounded pleased all the same. He waited at the wheel for the traffic light to turn green.

"I wanted to, so why shouldn't I? You helped me move the furniture around, and I wanted to pay you back."

"People don't have to be paid back. Sometimes they just do things because they feel like it."

"Obie actually got me the tickets. He says they're the best seats in the Sports Arena."

"How was your Christmas with them?"

"Not much of a celebration. Ruth went out and bought a lot of clothes that were supposed to be Obie's gift to her, and Obie went out and bought himself a rowing machine as her gift to him. They're not what you'd call sentimental. It was kind of," she searched for the word, "arid. It would have been more fun if you'd been able to come."

Mike's eyes were on the road. "I told you, Gloria had been planning her party for a long time. I couldn't get out of it." He changed the subject discreetly. "Did you get any good presents?"

"That TV and stereo console you saw in the living room was from the Major. It even has a section for tape cartridges. There are so many knobs I feel like I ought to have a pilot's license to run it."

The Major's gift had come at just the right time. Laura had studiously watched three basketball games on television, preparing herself for this evening. There had been other gifts. Obie and Ruth gave her a solid gold key to her apartment, with her initials set on it in rubies. There was a silver tea service from a group of theater owners, a dozen silver water goblets from her latest producer and director, a set of luggage that she did not need from someone whose name she did not recognize, plus a complement of blending, slicing, and mixing appliances, all from the manufacturer. From various sources came the usual cellophane-wrapped baskets of tinned preserves and hors d'oeuvres, not to mention several cases of wines and liquors. One large, elaborately wrapped parcel had arrived without a card. Inside, Laura found the scripts from all her films which Drucilla had had elegantly bound in gold-tooled red leather. She rewrapped the box and had it returned by messenger.

Mike was asking her a question. "Which float are you riding on in the parade tomorrow?"

"I forget. They sent me a letter with all the information, but I lost it someplace. I have to get up at five in the morning. They're sending a car for me. It may turn out to be fun. I've never been to a Rose Bowl parade, only seen them on TV."

"Then we'd better make it an early evening," declared Mike. So much the better, he thought. That would still give him a chance to reach Gloria's before midnight, if the basketball game didn't run late. He had begged off joining her earlier, saying he was having New Year's Eve dinner with his mother in Burbank. The situation with Gloria was becoming stifling. He had accepted Laura Curtis' invitation as a relief from Gloria's increasing demands on him.

"Tomorrow night I leave for Chicago, New York, and Florida," Laura told him. "I won't be back until March." She hoped Mike would say that he'd miss her, but instead he only turned on the car radio. "It'll be a long trip. I've never traveled alone before."

"You won't be alone," he corrected her. "There will be people from the studio taking care of you in every city."

"Only during the days, when I'm working. At night, I'll be sitting alone in a hotel." The thought depressed her. At least with Drucilla along on the other trips, there had been another person for company.

"You'll get used to it." He turned into the parking lot, already crowded with cars and streams of people heading for the brightly lit dome of the Sports Arena.

Laura tried a casual tone. "If I get lonely, may I call you?"

"Sure."

He hadn't sounded very enthusiastic, but it was better than nothing, knowing there was somebody she could talk to. As Mike helped her out of the car, several people saw her and pointed. A couple asked for autographs, having neither pencil nor paper for her to sign with. They went away, disappointed. It seemed fans always expected stars to travel fully equipped with autographing paraphernalia.

They neared the entrance and the crowd became thicker. Mike threw a protective arm around her shoulders and herded her through the press of people surrounding them. He hadn't bargained for this. Gloria would blow her stack if she found out where he'd been. He glanced covertly around but saw no familiar faces.

"I'm sorry," Laura said as they boarded the escalator. She pushed a loose strand of hair away from her face. "I hope you weren't embarrassed."

"Is it always like that?" He couldn't help being impressed by her reception.

"I'm used to it. It doesn't bother me anymore."

Though he was accustomed to having fans approach Gloria when they went out, the enthusiasm Laura Curtis inspired was new to him. Perhaps it was because Laura's fans were a younger group. Those who recognized Gloria tended toward middle age and showed her a distant deference. He wondered how old Gloria was. About thirty-eight, he guessed, six years older than he. The occasional flash of pity he felt for her depressed him. It must have played hell with her pride to accept the role in this picture, to play a fading movie queen. Though she took pains to obscure her financial situation, he knew she had accepted the film in a desperate effort to prove to Hollywood that the glamour was still there. The trouble was, audiences nowadays had grown sophisticated. They looked deeper than a clinging sequined dress and rented jewels. They demanded a new naturalism that Gloria, with her carefully lacquered coif and her deliberate, speech-tutored delivery, had never mastered. How ironic, thought Mike, that Gloria's famous, husky tones had been so widely imitated that now, when she opened her mouth, she appeared as a grotesque caricature of herself.

Laura glanced around. "Which way do we go?"

He looked at the tickets and, taking her arm, hurried toward the far end of the corridor. "Come on. They're already playing the national anthem. We'll be late."

Laura stood on her balcony, staring absently at the lights dotting the bay. A soft breeze was blowing, but it failed to refresh the humid night air. She brushed away the hair that clung to the back of her neck in the dampness. For the first time in her life, she was homesick. The crowded schedule of the day had only made her nightly solitude more oppressive. There was a cocktail party downstairs in the hotel which she had attended briefly. After a long day of personal appearances, she wanted nothing more than peace and quiet, yet the sounds of the gaity below made her a bit melancholy. Never mind, she couldn't have stood the party a minute longer, not with her feet so swollen from the heat. She came back inside the room and glanced at her travel clock on the bureau. It was almost nine thirty, almost time to call Mike. At the beginning, she had called him later in the evenings, just before she went to bed, but he was never home. She had become embarrassed at leaving nightly messages with the same brusque lady on his answering service. Finally, it was he who had suggested she call at six-thirty California time. That way, he explained, he'd be sure to be home, having just come from the studio to shower and shave before going out for the evening. Laura never asked him where he went. She suspected it was to see Gloria French, although the vision of Mike, young and handsome, with someone so faded seemed hardly believable. What was more puzzling was the fact that Gloria French was, in a word, common, and Mike, with his expertly custom-tailored clothes and polished manners, seemed hardly to have those tastes.

Laura gave a desultory glance at the typed schedule of her appearances tomorrow.

8:00 Breakfast, Conch Room, informal TV interviews . . . 10:00 Hal Castle radio show, live from Victoria Park . . . 10:45 Autographing Party, Victory Park Cinema Arcade . . . 12:00 Press Luncheon, Victory Park Holiday Inn, main dining room . . . 2:00 Assembly for opening day parade, S. M. Victor,

Grand Marshal (Laura Curtis, car # 3) . . . 5:00 Cocktails
for visiting celebrities, hosted by His Honor, Mayor Worth . . .
8:00 Testimonial Gala for S. M. Victor, Galaxy Roof.

Laura tossed the list on the bed and ordered a steak from
room service. Personal appearances were more exhausting by
far than making pictures, and tomorrow promised another day
of fatigue masked by the constant, cordial smiling that left
her face aching.

She gave Mike's number to the hotel operator and waited.
He answered the first ring.

"You sound beat," he sympathized.

She related the events of the day, the interviewers who in-
variably asked the same questions, the banquet lunch, like
every other banquet lunch, the rush from place to place to
meet the scheduled appointments, and the cocktail party she
had ducked out of quickly.

"Aren't there any people there you enjoy?"

"They're all nice enough, I guess," she allowed. "Colin
Kirkwood and the Major arrived today with a bunch of pretty girls. They're all under contract to the studio, but I never
saw any of them before. I swear, I don't know where he
finds them."

"Don't worry. They find him."

"Mike, I am so tired of being in this rat race. It's been one
stop after another, and all like this, ever since I last saw you.
That's almost eight weeks. Sometimes, I just want to burst
into tears, I'm so tired and lonely."

"Well, don't do that. You said it makes your eyes swell
up."

"Yes." She had a thought. "How much longer are you on
your picture?"

"About another ten days."

"Mike," she said delightedly, "I have a great idea. I have
to be here through the weekend before I go back to New
York for the Sullivan show. You get someone to replace you
Friday, and I'll have the studio fly you in for a long weekend."

"Are you serious?"

"Sure. All I have to do is tell them I'm unhappy and I want
my friend here. You can pick up your ticket in the administration building Thursday and fly here straight from work
that night. It's a beautiful hotel," she urged enthusiastically.

"We can have a wonderful time, and if I have to run around for interviews, you can go to the beach or play golf."

There was a pause at the other end of the line. "No," he said slowly, "I think I'd better not. But thanks."

"Mike, please."

"You'll have to take my word for it, Laura. It wouldn't be a good idea."

"But why not? It's so easy for me to do, and I'd love to see you."

"You'll be home soon, another three weeks. I can't just walk off the picture to go away for the weekend, not when we're so close to the end."

He wasn't coming. When she had replaced the receiver, Laura lay back on the bed. She wondered if that had actually been his reason for turning her down. Surely there were any number of people who could substitute for him. It was only one day.

She picked up the telephone and called room service again to ask where her order was. The man who answered had a heavy Spanish accent and seemed thoroughly confused. Laura got into a loud argument with him and slammed down the phone in his ear.

She peered into the bathroom mirror and, with an index finger, wiped at the smudges where her mascara had run. The color lights at CBS had been relentlessly hot and, not to help matters, the air conditioning had broken down just before air time. After the show, she had dismissed the limousine and walked crosstown from the theater on Fifty-third Street to P. J. Clarke's for some dinner. Milton Donner, one of the Victory's Studio's New York men, had accompanied her, with a garrulous stream of compliments on her performance.

Laura had actually no idea whether she had been good, adequate, or bad. It was one thing to be able to listen to playbacks when you recorded a song and to judge the merits and faults of each tape, secure in the knowledge that the best portions of each of the tapes could be combined for the final product. It was quite another to perform live with no electronic miracles to back you up. She had worked with the vocal coach all week, perfecting her style of delivery. After film work, the mannerisms seemed exaggerated and obvious. Laura wondered if the whole thing had been worth the effort.

She gave her shoes a savage kick, and they landed across the room. Once this God-forsaken trip was over, she'd stick to movies, where she belonged.

Collapsing onto the bed, she leafed through the messages she had picked up at the desk on her way upstairs. Among them were calls from Obie and Claire Poland. She glanced at her new wristwatch. In a moment of depression, feeling she owed herself a little pleasure, she had ducked into Van Cleef and Arpels during lunch time and bought herself a Piaget watch. Four thousand dollars worth of pick-me-up, she reflected, and she probably would have enjoyed a chocolate soda just as much.

It was eleven thirty. That meant the Sullivan show was in progress on the coast. She'd wait to call Obie after it was over. She gave Claire Poland's number to the operator. It would be good to talk to someone at home, even if it had to be Claire.

"Laura, darling."

"I just got your message, Claire. I was out doing *The Ed Sullivan Show*." Laura lit a cigaret and prepared herself for the usual barrage of questions.

"I know. Your hotel said you were there. I didn't transfer the call because I didn't want to get you all upset before you went on the air." Her voice held a tinge of condolence.

"Upset?" Laura asked uneasily. "Why?"

"Now, dear," Claire took a pause to consider her approach, "you and I have always leveled with each other, right?"

"Yes," replied Laura guardedly.

"Well, one of the boys down at the paper called me today with an item that confuses me. It could be nothing," she said hastily. "It could be a foolish fantasy on this woman's part. There are people like that. Every once in a while somebody pops up claiming to be Cary Grant's long-lost brother or something."

Whatever it was Claire was getting at, she had already managed to unsettle Laura. Masking her apprehension, she asked, "What's happened, Claire?"

"An accident. There was a car crash on the coast highway near San Onofre." She let the information sink in, but it still made no sense to Laura. "Four people were killed, one of them a woman who was a civilian employee at the Camp Pendleton Marine Base. Do you know a Lucy Maxwell?"

"No." Then suddenly, it all came together. Laura broke out in a cold sweat.

"She was the common-law wife of a Sergeant Carl Maxwell. He died in the crash with her. It seems that among this woman's effects were a lot of clippings from papers and magazines, all about you, and two old photographs. On the back of one picture was written, 'Laura-Louise, age one, at the folks' place.' On the other it said, 'Laura-Louise, fourth birthday, Devon.' They were both photos of the same little girl. Laura, isn't Devon the place you come from? Of course, I'm sure there are lots of Devons . . ." Clara trailed off, waiting for an answer.

The phone was slippery in Laura's moist hand. "Claire——" Her voice sounded strange in her own ears. She took a breath and tried to steady herself. "Claire, it's possible," she said finally.

"I see." There was a silence. Perhaps she was writing.

"Claire?"

"I'm here. I was rechecking your studio biography. It's quite specific about your being an orphan. I suppose they had a reason for that."

She hesitated. "It was Drucilla's idea, a long time ago," she explained weakly. "My mother left me. I don't remember her at all. Please, Claire——" She couldn't finish the sentence.

"Look, sweetheart," consoled Claire, "I'm only checking out a possible story. If there had been some quarrel, some estrangement between you two, this would be a big item. As it is, it's a good item, but not a great one. I mean, the woman was a virtual stranger to you. She never attempted to contact you, did she?"

"No. Never."

"Well," she continued, "I can't promise that the fan magazines won't get hold of this. It's the kind of thing that's their bread and butter. For my part, I'm willing to let it go. It's been a busy news week here, and I've got more material than I can use, for a change. However," her tone turned brisk, "I want you to promise me that when you have a really big story, you'll think first of your friend Claire. Even if you run off secretly and elope or something. I want your assurance

that I'll break the story. A firm and binding understanding.
Do I have that?"

"Yes," she agreed feebly, "I promise."

"That's a dear. Now you get some rest." Claire hung up.

Laura bolted for the bathroom, retching uncontrollably.

When the phone rang again, she was lying on the bed, staring numbly at the ceiling.

"You were sensational!" Mike shouted happily.

"Mike." She began to sob. "Mike," she repeated.

"Jesus, Laura. What's wrong?"

She told him everything, beginning with Claire's call and going back to Devon, her grandparents, and life with Drucilla. For the first time, it all poured out of her until, exhausted, she had finished and lay back, weeping softly.

Mike finally spoke. "You poor kid."

"Mike, I don't understand it. I never even knew her, but I feel so terrible. I feel so all alone."

"I'm right here, aren't I?" Talking gently, he alternately comforted and reassured her. It was not easy. At last, after almost an hour, she seemed to have calmed down sufficiently, and he asked, "Did you hear what I said when I called? You did a terrific job on the show."

She sounded steadier. "Did I really?"

"And how. When are you coming back?"

"A week from Wednesday. I have to begin fittings for the new picture. Did you finish shooting?"

"We wrapped Friday. It's in the can. I'll be lining up at Unemployment tomorrow."

Laura propped herself up. "But Mike. My picture starts at the end of next month. Maybe they haven't got a dialogue coach yet."

"I heard on the grapevine that Alice Emerson is doing it."

"Never mind. Wait till I get back. I'll have her replaced."

"Laura, don't do anything that's going to make waves."

"Don't be silly. All I have to do is say the word." She felt better now, knowing that she could do something to repay his friendship and knowing that he'd be close by if she needed someone to confide in. As an added thought, she asked, "Will you do something for me?"

"Of course, if I can," he offered.

"Would you take me to the Academy Awards week after next?"

"Damn," he said disappointedly, "I can't. I've already agreed to take someone else. Laura, you know there's nothing I'd rather do than take you."

"Can't you get out of it?"

"I'm afraid that's impossible."

"It was just a thought."

"A nice thought. How's this for an alternative? The night after the Awards, why don't you have dinner with me? Any place you say."

"Chasen's?"

"Chasen's it is."

Several times during the night, Laura woke with nightmares she couldn't remember. When she had finally gotten up and taken a sleeping pill, she lay in the quiet darkness going over their conversation. In spite of the distance between them, she felt closer to Mike Stanton than she had ever felt to anyone in her life.

As it happened, Laura was escorted to the Academy Awards by no one less than the Major himself. She had already thrown away her invitation and made up her mind not to go when his secretary called with the request. She had smiled to herself, thinking of the look on Mike's face when she showed up with S. M. Victor. She accepted. Laura was sure that Mike would be with Gloria French who would probably give her own left arm to be escorted anywhere by the likes of the Major.

She chose her costume with great care. Gloria, as always, would be well corseted and resplendently frosted with beading or sequins. Laura picked out a simple pale blue jersey gown, draped in the Grecian style. It clung close to her body and demanded no undergarments. After a prolonged argument with her hairdresser, she convinced him to forgo his intricate fancies in favor of an elegant simplicity. Her hair, seemingly carelessly arranged, hung in a few loose coils at the nape of her neck, cascading down over the back of her dress. The total effect, she hoped, would make Gloria look hopelessly vulgar by comparison.

There was something a little foolish about being in full evening dress at six in the afternoon with the sun still shining brightly. Nevertheless, the Major's compliments on her appearance as she stepped into the car assured her that she had been right. Laura assumed he had invited her as part of the buildup for this next picture. He had already spread the word that he expected to be a candidate for several awards next year. Perhaps he thought to tantalize her with the triumphs that might lie in store for her when the time came. Whatever his intentions, the only thing that mattered to Laura was a triumph over Gloria French.

They passed by the bleachers of applauding fans and into the auditorium. Here and there people embraced in the familiar Hollywood salutation, cheek to cheek, each looking over the other's shoulder to see if there wasn't someone more important they should greet. In the aisle seats, those who had received nominations thanked their well-wishers with tense, disconcerted smiles. It was a unique tribal spectacle, especially harrowing for the nominees whose films, made so long ago, now seemed like meetings with half-remembered strangers for which they were being called to account.

Laura settled into her seat beside the Major. Lisa Taylor and Marty Tabor, in the row behind them, leaned forward to exchange a few words.

"Where's Jack?" inquired Laura.

"Where else?" Lisa said. "Another location."

"We all share your disappointment that he can't be here," the Major sympathized. "I hope you have your speech ready in case the picture wins."

"She's going to make it a missing persons bulletin," laughed Marty.

Laura glanced around surreptitiously to see if she could spot Mike, but she had no luck. Their seats were very close to the stage. Probably Mike and Gloria were somewhere in the crowd behind them. The lights dimmed, and she turned to face the podium.

It wasn't until they disembarked from the long trail of limousines at the Beverly Hilton that she caught sight of them. She suppressed an exultant smile. Gloria's full-blown figure was sheathed in a strapless gown of scarlet lace reembroidered with glistening bugle beads. To Laura, she looked rather like an overripe tomato that threatened to burst at any moment. She noted with satisfaction that Gloria and Mike were seated at a table adjacent to hers which held a few lesser-ranking studio executives and some members of the

Victory technical departments. Laura inclined her head and nodded a greeting to Mike. It did not escape Gloria's attention. She had not intended that it should.

With a cool, professional eye, Gloria took in the political strength assembled at the Major's table. Already people were dropping by to pay court to S. M. Victor, Laura Curtis, Marty Tabor, Lisa Taylor, and the few chosen highly-placed producers who, with wives and girlfriends, occupied the remaining seats. Obie Straus was chatting with Laura. Gloria excused herself from Mike on the pretext of wanting to speak to Obie and maneuvered her way to a spot beside S. M. Victor's chair. She was delighted when Obie steered Laura toward the dance floor, leaving a vacant place next to the Major.

"I'm sorry Jack's picture didn't win," Laura was saying. "I guess Lisa was disappointed."

Obie shrugged. "She'd be satisfied just to have him home for a change, win or lose."

"Did they get married yet? I didn't read the papers while I was away."

Obie nodded a greeting to someone at a nearby table. "Jack's divorce isn't final. In four or five months, I think."

Laura looked back toward her table. Gloria was deep in conversation with the Major who seemed oblivious to the ample décolletage she was displaying. "Gloria French is a client of yours, isn't she?" she asked pleasantly.

"For years."

"Do you know," she said thoughtfully, "I heard about a picture that she'd be just right for."

Obie's attention sharpened. "Which one?"

The Captive Legion. Have you seen a script?"

His enthusiasm wilted perceptibly. "It's one of those old tits-and-sand numbers."

"Who cares? She'd be perfect for the part of the desert queen. Come on, Obie," she continued, assuming a confidential tone, "we both know she doesn't work all that often anymore. Why, this picture she just finished was her first in a long, long time. I'd think she'd be dying to do *The Captive Legion.* Does she know about the part?"

"I don't think so. They're late casting. It starts shooting in two months on some God-forsaken Spanish plain." He waved absently to the bandleader as they danced by the stand.

"Maybe Gloria would like a trip to Spain," she offered,

glancing back at the table. Mike was standing next to Gloria's chair. "Shall we go back now?" Laura asked. "This floor is getting awfully crowded."

Threading her way through the crowd, she inquired, "Obie, just how old is Gloria French, anyway?"

"Only her astrologer knows for sure."

"In any case," she told him, "I intend to put a word in to the Major about her doing that picture. It's going to be a Victory release. Don't worry, I'll do everything I can to see that she gets the part."

"Thanks," said Obie amiably. He nodded to the assemblage at the table and left.

Laura greeted Mike cordially, waiting for Gloria to relinquish her seat. He looked slightly sheepish at the encounter but recovered enough to introduce them.

"Laura, have you met Gloria French?"

Laura smiled warmly, seemingly unaware of Gloria's outstretched hand. "I always enjoyed your performances so much," she said brightly. "You're looking wonderful."

Gloria was silent as Mike escorted her back to their table.

"What is it?" he asked.

Gloria gave a grim smile. "She left off the rest of the sentence. She meant to add 'for your age.' "

6

Gloria

3:00 P.M.

CAPRICORN: *Look to associates, friends for assistance in fulfilling domestic obligations. Tend to health matters.*
Bullshit. *I can just picture my friends and associates fulfilling domestic obligations. Six producers and a casting director having a quilting bee. Tend to health matters. Like what? Get a gang together and we'll all go have high colonics? Jesus, if it were only that humorous. Face it, Gloria. This is another unfunny day in a big desert of unfunny days. Some great life, sitting here at three in the afternoon with nothing to do but read the evening newspaper with its glorious front-page spread of the grieving widow entering the church. Tough luck, chickie-baby, now you've lost him too. Think of the money you'll save. What a taker he was. The champion son-ofabitch taker of the Western world. Take 'em, use 'em, and toss 'em away like old Kleenex.*

Christ, I'm going to go nuts if I don't think of something to do. I need an activity. Why can't I take up needlepoint like those classy broads in the society pages? Or go to the art museum. The art museum. Not yet. It's not time. I'm still saving it. There always has to be someplace, just one place, that's left for an activity. If you use that up, then there's nothing left to plan for. You always have to save one thing. I'm saving the museum.

Sleeping late is the essential rule. That wipes out the morning. Who knows, maybe it's even good for you. After that, a couple of hours of makeup. Inspecting the new lines that weren't there yesterday. That bastard doctor said the work would last five years. That makes two years he owes me. The least he could do is take a few tucks in the worst places. I could get rid of the aquamarine ring to pay for it.

I should have married that crazy Brazilian. Funny, I can't even remember his name. What a sight he was, dashing onto the plane just as the load of us were taking off from the film festival. I'll never forget the looks on their faces when he opened that shoebox and all those stones spilled into my lap. Topazes, amethysts, aquamarines, and him standing in the aisle yelling, "Now will you marry me?" Poor schnook, they had to drag him off the plane in tears. Mad as a March hare. I sure as hell could use him now, him and his jewels.

So what's left? You put on the makeup and go to the hairdresser for the daily comb-out. Sometimes the only person I speak to all day is that pansy Phillipe. In the afternoon you cruise the stores, pretending to be interested in the merchandise so you can have a little conversation with the salesgirl, maybe get asked for an autograph. Twice a week there's the health club and the massage. God, but it feels good to have a pair of hands on your flesh, even if it is that buxom Swede with her halitosis.

That's what I need. I could call Mickey. Sure I could. He always has somebody. If he can't get hold of one of his boys, he'll come himself. Hell, it shouldn't be a problem in the middle of the afternoon. I just wish it didn't leave me so depressed afterward.

Remember when it didn't cost? When all those beautiful young studs hung around like bees around the queen, just so they could get themselves known at the studios? All those beautiful young fringe benefits of being on top. Who are they brown-nosing now, I wonder, the Mike Stantons of this world? Star-fuckers, all of them, but at least you got laid. For free. Once in a while you'd give a pair of cuff links, a key chain, a money clip. Mike cost me a morocco leather script binder. And the television set, chalk that one up to him too.

Christ Almighty, but it's quiet in this house. I need some music. Put a couple of records on, change into something sexy—and what? Call Mickey. But afterward. Afterward. Never mind, by then it'll be time to drink. That's part of the rules, no drinking until after six. Where the hell is that goddamn number?

"Mickey?"

"Princess."

"I'm feeling low, Mickey."

"You called the right place. Did you like Roger?"

"Roger?"

"The fellow from two weeks ago."

"Oh, Roger. Yes, I liked him."

"Say in an hour?"

"Make it an hour and a half. I want to take a bath and change."

"Princess, it'll be twenty-five this trip."

"Twenty-five?"

"It's the rising cost of living. It hits us all."

"So I've heard."

"Have fun, Princess."

SHE sat in the semidark living room, her eyes on the telephone. Curled up on the sofa, tensed, she resembled a crouched cat eyeing a blackbird. Willing the damned thing to ring was obviously not going to work. Restlessly, she snuffed out her cigaret and wrested herself from the cushions. She stalked to the plate-glass doors and caught herself reflected against them. Reaching out, she placed a finger against the glass and traced the curves of her body. It was all still there, still good. So, you s.o.b., she thought, why aren't you here enjoying it? Look what you're missing. Impatiently, she flicked on the outside lights and leaned against the coolness of the window, staring at the patio beyond. The jacaranda tree was shedding into the swimming pool again. A sprinkling of purple blossoms floated on the azure water. Beautiful, but eventually they would sink and gum up the filter system. Gloria let out a sigh of annoyance. The pool was just another pain in the ass. She had never been in it. She had never learned to swim. Swimming ruined your hair. It was enough to look good in a bathing suit. But, Hollywood being Hollywood, you had to have a pool. That meant you had to have a maintenance man for the pool. And a gardener for the patio around the pool. And a cleaning woman for the house with the patio and pool. It was like a goddamn nursery rhyme, she reflected.

The jangling of the telephone shattered the silence. She sprang for it. Then, stopping, she let it ring two more times. Her first agent had taught her that. Never answer too quickly. With deliberate languor, she put the pink receiver to her ear.

It was a wrong number.

The house seemed overly warm. Gloria slid open the door to the patio. From some neighboring house came the sounds of a party, punctuated by hearty male laughter. With a slam, she closed the door.

Who was he that she waited here like some caged animal for his handouts? It had all been so casual at the start. He was young and beautiful. He amused her, made her laugh. Nothing complicated, just some fun and games. Somewhere along the way, she had no notion of when it had happened, things had changed. The luxury had become a necessity. It was as if she would waste away without the nourishment he provided. She loathed the fact of her dependence on him. She reproached herself a dozen times a day. How had someone so smart gotten suddenly so dumb? She had always been so careful never to need a man. She had let them use her, and she had used them in return. That was the way the game was played, but never, never, did you get hung up on one of the bastards. People who fell in love became hostages, vulnerable to a thousand casually administered cruelties. Idly, she traced the window glass. "All men are pricks," she wrote.

She should have known what he was when she met him. Him with his society girl friend. Virginia, that was her name. She had set him up in style, that one, with the English tweeds, the Gucci shoes, the Vuitton luggage. The wild thing was, it all looked so right for him. Mike had class, and he knew it. It was his stock in trade. Even now, without the girl's money, he maintained appearances. Gloria knew he was deep in hock. The Bentley had been sold for a secondhand MG that needed constant repairs. Still, he hung onto it. He couldn't afford payments on a new car. Whenever they went out, he drove her Caddy, never failing to make a few deprecating cracks about "American cars." The MG, crate that it was, still held the rank of a foreign car. He played his angles well, she had to hand him that. He lived in one of the fashionable new towers on Wilshire Boulevard. It gave him a smart address to drop in conversation. What did it matter that his apartment was one and a half rooms on the second floor rear with a view of the blank wall of the building next door?

"Christ Almighty!" she burst aloud. "Where the hell is he?"

As if in answer, the phone rang.

"I called you almost three hours ago."

"I know," he answered easily, "I got the message."

"Thanks for returning the call so fast. I'm glad it wasn't a matter of life and death."

He ignored her tone. "I figured it wasn't," he said affably. "I was in a meeting with Walt Simons. He's directing the Laura Curtis picture."

"I know who he is," snapped Gloria. "You don't have to tell me."

"I thought you'd want to know I'm doing the picture."

"Surprise, surprise." Instinctively, she felt a tightening in her stomach. "I should have seen the writing on the wall the day you drove out of the Victory parking lot without waiting for me like you'd promised."

"Oh, hell, Gloria we've been through this before. I told you, the kid was all shook up. She needed someone to talk to. I figured you were smart enough to find your way home."

"While you were being smart about charming your way into your next job? I should have had you fired on the spot." It was an empty threat, she knew. Still, there had been a time when a word from Gloria French meant your job. What a bitch, she thought bitterly, that when you most need the power, it isn't there anymore.

"You wouldn't have done that, baby," replied Mike, "not when we had such a good thing going."

Gloria reacted sharply. "Had?"

"Have," he corrected.

"Mike?" She took a softer tone. "Why don't you come over for a while?"

"It's getting late."

"What does that matter? Just jump in the car and drop by."

"Gloria, I'm a little tired, and I have this script to go over."

"Bring it here. We'll sit and read."

"You know damned well we won't."

"Well, is that so bad?" she laughed enticingly.

"Not tonight," he objected. "I can't. I have to stay here."

Her voice held a note of wheedling. "So I'll come there. You do whatever you have to, and I'll come over in an hour." There was no reply. "Mike?"

"Yes," he said, "all right."

It had come to that. Gloria steadied herself in the doorway

to the bedroom, trying to suppress the fear that lay like something undigested and uncomfortable inside her.

Laura Curtis. How old was she, nineteen? A fucking, goddam teenager. What could she have to compete with? How much can you know at nineteen? Not a hell of a lot. Maybe it wasn't so lousy after all to have been around the block a few times. At least you picked up a few tricks along the way. She smiled. Never, she thought, remembering the old joke, fuck around with the Lone Ranger.

Obie would laugh his head off if he knew she consulted Rex Leon about the script. But Rex was someone she couldn't do without. She pressed the door buzzer under the small nameplate which read "R. Leon, Astral Consultations."

Rex had been Gloria's hairdresser, back in the days when his name was still Frank Pinto. Then, he'd done his clients' horoscopes for free. When he finally realized he was getting more calls for readings than for stylings, he had changed his name to suit his birth sign, let his red hair grow to an approximation of a leonine mane, and set up shop in the garage at the rear of his house.

The door opened.

"Jesus, Rex." Gloria stared. "That's some outfit."

He was draped in a brilliant orange fabric from his shoulders to his ankles. Around his neck assorted talismans hung from several leather thongs. From his left ear dangled a single gold loop.

"African, dear heart," he explained, seating her by his desk. "You know, like us lions."

"You go out on the street like that, you'll have the vice squad on your tail."

"No time for chitchat, loved one. I sandwiched you in between two very big appointments." He rummaged in his files and withdrew her chart, scanning it with a practiced eye. "Tell me, what's on your mind?"

"A new script. And my love life." She watched as he made notes of figures on his scratch pad. "Well?"

"Is this picture being shot overseas?"

She nodded. "In Spain someplace."

He hummed a little tune. At length, he glanced up. "Hunky-dorey, sweets. You have this super ray from the sun to Uranus. That's good for the money angle. Also, pretty soon Neptune will go direct. There's your trip. Aren't you the lucky one." He seemed very satisfied with his discoveries.

"The love life," she prodded.

"That," Rex frowned, "is not so hot. See," he pointed to the chart, "you have this tacky square from Mars to your natal Venus. Not the least bit friendly. And Venus itself is due to turn retrograde momentarily. What sign is he?"

"Pisces."

He sighed. "My glorious Gloria, how could you be such a silly girl. They're weak, all of them. Nice speaking voices, you have to give them that, but dreamers, always building castles in the air. No." He slapped his palm on the desk decisively. "Not for you."

"But Rex," she put in feebly, "I don't want to lose him."

"Darling," he admonished, "the stars don't lie. I mean, there's that square, just staring you in the face. Of course, you goats are such determined creatures that you hate to believe you can't get where you want to go. What the hell, why not take your trip to Spain and see if he still looks good to you when you get back?"

"The way things are going," she said morosely, "it may be too late by then."

"But you'll have all that nice money to keep you warm." Rex rose and showed her to the door. In a courtly gesture, he kissed her hand. "Love you Capricorn glamour girls. Marlene Deitrich, Ava Gardner, and you, my Glo-girl. Smashing, all of you."

Gloria wondered grimly how their love lives were right now. Rex was correct, naturally. He always was. Take the money and run. It sounded so easy when he used it.

In spite of Rex's advice, she put off calling Obie. Let the producers sweat it out for a few days. If they thought she was holding out, there was a chance she might be able to pull a few strings. One little concession, she reasoned, that wasn't such a big deal. She had already dropped the hint to Mike on the telephone, and it had worked like a charm. He was so predictable when it came to rising to the bait.

Gloria inspected the contents of her closet and selected a black jersey dressing gown. It was eight years old, but it fitted like a glove and showed a very tempting amount of cleavage. That was good. It would be years before Laura Curtis had the stuff to wear a clinging black dress. Gloria gazed into the mirror, appraising what she saw. The bosom was still gorgeous, thanks to exercise. Laura Curtis was no match for that. The thighs pleased her less. She pinched one, feeling the flaccid, slightly waffled flesh. Goddamit, the time was going to come when she'd have to turn out the lights in bed. But not just yet, she determined, I've got a few left in me before I get to that point.

For a change, he was on time. On time and eager to perform. Gloria refused to believe that her veiled reference to boosting his career was solely responsible. No man could be stimulated to that degree of passion by ambition alone. No, she decided confidently, there were still enough sparks there to keep the fires burning.

She slid back into bed and handed him the glass of beer. Mike lay propped against the quilted pink satin headboard.

He gulped down half the contents of the glass. Gloria reached over and ran her fingernails lightly across his chest.

"Don't," he told her.

"You don't like it?"

"I'm bushed," he objected. "You broads forget we don't function on the same timetable you do."

"Sorry." She moved to lie closer beside him, feeling the warmth of his skin against hers.

"What was that business on the phone?"

"What business?" she asked evasively.

"You were acting very cagey about something. What's doing?" He reached for a cigaret and lit it.

"Oh, that." Gloria paused for a moment, wanting to keep him in suspense as long as possible. "Listen, how much are they paying you on that picture?"

He turned to her. "Same as last time. Why?"

"They shouldn't, you know. That picture has a much bigger budget than the one we did. Besides, you're very good at what you do. It should be obvious to them that you're worth more. Can't Laura Curtis get your salary raised?"

"She's not involved. She just suggested me for the job." He watched the smoke rise from his cigaret and disappear in the air over the bed.

"I heard she had someone replaced so you could take over." Gloria lay with her eyes shut, as if to prove the casualness of the conversation.

"Probably a rumor." Mike took a swallow of beer. "You know how those things are."

"Sure I do. Still, it seems to me that if she wanted you for the job enough to go to bat for you, she could have made it worth your while. Mike," she opened her eyes and glanced up at him, "how much money do you need?"

He grinned. "All of it."

"Seriously, how are things with you?"

"Seriously? Well," he examined the ash of his cigaret, "I could use a few thousand. The tailor, the car repairs—you know. I still have the membership at the golf club to fall back on. That's doubled in value since Virginia gave it to me. It's worth a few thou."

"I thought you wanted to hang on to that," said Gloria.

"I do. It's good for making the kind of contacts I need if I'm going to get where I want to get." He gazed into the now-empty glass.

"Where is that? Producing?"

"Yes."

"That's what I thought." She rolled over to face him. "How are you going to do it?"

He hesitated, looking into the glass as if the answer might lie among the dregs of foam at the bottom. "Wait for the right break, I guess."

Gloria moved closer. "Don't be a chump, Mike. In this life you make your own breaks. If a chance comes along, you grab it, and to hell with everything else. You have to push your luck for all it's worth."

"What's that supposed to mean to me?"

She gave him a slow, artful smile. "It means maybe there's a chance for you that you don't even know about." She paused to let it sink in.

Mike assessed her with a long, cool glance. "Go on," he said.

She nestled back into the pillows, pleased that, for the moment at least, all the cards were in her hands. "I've been asked to do a movie in Spain. I haven't accepted it yet," she added hastily. "I'm letting them sweat it out. But when the time comes that they have to have an answer, it just might happen that I attach a few conditions. Like, for instance, the fact that I'd feel more comfortable about the project if one of my people was somewhere on the production end to look out for my interests. Spain being a foreign country and all that, I'd have more confidence in the picture if someone with good old-fashioned Hollywood experience was on the team. So?"

"Do you think you can do it?"

"Associate producer? It shouldn't be too hard." Gloria affected a note of confidence. It would be harder than he knew, but it would also be worth it, even if it meant a slight cut in her salary to defray putting him on the payroll. There was no reason to mention that part.

"When does it go? I've already got myself committed to this picture."

"Then get yourself uncommitted. How many chances are you going to get? When you see a break, go after it. That's the only way you'll ever get to the top." Gloria brought herself up on one elbow and eyed him impatiently.

He spoke slowly. "I don't know. I agreed to do this. It took a little arranging on Laura's part."

"Jesus Christ!" interrupted Gloria. "She sure as hell didn't bother to arrange much, not even a raise in pay! It's not as if she cared enough to put her ass on the line for you. Where did you catch this sudden epidemic of loyalty? Or," she keyed herself for the thrust, "is it something more than that?"

"Skip it. Lay off. She's a kid. She's had a rough life, all alone, nervous, sick with exhaustion half the time———"

"—And very rich."

"Don't be a cunt. You can't help feeling a little sorry for her."

"I can too. Does that mean you don't want me to bother trying to get you on my picture?"

"I didn't say that."

"So you didn't." If there was one thing about Mike, she thought sourly, it was that his character was consistent.

"But I'll have to think about it. There are no guarantees."

"There never are," she acknowledged drily, adding, "not with Laura Curtis, either." She rolled away from him and, wanting to change the subject, switched on the bedside radio. A strain of melody filtered into the room. Gloria lay moodily at the edge of the bed, wondering just how much of a lead she had scored. It was, at best, tenuous. An acrid taste filled her mouth. She listened to the music, realizing suddenly how familiar the song was. Maybe it was a good omen. Out of the corner of her eye, she saw Mike glancing at his wristwatch.

Quickly, she said, "Did you know this song was written for me?" She hummed the tune for his benefit. "I was wearing a silver dress and I danced down a white staircase two stories high. Two stories high," she repeated.

"I remember. You were surrounded by a bunch of light-footed faggots in top hats."

"Don't, Mike. It was a beautiful scene. And I carried a huge fan. Ostrich plumes."

He was silent.

"Mike?" She moved back toward him. "Couldn't we have fun in Europe? Wouldn't it be a ball?" Without waiting for his answer, she lowered her head to his thighs.

Two days passed before he bothered to call her back. He still hadn't made up his mind, he said. Though Gloria had to fight to keep her anger under control on the telephone, the delay actually worked in her favor. She had broached the subject to Obie whose initial reaction was negative. "They'll never stand for that," he told her flatly. She begged him to make the attempt, to feel them out. Maybe they even needed an associate, who knew? If it was at all possible, she had told him, she'd even go so far as to pay part of Mike's freight herself. Obie, protective of his clients as always, had rebelled at the suggestion. "What the hell is this guy, some sort of superman?" She had laughed. Mike was no superman, just young and handsome. The day came when you had to lower your sights from the supermen and settle for what you could get. To be young and handsome was sufficient.

Gloria slipped out of her slack suit and into a robe. The sun still made patterns on the bedroom rug, a sign, at this hour, that the days were growing longer. Christ, but the lengthening twilight hours were hard to take. It didn't seem right to swallow a pill and go to bed while it was still light. She glanced over to where the bed lay waiting, empty, satin-spread, like a goddam pink-lined coffin. Repelled, she turned away and hurried downstairs to the living room. The house was silent. She stood in the center of the room, hearing only the sound of her own heartbeats. The familiar panic seized her. Rushing at the television set as if it were life-giving, she flicked it on and relaxed as the room filled with noise. Gloria gathered her robe about her and settled herself in a large chair.

A fair-haired girl cavorted over a meadow with a young man in a cigaret commercial. She had been a fair-haired girl once. Now, every time she looked at TV she saw a generation of new faces, bland, unlined, cream-puff faces. Soft, pouty-lipped ingenues, barely able to speak the lines they were given. Beauty-contest winners, perhaps, inexperienced and untalented. Where was the glamour? Where was the magnetism, the star quality that set audiences to worshipping at your feet? Not one of these wan, vapidly smiling faces had an ounce of it. Lightweights, all of them, each undistinguishable from the others. She turned away in disgust.

Gloria went into the pantry and poured herself a glass of wine. She wondered if maybe she was drinking too much. What the hell, it was only Chablis. Besides, it helped her sleep. Wine wouldn't ruin your looks, not like the hard stuff. Still, you had to keep an eye on yourself. Returning to the living room, she reached under the sofa cushion and pulled out the face exerciser. She plugged it in next to the TV as she always did and propped her feet up on the sofa. The remote control for the set lay beside her. Her eyes fixed to the television, she sipped her wine as the electric current tugged away at the muscles of her face.

Gloria inspected herself in the hall mirror. No question about it, she looked great tonight. She doubted that there would be anyone but her and Mike in the projection room, but you never knew. Because it was a first rough cut of the picture, the Major might even show up. She scanned the clock. Damn Mike. He couldn't even be on time when it was his own picture. She prayed it would be good. Maybe it would remind him of how it had been between them when they were working together.

She waited another fifteen minutes before he finally arrived and hustled her outside.

Gloria halted in the driveway. A sleek white Jaguar XKE was parked at the curb. "Where did this come from?" she asked, as if she didn't know.

"It belongs to a friend. I'm taking it to my mechanic for a five-hundred-mile checkup." He got in beside her. "It's just being broken in. These things are highly tuned, and they need a little expert care." Mike gunned the motor as if to emphasize his point.

"And you're an expert, I suppose." Her voice betrayed a slight acidity.

"I'm helping to break it in," he replied pleasantly. "Any news on the picture deal?"

She wondered how long she could stall him. "They're talking it over. Maybe you should speak to someone about getting a replacement for the Curtis picture." Even to her own ears, the words sounded empty. The chances of Mike getting a job on the picture in Spain were next to hopeless. Only this morning, Obie had asked her to lay off her demands. "Don't press them any more," he told her, "or you'll antagonize them to the point where they'll hire another actress." They both knew this was something she could not afford.

"Maybe the Major will be at the screening," she said by way of conversation.

"I doubt it," said Mike. "Didn't you hear the news?"

"What news?"

"It was on the car radio when I drove over. Something about Helen Farmer being in the hospital and the Major rushing over with his own surgeon to treat her."

"Good God. What happened?"

Mike shrugged. "A freak thing. Hans Deitrick's German shepherd went for her face. I guess she's pretty badly disfigured."

Gloria shuddered. "How awful." Jesus, she thought, of all the hideous things to happen to an actress. It reminded her there were worse things than the possibility of losing Mike Stanton. Immediately, she felt guilty that her anxiety had been lessened at Helen Farmer's expense. Again, she shuddered.

They said little about the picture on the way home. Maybe it was better that way. Mike was distant. She did not know whether it was because he hadn't liked it or because he, like Gloria, had been struck by the camera's cruelty on her face. She had been shocked at the results of the lighting. Every unflattering line was harshly etched on the film. Gloria had almost burst into tears when she saw the first closeup. Relentlessly, horribly, the reels had rolled on with shot after shot aimed at tearing her face apart. She appeared as a pathetic pasteup of decaying glamour. The knowledge that she had never performed better gave her some satisfaction, but it was no match for the depression she felt. It occurred to her that, after what he had seen on film, Mike would not, could not, possibly make love to her tonight.

She went to the refrigerator to get him a beer. In the living room, Mike was dialing the phone, calling his service most probably. On an impulse, she set the beer can down and gently raised the receiver on the extension. A woman's voice was telling him that Miss Curtis had called twice and wanted him to return the calls, however late he returned. Gloria leaned against the counter. No matter what, she told herself, you can't fall apart tonight. It would only remind him of the harridan she had been on film. She took a deep breath, fighting for composure.

"Here," she said brightly, bringing him the filled glass.

"Thanks." He remained standing as he drank. "I've got to be on my way." He handed her the rest of the beer.

"Oh? Somebody whistled for you?" No, she cautioned herself, don't. Whatever you think, don't say it.

"Early day tomorrow."

"I understand." She opened the door for him. They were both acting, and they both knew it. Mike paused and gave her a perfunctory kiss, brushing her lips quickly as if, she thought, he were afraid I might hold him here.

She leaned against the closed door. The silent house. The empty room. There was a rip in the sofa slipcover that she had not noticed before. She took in the room, realizing with a dawning distaste that its furnishings looked tired. It appeared to her suddenly like a slightly worn stage setting, deliberately dated. Everything, everything was slipping through her fingers.

"I heard about Laura Curtis." Gloria was standing at the window, looking down at the street below. "Is she very ill?"

Obie pushed his chair away from his desk and leaned back, lighting a cigaret. "She's sick, but I don't think it's too serious. Some kind of kidney infection. She's in for observation. My hunch is that the Major thought it would do her good to spend a week in the hospital before she starts this picture. That way she'll be forced to rest. The girl drives herself too hard."

Gloria continued to stare out the window, her back to him.

"Gloria, let's get to the point. I have to give those guys

your answer by this afternoon. You can't drag your ass any longer, no matter what's eating you."

"I know," she answered faintly.

"One of the ways I earn my pay is by giving advice to my clients." He looked at the cigaret as if he had not noticed it before and snuffed it out in the ashtray. "You and I both know that you can't afford not to do this picture. I don't give a damn how hung up you are with Mike Stanton. In dollars and cents, he's worth nothing to you, and this job is worth a lot. That's all there is to it. I want you to say yes. Now." He waited.

She turned to him slowly. Obie noticed that her eyes were glistening with tears. "Are you sure," she pleaded, "that there is no chance for him to come too?"

"Shit!" He slammed his hand on the desk. "What do I have to do to convince you? It's no! How many times have I told you? Absolutely not. Jesus Christ, Gloria, do you want it in writing or something?"

"All right." She collected her things from a chair. "Tell them I'll do it."

Obie's tone gentled. "You're behaving as if this was a disaster. You've landed a picture, a picture you needed. It's not as if you'd lost out."

Gloria paused in the doorway. "No," she said, and started to add something else. Thinking better of it, she turned and left the office.

Obie stared at the closed door. It had been like pulling teeth, for God's sake. A ridiculous, small-potatoes deal like this, and he'd practically had to hit her over the head to make her accept it. He knew the score, of course. It was plain she'd gone off her tracks for Mike Stanton. One last, desperate attempt to prove she could still appeal to a good-looking young guy. Obie wondered if she was aware of how much time Mike was spending at the hospital with Laura. From what Laura said on the phone, it seemed as if he was there day and night. She didn't just talk about him, she effervesced. She repeated his anecdotes to Obie as if they were gems of wit. Sometimes, when he called her, she would break into laughter at some irrelevant aside from Mike who was also in her room.

It was just as well, Obie thought, to get Gloria out of this situation. Things could only become worse. From the look of it, Mike had transferred his allegiance to Laura Curtis without a backward glance. Sending Gloria off to Europe was an act of mercy.

"Can't it wait?" Mike asked.

Gloria gripped the phone. "No, damn it, it cannot. I want to see you."

"But I'm supposed to be someplace in half an hour."

"Mike, I have to see you. Right away."

He hesitated. "I can't stay long."

"Just get over here."

"Only for a few minutes."

"Christ! I'll set a timer!"

Gloria was trembling when she hung up the telephone. Why the hell had she called him in the first place? He hadn't phoned to check on the possibility of going to Spain since the night of the screening. It was an empty gesture, getting him to come over. Empty, yet somehow essential that she be able to summon him here, that she be the one to turn him down, to tell him they had no use for him on the film. She couldn't bear the thought that, had she not phoned him, he never would have called again at all. He would have let the whole thing die without a word, never making any attempt to contact her. No, she couldn't take that. It was important for her to end it her way, neatly dismissing him. It was a matter of dignity. No lousy, ass-kissing sonofabitch like Mike Stanton was going to dump her, not if she could help it.

When she reached for the knob, it only slipped against her moist palm. Hastily, she wiped her hand against her blouse and opened the door.

Mike strode past her without a glance. He tossed his jacket on the living-room sofa, waiting for her to join him. "I can't stay long."

"You said that. I wanted to talk to you about the European deal."

"What about it?" He remained standing as she seated herself on the sofa.

"Obie's been discussing it with the company." She stopped, torn between the truth and the desire to make the moment last. "They've been talking back and forth."

Mike said nothing, waiting. She glanced up at him. How

cool he looked, how self-confident, as if the opportunity hardly mattered to him. "Well?" he said finally.

"I knocked myself out, Mike," she said truthfully. "I pushed it to the limit, even to the point of offering a few concessions if they'd include you in the deal." In spite of herself, her voice started to break. "I went so far as to risk losing the picture, but——" she paused, shaking her head.

He stood there above her, wordless. Gloria reached out and touched his leg. Instinctively, he started to draw away, but, catching himself, turned the movement into a gesture of resignation. Gloria perceived the maneuver.

A sharpness came into her tone. "They said you were too inexperienced," she told him. "They didn't feel that having been a B-picture actor as a kid had much value. They said that having produced one documentary short that never sold was hardly a recommendation. Neither was having operated a shoestring theater that flopped. They just didn't think you had the stuff." She leaned back against the cushions, waiting for his reaction.

After a moment, he reached for his jacket. As it brushed by her, Gloria felt the familiar rough tweed and caught the scent of him on the material. She reached for it and held on. Mike glanced at her.

"Please." She tried to take it from him.

"Don't," he commanded and pulled it from her. A small box tumbled out of one of the pockets and onto the floor. Two gold earrings spilled out. Mike bent to pick them up. He did not look at her.

"A gift?" she managed.

"Her birthday is next week."

The ring of the telephone spared her. Her back to him, she made her way to the table to answer it.

"It's for you." She held the instrument out at arm's length as if wishing to rid herself of it.

He listened for a moment, then said, "No, it's all right. I told my service to give you this number. I didn't want you to think I'd forgotten what I'd said." After a pause, he spoke again. "When did it happen?" he demanded. "What do you mean they won't give you anything? No medication? They're insane. I'm coming right over. Don't worry." He slammed down the receiver.

Gloria was watching him. "Never stray too far from the feedbag, do you?"

"She's ill, for God's sake." He slipped into his jacket. "She needs me."

"Mike!" She followed after him.

He stopped at the doorway. "What?"

"Didn't it ever occur to you——Has it never occurred to you that I might need you?"

"Don't be silly. You'll find someone else. You're still a good-looking woman, Gloria." He turned and was gone.

The words stung like a slap. Perhaps it was not even the words themselves, but the cold lack of concern with which they had been delivered. Her life meant no more to him than that of an ant, carelessly demolished beneath his foot as he went on his way. She stood dumbly in the hall, too angry even for tears. Christ, how stupid she had been, thinking all this time that she was stringing him along, keeping him on the line with the promise of a job. It was herself she'd been stringing along, holding on for dear life to the hope that his own selfish motives would be sufficient to sustain his attentions. Jesus, she thought bitterly, I crawled for the sonofabitch. I groveled for that stinking bastard.

But all the rancor in the world did not make the silent hallway less empty.

Obie drove her to the airport. She said little, answering only when spoken to. He figured there had been a scene between her and Mike but chose not to bring up the subject. The last thing he wanted was to send her off in tears. He suspected she had had a few drinks earlier. Her face was flushed, and she seemed a little hard to reach. What the hell, maybe the plane flight scared her. A couple of belts before takeoff would ease her nerves. He glanced over to where she sat, uncommunicative, staring out the window at the freeway. He looked up at the clouds overhead.

"At least you won't have to face June in L. A.," he said. "Seems you could go anyplace and find better weather than this."

She nodded. She was glad to be getting out of the oppressive dampness of May and June. The heavy, gray layers of cold fog only depressed her more than ever. Once in a while a weak and watery sun showed through for an hour and was gone again. Bleak weather had settled over the city. She had to escape.

He walked with her to the departure gate. "Got all your papers, the script?"

"Yes."

"You need anything? Want me to pick up a couple of magazines?"

Gloria didn't reply. She gazed vaguely around her at the flow of movement in the waiting room. "I could use a drink."

"They've announced the flight. Better wait until you're on the plane. Listen," he said, "you'll have a good trip. The picture will be a smash. If you need me, just shoot me a cable or give me a call."

She looked at him a moment, unsmiling, and walked toward the passageway to the phone.

A zombie. She was like a goddam zombie. Obie strode hurriedly out of the terminal, relieved at having executed his duties. Gloria had damn well better snap out of it before she screwed up the picture and got herself canned. He shook his head. No, she was a pro. These broads were like trained animals. Once that film started to roll, they turned on the old stuff. If nothing else could help her, the simple fact of being in front of a camera would do the trick. He hoped.

The fact was, she had even enjoyed the picture. It was a piece of crap, she knew, but that had its advantages. Knowing it wasn't worth shit, she had no conscience about doing as she bloody pleased, though that usually meant turning up on the set the next day with a God-awful hangover. The night-life started late and increased in pitch until the early morning hours. Then one of them, Luis, Carlos, Diego, whatever their names were, would take her back to her hotel suite and spend the night. They had ready smiles and white teeth and treated her with a gallant deference. Once in bed, they murmured words she did not understand as they performed. Most of them wanted jobs as extras. She was glad to help. At least they had been plentiful and attentive.

To them, she was the senorita star. Some of her old pictures were still playing there in dubbed versions. She had gone one night to a crummy, rundown movie house with one of the smiling young men. It had sounded odd to hear herself speaking the lines in Spanish. She watched the film intently, while all the time, the dark-haired fellow stroked her thigh.

The suite in Spain had been three rooms. Now here she was holed up in one lousy room at the Plaza. Some swell welcome. New York was shut down for the Labor Day weekend. Hardly a soul walked the steaming streets. She glanced out of the window and watched the waves of heat rising from the pavement below. Across the way, in the park, the trees drooped listlessly above some few shirtsleeved people who lay with their eyes closed on the grass, immobilizied by the temperature.

Why the hell, she wondered, was she glad to be back? Over there she could still command her following of willing admirers. Here, she realized, only the inevitable, dreaded emptiness of the house on the coast awaited her. She supposed it had been the language that had eventually got to her. There was something about not understanding what the hell a guy was moaning when he came that had made the whole thing ridiculous after a while. All their grinning spic faces had begun to merge into each other, until she couldn't remember whether or not this one or that one had already had her.

It was good to hear people speaking English again. She turned from the window and switched on the television. Going to the dresser, she extracted a few cubes from the ice bucket and poured more vodka into her glass. On an impulse, she called the front desk and asked for the number of the nearest delicatessen.

She ordered greedily. She'd have a cheeseburger, chili, dill pickles, potato chips and, for good measure, a couple of cabbage rolls. Christ, she thought in anticipation, it is nice to be home. She settled back to wait for her order, idly enjoying the sound of her own language on the television. Eagerly, she watched the news, as if to catch up on everything she had missed in the time away. By the time the ball scores came on, she had poured herself another drink. She was aware she was getting a little loaded, but the food should be arriving soon. That would take the edge off. She eased into the chair again, balancing the glass precariously on its arm.

"This holiday weekend," the newscaster announced crisply, "had an especially festive note on California's Santa Catalina Island. The luxury yacht of film titan S. M. Victor was the site of one of Hollywood's fabled royal weddings." The camera traveled the length of the hulking white ship, flags fluttering from bow to stern. Gloria hunched forward in her chair, spilling part of her drink on the upholstery.

"The bride was movie princess Laura Curtis, and her groom, as in all such stories of make-believe, a mere commoner who managed to catch her eye and win her heart."

There they stood, kissing for the cameras. They drew back, laughing and kissed again while more flash bulbs popped. Mike's hair was disheveled. Laura reached up and smoothed it. Someone moved the Major into the picture, and he brushed at Laura's white veil which kept blowing across his face.

"The lucky man is former child actor Mike Stanton who was involved in the production of Miss Curtis' latest film. He is thirty-three. His bride is twenty. After a three-week honeymoon in Hawaii, the happy couple will journey to Mexico for an upcoming picture. *Amor*, as they say, *vincit omnia*. And now for the news of our metropolitan weather . . ."

For a moment Gloria sat perfectly still. Then, quite deliberately, her eyes on the set, she drew back her arm and aimed. With all her strength, she hurled the glass at the face of the screen, smashing them both to bits.

7

Lisa

3:15 P.M.

"Mrs. Haller?"

"What is it, Teresa?"

"There's a Miss Swensen on the telephone. She's trying to reach Mr. Haller."

"Tell her to call him at the studio."

"She did. They told her he was at home. She said to tell you she wants to borrow a print of a film she made for him. What should I tell her?"

"Try the office again. He's probably back there by now."

"Yes, Mrs. Haller."

"That damned Astrid. She's got a hell of a nerve calling Jack here. She thinks of Astrid first, and to hell with the rest. Even her own son. How could someone like Jack have fallen in love with Astrid in the first place? He must have had an inkling of what she was like.

But I didn't. Before I met Astrid I was scared to death of her. How well I remember the photographs. That beautiful porcelain face and masses of blonde hair. Those unbelievable legs, miles of them, and that svelte stretch of body. Ridiculous, isn't it, how insecure beautiful women are. Perhaps it was because her looks are so different from mine that I thought she could just wiggle her finger and repossess Jack. That, and the inescapable fact that she is the mother of his child. If only I had known her then. How different things might be. If I had met her then, seen for myself how uninterested she is in anything or anyone except Astrid Swensen, how changed all our lives might be. But no, all I knew was from photographs. Of all the times to have been such a damned fool. What a mess I made of things.

There it is again. The truth does exist. It is untidy. We cir-

209

cumvent it, politely trying to ignore it. And so, to all appearances, life goes on unchanged.

What a privileged class we are. Laura, me, all of us. . . . Elevated by success. We have our little armies of publicists and attorneys who issue polite stories to the press. And somewhere, safely insulated behind each convenient new truth, we live out our less than perfect lives.

There isn't one of us who would attempt to upset the system. Because there isn't a single closet without its resident skeleton.

All our safety lies within the system of privilege, and privilege lies with success. And nothing could possibly be wrong with that. It's positively wholesome.

Christ, what I wouldn't give not to be a cynic. But then, everything exacts its price, doesn't it?

"HAVE you heard from him?" Marty asked, handing Lisa a snifter of brandy.

"If you can call it that. Some ham operator halfway around the world acted as a relay. It was a pretty fitful dialogue, both of us yelling 'Now can you hear me better?' We had to take turns because of the radio hookup." She swirled the amber liquid and stared into the vortex. "It was a very stilted and antiseptic conversation."

"Where are they now?" Marty settled herself in Jack's Eames chair and propped his feet up on the ottoman.

"Still in the desert. Jack says that water has to be flown in daily and that half the company is sick with one thing or another. Things are going very slowly, he said."

"It sounds to me like a bitch of a location. You should be thankful you're here."

"I suppose so."

"Nothing's gone wrong with you two, has it?"

"Hardly. He hasn't even been around long enough to get into an argument."

"Do you want out?"

"No!" she flashed. "Of course not."

"Then I don't see why you're letting it upset you." Marty looked at her intently. "You went into this with your eyes open. It's not as if you were two kids. You're both professionals and you know the lumps this business can hand out."

Lisa was silent. Marty sensed the accumulated tension behind the facade. "Be honest with yourself. You knew there would be times like this."

"Goddam it!" She set her glass down hard on the table. "Why can't he be like other producers and oversee his locations by telephone?"

"You just told me there was no phone where he is. Lisa, you're acting like a spoiled child."

"Am I? Well, you try it like this for a while and see how you like it."

He attempted a good-natured smile. "Where's that spirit of giving that's supposed to be in these relationships?"

"Giving. It seems that's all I've been doing. Giving and forgiving. What I want to know is," she took a swallow of the brandy, "when is it going to be my turn for a change?"

"Aren't you planning to join him when they finish this location?"

"I was. We were supposed to meet in Yugoslavia two weeks from now, but that's all changed. They're behind schedule, and by the time they get there I'll have to be here to start shooting at Fox."

"That means postponing the marriage plans."

Lisa said nothing. He had struck the target. If Jack had only waited three weeks before leaving, his divorce would have been final and they would already have been married. But no, the film was too important and Jack had a responsibility to Victory Studios and the millions of dollars they were pouring into his project. When would he feel some sense of responsibility for her? Or would there always be another film, another excuse? It was not a need to be married now, this minute, that rankled. It was, rather, that Jack could tune out their plans with such facility.

"What are you thinking?" Marty asked.

"I'm beginning to wonder if Jack wants to be married at all." When she spoke again, her tone was clinical, as if she were holding the words at arm's length. "He took his and Valerie's breakup very hard at the time. I've heard the stories. Perhaps he took it harder than I thought." She gazed into her empty glass.

"Not that I'm agreeing with you in the least, but if worse

came to worse and that were the case, what's so wrong with just continuing to live together and taking life as it comes along? Is the ceremony so important?"

"It is if you want to have a child."

"Yes, I guess it is then." He glanced at his watch and eased himself out of the chair. "It's after midnight, and I have an early call in the morning. Lisa," he gave her shoulder a brief squeeze, "just because you're sitting here alone in this big house with nothing but your fantasies to entertain you, don't let those fantasies get the upper hand. Everything will be all right."

She had a sudden thought and shook her head regretfully. "Marty, I'm so sorry. I was the one who was supposed to cheer you up tonight."

"That's all right. If things had been meant to work out between Janet and me they would have."

"Still, it's hard to break up with someone you've been seeing for a long time."

"These things happen."

She listened to the sound of his car as it pulled out of the driveway. She began turning off the downstairs lights. Men were so sensible about things. To them, something either worked or didn't. They made it all so simple. It was black and white to them, but to a woman it would always be foggy, elusive shades of gray. It isn't sex we need them for, Lisa thought wryly, it's balance.

A Santa Ana wind was blowing, filling the air with fine, gritty dust. The dry hail pitted car windshields. It made eyes run red and throats go dry. It ground sandily between the teeth. As always with a Santa Ana, people became jumpy, and tempers were on a short fuse. The neighborhood dogs prowled restlessly and split the air with baying. Sleepers, roused by the roar of the wind through the twisting trees, lay awake, unable to doze off again.

Lisa rolled over in bed fitfully and, resigned to insomnia, folded her hands in back of her head and stared up at the dark ceiling. Outside, the ivy on the walls scratched against the side of the house. The sound was beginning to get on her nerves. Where in hell was her call? She had placed it with the overseas operator over five hours ago. The last time she had spoken to Jack in Belgrade the call had gone through in half an hour. She reflected uneasily on the headlines in the afternoon's paper. Was it possible that the border situation was spreading to Yugoslavia too? Surely nothing would happen to an American film company. Still, she would feel a lot better if Jack's voice were reassuring her. The paucity of information was frustrating. She had telephoned an AP reporter she knew to see if the wire service had any additional details, but the sudden exercise of strict press censorship around the satellite countries left little but rumor and speculation.

At six fifteen her alarm rang. Lisa dressed and drove to the studio. The wind had toppled trees and torn off branches. In the makeup department people cursed the Santa Ana and told exaggerated stories of its damage in attempts to top each other. Lisa made the effort to listen, but her attention wandered impatiently. Between hairdressing and makeup, she stepped into the department office and called the overseas operator once again. The lines, she was informed, were still tied up. She gave the number of her dressing room on the sound stage and said to keep trying.

Keith patched up the circles under her eyes without comment. The wardrobe woman clucked over the fact that she was losing weight and the clothes might have to be refitted. She instructed Lisa to drink a chocolate malted with an egg in it. The thought turned Lisa's stomach.

The morning dragged. She was chain-smoking, much to her annoyance. The prop man laid a supply of cigarets in front of her. Keith said a few words to the gaffer who glanced in her direction and nodded. "Give me a magenta for that eyelight," he ordered. "Looks like we have to add some sparkle to her baby blues." Twice Lisa blew a take for no reason. Several times she asked the hour, only to find out that it was not yet even eleven o'clock. Distractedly, she rehearsed a new camera setup. "Buoyancy," the director was saying, "buoyancy is what we're going to need here. It's a key comedy scene, and we can't let it go flat on us." She nodded. "Second team," called the assistant, and Lisa stepped out as the stand-in took her place. As she walked into her dressing room, the telephone was ringing.

"Are you all right?" was the first thing she said.

"Yes." Jack's voice was slightly muffled by the distance. "So far things are pretty cool here. There's some tension in the air, but everything, the newspapers, the radio, the transportation, is functioning as usual. We're operating as if things were perfectly normal."

"But what if something happens?"

"Then we'll pack up and get out."

"Will you be able to do that?"

"Let's hope so. At the most, they wouldn't do more than detain us a few hours. The move would force us to scrap a lot of shooting, though. I'd rather not think about that possibility."

"Jack, for God's sake," she said, "here I am worried to death about your safety, and you sit there thinking about your cans of film."

"That's my job. Besides, this country has a record of not getting pulled into these skirmishes. My money's on the Yugoslavs. I wouldn't worry, if I were you."

"All the same, I do."

"That's because you're so far away. Look," he reassured her, "it's a beautiful cold clear night here. From my window I can see the city lights and plenty of cars on the streets and people walking on the sidewalks. What could be more ordinary?"

"I hope you're right. Jack, I have a piece of good news. It looks like I'll have the week before Thanksgiving off from work. They're shooting some stuff that I'm not in."

"Good. You'll have yourself a paid vacation."

Lisa caught her frowning reflection in the mirror above the makeup table. "Jack," she began again, "you know I want to be with you. Couldn't I join you, even if it's only for a few days?"

There was a moment's silence. "Lisa, I don't think that would be wise. After all, we are on sort of a standby alert here."

"But you just said nothing was going to happen!"

"I said it looked as if nothing would happen, but I'm not God. I can only make an educated guess. It's one thing for me because I'm already here. It's quite another thing for you to decide to take a pleasure jaunt in the middle of an international crisis. It's sheer foolishness."

"It's no more foolish than you staying there pretending nothing's going on when you may be sitting on a time bomb."

"It damn well is. Use your head. I have a responsibility here."

"I'm sick of your responsibility!" Then, lowering her voice, she said, "Jack, I'm sorry. I didn't mean it. It's just that I've been worried and I miss you. We have a Santa Ana wind here that's making us all jittery."

"If it's any comfort," he told her, "I just realized that the week you're talking about we'll be out in the countryside. You'd be bored to death spending your days alone in Belgrade while I was off filming chase scenes."

"I suppose." Lisa didn't want the conversation to end on a depressing note. "What else is happening over there?"

"Nothing but aggravation. Carmela Conte is giving us trouble."

"Your sexy lady spy? I didn't think she was shooting yet."

"She isn't. The unit publicist went to Rome last week and happened to run into her. He says she's gained at least ten pounds since we cast her. Looks like Miss Pasta, he said. We sent word to her to knock it off before she gets here. The last thing I need right now is a chubby spy. Now tell me, what happened to the Rams on Saturday?"

"They won."

There was a knock at the dressing-room door. "We're ready out here."

"Jack? I have to go."

"Okay. You just got me a free bottle of Polish vodka. I had a bet on the game with our cameraman."

"Wonderful," she said with more than a trace of bitterness.

He seemed not to have noticed. "Take care of yourself and don't worry anymore."

"I love you, Jack."

"Ditto." He hung up the telephone.

Ditto, for Christ's sake, thought Lisa. For Christ's sake.

The wind abated a day later. Despite the balmy, sunny days of California's subtle autumn, Lisa remained tense. The film was going well. It wasn't that. Her days were relatively bearable. The nights were not. She dined out occasionally with friends, but increasingly she missed the closeness of her man. Polite table conversation was no substitute. The overseas calls only served to emphasize the distance between her and Jack. Regardless of the phone company's slogans, there was no next best thing to being there. You can't, she began to realize, maintain a relationship by long distance.

It was almost nine in the morning when Lisa and Keith stepped out of the makeup department into the glaring sunshine. They headed for the stage, discussing the day's work. Behind the administration building a small group had clustered in the street. One of them called out to Keith and pointed to the north. They turned to look. A small wisp of smoke curled gracefully upward from the hilly horizon.

"Where do you think it is?" Lisa asked quietly.

"Hard to tell for sure. Near Mulholland, maybe up at the reservoir." He watched the pale gray plume puff its way silently up into the brilliant blue sky. "Has anyone reported it?" he asked the group at large.

"Fifteen minutes ago," someone said. "It was only half the size it is now."

"Let's get to the stage," Keith urged. "I think I'd better call home. It looks like it could be fairly close to us."

There was already a line of three or four anxious people waiting to use the phone on the set. Lisa stepped outside while Keith dialed from her dressing room.

"Nothing," he said as he exited. "Mary says she heard the engines, but they didn't seem to be nearby."

"That's a relief."

"Those hills are too damn dry for comfort, and that wind we had dried them out even more. There's nothing but greasewood growing up there, and that stuff goes up like a torch."

"I know," said Lisa, "but if worse comes to worse, they'll send up the borate bombers from Burbank. Come on," she smiled, "Mary would have told you if there was any danger."

The morning's work went as expected. One of the extras had a transistor portable and was keeping tabs on the fire. So far the reports had it well under control. It was a small flareup in the brush near the top of Sepulveda Boulevard. The fire department had it contained between a fire break and the concrete stretch of the San Diego Freeway. Within the dusky stage, immersed in the light business of comedy, everyone was pleasantly insulated from any great degree of concern. Nevertheless, Keith left early before the lunch break to drive home and take a look for himself.

The smoke had grown thicker. On the way to the commissary Lisa noticed that the sun had been turned almost blood rcd by the haze of the fire. It was reflected rustily against the windows of the administration building. That color of sun was a phenomenon that brought uneasiness to anyone who had ever seen it before. Lisa found it difficult to enjoy her food. She sipped distractedly at her coffee and finally got up and paid the cashier.

A curious sight stopped her on the commissary steps. Several cars passed by on the studio street, each crammed with books and furniture. A few feet away, her assistant director stood observing the caravan. "Charlie?" she called out. "What is it?"

"The fire jumped the freeway half an hour ago."

"But how could it? It's not possible, is it?" She ran toward him. "There's hardly any wind today."

He nodded grimly. "These fires make their own drafts. Sometimes the damn things blow close to cyclone force."

"Jesus."

"Look." He pointed at the smoke-shrouded hills. The flames themselves had become visible, spouting into the sky. From the valley side of the mountains two bombers, small and copper-colored in the distance, flew low over the terrain, dropped their cargos of borate and circled back toward the airport to reload. "Those bastards have all the guts in the world," he said admiringly. "Let's get back to the set. There'll be a few replacements on the crew this afternoon. They're evacuating the houses between Sepulveda and Beverly Glen on both sides of the hills. Some of our men have gone home to help."

"Where's Keith?" the sound mixer asked Lisa as she came through the stage door. "His wife's on the phone."

"I'll take it," she told him, lifting the receiver. "Mary? It's Lisa Taylor. Where are you?"

"I'm at the synagogue on Wilshire Boulevard in Westwood. The Red Cross has set up a center here to assign evacuees to motels and hotels. Where is Keith?" She raised her voice above a background of babble.

"He went home over an hour ago. He was worried."

"I don't think he'll get there. They've set up roadblocks to keep people out."

"Where are the children?" Lisa couldn't keep the fear out of her tone.

"Their school was the first thing to be cleared out. The

classes were split into two groups. They're either at UCLA or one of the churches in Westwood. When I find out which, I'll pick them up and take them wherever we're told to go."

"Do you need anything? Were you able to pack?"

"There wasn't any time." Mary's voice wavered slightly. "I looked out the kitchen window, and the smoke seemed quite far away. Then ten minutes later the police rang the doorbell, and when I answered I could see the flames only two blocks up the street. All I have is the clothes on my back and the children's christening mugs. The dog ran away. I had to leave him."

"God. Mary, is there anything I can do? Do you want to come and stay at my house? It's close to Sunset Boulevard, right near UCLA. I'm sure it's safe."

There was a pause at the other end of the line. "Lisa?" Mary asked tentatively. "Have you checked to make sure?"

"Of what?"

"Don't take my word for it," she said hesitantly, "because there are so many rumors flying around, but I think you'd better call the police. I heard they were clearing out the Bel Air Hotel. That's near your place, isn't it?"

Lisa felt a sudden constriction of fear. It couldn't be true. "Mary," she said quickly, "I'll have someone tell Keith to call you."

Her hand shook slightly as she dialed. The house was the one tangible, solid thing that she and Jack shared. In the lonely evenings she would wander through it from room to room, occasionally touching the walls or a piece of furniture tenderly. Here was the bed they loved in. Here would someday be the nursery. Here would lie their future, under this roof. With Jack gone, Lisa took her reassurance from the presence of this place, these things that they had brought together and among which they would live out their lives. It had become the sole symbol of her security.

"I'm sorry," the voice was crisp, "but that area was evacuated a short time ago. Your radio and television will keep you posted."

She hung up. For a moment her mind was blank then, panicked, she remembered the closets in the study. Locked inside them were all of Jack's business papers, his tax records, his contracts, outlines of scripts, cost breakdowns, all the paperwork on which his company was structured. It was irreplaceable. She bolted for the door of the stage.

"Lisa," Charlie stopped her, "we're closing down for the day. I just got the word from the front office."

She brushed past him without a response.

In spite of the fact that it was only early afternoon, the light outside resembled sunset. Smoke had darkened the entire sky, all but obscuring the deep red disc that glowered above the blazing hills. A fine fall of ash was sifting out of the air. The green of the box hedges lining the walkway was fading to a dull gray. Her sweater brushed the flat-cut top of a bush and became soiled with cinders.

Lisa halted her car at the police roadblock and got out, but no amount of persuasion or argument was successful. She was not allowed through. Wheeling around, she drove quickly into the nearest driveway and abandoned the car. She stopped a moment to get her bearings, then raced through the driveway and into the rear garden of a house that belonged to no one she knew. Frantically, she made her way through a series of back yards, their flower gardens drabbed by the pall of gray. At one point, faced with a high wall, she dragged some pieces of metal patio furniture against it and, piling a chair on top of a round table, lifted herself up and over. Swimming pools lay placidly unoccupied, their small waves lapping at the coping. Houses had been deserted in the midst of daily activity. Here a door had been left open. Here a basket of needlework and one half-darned sock rested on a porch table. It seemed totally unreal that she, Lisa Taylor, filthy with soot, should be running, gasping for breath through the premises of strangers, alone, as if she were the only human being left to trespass on these vacant lawns.

She could hear the fire now, crackling ominously somewhere in the hills above her. In the streets, the wail of sirens and the shouts of men seemed closer. She pushed open the service gate and stumbled up the rear steps to the house.

In the pantry the ironing board lay open, a partly pressed sheet over it. Lisa grabbed the laundry cart and overturned it spilling the wash onto the floor. The maid, Teresa, was gone. Lisa rolled the cart ahead of her into the study and unlocked the closets. She filled the cart with Jack's papers. There were too many. She had to stop and select those she knew were most important. What she could not get into the laundry bin she stuffed into a pillowcase retrieved from the pantry floor. She dumped the lot at the front door and ran into the dining room. All the silver was stored in the sideboard. She pulled out each drawer in turn and, staggering under the weight, went through the open door to the patio and threw the contents into the swimming pool.

Lisa knew she had to get out. She shoved her load of precious papers ahead of her down the brick walk to the street. A piece of flaming wood fell at her feet. Across the way two firemen stood on the roof of her neighbor's house, wetting down the shingles. She noticed they did not have sufficient water pressure for the job. The street was snaked with hoses. Near one of the engines, men were hurriedly setting up a portable pumping unit to drain the water from an adjacent swimming pool.

"Christ, lady!" a patrolman grabbed her arm. "What the hell are you still doing here?" Not waiting for an answer, he maneuvered her to a police car. She pushed Jack's belongings onto the rear seat. Wordlessly, the cop piloted her back down toward Sunset Boulevard. He swerved the car to avoid a flock of animals. There were darting cats, a few panicky yelping dogs, rabbits with their fur singed. She turned away from the spectacle only to catch sight of another pack of animals. They were fleeing down a driveway and into the rain gutter. Lisa thought at first that they were small rabbits. She looked closer. They were rats, running down from the hills ahead of the flames. Nausea seized her and she gagged.

She was deposited at her car. She thanked the cop briefly and watched him as he turned back toward the smoking street. Resting her head on the steering wheel, she tried to take a deep breath. She glanced into the rear-view mirror and hardly recognized her besmirched face. From somewhere in her throat came a wild, uncontrolled laugh, and Lisa sat there in the car, howling, surrounded by her stacks of paper until, finally, her hysteria turned to tears and subsided.

"Your maid called," Marty told her as she came from her shower. "She's at her sister's."

Lisa paced to the window. The night sky was illuminated by a hazy pink glow that glimmered and flashed like an aurora borealis.

"Beautiful, isn't it?"

"It's almost difficult to comprehend something that lovely being so destructive." She sagged onto the sofa.

"Want a drink?"

"I could use one. God, but I hope nothing has happened to the house. It seems as if all our hopes are locked up in that house. I'm not even through furnishing it."

"That may turn out to be a lucky break." Marty handed her a glass.

"Don't try to prepare me for the worst. I've already faced up to the fact that there may be nothing left. Marty, turn on the television while you're up. I want to see what's happening."

For two days she knew nothing. The entire city stayed by its radio and television sets. Scene after scene recorded only the ugly stumps of chimneys protruding from flattened, still-smouldering ruins of what once were homes. There were camera shots of pedestrians applauding and cheering the exhausted, soot-encrusted firefighters as they passed in their trucks. Commentators voiced dark warnings of floods to come, once the winter rains hit the now barren earth. At night, as the photo helicopters cruised above the charred streets, there would be an occasional explosion of flame as another house burst and burned. Only rarely was an address given, a precaution against the possibility of looting. For the evacuees, the suspense was almost unbearable.

"Have you spoken to Jack?" Marty asked.

"What would I tell him? I don't know anything yet. He has enough on his mind without this."

"He may be worried about you if he's heard about it."

"He couldn't have. He would have tried to reach me at home, and when he couldn't he would have called you. I'll wait to phone him until I know what's happened. Look," Lisa pointed to the TV set. Four firemen were working a small section of brush which suddenly, without warning, leapt into house-high flames, lashing at their clothing. Breaking into a run, they rushed to safety, chased by a wall of fire.

Lisa shook her head. "I don't know how they do it." They passed by the television camera, their faces bleary with fatigue. "They keep the rest of us going. Anyone who complains has to feel like a fool when he sees what those men are doing up there."

"Agreed. Come on, Lisa, let's get away from it for a while.

It's beginning to get us both down. I'll take you to La Scala for dinner. It'll keep your mind off things for a couple of hours. Have you got a dress to wear?"

"I borrowed some clothes from the studio. But I don't know—" she hesitated.

"Don't be an ass. We still have to eat. Go get dressed."

They ran into several people they knew. A macabre carnival atmosphere prevailed. High-strung by the shared tension, with no homes to go to, they spent a long evening cheering each other with lame jokes and anecdotes of the absurdities they had found themselves performing in the frenzy of evacuation.

The news came over the car radio as Lisa and Marty were driving home. Late in its third day, the fire had been contained. Residents were asked to check their local police stations for information as to when they would be allowed to return to their particular areas.

For Lisa there was no feeling of relief. She still did not know what, if anything waited for her on the hill. She pictured herself going back, driving up the road toward a house which might be there and might not. What words were there, she wondered, to break the news to Jack if all their plans and hopes had been reduced to nothing.

But it was there. The ivy on its walls had been baked dry in the heat of the flames, and the paint on the doors and shutters had bubbled. The rose bushes in the garden had dried up and were covered with a thick layer of cinders. Along the roof line, the shingles were charred. Inside, the house reeked of smoke. Nevertheless, it had fared better than most on the street. The fire had been stopped two houses away by a shift in the wind. Only that sudden caprice had spared it.

Teresa opened all the windows and set herself to the job of washing them clean again. By the time Lisa came from the studio, the house had taken on a semblance of normalcy, despite the fact that the street outside still looked like a seared battleground. The telephone company had strung lines to those homes still standing. The postman, Teresa reported, had delivered four days' mail.

Lisa poured herself a Scotch, if only to get something other than the flavor of smoke in her mouth and nostrils. She dumped the mail on the desk, and, checking her watch, put in a call to Jack. As she held the phone to her ear, listening absently to its static, she glanced over the mail. An item in the morning's *Variety* caught her attention.

SWENSEN SIGNED

Astrid Swensen, internationally known fashion model, has been signed by producer Jack Haller to make her film debut in *The Jonas File* currently shooting in Yugoslavia. Miss Swensen replaces the ailing Carmela Conte.

Lisa stared at the page in disbelief.

She tried to keep her voice even. "Did I wake you?" she asked apologetically.

"That's okay." Jack yawned audibly.

"I thought you'd want to know that things are fine here."

"I figured they were." He yawned again.

"No," explained Lisa, "I mean about the fire. I guess you couldn't have heard. We've had a dreadful fire here. Hundreds of houses are gone." Her voice began to rush the words. "I didn't call you before because I had to evacuate and I didn't know until today that we still had a home. I didn't want to worry you if I could help it."

"I wasn't worried," he said pleasantly. "I knew about it. A couple of people on our crew got calls from home. I knew from what they told me that you must have been evacuated too."

Lisa halted. "But you didn't feel it necessary to call?"

"I figured you could take care of yourself. Anyway, how would I know where to reach you?"

"You might have called the answering service or tried Marty."

"But why? You just said that you wouldn't have been able to tell me anything. I knew that when you had the score you'd call or cable."

"I was very frightened, Jack. We had so much to lose, especially your things, your papers. I managed to get most of them out. So many of the people around here haven't anything left."

"Well, there wasn't much either one of us could have done about it, was there?"

"No, I guess not." Yet she was stunned that he had known

what was happening and never tried to contact her, to find out if either she or their home had been in danger. The telephone rested coolly against her cheek, as if to emphasize the lack of warmth she felt.

"Are you there?" Jack asked.

"I'm here. I read an interesting item in today's *Variety*. Is it true you've signed Astrid Swensen?"

"It's true. We had to replace Carmela."

Lisa fought to keep her tone conversational. "What was the matter? It said she was ill."

"Ill, hell. She was four months pregnant. Claimed she didn't know it, the bitch."

"Who got the bright idea of using Astrid?"

"Don't get sarcastic on me, Lisa. It was the Major's idea. He had just seen a test of her that was made in Rome. He's signed her to a picture deal."

"You were quite specific about wanting a big European name for the part. You said it was important for your overseas grosses. You mentioned that several times."

"True, but with Victory studios launching one of their blockbuster publicity campaigns, Astrid will be as popular as Coca-Cola by the time the picture comes out. She's really quite good. I was pleasantly surprised."

There was a silence as Lisa tried to sort out her thoughts. She couldn't contain herself. "I wondered if that might be the reason you hadn't called to see if I was safe."

Jack sighed tiredly. "Don't act like a fool, Lisa. I knew I'd hear about it if you weren't. It would be front-page news if you went up in smoke."

"Jack! Jesus Christ, what the hell kind of thing is this to joke about? You almost lost everything you own and you're acting as if you couldn't care less! What in the name of God is the matter with you?"

"I'm sleepy. Exhausted. Things are still unsettled here, and I've been knocking myself out to get this picture shot. I don't need you shrieking at me like a fishwife in the middle of the night."

"You're a callous bastard. Don't you give a damn about anything?"

"Yes. I give a damn about getting this show wrapped and getting back to California as fast as I can. Does that satisfy you?"

"Don't try to satisfy me. You wouldn't want to blemish an unbroken record."

"Didn't anyone ever tell you that caustic women are not attractive?"

"Thanks for the information. How do you expect me to react when I find out that you and your girl friend are sitting there together while your home almost burns to the ground?"

"For Christ's sake, is that what's bothering you, Lisa? Listen, I'm a lot more concerned with the snow that's falling and our camera motors freezing up than the charms of Miss Swensen. Now, will you drop the subject?"

"Did she bring her child with her?"

"No, she did not."

"When are you coming home?"

"At this point it's hard to tell. This freak weather is giving us trouble. I'd say shortly after New Year's."

"But that's almost two months away! Won't we have Christmas together? I'll be off the picture by then. I could fly over for the holidays."

"Wait and see. With conditions the way they are now, we may be buried under ten feet of snow."

"Wait and see?" she repeated.

"Wait and see."

"Goodnight, Jack." She hung up the phone, buried her face in her hands and burst into tears.

The instrument at her side rang shrilly. She grabbed for it, but it was only Obie on the other end.

"I conclude your place is still there, seeing the telephone is intact."

"Yes, we were lucky."

"Did I wake you? Your voice sounds odd."

"No." She cleared her throat. "Is that better?"

"It sounded strained. Not that I blame you. These past few days must have worn your nerves raw."

"I guess they did."

"Ruth and I weren't sure we'd be able to reach you, but we decided to give it a try and see if you'd join us for dinner tonight. We're going to Scandia. Shall we pick you up at eight?"

She probably never should have gone. She had been tired to begin with. Whether it was simple carelessness or an attempt to relieve the accumulated tensions and disappointments of the last few days, Lisa didn't know, but she found herself drinking more than usual. First there were the cocktails, then wine with dinner, then brandy with their coffee. The brandy gave her insomnia. Or perhaps the brandy was not what gave her the insomnia at all. At any rate, in the morning she had a blinding headache. At least it was Saturday and she didn't have to go to the studio. She had, in fact, nothing much to do except to drop in at the Marvin Newman Galleries and inspect some dining chairs she was thinking of buying for the breakfast room. She wanted to give them a second look before making any bids.

She slid her dark glasses up into her hair and bent down to scrutinize the needlepoint on the chair seats. It was slightly worn but had an antique charm that pleased her. Having nothing better to do, she wandered through the cool, softly-lit gallery, aimlessly inspecting various pieces that caught her eye. She had a vague, diffused feeling of malaise, of being without a sense of direction. Readjusting her sunshades against the daylight, she left the building.

"Give me a hand with this, will you?"

Lisa turned. "I beg your pardon?"

His head appeared from behind the trunk of a red Mercedes coupe. "It's me, Lisa. Mike Stanton. Hold this trunk open, will you? It keeps closing on me."

She held it up for him. "What have you got there?" she inquired as he hoisted several newspaper-bandaged packages.

"When I get it assembled it'll be a chandelier that'll knock your eyes out. There are so many prisms it looks like an ice storm." He placed the first bundle gingerly inside the trunk.

"Aren't you afraid they'll get broken riding in there?"

"Jesus, I hope not. The goddamn thing cost a fortune. It's something old man Hearst bought in Europe and never lived to install."

"Maybe you ought to put it in the front seat."

"I'd still have to hold it steady. How would I drive?" Mike straightened up and surveyed the contents of the trunk. "You're right," he said reluctantly. "Can't leave it like that. Lisa," he turned to her, "I'll make you a deal. Get in the front seat and let me pile this stuff on your lap and on the floor between your feet. Help me take it up to the house, and I'll buy you lunch and bring you back to your car."

She couldn't see that he had any alternative if he were to get his precious cargo home intact. "Okay," she shrugged and got into the car.

The house was a splendid Regency off Coldwater Canyon. Lisa remarked on its elegance.

"I know. It's too damn much, isn't it?" Mike said proudly. "Laura has this idiot New England thing about vine-covered cottages, but I finally persuaded her that she needs a home that's a little more imposing. In keeping with her position, if you follow me."

"I follow you," she said, which was a fact, as she trailed after him through the cavernous foyer into a pastel-and-gilt salon.

"This is the reception room. Like it?"

"Who wouldn't? It's beautiful. Laura's done a fantastic job of decorating." Her eyes traveled over the damasks and the Aubusson carpet.

"Laura, hell. I worked with the decorator. Laura's too busy with scripts to fool around with this stuff. Anyhow, she doesn't know enough about antiques. As far as she's concerned, all this stuff could have come from the prop room at the studio. Besides, she has no patience. She wants it all done yesterday."

"Where is Laura?" Lisa thought to ask.

"Mexico. Sit down." He lay back on the green silk sofa and propped his feet up on a Chinese jardiniere that held a small lemon tree.

Lisa joined him on the sofa. "Do you have any trouble getting help up here?" she asked vacantly. "Cabrillo Drive is pretty far from town. I hope your maid drives." What an inane conversationalist I am today, she thought.

"It's a bitch. That's one of the reasons I came back. The couple we had called us in Mexico to say they were quitting. I came back to interview people so we'd have someone by the time Laura comes home next week. So far I haven't come up with anybody." Mike lit a cigaret, crumpled the empty package, and tossed it into the jardiniere.

"Did you enjoy Mexico?"

"Yes and no. I took it for a month. The first couple of weeks were okay. Then it got to be a drag." He brushed a shred of newspaper off his shirt.

"Where were you?" Dull, thought Lisa. I am dull today.

"Mexico City, at the Maria Isabel."

"But that's a beautiful place. How could you not like it?"

"Not enough to do."

"You can't be serious." She gave him a look of disbelief. "Didn't you see the Pyramids of the Sun and the Moon? Did you go to Chapultapec Park, to the museum? You must have shopped along the Niza. And the marvelous restaurants. There's so much to do in Mexico City, how can you say that?"

"Easy, I got bored stiff hanging around Cherubusco Studios. Christ, Laura's got her hairdresser, her makeup man, her wardrobe mistress, a stand-in, a secretary, a dialogue coach, and an interpreter. I damn near got lost in the crowd. I'm not going to end up being somebody's gofer, ferrying cups of coffee to her retinue. I cut out." He threw his cigaret into the jardiniere.

"Doesn't Laura mind being alone?" she asked quietly. "I do."

"She hates it, but somebody had to come back and look after the house. It's just as well. Things were getting tense between us. All that spare time got on my nerves."

Lisa couldn't resist the impulse. "Really?" She glanced at him draped languidly across the sofa. "It doesn't seem to be killing you now."

"It was different down there. I became like an extra piece of baggage. I felt like some sort of appendage. If Laura had had any sense, she'd have had them put me on as associate producer." As an afterthought he added, "I could have smoothed things out for her and made it an easier job. She needs that."

"Maybe you do too."

"Sure I do. A guy has to keep up his standards. The last thing I thought was that marrying Laura would hurt my career." He stretched impatiently. "I'll show you the rest of the house before I take you back," he said, as if the tour were an expected part of the package.

"Like it?" Mike was pointing to the Meissen china ranked for display behind its glass cupboard doors.

"Nice."

"These are Baccarat." He flicked the side of a goblet with his thumb and forefinger and listened appreciatively to its pure and resonant note. "But this," he paused in front of a large double-doored closet, "is the pièce de résistance. Get a load of this." He opened the doors wide and stepped back. From floor to ceiling, the closet was crammed with gleaming vermeil of every shape and size. "Flatware," he indicated, "plates, candlesticks, tea service, centerpieces. It was part of an estate. I didn't want to see it get broken up."

"You're a regular magpie, you know that?"

He turned. "What the hell do you mean? Don't you like it?"

"Of course I like it. What's not to like? It's just that you act like a Midas, roaming around this huge house, gloating over the bright shiny objects you've amassed."

Mike gave her a long cool look. "Just what the fuck is eating you, lady? What is it with these smart-ass remarks? I offered to show you around the place. I didn't ask for any editorial comments."

"You did not offer," she countered. "You didn't give me any alternative."

"I'm giving you one now. Fuck off." He slammed the closet doors.

"Take me back to my car," she demanded.

"Call a cab. There's the phone."

"Damned if I will! You're going to take me back to my car! You're just angry because I exposed you for what you are!"

"Which is?" he asked softly.

"You're an arrogant, greedy social-climber."

He slapped her hard across the face. Just as hard, Lisa struck him back. Suddenly, she hid her face in her palms and cried. "Damn. Shit. How stupid."

"Then what made you do it? Answer me, you bitch!"

"I don't know." The tears streamed down her cheeks. "I'm sorry, Mike. Nobody has any right to comment on anyone else's marriage. I'm sorry."

"Damn right. How would you like some loudmouth taking potshots at your marriage?"

"There may not be one." She stopped, stunned by the words that had come out.

"Oh, for God's sake, is that what's eating you? Why didn't you say something before?"

"It's none of your business."

"It is now. You made it my business when you started taking it out on me. Wipe your face. I'll get us a drink."

She sat beside him on the green sofa. Mike poured the last drops from the bottle of Château Lafite Rothschild '61 into their glasses.

"We're in the same boat, baby. Jack and Laura are just too busy for us. Bruises the ego, doesn't it? What do you recommend we do about it?"

"I don't know," she said tiredly.

"You'll think of something."

She glanced at him sharply.

Very slowly, Mike smiled.

"You're crazy," she said.

"I don't think it's such a crazy idea. After all, what better way to while away a lonely afternoon?" He watched her face expectantly.

"It's time for me to go." But she hesitated a moment.

"Uh-uh." Mike shook his head and slid toward her, covering her mouth with his.

Lisa lay among the twisted sheets, inert. It frightened her a little that she did not feel guilty.

"What are you thinking?" Mike asked her.

"Not a hell of a lot." She closed her eyes.

"Did I tell you this bed was part of Hearst's stuff too?"

"Good Lord," she said, her eyes still shut, "don't you have anything that isn't labeled?"

"Don't start that crap again."

"What is it with you? You've been married two months and you're lying in bed with another woman."

"Are you complaining?"

"Hardly."

He was silent for a moment. "It's difficult. Especially with her. Laura's never had anyone she was really close to. Sometimes she overcompensates. She gets so possessive, I think she's going to suffocate me." He scratched his chest pensively.

"I know what happened. You woke up one morning all clammy with the realization that you were suddenly supposed to be a responsible married man. It scared you to death, and you're trying to outrun the feeling."

"How do you know so much?"

"Just lucky I guess. Why did you get married if it's so abhorrent to you? There are other ways of collecting vermeil." She took a calculated pause. "As you well know."

Mike glanced over at her. "You don't like me much, do you?"

"I would say," she smiled slightly, "that horizontal you are terrific. Vertical, I suspect you are a bit of a shit."

"She needs me," he said simply.

"For this?" Lisa's gesture took in the bed.

Mike ignored it. "She needs someone who puts her interests ahead of anything else. It's not a question of having an agent or manager. She needs someone to protect her from things she shouldn't have to be bothered with." He rolled over and lit a cigaret, balancing the ashtray on his bare stomach.

"Such as?" persisted Lisa.

"Buying this house. Getting it furnished and staffed. If I'd left it up to her, she'd have a goddamn Cape Cod cottage and the realtor would have taken her for every cent. The only trouble with this place is that there's no room for a tennis court."

"How awful," said Lisa drily.

"Not really," he rejoined pleasantly. "We didn't plan for this house to be anything permanent. Laura's got a bundle of cash coming to her. When we collect, we'll find something more suitable."

Lisa appraised him with an incredulous look. He was dead earnest, probably counting dollar signs in his head as he watched the smoke unfurl from the tip of his cigaret. "What money is that?" she asked him.

He inhaled deeply. "Some toy company failed to get proper authorization for a Laura Curtis doll. The suit has been hanging fire for a few years. Now it looks as if we'll have a settlement in six months. The attorney says we can expect about twenty thousand dollars."

"That'll buy a lot of chandeliers, won't it?"

"Cunt."

"Give me one of those, please." She raised her head off the pillow while he lit her cigaret. "I just find you appallingly acquisitive," she dropped back onto the sheets, "that's all."

"Marriage is a bargain, fifty-fifty."

"So we've all heard. Tell me," she rolled over on her side and faced him, "what does Laura get for her fifty percent?"

"Plenty. She gets someone who puts her interests first."

"I know, I know. You hire and fire the household help."

"Listen," he propped himself up on his elbows, "Laura has a fantastic career ahead of her. Those idiots at Victory haven't even begun to scratch the surface of her talents. All they're interested in is exploiting her for the quick and easy buck. And Obie's not far behind. He'd rather not rock the boat where his ten percent is concerned. She needs someone who knows what she's really capable of doing, someone who channels her artistic ability into the areas where it'll be most productive." He gave an emphatic nod.

"How do you plan to do that?"

"I've already started. I pick out the songs she records. Hell, I know her better than anyone else. I know what fits her personality. I give her the advice she needs on packaging her image. Christ, what a hassle I had with that faggot costumer in Mexico. You should have seen the junk he planned to hang on her."

"Mike," she asked casually, "do you have any plans to produce?"

"Damn right. Laura and I are going to form our own company. She should have better scripts than that crap she's getting from Victor." He stubbed out his cigaret with firm little jabs. "When we get some black ink into the company books, we'll buy out the rest of her contract with the Major. Then watch us take off." His hand made a swooping motion.

Lisa smiled.

He leaned over and flicked her nipple with his tongue.

"No."

"Shut up."

He excited her with subtle skill, his hands and mouth teasing her flesh. She let out a moan, and he covered her mouth with his hand. Lisa felt her body began to twist involuntarily. Her tongue tasted his hand strong with the scent of tobacco. Mike pulled it away and reached between her legs, stroking the pink tip of her clitoris with his moist fingers.

"Please."

He did not answer.

"Please!" And finally, "Inside me! Inside me!"

He kept silent, increasing the rhythm of his fingers.

"Mike! Now!"

He thrust his hand into her with such force that she emitted a groan of pain as she exploded hotly, uncontrollably, in a mindless spasm.

He withdrew his fingers and looked down at her without expression.

"You bastard."

"You enjoyed it."

"I want to wash." She raised herself unsteadily from the bed.

"Suit yourself. It's that door there. But don't go away." He grinned. "I haven't finished with you yet."

When she returned she held an outstretched palm under his face. "I doubt that this is Laura's, and it's too small to fit a man." She dropped a ring onto his bare chest.

Mike examined it. "Fairfax High. Oh, Christ, that would have been hard to explain. She was a carhop. Goddamn lucky you found it." He dropped it into the ashtray.

"What exactly do you do with your days when you're not busy in bed?" Lisa stretched herself across the sheets.

Mike laughed. "Shoot rabbits."

"You what?"

"They tear up the garden. The place is overrun with them." He reached into the bedside table and withdrew a revolver. "See? I get my target practice, and the plants don't get chewed to bits." He dropped the gun back into the drawer.

"God, that's an ugly thing. I'd be afraid to have one in the house."

"We had prowlers when we first moved in. Probably just kids, but you never know." He shrugged. "Fired a shot in the air, and they took off like big-assed birds." He reached over and buried his hand in her hair, grasping it tightly. He pulled her to him, parting her legs. They lay facing each other, silently, with a mixture of hostility and lust. Very slowly, he drew his penis back and forth across her soft lower mouth, neither of them granting the other the concession of a reaction. When he finally took her, it was with such a release that they went at each other like two furious animals.

Lisa was slipping into her clothes. "When is Laura coming home?"

"Next Thursday. She has a week or so of exteriors to shoot here, and then around the first of December we're going to Vail. We'll stay through the holidays." He pulled a sweater over his head. "Don't worry," he assured her, "we'll have another round before she gets back."

"I think not. I don't really like you, Mike. Moreover, you could become a habit that might be hard to break."

"I wonder which one of those you really mean."

She turned to him. "Both."

"Have it your way."

Lisa wasn't sorry she'd done it, nor had she any urge to repeat the encounter. It had served its purpose, a moment's revenge for Jack's callousness, a reaffirmation of her female appeal. It was reasonable enough and quite uncomplicated. She decided to forget about the whole thing. As far as she was concerned, she and Jack were even, and he no wiser. It seemed so neat, so expedient. She dismissed it from her mind.

"It's a relief to see you cheerful for a change," Marty smiled over his coffee cup. "You haven't shut your mouth since we sat down to lunch."

"Haven't I? I am sorry." Lisa laughed at herself. "I'm afraid it's not all me. I took a Dexamyl earlier. I've been feeling so bushed lately that I can hardly stay on my feet."

"You're skinny as the devil. Jack is going to have to beat the sheets to find you, if you don't put on a few pounds before he comes home."

"I'm just not very hungry," she apologized. "Sometimes I feel too tired to eat."

"Well, do something about it. You're beginning to look a little haggard." He rose and glanced at the check.

"Walk you back to the stage?" he offered as they exited the commissary.

"Thanks, but no. I have to stop by the dispensary to see the doctor. I've been meaning to go for two days, but I just haven't had an hour off from shooting."

"Make the old duffer give you some vitamins."

"What do you hear from Jack?" the doctor inquired without looking up from his prescription pad.

"I spoke with him night before last. He's got problems on top of problems."

"Things are still the same between you two, I take it. You haven't started seeing other people in his absence?" He gave her an indulgent smile.

"No," she said wearily, "I've yet to meet anyone who is

any threat to Jack. But it is difficult," she admitted. "At the moment, we might as well be total strangers. It's like having a pen pal you've never met," she added ruefully.

"All the better to get reacquainted when he comes home."

"Doctor Berg, your bedside manner is showing."

"Here, take this to the pharmacy." He handed her the slip.

"What's it for?" She glanced blankly at the hieroglyphics on the sheet.

"Hormones."

Lisa frowned. "They won't scramble up my system, will they? I've never fooled around with these things."

"Rest assured, my dear. They'll have you shipshape in a couple of weeks. When did you say you had your last period?"

"Ten days ago."

"Right. And when did the hemorrhaging start?"

"Two days ago."

"Exactly. No problem. These cysts are common as salt. Take the hormones as directed, and it'll all disappear with your next regular period. Now, my dear, anything else I can do?"

"I am awfully tired," she confessed. "Maybe some vitamins—"

"Easily done." He unlocked the doors of a large cupboard. "Multivitamins, timed release." He handed her the jar of varicolored pills. "For good measure," and he extracted another bottle, "protein tablets. Need anything else?"

"I'm almost out of Dexamyl. I've needed one every morning for the past two weeks."

"Don't overdo," he warned, pouring the green-and-white capsules into a small plastic vial. "If you have to take these things, make sure you force yourself to eat three balanced meals a day, otherwise, you'll whittle down to nothing. You don't normally have a weight problem, do you?" He gave her an appraising once-over.

"No."

"Then take these along too." He took a cardboard cannister from his desk drawer. "My own formula for energy. Plenty of yeast, wheat germ, all the things you need. Nibble them between takes." He put the lot in a large manila envelope and gave it to Lisa. "Be sure to remember me to Jack when you speak to him."

"I will," replied Lisa, reflecting that the only thing wrong with the studio doctor was that he always gave you too much of everything, whether you wanted it or not.

"Please," Lisa begged Marty, "don't make me laugh. Last night Obie started doing old burlesque routines at dinner, and I laughed so hard my stomach actually got sore. It still hurts. I'll thank you not to break me up." She dabbed at the tears of laughter in the corners of her eyes.

"It is a hell of a funny story, you have to admit." Marty had just regaled her with a description of Claire Poland's latest social pratfall.

"I swear," said Lisa, "that woman is carnivorous."

"You're looking a little better than when I saw you last week," he commented.

"Think so? I've been making myself eat, hungry or no. I gained two pounds back."

"What are you doing Saturday?"

"I thought I'd get an early start on Christmas shopping. For a change," she smiled.

"When you come to my name, find me a sexy broad who can cook and who speaks only when spoken to."

"That's not Christmas shopping, brother, that's pimping. How would it look for me to spend the holidays in jail?" She suppressed a yawn and grimaced.

"What's the matter?"

"I told you. I must have really laughed my guts out last night. It hurts me to yawn or cough." She reached over and turned off the late show which neither of them was watching.

"You must have strained something." Marty drained the last of his Scotch.

"Probably. Why did you ask me about Saturday?"

"I thought you might want to drive up to Santa Barbara for some riding. Friends of mine have a ranch up there." He rose and stretched.

Lisa led the way to the front door. "I really would rather spend the day out in the fresh air than in the stores. Maybe I'll have time to shop at night this week. I think the stores stay open late. Give me a call early Saturday morning, why don't you?"

"Will do. Thanks for dinner." He was off into the cool, clean-smelling winter evening.

It was Teresa who answered the phone when he called.

"Mister Tabor? Is it you?"

"It's me, Teresa. Is Miss Taylor there?"

"Mister Tabor, I didn't know if you'd be up so early on a Saturday," she apologized. "I was waiting."

"What is it, Teresa?"

"Miss Taylor. She's not here."

"Where is she?" he demanded.

"They took her away in an ambulance at three in the morning."

"What's wrong?"

"I don't know. She couldn't breathe right. I didn't know if I should call you and Mister Haller."

"Do you know where they took her?"

"I'm not sure. Is there a Saint something?"

"Saint John's?"

"I think that's it. I'm sorry . . ."

"What's the name of the doctor my sister uses?"

"Doctor Green," she replied promptly. "I'm sure of that."

Marty dialed Saint John's Hospital in Santa Monica. The floor desk crisply confirmed that Miss Taylor was a patient. She was, however, accepting no calls at present, nor any visitors. Beyond that, all inquiries would have to go through the patient's physician, Doctor Eliot Green. Marty rang the doctor's office.

It was mid-afternoon before Green returned the call. He asked several pointed questions as to what Marty's interest was in Miss Taylor. "Sorry," he excused himself. "We doctors all get a little gun-shy about talking to strangers in this town. There's not one of us who hasn't inadvertently leaked at least one story to a columnist."

"Forget it," Marty overrode him brusquely. "What the hell is wrong with my sister?"

"Peritonitis, I'm afraid. We're pretty confident that it's localized, however."

"Peritonitis?" he repeated.

"She said something about an ovarian cyst. Looks like it got the best of her."

"What are you going to do?" Marty wondered if he should try to contact Jack.

"We're not sure of anything. There are a couple of other

alternatives. We're running some tests." Marty could hear the
doctor shuffling through some papers. "It may be that we
have to operate."

"When will you know?"

"A few days perhaps."

"The maid said Lisa couldn't breathe. What was that all
about?"

"It's not that she can't breathe," he explained. "It's just
that it gives her severe pain. She has to take very shallow
breaths. Don't worry." Professionally, he anticipated what
the next question might be. "We're keeping an eye out for
chest congestion. We force a cough out of her at intervals.
There's no danger of pneumonia."

The doctor, Marty realized, obviously knew what he was
doing. He felt somewhat reassured. "When will she be able to
have visitors?"

The doctor spoke to someone in his office. "What?" He returned to the phone. "You may drop in on her if you like.
Don't stay long. She's under sedation for the pain and she's a
little sleepy from the anti-nausea shots."

Lisa whispered his name as he entered. "Sit where I can
see you. I can't move anything but my head. It hurts too
much to move."

"For God's sake, what happened?" Marty stared at her
dead-white face drained of strength. "You were fine on Tuesday night How could this happen so fast? You look like
hell!" His candor escaped in spite of himself. He was shocked
that anything could have made her deteriorate so fast.

"Thanks," she attempted a smile. "I just kept on getting
worse and worse. I didn't have time to go to Doctor Green
during his office hours, I took Darvon and hoped that would
kill the pain enough so that I could go on working. I never
should have gone to that idiot pill-pusher at the dispensary."

"Berg is a quack. I wouldn't trust him with anything more
than a stubbed toe." Marty noticed tears in her eyes. Wordlessly, he reached for a tissue and put it in her hand. "Hurt
bad?"

She nodded. "Wipe, would you? I can't even move my
damn arms without having to scream."

A businesslike nun came into the room, followed by a

young intern. She pushed up Lisa's sleeve. "We need some more blood from you."

"Vampires," Lisa whispered, smiling weakly.

Marty did not stay more than ten minutes. It was plain that it was too hard on her to have to talk. Out in the corridor, he heard Doctor Green's name and saw one of the nurses approach him with a message. Marty introduced himself. "Is there anything else that can be done?" he demanded.

"Tests. We're doing our best. So far the infection seems localized."

"Please keep me posted," said Marty. "I'll leave my number at the nurses' station."

Marty stood with his back to the room, watching the stately sway of the palms outside. Their fronds glistened green against a pure and cloudless sky. "I still think," he said to the figure in the bed behind him, "that we should call in another doctor for an opinion. It's been almost a week that you've been lying there. Your color is lousy, if you want the truth, and you've lost so much weight that it's frightening. I'm giving you the facts, Lisa, because somebody has to goose your Doctor Green, and you don't have the strength to do it. What the hell has he been doing all this time?"

"Tests," she whispered.

"What kind of tests?"

She took in a breath. "Don't know."

"Is that all?" Marty turned and glanced into her face, taking in the purplish smudges of the circles beneath her eyes. Her skin was pale and sallow. She had the translucent cast of a piece of Belleek china and looked, lying there just as fragile. "For Christ's sake," he said impatiently and moved to sit beside her.

"Doctor Green," she inhaled carefully, "sent the head of surgery down."

"What for?"

"He was here a couple of times. He prodded me all over."

"Did he say anything about operating?"

A shaft of light came from the door as Doctor Green let himself in. "No," he answered, catching Marty's query, "that's not going to be necessary." He stood at the foot of the metal bedstead. "How long did you tell me your fiancé has been away?"

"Almost five months."

"What in hell has that got to do with the price of eggs?" interrupted Marty.

"I'd rather talk to Miss Taylor alone."

"No," she whispered, "I don't mind."

With noticeable reluctance, Green returned his attention to Lisa. His tone was antiseptic. "You were admitted to this hospital with the tentative diagnosis of an ovarian cyst for which you had been under treatment by your studio physician. The puzzling fact was your lack of response to treatment and the resulting peritonitis. That hinted at some other cause, an atypical appendicitis, perhaps, or some atypical g.c. infection."

"Shit," snorted Marty. "Clap? That's ridiculous."

"No worse than a bad cold," Lisa joked feebly.

"Both of you are dead wrong. At first glance it seemed nonessential to run a culture. I was aware that your fiancé was in Europe and had been for quite some time. I was also aware of your great attachment to him." He paused. "Nonetheless, we like to be thorough. We've run several cultures with no results, but that's not surprising since these organisms grow only under optimum conditions. In certain cases, even when the diagnosis is perfectly clear, we never achieve results. However, I have this morning received a report from the laboratory. They've isolated the organism, and it is definitely gonorrhea."

Marty, motionless in his chair, edited the questions that could wait. "Why," he asked Green overlooking Lisa, "is she so damn sick with something like an ordinary, garden-variety dose of clap?"

"It went unchecked for quite a length of time," he admitted. "She's already receiving antibiotics. It won't be long now, a few more days, perhaps, before she can leave the hospital."

Lisa spoke quietly. "Then everything will be all right?"

"Do you want honesty or optimistic phrases?"

She lay silent.

"I would not," he seemed to be choosing his words with great caution, "be entirely truthful if I gave you the impression that there will be no residual effects. In cases like this there is little chance of escaping some damage." He halted.

"Tell me," said Lisa.

"We won't know for some time," he hedged, "until after further examination."

"Tell me," she repeated.

"The damage is to the walls and openings of the fallopian tubes. There are incidences of abnormal bleeding, low backache. Sterility," he said abruptly.

"When will we know?" she asked softly.

Green cleared his throat again. "Perhaps," and for the first time his voice was without its mechanical tone "there is an overemphasis on the biological aspects of motherhood. Before you leave here, Lisa," he said gently, "I'll take you down to our nursery and point out a number of infants who will be released to adoptive parents. Handsome, healthy babies." He glanced awkwardly at his watch. "I'll drop in on you later in the day," and he turned to the door.

In the silence that followed, Marty rose from his chair and, for lack of any purposeful movement, returned to the window. "What do you want me to tell Jack?" he asked finally. "You know he calls me every night to check on how you're doing."

"He thinks it's a cyst, doesn't he?"

"Yes. Because that's what we thought."

"Leave it like that."

"Do you think," he inquired deliberately, "that that's fair?" Marty faced her.

"Marty," the tears were running onto her pillow, "it has to be like that. Don't you remember what Valerie did to him?"

"I remember she put horns on him all over town."

"Yes."

"However you want it. It's your life." He scooped up his jacket from the arm of the chair.

"Something else."

He glanced up.

"Get hold of Mike Stanton. He's off skiing someplace. Obie will know where to find them. There's no sense in the same thing happening to Laura."

He just stared at her. Very slowly, he shook his head. "Of all the fucking idiots . . ."

"You found him?" Lisa was sitting up. The last rays of a pale winter sunset striped across the blanket.

"They're in Colorado." Marty's mouth had a grim set.

"The conversation was rather stiff. I assume Laura was in the room with him. He said, and I quote, 'I'll handle it.' " He sat down and lit a cigaret.

"That was it?"

"That was it. No messages. No apologies. No best wishes for a speedy recovery."

She wrapped her arms around her shoulders and stared at the foot of the bed.

"Mister Wonderful," Marty said.

"Shut up, will you? It was an accident. I'm sure he had no idea at the time. I've never been crazy about him either, but I'm sure it wasn't intentional."

"Are you, now? Christ, but you are naïve. Sometime between then and now he had to know. All it would have taken was a dime in the phone slot and you wouldn't be in the shape you are. Don't try to pin any nice-guy labels on him. You picked yourself a real winner." He looked at the cigaret with sudden distaste and stubbed it out. "I hope to God Jack never finds out. He's the best friend I have, and I don't like to think of him being hurt."

"He won't find out."

"You'd better make a goddamn career out of being sure he doesn't."

Lisa turned on him. "That's enough! Keep your damn mouth shut, once and for all. As far as I'm concerned, this is the last mention of the subject. The last. Am I making myself clear?"

"Good thinking," he said tersely.

8

Obie

4:30 P.M.

"Obie? I called you to find out if you know whether or not Laura still intends to fly to San Francisco for the film festival this weekend."

"Jesus, Jack, I'd forgotten. Have you spoken to her about it?"

"I was down on the set a few minutes ago. It occurred to me to mention it, but I decided not to. You know Laura. If anyone so much as inferred that she had a commitment, she'd get up from her deathbed to appear. I didn't want to put pressure on her, not when she seems to be making out so well."

And risk the fact that she might be too overwrought to cut the mustard when she came back to work next Monday morning. Don't pull this altruism crap on me. *"You've got a point, Jack. We can't let anything send her off course right now."*

"There is the insurance problem."

Now you're being honest. *"You don't have to explain it to me."* Not when I have all those medals for hand-holding and well-wishing.

"Understood. What can be done about San Francisco?"

"I'll call the festival committee. They'll settle for another name with equal clout. I'll tout them on someone else. Under the circumstances, I don't see how they can object. Not if I play up the tears."

"But will Laura object? To your going over her head, I mean. I'm serious about not upsetting her in any way, however small."

"Hell, I'll simply tell her it was their suggestion. An expression of their understanding of what she's going through."

"Right."

243

"Hold on, will you, Jack? I have another call. Yes, Julie, who is it?"

"A Frank Whitman, Mr. Straus. He says he's from Life magazine."

"I'll be with him in a minute. Jack, you there?"

"Yes. That's all I wanted, Obie. That, and to let you know she's holding up like a champ."

"Good. Talk to you later. Mr. Whitman? Obie Straus here. What can I do for you?"

"I'm calling in regard to Laura Curtis. She's your client, I believe."

"She is."

"I'm sure you realize that at the moment she has the sympathy of the entire American public."

An unctuous voice. Never met the guy and already I don't like him. "I'm sure she does."

"While the situation is still pertinent, I feel the public response to an in-depth article on her tragedy would be tremendous."

I'll bet you do. "Tremendous for whom, Mr. Whitman? For Laura? For the public? Or for you?"

"Well, I suppose it would be of interest to all of us."

"Why haven't you taken this up with someone more appropriate, like her studio publicist?"

"I'm sure they're overloaded with requests for stories. I didn't want to get lost in the shuffle. This wouldn't be just another fan magazine piece. This would be quality stuff, first class. We might even make Life with it. I wanted to approach her through a more personal source."

"I thought you told my secretary that you worked for Life."

"I have. I have. Many times. Free-lance."

"I'm not interested in any speculative piece on Laura. Neither would she be."

"Now, that's what I call a mistake. Mr. Straus. You know as well as I do that articles will be written. Most of them for the fan mags and the tabloids. 'I Watched My Husband Die.' That sort of thing. A piece with class, placed in a top-notch magazine can help offset those. I don't need to tell you there's been a lot of speculation, a lot of talk. Every reporter in town will be covering the inquest."

"When you've made your deal with Life, then we'll talk."

"*I'll be writing the story believe me. But, of course, I'll be able to be a lot more sympathetic to her if I've had her cooperation. A lot more sympathetic.*"

"*And if she's not available?*"

"*Well, you just never know. Sometimes these things seem to almost write themselves. The facts do tend to sensationalism. I'd hate to have it turn out differently from my original intent.*"

"*Which, as I understand it, is to virtually blackmail your way into a piece which you can sell to the highest bidder, thereby landing yourself a fast buck and a fancy byline. Right?*"

"*That's an overly harsh judgment, Mr. Straus. Of course, I wouldn't be averse to paying you for your services in handling the matter, but it was my primary thought that Miss Curtis' interests deserved protection.*"

"*And that, buddy, is what they're getting! The conversation is over. Your three minutes were just up. Don't call us, Mr. Whitman, we'll call you.*"

A knife job. The sonofabitch is going to do a knife job.

"*Julie, get me Marcia Wheeler at* Life *magazine.*" I hope to hell she grabs at the idea. One thing's for sure, her opinion of me is going to take a dive for wanting to expose my bereaved client to the glare of her glossy pages. "*Marcia, dear.*"

"*Obie, I hope you're calling to say that Colin Kirkwood has reconsidered.*"

Seek and ye shall find. If you had the lever you could move the world. And I just found my lever. "*I think he's thawing, Marcia. I knew you'd want to be kept posted. Give me a few more days so I have the opportunity to approach him at just the right time, and I don't think that set will be closed to you anymore.*"

"*But it will still be a closed set to the rest of the press.*"

"*The coverage will be exclusive. Only your people will get in.*"

"*New York is going to be very happy about this. They've been pressing me pretty hard.*"

"*Tell them you're too nice a girl for them to treat you badly. By the way, you might also tell them that I've been in conference with some of Laura Curtis' advisers, and it's our view that there'll be a rash of sensational and blown-up arti-*

*cles in the wake of the accident. Never mind that it could
have happened in Hoboken. The hatchet boys will try to
make it a slap at Hollywood. That's the kind of slanted jour-
nalism that gives the industry a big pain. We were wondering
if an in-depth piece, written in the best of taste, about the
tragedy of the thing might offset some of the shabby stuff. It
was my idea to give you and your people first crack at it because you have the first-class writers. We want quality, only
the best, and that's you."*

"I'll call New York on it first thing in the morning."

"At the moment Laura has the sympathy of the entire
American public."

"Yes, if I get the go-ahead, we'll want to do it immediately. When is the inquest being held, do you know?"

"The end of next week. I'll be waiting to hear from you.
Good-bye, Marcia."

*That's one down and two to go. Now it rests with getting
Colin Kirkwood and Laura to fall into line. Christ, sometimes
I feel like a goddamn juggler with too many Indian clubs.
Kirkwood has to come through. The drunk-driving arrest last
week was his fourth. If it weren't for my doing some fast
palm-crossing with that hungry little putz in the D.A.'s office, the charges wouldn't have been dismissed, and Colin
Kirkwood would be spouting Shakespeare from a cell. There
won't be any trouble with Colin. Laura I'll get to later.*

"Julie, see if you can locate Mr. Kirkwood. Then bring me
a Maalox."

"There's Gelusil in the washroom."

"That, then. I can't afford to be choosy."

OBIE pocketed the car keys and walked across the macadam
driveway toward the front door. The poinsettias, tall as he,
were in full waxy bloom under the outside lights. He thought
how artificial they looked. Thirty years he'd lived in California, and flowers in the winter still seemed unnatural. He
paused and took a breath before turning the doorknob, aware
that some sort of a tempest awaited within. When he'd
phoned Julie for his messages, she'd told him that Ruth had
called twice, frantic to find him. The entire day had been
wearing. First there had been the message from the studio

that unless Laura reported to work for her retakes within forty-eight hours she would face suspension and a lawsuit. Then there had been the coincidence of the two writers both calling, looking for Mike and Laura. Worst of all was Mike's evasiveness. For five days now he had frustrated Obie in his every attempt to speak to Laura directly. "I'll handle her," Mike kept saying. Handle, my ass. Obie gave the door an angry jerk.

"Oscar?" Ruth's voice was tremulous. "Oscar!" she wailed as he walked into the living room.

"What the hell is going on here?"

She pointed, speechless, toward the garden. Obie squinted through the window, but it was getting too dark to see whatever was out there.

"I told you!" She pitched the words at him. "I told you not to get rid of Mr. Takemoto!"

"The gardener? I didn't think he deserved a raise. That's all there was to it."

"And he quit. And we had to get that dreadful Mr. Mendoza!"

"For God's sake, Ruth, sit the hell down and tell me what you're shrieking about. I've had a rough day." He gave another glance toward the darkened garden but saw nothing.

"Federal agents!" She thumped her body down on the sofa. "Federal agents. Digging up my garden!"

"What?" he croaked.

"I went to do an errand at Tiffany's, and when I got back Rosita was in tears, and there were three men rooting up the garden. That terrible Mendoza!" She poked distractedly at her hair. "He's been growing marijuana in our garden! Ours and a lot of other people's. And he sells it!"

"Oh, shit." Obie let out a long breath. "Oh, shit," and he began to shake with laughter. Hooting, he collapsed into a chair.

"What's so funny about it?" Ruth shot.

"Are you kidding?" he managed to gasp. "It's bloody hilarious, the picture of that crazy Mexican having a junk route. And our garden, yet."

"You won't think it's so amusing if it gets us into trouble," she said angrily.

"So what kind of trouble? It has nothing to do with us. Let

the lawyers handle it, Ruthie. Relax." He wiped away the tears of mirth.

She made a petulant face. "Those men stepped all over my chrysanthemums."

"So sue. Write a letter to the Department of Agriculture. Hell, it's the only entertaining thing that's happened to me all day."

She fixed him with a withering stare. "I'll go see what time your dinner will be ready." When she was angry, it was always "your" dinner.

Obie sat for a moment, relishing the story. The ring of the phone interrupted his enjoyment.

"It's Julie, Mr. Straus. I found out what you wanted to know. I phoned my aunt in Denver, and she called a friend of hers."

"Wait until I get a pencil." He rummaged in the drawer of the table. "Okay, shoot."

"There's a local clinic in Vail. Next to that, the other place to try would be the hospital in Glenwood Springs, Colorado. You don't think anything's happened, do you?" she added worriedly.

"Something has. Let's not assume it's a catastrophe until we learn more. Not a word about this, Julie."

"Yes, sir." She hung up the phone.

If it were anything as obvious as a skiing accident, there would be no reason for Mike not to have told him about it. So that was out. Already three other possibilities had occurred to Obie. Laura might have had a nervous breakdown. It wasn't impossible, considering her behavior after that business with Hans Deitrick. Then again, maybe she and Mike had had a roaring fight and he'd broken her jaw or slugged her in such a way that she was too bruised to film. That would account for Mike wanting to keep her under wraps. Or maybe, Obie frowned at the thought, they'd had a fight and Laura had left him. What if Mike didn't know where she was either? He'd been stalling, of that Obie was sure.

Obie's view of Mike Stanton had dimmed considerably after talking to the two writers, neither of whose names had the slightest familiarity for him, or, in fact, for the boys in the literary department. If Mike's idea of handling Laura's interests was to fork over substantial sums of money to option a couple of unknown and unproduced plays, someone, himself if necessary, ought to take a closer look into her affairs. Obie heaved a sigh of aggravation and dialed the operator.

The call to Vail had yielded nothing. "Yes," he repeated into the mouthpiece, "person to person."

Ruth was poised in the doorway. "Are you calling the attorneys?" she wanted to know.

"Glenwood Springs, Colorado."

"Who's in Colorado?" she puzzled.

"Hold it, will you, Ruth?" He made a silencing motion. Obie listened intently. "Operator," he demanded, "please find out when Mrs. Stanton will be accepting calls." After a minute's confusion, his call was transferred to another floor. "You have a Laura Stanton as a patient there?" The answer was affirmative. "I'm told she's not taking phone calls," Obie broke in over the operator's voice. "This is a business emergency. Can you tell me when I'll be able to be put through to her?" The nurse conferred with someone else close by the telephone.

"You'll have to speak to Doctor Brower," she came back.

The long-distance operator requested a transfer. Obie tried to make himself more comfortable in the chair. At least he'd located her. That was a start.

Ruth stood at the glass doors to the patio, shaking her head disapprovingly as if she could discern the damage beyond.

"Yes, I'll speak with him instead of Mrs. Stanton."

Ruth flicked on the outside light and let herself out. When she returned, she announced, "Oscar, it's absolutely criminal what they did."

In response, he slammed the phone into its cradle.

She was startled. "I hadn't realized you had got that angry, too."

"What?" he asked abstractedly.

"You're angry." She was actually quite delighted.

"I'm upset."

"Upset, then."

"Damn right I am." He flipped his lighter impatiently and finally resorted to matches.

Ruth perched on the edge of the sofa.

Obie thought for a moment. "I'm going to Colorado," he declared.

She simply looked at him.

"That," he glanced at the phone with marked annoyance, "was the most unsatisfactory damn conversation I've ever had."

Ruth was still at a loss. "But why Colorado?" she inquired weakly.

"Laura Curtis. She's ill."

"Oh. Is it serious?"

"The doctor said next to nothing. He was too damn vague for my tastes."

"But if it's not serious . . . "

"Believe me, Ruth," he interrupted, "one way or another, it's serious. If she's well enough to work and doesn't show up at the studio, they'll sue the bejesus out of her. If there's something radically wrong with her, I want to find out the nature of the problem." He neglected to enumerate the possibilities he'd considered. There was too much hairdresser gossip in this town.

"But what about Mike? Have you talked to him?"

"He's doing a lot of bobbing and weaving. He wouldn't even admit she was ill as late as this afternoon."

"But Oscar, Colorado? Be sensible. We have enough trouble of our own right now. What can you do there? You're not a doctor," she pointed out.

"Ruth." Obie was suddenly overcome with weariness. "I have to call Laura's producer, the airline, and half a dozen other people. Why don't you go ahead and start dinner without me. Please," he added for emphasis.

She moved reluctantly toward the door to the dining room. "Vickie Mann phoned for you today. She's finally finished that book she's been writing for over a year. She wants you to read it before she starts her revisions. She wants your opinions."

Obie stared after her as she walked out of the room, wondering wistfully that there had ever been a time when he and his wife spoke the same language.

Obie maintained an innate suspicion of aircraft which precluded his enjoying any flight, however smooth. The United flight to Denver had been unpleasantly rough in spots. There had been a long wait for his rented car, and the drive to the hospital, through a graying afternoon punctuated by occasional swirls of snow, was tiring. Somewhere out there among the lowering clouds there was spectacular scenery. He saw none of it.

He entered the hospital, stamping the snow from his shoes. After inquiring at the desk, he received directions to Laura's floor and left a message for Doctor Brower.

At the end of the corridor, outside what he took to be Laura's door, waited Mike. Even at a distance of thirty feet, Obie saw the look of fury that passed over Mike Stanton's face. By the time he drew closer it had been replaced by an appearance of mild curiosity.

"What brings you here?" Mike asked smoothly.

"The mountain air," retorted Obie. "There was too much smog in L. A." He resisted the urge to seize Mike by the shoulders and shake him. "I want to know," he began, "what kind of crap you've been giving me. What the devil is the matter with Laura?"

"She was operated on this morning. They took out her appendix. She'll be all right."

"Christ!" he exhaled and leaned tiredly against the wall behind him. "Why didn't you say that was it? Why such a frigging mystery? You behaved like a goddamn jackass, Mike! Don't you know Laura's facing a suspension? Why in God's name didn't you just explain how ill she was?" His look demanded an explanation.

"Because," said Mike, "I was sure she'd pull out of it. I thought she'd get better instead of worse."

"Then, for pete's sake, when she did get worse, why didn't you notify someone? The insurance would have covered the cost of holding the other people on the picture until she was well enough to work."

"Think again. The studio can't get insurance on Laura. Have you forgotten the recurrent problems with her insides? The pneumonia? The kidney infection? Not to mention the publicized suicide attempt. That was the capper."

"But that was a year ago!"

"That's right. They haven't had her insured since then."

"Damn!" Obie shook his head. "Why didn't I know?"

Mike shrugged. "Beats me."

"Mr. Straus?" The white-jacketed man approached them and extended his hand. "You left a message you'd like to see me. I'm Doctor Brower. If you'll come with me, I'll find a place where we can sit and talk." He nodded at Mike who stepped aside for them to pass.

Obie halted. "By the way," he turned back to Mike. "I want to speak to you about your writer friends before I leave."

His look was blank. "My writer friends?"

"Yes. Those two novices that you're supporting in such grand style." Not waiting for a reaction, he walked away following the doctor.

"You are her agent." Brower settled back in the chair.

"Yes."

"What is the purpose of your visit?"

"I'm here because my client is ill."

"You want to see her back at work."

"Look," Obie flattened his palm on the desk, "I don't know or care what you've heard about agents. This girl has a risky medical history. She's alone in the world except for her husband, and . . ." Discretion overtook him.

"Go on."

". . . And nothing. I'm concerned for her welfare. Part of that is my job. Part of it is a personal interest. I felt I should be here. I wasn't completely satisfied with our telephone conversation. Frankly, it sounded like a lot of double-talk to me."

The doctor failed to show if he was annoyed by the remark. "It was a difficult diagnosis. By the time she was brought here, she was suffering from a severe internal disorder. So severe, in fact, that it was very tricky to isolate the cause. Some things are never as clear-cut as we doctors would like to have them," he said regretfully.

Obie waited. Brower seemed to be reflecting about something. After a moment, he went on.

"Mrs. Stanton had taken it upon herself to assume she had an ovarian cyst. In all fairness to her, it seemed she was correct. She has had these troubles in the past, and from the symptoms, even a trained physician might have reached the same conclusion. She had some of her hormone pills in her traveling case and she treated herself. Unfortunately," he stared down at the desk, "that was not the case. The improper treatment failed, of course, and by the time she collapsed and had to be hospitalized, she was suffering from peritonitis."

Obie glanced up sharply, but the doctor was not looking at him. He was gazing out the window, lost in some thought. "We had no reason to believe that the only other alternative cause wasn't appendicitis."

"But will she be all right?" Obie broke in.

"She's on antibiotics now." Brower turned to him. "She'll be all right." He tapped his fingers on the top of the desk. "I had rather a long talk with Mr. Stanton after the operation." He paused briefly in reflection, then continued, "He asked me to telephone his wife's physician in Los Angeles to acquaint him with the facts in case any residual problems might occur. I have already done that. It's a closed matter," he said abruptly and rose.

Obie persisted. "What kind of residual problems?"

"Nothing for you to worry about." He opened the door and ushered Obie into the corridor. "Sorry you had to make such a long journey. If you'd waited a day, you could have saved yourself the trip."

"I'd like to see Laura before I leave."

Brower hesitated. "I suppose you may. She'll be a bit groggy. Don't stay more than a couple of minutes." As an afterthought, he laid a hand on Obie's arm to stay him. "By the way," he asked quietly, "what about this suicide business?"

"What suicide business?"

"I was led to believe by Mr. Stanton that his wife had self-destructive tendencies."

"I would hardly call it a tendency," Obie replied testily. "Yes, she did attempt suicide once that I know of. That was about a year ago. Why?"

"Her husband said she'd been under treatment by a psychiatrist. He seems to be extremely concerned that she shouldn't be upset in any way. I believe the phrase he used was 'disturbing the delicate balance.'" Brower looked at him questioningly.

"Damned if I know. Maybe things are worse than I thought. Maybe they're not telling me everything. What's this got to do with her operation?"

"Rest," he answered quickly. With a vague gesture of one hand, he added, "Not returning to work too quickly. You know, that sort of thing."

Obie watched him stride away down the hall. "The goddamn Mad Hatter's tea party," he muttered.

The room was dark, save for the small lamp set in the wall over Laura's bed. It took a second or two for his eyes to adjust to the shadows. Mike looked up at him from a chair, saying nothing. In the bed, Laura lay apparently sleeping, her hand in Mike's.

Mike opened his mouth to speak, but Obie quietly overrode him. "I know. Only for a few minutes. Has she come around yet?"

"She drifts in and out."

"Listen, Mike," he kept his voice low, "is there anything I ought to know? Laura hasn't been depressed again, has she? Brower just intimated that you thought she was unstable." Obie squinted in the dimness, trying to make out Mike's reaction. "If she's gone and freaked out again on us, I think you'd better tell me about it."

"There's nothing to tell. You know Laura. She's as neurotic as any other actress, maybe a little more. She has her problems but——" He broke off as Laura made a sound.

"Oh, God," she groaned, "it hurts. What did they do to me?"

"Take it easy, baby." Mike stroked her hand. "It won't be for long. Obie's here to see you."

"Obie? Where is he?" she asked dazedly, opening her eyes.

"Right here." Obie stood next to Mike.

"Is Ruth coming?" she whispered.

Obie looked at Mike.

"No, darling. Ruth is in Los Angeles. We're in Colorado, remember?"

"Don't go to Los Angeles," she said fuzzily. "Don't leave me, Mike. Please, don't leave me."

"I'm not going anyplace. I'm staying with you."

"I wish it didn't hurt so much."

"The nurse said she'll bring you something in a while. That'll help. Close your eyes and try to rest." He smoothed the pillow under her head.

"Will you be here when I wake up?"

"I'll be here."

"Promise. Don't go away."

"I won't, sweetheart. I'm right beside you."

She closed her eyes and lay still.

Obie gazed down at her. She looked like a little kid. Her hand still rested in Mike's. There wasn't, he realized, any point in remaining here. He touched Mike's shoulder. "Let me know how she is. I want to hear from you every damned day until she's out of this hospital. Is that clear?"

"I'll call your office tomorrow afternoon."

"I'll be expecting it." He added a hushed good-bye and left the room.

It was not until he was checking in his car at the airport that Obie remembered the subject of the writers. It had escaped his mind completely. He jotted a note to himself to mention it to Mike when he phoned.

"But why didn't somebody say something?" Claire demanded. "Not a word! I'm quite put out with all of you." She looked at her hors d'oeuvre distastefully, then popped the whole thing into her mouth.

"We didn't want a big fuss," explained Lisa.

"That was the plan," put in Jack, "ten minutes in the judge's chambers, and here we are." He put an arm around Lisa's shoulders and gave her a possessive squeeze.

"Then it's the Strausses' fault," decided Claire. "All their invitation said was 'cocktails and buffet,' nothing about it being a wedding reception." Her tongue flicked out to catch a speck of puff paste at the corner of her mouth.

"That's because we wanted things this way," insisted Jack in a tone commonly reserved for the very young and the slow-witted. "We asked Obie and Ruth to forget the fanfare."

The combo in the corner of the living room resumed its music. Raising her voice, Claire inquired, "How is *The Jonas File?* Are you pleased with it?"

"I'll let you know when we're through cutting it together."

"How did the girl come off, Astrid Swensen?" she asked loudly watching Lisa for a reaction. There was none. "I hear she's going to make it big."

"That's for the public to decide," Jack said.

From across the room, Obie looked at the three of them, deciding that Jack and Lisa had been in Claire Poland's grasp long enough. The woman never knew when to let go. It was like watching a tramp poke persistently through a trash can, sure that if he probed long enough he'd discover something of value. "Ruth," he said quietly, "why don't you show Claire what you've done with the garden?"

"Well, I'm not going to tell her why we had to redo it!"

she flared at the thought. Then, "Do you really think she'd like to see it?"

"I'm sure." He watched as she separated Claire from the Hallers.

"Darling," Claire paused beside him on her way to the patio, "it's a lovely party. And what a surprise," she added pointedly.

Obie overlooked the jab. "I'm glad you like it."

"Incidentally," she went on, "Aces Norton phoned me yesterday to say his daughter is getting married." She waited to let the message strike home. "He's looking for a good gag writer to come up with a few jokes for the wedding dinner. Says he'll go as high as a thousand. Maybe one of your clients?" she suggested.

"I'll see if I have anyone." To himself, Obie dismissed the idea. Norton, like all comics, had to be on stage every minute, even at his daughter's wedding. Let him write his own material. No client of the Straus Agency was quite that hungry.

Vickie Mann pecked him on the cheek as Bob, heading for the bar, waved a greeting. Vickie squinted myopically at the throng. "Wow," she breathed, "I'll just never get over it. I just never will. Did you ever see so many famous people? Do you think I could get Colin Kirkwood's autograph for the kids? Would he mind?" Reassured by Obie, she hustled off.

Threading her way through the increasing press of the crowd, Tula Jackson came to greet him. Almost six feet tall, she moved like slow, dark syrup. She bent to kiss him, and Obie cast a glance at the exquisite cleavage between those black breasts.

"Easy, baby," she chuckled throatily. But, whether or not it was because of the close quarters, he didn't know, she moved nearer. She seemed not to notice that their legs were pressed close. Tula was taking inventory of the guests. "How integrated you are," she pronounced. "The room looks like a regular marble cake."

"Who counts?"

She gave him a long smile. "You count," she said.

She was coming on strong. He couldn't help wonder, why him? Tentatively, he reached for a cigaret on the table, allowing his hand to brush over her rear.

"Nice," said Tula.

He lit the cigaret.

"I hear tell you never screw a client."

"Exactly how do you mean that?"

She laughed. "Take it how you like. I'm thinking of changing agents. Interested?"

"I'm always interested in you, Tula, and," he added, "I make it a rule not to fuck clients."

"Well, then," she drew back from him, "I guess that's the end of a beautiful romance and the beginning of a new contract."

"Come into the office Monday." A twinge of regret accompanied his words.

Obie spoke briefly with Ian Driscoll and his companion, another ravishing look-alike for Christy. From the series of girls Obie had seen with Ian since the divorce, he entertained the wild thought that Ian must have had Christy run through a Xerox copying machine.

"Wonderful, wonderful," Claire had returned from the patio. "Look at all these people."

Obie returned Gloria French's effusive hug of greeting. Over her shoulder he spotted Mike and Laura in the doorway.

"Hello, Claire," Gloria greeted her warmly.

Claire favored her with the most fleeting of smiles, easily to be mistaken for a slight facial tic. Her eyes roamed the assemblage for bigger fish.

By the time Obie managed to reach the entrance to the foyer, they had moved elsewhere. Finally he saw Laura with Mike, snaking her way through the group pressing congratulations on Jack and Lisa. Obie followed.

"It's terrific!" Laura was beaming happily as she bussed Lisa on the cheek. "One for you, too." She kissed Jack whose reddened cheek had become a tally of well-wishing women.

Mike wore a pleasant smile, saying nothing. Jack extended his hand and Mike shook it. "Where does one get a drink?" Mike asked him.

Jack laughed. "That's something I'd like to know myself. I think it's somewhere in that direction," he indicated. "If you get there alive, bring back a Scotch and soda, will you?" He turned to Lisa. "Anything for you?"

"No, thanks."

"Obie," smiled Jack, "it's a hell of a party. That's in case we forgot to thank you before."

"Marty sent a cable from London," Lisa interjected. "Ruth just handed it to me. He said how sorry he was to miss the celebration."

"For a role like that he would miss his own wedding," returned Obie. "Laura, you're looking good. Big improvement over the last time I saw you."

"You know," she said, "I don't even remember your coming there. I must have been really knocked out."

"You were." He drew her aside. "Feeling better?"

"A little tired now and then, that's all."

Obie led her to a comparatively quiet corner. "I don't just mean physically. How are your spirits?"

"My spirits? I guess my spirits are fine. Why?"

"Well—— Well, it was only a little over a year ago that they were pretty low."

"Forget that."

He changed his tactic. "It's just that I have another client with some personal problems. I wanted to ask you if you thought the psychiatrist had been of any help to you."

"The psychiatrist?" She looked at him blankly, then remembered, embarrassed. "Don't ask me. I only saw him that once. I suppose those doctors can do something, but that stuff's not for me. If I need to confide in someone, I have Mike. He's all I need," she smiled.

After the slightest pause, Obie complimented her on her dress.

"Mike picked it out," she said proudly. "Listen," she had another thought, "what's this business about your not sending me the script for that African picture that Paramount is doing? Mike said he'd have thought you'd set me for it. I know Victory doesn't have anything for me right now, so that's no problem."

"You're out of the hospital three weeks and you want to go to Africa? You must be nuts!"

"It's a great part," she countered.

"It's a rough part. They're going to shoot in some remote place nobody ever heard of. Why would you want to spend all those months crawling around in the jungle?" She was right, of course. The producer would sell his soul to have Laura Curtis, but the physical demands of the role were such that Obie had ignored the request. Rest, Doctor Brower had said.

"You don't want me to go broke, do you?"

"Why the hell would you do that? You've got plenty of money."

"There's some in litigation, but it'll be months before I can get it. Everything else is invested. Mike bought a chain of bowling alleys and a gas station. The rest is in stocks, except for some that's in land up near Solvang."

"But that seems ridiculous, Laura. You shouldn't be strapped for cash."

"You'll have to talk to Mike. He handles everything. All I know is that it costs us two thousand a month to keep his mother in the nursing home, what with the private nurses around the clock. Then there are the expenses on the house. He doesn't think we should settle for anything less than the best. Fine furnishings are a great investment," she insisted.

"Like what fine furnishings?"

"Like, oh, you know, Aubusson, Chinese porcelains. These things cost money."

"I think I'd like to view all this magnificence sometime. Invite me over, will you?"

"Sure. When Mike's finished with it, he says we'll have a big party. Now, what about the African thing? I want to see the script."

Obie nodded without enthusiasm. He saw Mike heading in their direction, but before he reached the corner he was halted by Claire Poland. With a jerk of his head, Mike beckoned Laura to join him.

"You won't forget," she admonished Obie as she left him.

He watched Mike slip an arm around her waist. What the merry hell, he wondered, is going on here? Then, remembering the oldest advice, he reprimanded himself. Don't mix in.

That didn't look as if it was going to be easy.

But, as he recalled later, excuses had been plentiful. The office was so overloaded with business that spring that he had been forced to take on two more agents and another secretary. While other talent agencies floundered and laid off personnel, Obie's dealings, for a time at least, seemed to be multiplying. It was ironic, therefore, that his personal fortunes should be left behind in the upswing. Why was it that you could never get lucky at cards, horses, and business at one and the same time? The more he made, the more he lost. Yet, always, there was that chance that luck might reverse itself.

Ruth basked in the reflected prosperity of the agency, and, as he always knew she would, finally had her way about moving into Trousdale Estates. The place was a foreclosure, a real bargain, he repeatedly told himself at a hundred eighty thou.

With Mike and Laura out of the country, his worries about her could wait until they returned. There wasn't any reason to be involved. Perhaps, by the time they got back there would be no need for concern at all.

He was wrong. He fingered the two manila envelopes Laura had just handed him and listened dourly to her rapid-fire announcement. They were selling the house and moving to Bel Air. "How," he asked, "did this come about?"

"We didn't take it seriously at first. When we got back from Africa and I collected the payment from the lawsuit, Mike said wasn't it too bad we hadn't had the extra twenty thousand dollars last year because we could have bought a house with a tennis court. Then he came up with the idea of listing the house with a realtor, just to see if we'd get a nibble. First thing we knew, some electronics manufacturer offered us ten thousand over what we'd paid for it. How could we turn him away? He's giving us seventy-five thousand cash down." She smiled and shielded her face from the sun which angled through the window. She wanted Obie's reaction.

He adjusted the blinds. "That better? You and Mike put a lot of money and effort into that house."

She was disappointed. "I thought you'd be pleased that we made so much on the deal."

"I'm not so sure you did. As I said, you put a great amount into that house."

"But that's furniture. It's all movable," she protested.

"All of it?"

She hesitated. "Well, most of it, except for a few things we had built in."

"Moving itself costs money. Not to mention any changes you might have to make in a new place. Laura," he leaned toward her over the desk top, "God knows I'm in no position to sermonize on domestic thrift, but perhaps you should have considered renting out your house for a year or two and giving this fellow an option to buy. That would have been a much better deal for you financially. It would have allowed you a substantial tax deduction for the improvements you've made on the property."

"It would?"

"Didn't Mike mention that alternative?"

"I don't think he knew about it. The tax benefit, I mean." She gave a little shrug and brushed her hair back from her face. "Anyway, it's done now. Come to think of it, we couldn't have rented it. We need the cash from the sale to put into the new house on Copa de Oro."

The address, Obie noted, was one of the most elegant in already elegant Bel Air. That did not surprise him, but the rest of it did. "You sit here and tell me that you have a total of ninety-five thousand dollars in cash and you're putting all of it into a house?"

She was plainly irked that Obie's reaction had been so negative. Somehow it tarnished the brightness of the new acquisition.

"Do you mind my asking how much it's costing?"

"Four hundred ten."

He let out a low whistle. "I didn't know Marie Antoinette was moving."

"Oh, cut it out. You haven't seen it. Obie," she enthused, "it has everything, pool, cabanas, tennis court, billiard room, projection room, even a conservatory."

"I'm speechless."

"Wait until you see the boiserie. And there's a fountain in the entrance foyer that was brought from an old monastery."

It was, as she had pointed out, done. "I hope you'll be very happy there."

She smiled and rose. "We will. I know we will. The house is Mike's birthday present to me."

"Thursday, isn't it?"

She nodded. "Silly, to be just turning twenty-one when I feel as if I'd been an adult all my life."

Obie made a mental note to send her something special.

When Laura had left, he returned to his chair and swiveled around to stare out the window. He found himself shaking his head slowly from side to side. Her birthday present from

Mike. What Obie wondered wryly, was Mike planning to give her for Christmas? Disneyland? He glanced briefly at the two scripts Laura had brought him. First drafts, she had explained, of the properties Mike had optioned. He wondered if she was aware that he knew Mike had brought his writers out from New York, all expenses paid, and established them in a comfortable suite of offices while they worked at their screenplays. He slipped the manila envelopes into his attaché case. He'd go over them Friday on the plane to Vegas. Maybe everyone's luck was due for a change.

Although Obie spoke to her several times, he didn't see Laura again until the summer was almost over. When he did, he remarked on the fact that she had changed the color of her hair.

"Mike's brainstorm," she said. "He didn't like me all blonde. He says that streaks are more chic."

They stood outside the Century Plaza Hotel, waiting for Laura to be called in front of the cameras. *The Century of The Curtis,* the show would be called. It was a flashy TV special of singing and dancing numbers staged among the glossy modern buildings, flowered walkways, broad avenues, and skeletal construction sites that formed Century City.

"Are you happy with the show?" It was the obligatory question to be asked on the agent's obligatory visit to service his working client.

"It's tiring, that's for sure. When I first started the dance rehearsals, I thought I'd die of exhaustion." Laura had never done a musical special before. Obie hoped she wasn't trying to spread herself too thin. "Mike said this will show the public a whole new facet of me." It seemed to Obie that everything Laura told him these days was prefaced by "Mike said."

"How is Mike?" This, too, was obligatory.

"Fine. Working hard. He has to ride herd on all those workmen at the house. It's driving him crazy because he's supposed to be working with the writer to get a final shooting script on his picture." Laura smoothed the wrinkles out of her opera hose. A hairdresser approached and secured a stray lock with a bobby pin. Laura thanked her. "The breeze keeps undoing me," she laughed to Obie. "What I'm really afraid of is that when we do the big production number in front of the fountains the wind will blow the spray all over me. If that happens, it'll take a couple of hours to set and dry my hair again. The network man is panicky at the prospect. He won't even watch, just sits in the hotel lobby contemplating all the money his company's spending."

"Tell me," said Obie, "which script is Mike working on?"

"*Day After Tomorrow*. We've put the writer up at the Bel Air Hotel. It's too noisy for him at our place with all that hammering and sawing going on." She returned the wave of a hotel car valet who recognized her.

Obie had told Mike exactly what he thought of the two projects he was underwriting. *Day After Tomorrow* was a dreary soap about a beautiful girl struck down by leukemia on her honeymoon. The other property was a tired melodrama about twin sisters in love with the same man. It had been done before, and better. He had tried to discourage Mike from investing any more time or money in either story.

"Are you going to do the picture?" Obie asked cautiously.

"Mike says we'll get the best financing if they know I'll play the part." This fact was something Laura herself knew, yet again it assumed added authenticity because "Mike said."

Obie doubted that even with Laura Curtis fronting the venture anyone would be fool enough to invest in such a sure loser. For Laura's sake, he hoped the project would die on the vine. It was his job to protect his client from appearing in a film in which no one, not even Duse herself, could receive decent notices. In this case, it might be one hell of a struggle.

"Mike's already given out the story to Claire Poland."

"He's what?"

"He let her have an exclusive on the item that we'd formed a company and I'll star in the first picture he produces. Of course, I have one to do for Victory before I'll have time for our film," she chatted on.

That was enough for Obie.

"Where are you off to?" she asked.

"Del Mar. Got to make it in time for the double." He glanced at his watch. "I'll be back Sunday."

"Luck!" Laura called after him.

Luck. He'd had luck, all right, but the wrong kind. Before checking out of the hotel at La Costa he'd filled the wastebasket half full of elastic-wrapped packets of uncashed ten-dollar tickets. Now he patted his pocket again to make sure he hadn't overlooked any. Ruth always checked his clothes before sending them to the cleaner.

A bum trip, he reflected, all the way around. Not even the steam and massage had revived him. He turned off the La Costa road and onto the freeway. It was past noon, but the morning mist remained. It hung so low to the surrounding fields that it looked like a smouldering swamp fire. Beside him on the front seat of the car were piled Vickie Mann's revised manuscript and the notices for Jack Haller's *The Jonas File* which Julie had culled from newspapers in the several cities where it had opened. A bomb. A flat-out catastrophic thud. The damn thing had run a fortune over budget, costing both Jack and the studio plenty. Obie took it for granted that Victory Studios which had been having a rough year would now blame most of its annual losses solely on Jack's picture. Jack seemed to be taking the raps philosophically. He was busy cutting his third film under the Victory deal, and his enthusiasm for it mitigated the disappointment he must have felt. Only Astrid Swensen had escaped the attacks of the critics. She was unanimously praised for her beauty and the sexy delivery of her lines which, as one reviewer wrote, "could not be spoken straight-faced by an actress of less than Miss Swensen's considerable talents." "The most exciting Swedish import since Garbo," another said. None of it would do Jack much good.

Near San Clemente a watery sun began to penetrate the fog. The traffic moved well. Obie enjoyed this part of the drive, especially now with the hills and highway bathed in the thinning silvery mist that gave a glistening iridescence to the coastline. At least Vickie's manuscript had proved a bright spot in the weekend. Her revision was trim and slick. Somehow, despite the kids, the house, the PTA, and being the wife of the glamour set's pet dentist, she had pulled together enough time over the past couple of years to produce a creditable novel. It was not what Obie would call a man's book. The pages of *The Marriage Trade* contained the life cycles of intermarriages within the international set. Its characters had just enough of a passing resemblance to actual notables to lead the reader into thinking he was getting an insider's exposé of café society. That, and a generous lather of sex, increased in the rewrite at Obie's insistence, ought to buy Vickie a sale. He'd call her as soon as he reached home.

Obie stepped up his speed as he turned inland and the drive became increasingly unattractive. Miles of identically vulgar houses had been thrown up, cheek by jowl, over the once verdant hills. These gave way only to the oil fields, lying tarnished under a film of acrid smog. Through the yellow vapor he could see the pumps bowing up and down continuously like obsequious praying mantises. Obie rolled up the window, closing out the foul smell, and turned on the radio.

The news came on as he drove through the Trousdale gates and up Loma Vista to the house. For the money, he thought as he pulled into the carport, you'd have expected the place to have a proper garage. He reached to switch off the radio, but something stopped him. "Actress Laura Curtis," the announcer read, "was admitted to the hospital in Los Angeles this afternoon. She faces the prospect of major surgery within twenty-four hours. This is the latest illness for Miss Curtis whose health problems . . ."

Obie swore under his breath.

He tucked the phone between his chin and shoulder and tore at the fresh pack of cigarets with both hands. "What I can't understand," he was saying to Mike, "is why she didn't say anything about it on Thursday. You can't tell me she didn't know. Partial hysterectomies aren't usually done on the spur of the moment, are they?"

"She knew," said Mike. "We'd just decided to keep it quiet. We told Claire Poland she could have an exclusive on it for Monday's paper. Probably someone at the hospital leaked it to the press."

Obie stared incredulously at the instrument in his hand. "Do you mean to tell me that Laura was knocking herself out with dance routines when she was about to go to the hospital with a tumor?"

"She's what you call dead game, you have to say that."

"Damned if I have to say anything of the kind! I think it's criminal. What's more, I think you're both insane."

"Take it easy, Obie. We talked it over and decided that as long as the doctor didn't object too strongly Laura should go ahead with the show. It was important, a whole new departure for her. It showed the public that Laura Curtis had talents they'd never seen up to now. It was tailor-made for Laura. We figured there'd never be an opportunity as ideal as this one."

"Christ!" muttered Obie.

"She had no complaints. No ill effects. She'll come out of this fine. She always bounces back."

Obie checked his impulse to say "fortunately for you," and instead gave Mike a curt good-bye and hung up the telephone. He stared at it a moment, let out a quiet curse and, shaking his head unbelievingly, dialed Vickie Mann's number.

Since Vickie was a personal friend and Bob's wife, Obie bypassed his literary department and submitted the book himself. He chose to send it to the Nova Press. Their penchant for contemporary novels with a jet-set backdrop and their skill in promoting the sensational aspects inherent in books like Vickie's made them his first choice. He wasn't surprised when they made an offer on the manuscript.

"Got a present for you," he told her.

"Wait a minute, will you?" She turned away from the phone. "For the last time, Brad, get a napkin for that popsicle. It's dripping lime green all over the kitchen floor. And no, absolutely not, Penny, I told you you can't help me stuff the turkey until it's thawed out. Now leave me alone. I'm on the telephone. Are you still there?" Not waiting for his response, she groaned. "Thanksgiving recess. I tell you, Obie, I give my thanks the day they go back to school. That's my Thanksgiving. Are you still there?"

He laughed. "Sit down and take a deep breath. Nova wants the book. If it's all right with you, I'll drop by this evening after the kids are in bed and we'll discuss the details." Obie knew how impossible it was to carry on a conversation with the four Mann children bounding around the living room.

"All right? All right?" she exclaimed delightedly. "You better believe it is. Wait'll I tell Bob. Hey, it's champagne and caviar for us tonight!"

Obie smiled as he signed off. Vickie Mann, author of Nova Press' newest sexploitation novel, was about as exotic as scrambled eggs.

Julie buzzed him impatiently. "It's a Mel Presscott from Victory Studios."

He pushed the number three button. "Obie Straus here."

"Mel Prescott, Mr. Straus. We got trouble." He sounded dour. "She blew her stack again."

He sighed his annoyance. "I'll be right over."

For the first time in her life, Laura was showing signs of temperament. Last week she had seized the costume sketches for her new film from the hand of the designer and torn them to shreds in front of the producer and director. The next day she demanded that one of the dress extras be fired because she had shown up in a gown too similar to hers. A compromise was reached by placing the girl obscurely in the rear of a ballroom crowd. What had precipitated this latest crisis, Obie didn't know.

Mel was waiting for him outside the stage. He'd been Laura's assistant director on several of the Nikki pictures as he was on this one. He, like so many of the Victory regulars who had known Laura since her childhood, held her in a sort of proprietary affection. It was clear to Obie that Mel's feelings were being severely taxed.

"We can't get her to come out of her dressing room."

"Why'd she go in there in the first place?" Obie matched stride with Mel and passed from the bright outdoor sun into the quasi-twilight of the set.

"We were shooting the scene where she gives up the social-butterfly bit to devote herself to working with the war orphans."

"And?"

"She blew nine takes and then she walked out of the shot. Just like that. Ran off the set and locked herself in her trailer. Won't come out."

"Listen," Obie took Mel aside, "as long as the Major's enjoying himself out on the briny, let's handle this ourselves." If word of the incident were transmitted to S. M. Victor on his yacht, it would, Obie knew, assume larger proportions than necessary. "Is her husband here?"

"We couldn't get hold of him. That's why we phoned you."

"Okay. Where's her dressing room?" Obie followed Mel across the set. "Tell the crew to take a coffee break over at the commissary. No sense in having them all standing around gaping at her when she walks out of her trailer. Give us half an hour." Obie waited until he'd disappeared before knocking softly on the door. There was no response.

"They've gone, Laura." He spoke loud enough for her to

hear him within. "Everyone has left the set. If you wanted to be left alone, you have been. Now open the goddamn door."

He waited.

"Obie?"

"Yes, Obie. Open up. You can't stay in there for the rest of your life, you know." There were days when that ten percent didn't come easily. "Laura," he said louder, "I want you to cut the shit. Either open the door, or I'll break the window." He had no intention of anything as physical as that, but his patience at feeling like such a bloody horse's ass was limited. The approach might work.

After a moment, he heard the lock click. He tried the door and opened it.

She sat clumsily on the edge of her makeup chair, her arms crossed, hugging her shoulders. Obie balanced himself on the leather arm of the chair and patted her hand. "Something must have got to you. Want to tell me what it was?"

"The kids."

"The kids? You mean the children playing the war orphans?"

Laura nodded.

"How, exactly?"

"I don't want to be around them now."

"Laura, I don't understand."

Arms around herself, she moved back and forth in the chair, rocking. She hid her head in her folded arms. It seemed she had forgotten she was not alone. Obie had the strange impression that if he did not stop her, Laura might draw away from him completely, retreating so quickly and so finally that, unless he reached her, she would pass beyond recall.

"Laura!" he shook her roughly by the shoulder.

She glanced up at him and waited. Her wet cheeks were puffy and streaked with makeup.

"You forced yourself to start this picture when you know damn well that you should have spent several more weeks at home resting up first. You came back to work too soon out of the hospital. After a partial hysterectomy, for God's sake. You've been in almost every scene for the past six weeks, and it's been too hard on you. You needed more time to recover, physically and emotionally. Do you think," he argued, "that a bunch of little kids could set you off like this if you were in good health? Bullshit." Obie circled an arm around her shoulders. "I'm going to see if there isn't some way to reshuffle the schedule and give you a few days off. You pull yourself together and finish out the day. I'll go up to the front office and have a talk with them. I want you to spend that time doing nothing. Nothing. Then, by the time you come back to the studio, you won't fall apart like this. But mark what I say," he warned her. "Don't screw around with this resting bit. I'm going to have to give the front office a pound of flesh to get you any time off. You damn well better use it to advantage." As he rose, he realized that his shirt was soaked through with perspiration. Whatever it was that had happened to her a few moments ago had frightened him badly.

Mel waited for him by the stage door.

"Call me Dear Abby. You can send her makeup man in there now. She'll be ready to work. Come on," he told Mel, "you and I have to go upstairs and knock our heads together."

Her extended weekend in Palm Springs paid off. Laura held herself together until the end of the picture, in spite of the fact that she developed a recurring migraine condition. Obie began to wonder if all the brouhaha about psychosomatic illnesses was such a lot of crap after all. After the filming, she and Mike took off for St. Moritz to ski. He received a short note on the stationery of the Palace Hotel saying that they'd stay longer than expected. It seemed Mike was after some European financing for his intended movie. The next Obie heard, they were in Munich. Then came a letter from the Hassler in Rome. "Things look good for Mike. We'll know in about six weeks. Meanwhile, buying up antiques for the house. What fun! Will hate to leave, but expect us home around the end of May. Tell the Major I am getting work fever. Please have lots of scripts waiting for me to read." She signed it with several childish x's.

Evidently, Mike did not find his backing. Little was said about it on their return, but Obie gathered that Mike had shifted his sights to the second of the two properties. Not, in his opinion, much of an improvement. They saw Mike and Laura one evening at the Trader's. Laura, looking stunning in something very Parisian, was still bubbling over about their lengthy vacation, dropping an occasional titled name which Ruth received with unabashed awe.

Obie tentatively broached the subject of financing the films.

Mike cut him off. "Still up in the air," he said, refilling Ruth's wine glass. "By the way, we saw Jack Haller's latest picture on the plane coming back. Christ, they ought to hand out parachutes with that one."

Unfortunately for Jack, Mike was not alone in his opinion. Word of mouth was circulating to the effect that Jack was a one-shot talent. His first big picture had got him the Oscar nomination, but since then he'd been on a downhill ride. *The Jonas File* and now another turkey.

The pressure on Jack was beginning to show. Too much of his own money had been locked into his films. Obie knew that Jack had a modest family fortune to start with, but at this rate it couldn't last. Victory Studios had begun to make dissatisfied noises. Jack phoned Obie and asked him to drop by his office.

"I'll only be a minute," said Jack. He introduced the production man who sat on the arm of a leather sofa, nervously fingering the edges of an already dog-eared script.

"What's this," he was asking Jack, "about establishing a p.o.v. of city lights on that ride up to the lodge?"

"Can't we use stock footage?"

"Forget it. Just let one of the actors glance out the car window, whistle, and remark on the view." He tucked his script under his arm, nodded to them both and left the room.

Jack watched him go. "They're cutting back on me," he said, his eyes still on the door. "Would you believe that my seat in the executive dining room has been moved ever so slightly below the salt? What's next? They fire all my stars and use hand puppets?"

"You'll make it."

"It's getting to the point where I can't afford not to. The Major and I really went at it when the retrenchment started. I swear to you they're screwing themselves. They're ruining this picture with their goddamn sudden-thrift policy. Can you conceive," asked Jack, angry now, "of a film with elaborate production values in one scene and in the next looking like it was a quickie TV show shot with a frigging Brownie camera? Not to mention the fact that some of the scenes they're scrimping on are those that are weakest in the script and most in need of dressing up. Christ! Will these bastards ever learn?" He slammed the middle drawer of his desk in and out impatiently.

"No," Obie answered evenly, "they won't. You know that, and so do I. This is one of those times you just have to bite the bullet."

"Shit."

Obie nodded his agreement.

"Here's the thing," Jack said abruptly. "I'll be wrapping this picture the end of next month. The Major's putting a subtle squeeze on me to announce the next project." He paused to light a slim cigar and watched the smoke rise for a moment before he went on. "There's something brewing upstairs. Don't ask me what, because I don't know for sure, but it's there. I smell it. It's my guess that if I don't come up with something they like damn soon, they'll attempt to get out from under our agreement. Either that, or they'll deliberately throw me a property they know I'll refuse and then find an excuse to sue me for breach of contract. At this particular time it might not be easy for me to negotiate my kind of deal elsewhere. I'd have to rely on studio financing more than I have in the past, which would mean producing any piece of crap they forced on me. Damned if I'll give up my autonomy. I've worked too hard to earn it. I knew the risk I was taking by getting in so deep with my own money, but, Jesus, these are my pictures. I'm responsible. It's a personal commitment, and the financial investment is a part of that commitment. There are always dangers involved in a deal of this sort. I just wish to hell that I had more ready cash. Then I could tell the Major to go fuck himself."

"At least," Obie said, "you're accepting the facts realistically."

"What's the alternative? I need some fast action, Obie. I've got to come up with a property before the Major gets a case of the flop sweats and brings the roof down on me."

He spread his hands emptily. "You know I'm always looking. I thought you'd go for that chase script I sent you. It could have been a neat little package."

"No. The Major is leery of chases since *The Jonas File.*"

"I can only go on looking," apologized Obie. Briefly, he entertained a thought that passed through his mind, but no.

"The point is, lay a little steam on it, will you? There's a time element."

Again, Obie thought of the manuscript in his desk drawer at the office, but he remained silent.

The decision was made for him.

As Obie was leaving the house for Vegas, Ruth had stopped him in the hall. "Oscar, before I forget, the landscaping man has called twice. Remember I gave you the bill a couple of months ago?"

He didn't remember.

"I guess you forgot to pay it, because he sent another. I didn't want to trouble you again, so after he called I went to the bank to get some money from our joint savings account. They've got awfully dim young girls working there nowadays." She shook her head disparagingly. "I don't think any of them really knows how to run those complicated machines they give them." She opened the front door and bestowed a brief kiss on his cheek. "Anyway, this little girl at the window took the passbook and ran it through her machine to compute the interest. Then she handed it back to me. There was only a little over two thousand dollars in the account. The landscape man needs thirty-five hundred. I told her I thought the withdrawal entry was a mistake, but I didn't want to make a fuss until I'd asked you."

"I transferred some funds temporarily. Leave the green man's address on the phone pad, and I'll mail him a check when I get back."

Why was it, he wondered, that everything always seemed to happen at once. Just before Ruth had brought up the subject of the landscaping bill, Obie had called Cal to place a few bets and been reminded succinctly of his record of losses, unbroken for too long. He had been counting on this trip more than he cared to acknowledge. He needed Vegas. He was depending on the tables to help him recover.

How could it be, then, that now, not forty-eight hours later, Obie found himself being ushered ever so politely from the stark fluorescence of the manager's office back into the softly soothing illumination of the casino, numbed by what had just taken place.

"Cigar?" The manager made a conciliatory gesture. Leaning close to Obie's ear, he added, "Cuban."

"No thanks."

Obie stood outside the closed door. For the first time in his life the music of the casino failed to excite his senses. The whir and jingle of the slot machines, the rhythmic incantations of the croupiers, the staccato clicking of thousands of chips, the murmured numbers of the hopeful, all of it might as well have been a million miles away. Gently, courteously, he had been informed that his credit had been shut off. Like that. Period. He had been so damnably sure his luck had changed. Last night before the dinner show, he'd piled up over fifteen grand. Just as easily, between then and now, he had lost it all. And more, much more.

For nearly two hours, he paced the hotel grounds. Around him the flat, baking desert sent up shimmering waves of heat. His shirt was soaked through. He removed his tie and jammed it into the pocket of the jacket slung over his arm. Always before, something had bailed him out when things got tight. A few nights of poker at the club perhaps. Only a matter of a few fortunate hours. Enough to have a backstop. But now, the thing he had never believed could happen had happened. There simply wasn't any more. He forced himself to review the concept over and over in an effort to convince himself of the truth. It couldn't have come to this, not here in Vegas where money lay thick as the sand. The fact was unacceptable. But it was there. Like a man faced with a diagnosis of a terminal illness, Obie reacted with utter disbelief that anything this conclusive could have happened to him. But it had.

He paused on the side of the fairway, absurdly, dazzlingly green under the searing sun. Personal loans were taboo. His closest friends were also his clients and, above all, their confidence in him could not be shaken without irreparable damage to his business. The agency and its reputation had to be protected. A bank loan was out of the question. As for the house, it already had a third mortgage on it. The few remaining stocks in his name were not sufficient to meet his outstanding debts. That meant going to Ruth with the truth and asking her to cash in the securities he had bought in her name.

Still, there might be one other way. Like a stubborn piece of flotsam that refused to go under, the same idea surfaced again and again in his mind, and, like the drowning man he was, he reached for it. It was just possible that he could save both himself and Jack Haller in a single stroke. It was not illegal, he reassured himself, merely unusual. That was the word. An unusual procedure. Jack was in no financial position to bid competitively on any of the hot literary properties up for sale. Yet Obie, in his desk, had both Vickie Mann's galleys and the letter he had just received from Nova Press informing him of their plans for the book. They were convinced that it would be an exploitation blockbuster, so convinced that they planned to mount the most intensive publicity campaign in their history.

Obie turned and walked back in the direction of the hotel. The combination was his ace. His pace quickened. Once inflated by the publicity barrage, the book would be sought after by every producer in town. The price would skyrocket. But that was months away, too far in the future to do either him or Jack any good. It was now that he needed to act.

And what would it matter to Vickie if she didn't make a fortune from the sale? She didn't need money. Bob Mann was well fixed. For Vickie the fame would be enough.

It would be a simple procedure to offer the property to Jack before Vickie really knew what she had. Obie had yet to show her the letter, an unintentional oversight. He would present the book to Jack without exposing it to competitive bidding. Jack, instead of having to pay an exorbitant sum, would get gold for the price of tin. Vickie would get enough to be satisfied. And he, Obie, would receive a consideration from Jack. It was, he told himself, merely an expedient course of action for them both. None of it was illegal. Unusual, perhaps.

By the time he reached the air-conditioned lobby, the device did not even seem unusual anymore. He took the elevator to his room, put in a call to Jack, and began packing.

Obie's security lay in the fact of Jack's one-track mind where his work was involved. Now, with a gun virtually at his back, he was more coolly pragmatic than ever. He accepted the manuscript without glancing down at it, opened a desk drawer, and slipped it inside. He locked the drawer. "When would you like to have your answer?"

"As soon as you've read it and gotten the okay from the Major. Soonest."

"We're going to want to talk to the publisher. I realize that exploitation is Nova Press' specialty, but we'll need to get a clear-cut concept of just how big they're going to go with this."

"They're pulling out all the stops."

"Nevertheless."

Obie made a gesture of agreement. How like Jack that there had been no questions as to the reasoning behind his suggestion. Business was business, and getting off the hook was all that mattered.

Jack stepped from behind his desk and escorted Obie to the office door. "Good title, *The Marriage Trade.* You seem to have a lot of faith in this property," he observed.

"I think you'll find yourself in accord."

"I sincerely hope so."

Nobody was disappointed. Jack paid a fair price with no complaints. Vickie would collect seventy-five thousand for the movie rights, minus, Obie reminded her, the agency's commission. She remained speechless at the figure. He neglected to mention that if the book were anything near the colossal success Nova expected, she might have grossed at least a hundred thousand more. No matter. She was thrilled.

For what Jack referred to as "special services," Obie was handed two checks, each made out to cash and each in the amount of twenty thousand dollars. He nodded his thanks and pocketed them without comment. Like himself, Jack was convinced of the success of the project. He had to be. And the Major, Jack informed him, had exhibited sufficient enthusiasm to reassure him that the Haller Company was off the danger list. Victor persisted, however, in hedging a bit when it came to stating the degree of Victory's financial participation.

"Is it going to be a problem if they want to keep the budget down?" Obie had never asked Jack directly how much money he had.

"It is," admitted Jack. "I'll be scraping to do it. Lisa has been a champ about this. Do you know what she said?" He smiled affectionately. "She believes in this property so strongly that she's willing to go back to work. Her agent is negotiating with the Major. It looks like a three-picture deal at a hundred thou per, one-third payable in advance. The check goes into the company account. Every man should be so lucky to have a wife like that when the chips are down."

"And the rest?"

"I'll refinance the house, sell my stocks, borrow." He dismissed the thought for the moment.

"I want to see this thing succeed." Obie was fond of Jack, that was true. But through his own actions, he was also involved up to his neck. He didn't like to think of having to deal with his conscience if, by some slim chance, Jack should fail.

"When this book takes off, it's going to rocket right to the top," insisted Jack. "We should have no trouble finding actors who'd rather have a piece of the action than straight salary."

"Right," Obie agreed. "No sweat."

The two men shook hands. The manner of Jack's acquisition of the manuscript was not discussed again.

9

Marty

6:15 P.M.

Edwin L. Montenegro, Attorney at Law. Very reassuring. It's reached the point where I'll settle for a bit of security from a sign on an office door. Every little bit counts, right?

"Ed."

"Come on in, Marty. Sit down. Fix you a drink? It's getting toward that time of day."

"No thanks."

"I figured I'd hear from you. It was all over the papers. Just wait until I put some ice in this glass."

"I want to ask you a few questions, for Lisa as much as myself."

"What's up?"

"It's what you read, that business about Mike Stanton."

"Suppose you tell me. I don't rely too heavily on the press for my facts."

"Lisa and I were there."

"In that house."

"In that room." *Blue. Laura's bedroom was pale blue. The walls and the carpet. I remember the stain looking muddy on that blue carpet.*

"Go on."

"That's it. We saw what happened. There's going to be an inquest, I'm told, and I'm not familiar with what that means. I thought you'd be able to fill me in."

"It's a routine procedure. Especially in cases where the death involved firearms, which I understand this one did. The county coroner assembles all those who were actual witnesses or who might have something to contribute that would clarify the matter. For the past couple of months the coroner's been getting a goosing from the news media, so it's only natural that when something this sensational occurs, in-

277

volving famous names, he'd play it for all it's worth. He's got his political position to protect. All the inquest really means is establishing that Stanton's death was a clear-cut accident. Look, Marty, maybe you'd better tell me all the facts. How do you fit into this?"

"I am—was—in love with his wife."

"Stanton's? You mean Laura Curtis?"

"It started several weeks ago."

"How many people knew about this?"

"Some. I don't know. A few know, and I assume that the rumors are making the rounds. They always do."

"Never mind the rumors. Let's stick to the truth. I want you to think before you answer this next question. Is there, could there be, any actual evidence presented that might indicate that either you or Laura Curtis deliberately arranged to get Mike Stanton out of the way so that you could continue your affair?"

"No. There isn't any evidence of that sort. I don't think either one of us would even be capable of considering such a thing. Jesus, Ed, you and I have known each other for ten years. Could you seriously picture me doing something like that?"

"Stranger things have happened. Usually where a triangle was involved. And I don't know Laura Curtis personally."

"I assure you Laura did not plot to kill Mike."

"What's this about Lisa?"

"She was in the room when the accident happened."

"Then both of you saw the same thing. You, Lisa, and Laura will simply testify as to what occurred, and the decision will be handed down. An accident, you said."

"But of course there will be talk. Some sonofabitch who says he works for Life has been poking around. He told me that he'd already spoken to Lisa and she'd given him 'the real story,' which I knew was a lie. I told him to go to hell. He said something about this being 'the biggest whitewash job since Tom Sawyer's fence,' that sort of crap. There's going to be any number of people like him trying to stir up a story."

"You have to expect that in a case that brings in so many well-known names. Suppose we get back to the accident. Tell me everything that happened, from the beginning."

Everything. From the beginning. Where to start? That Sun-

*day afternoon at Jack's? The night in New York? No. The
party. It always comes back to the party.*

"Go ahead, Marty."

*So I tell the same story, repeating the same lines. Once
again now, with feeling.*

"Hi, Mart," Lisa smiled. "Jack and the others are in the living room."

"Mind if I leave this here?" He put his tennis sweater on
the hall table.

"You look very handsome in those whites. Where were
you playing?"

"The usual Sunday game in Malibu. Who's here?"

"About ten people, most of the cast except Laura. Ian Driscoll is here. And Jack included Vickie Mann which I think
was a very sweet thing to do. She's so impressed with the job
Arnold Kramer did on the script that I thought she was going
to kiss him when they met. She's still overwhelmed by the
whole thing. Wait," she said. "Before you go in, help me
carry the coffee trays from the kitchen, will you? Teresa's off
this afternoon."

Marty followed her through the dinning room. "It must be a
hell of a kick for someone as star-struck as Vickie to suddenly become a celebrity herself."

"Obie said her husband's getting just as big a wallop out of
it as she is. He's hired the best publicists in town for her and
sits back reveling in the reflected glory. The cups and saucers
are up there," she pointed to the cabinet above the stove.

"There's plenty of glory to go around. The damn thing has
been on the best-seller list almost since it came out."

"Over two months. And three weeks now as number one.
Jack is really flying, he's so delighted." She filled the large
electric urn with water and replaced the lid.

"Things are looking up." He patted her bottom. "Where do
you want these?"

"On that silver tray there."

"Are you going to hang around for the reading?"

"Not me. It's strictly Jack's show. I'll be upstairs."

"Is Mike Stanton coming?"

She continued counting spoons. "He's the associate producer."

"I know. She finally did it for him, didn't she?" he said.

"It was the least Jack could do for her, Marty. She wants to do this picture very much. She's as enthusiastic about it as anyone. When Laura found out that Jack was having trouble squeezing money out of S. M. Victor, she went to the Major herself and asked to do the picture outside of her Victory contract. That means she'll still owe the Major another film this year. She's doing this one for Jack the same way you and some others are, getting one-tenth of the usual salary and taking a percentage. When she asked Jack one favor in return, he could hardly turn her down."

"I dare say Mike's nose is slightly out of joint. From what I hear, he could use a little more cash to finance his own project."

"I dare say. You can take those in now." She laid the last of the napkins on the tray. "Marty. Marty," she said suddenly, "good Lord, we haven't told you!" She laughed happily. "The news. Jack and I have applied to an adoption agency. We've already had one interview."

He put the tray back down and hugged her. "That," he smiled, "is going to be some lucky kid."

"Jack," he said, before greeting the others, "Lisa told me. It's great."

Jack beamed. "We've got a big house here. Time to start filling it up. Marty, you know all these people, don't you?"

He exchanged nods and handshakes with the two writers and the rest of the cast and seated himself next to Ian Driscoll. "I figure," he cracked, "the closer I can get to the director, the better off I'll be."

"You're looking very athletic," Ian rejoined. "One of the joys of California, being able to play tennis in mid-January. We English envy you that more than anything else."

"As soon as Laura gets here we can start reading," Jack put in. "I'd like to go straight through the script with no stops the first time around. Okay with you, Ian?"

"Right."

"Arnold and Vickie, sharpen your pencils. If you hear anything amiss or that strikes you as better said in some other fashion, start rephrasing. As a matter of fact, we'll listen to comments from any of you. This has become sort of a group effort." He seated himself and riffled the pages of his script. "The thing that matters, the only thing, is making this one hell of a fine picture."

"Hear, hear," Peggy Smart said quietly. People nodded. She joined Marty and Ian sitting on the sofa.

Marty gave Peggy a congenial wink and noticed with amusement that she flushed pink from her neck up to her white upsweep. Peggy was one of that elite reserve of magnificent character players often more respected in the business than the better-known stars. Marty was pleased that Peggy would be playing the part of the recluse millionairess. That meant his scenes with her would be something to remember.

"Dear Jack," Peggy asked, "have you any idea how long we'll be in New York? My grandson's doing a play in Pasadena. I'd hate to miss it."

"We're counting on no more than three weeks on location. I'll have shooting schedules for all of you in a couple of days."

"Does that three weeks include Acapulco?" someone inquired.

"The Acapulco stuff will be shot by a second unit. We'll do those scenes in process shots at the studio."

"Too bad. There goes our free trip to Mexico."

"I'm sorry I'm late." Laura stood in the doorway.

Marty tried to remember how long it had been since he had seen her last. A couple of years at the least. Actors moved in and out of each other's perimeter, not meeting for years at a time, yet always aware of the other's presence on film, in the news, on television, so that it came as a jolt to realize that they had not actually come face to face in so long.

Laura had changed. She appeared taller, perhaps because she was so slender. Marty observed her as she moved to kiss Jack on the cheek. She no longer walked like a self-conscious girl. She carried herself with a womanly awareness of her impact on others. Her dress, a short white knitted shift, skimmed lightly over her figure, giving the merest hint of curves. On her shoulders was draped a tailored leopard coat. Her hair, honey-colored, brushed the top of the coat and, as she spoke to Jack, obscured her face from Marty's view.

"Jack, darling, I think I've done something very clever for a dumb broad like me. It's called saving money."

"I'll see that you get a dozen extra closeups."

"There's a marvelous designer in town who's quit his old job and just started making clothes under his own label. He wants publicity. He's willing to do all my costumes for nothing. He can have the first six, the ones we need in New York, ready by the end of the week if you approve the sketches. The other ten will be waiting when we get back. That's about ten thousand bucks to the good, yes?"

"You bet, yes. Bring him into the office tomorrow. Ian," he smiled, "you heard the lady. Start plotting her closeups." Jack glanced over Laura's shoulder into the hall beyond. "Where's Mike? Isn't he with you?"

"He dropped me off. He had an appointment to go over the set designs."

"I'd forgotten. Have you met everyone?" He put an arm around her and turned her toward the group.

She was more beautiful than Marty had remembered. Her face had come into its own, cheekbones clearly delineated beneath the large, arresting green eyes. He noticed suddenly that her eyes were reddened and that a slight puffiness of the lids had been deftly disguised with shadow. He wondered if anyone else saw it.

"Trouble," Peggy whispered very quietly. Laura was across the room talking to Arnold and Vickie.

"Like what?" Marty wanted to know.

"I hear the husband's been interviewing," she put the word in quotation marks with her fingers, "girls for bit parts."

Marty had no reply. He rose as Laura came toward him with both hands outstretched. He took them in his and gave her a brief kiss on the forehead. Her skin smelled of flowers. Gardenias. The fragrance lingered in the air after she had moved on to greet Peggy.

"I think it's time we got down to the business at hand." Jack returned to his chair, and Laura seated herself on a bench in front of the fireplace, dropping her coat beside her. She took her script from one of its pockets and held it expectantly on her lap.

"Before we start the reading," he went on, "there are a few words I'd like to say. Certain of you," he glanced at Arnold, Laura, Ian, and Marty, "have taken a financial interest in this venture because you believe you're riding a winner. I want you to know just how much I appreciate that faith." The room was quiet. "Now," his tone turned brisk, "Fade in. Scene one."

As they played out their scenes, the words took on a promise of reality. Occasionally someone scribbled a hasty note on a page for future reference.

Jack read the directions on the last page. "Tony exits, closing the door softly behind him. Fade out. The end." He slapped his script shut and looked around the room.

"There won't be a dry eye in the house," commented Peggy.

"Let's hope not," Ian said. "If there is, we'll have mucked up somewhere."

Jack stood up and stretched. "Before we get to the comments, let's refill our coffee cups and have a few minutes' break."

They milled about, more familiar with each other now and with their shared purpose. The comments were helpful, a line changed here to give it a more specific meaning, a speech omitted in favor of a telling glance, a piece of business modified to make it more believable. Laura made several suggestions, accompanying a few of them with self-deprecating wisecracks. This side of her was new to Marty. She was sharp and rather amusing in her remarks, but he wondered why the flippancy. It was obvious she would give an excellent performance as Jennifer and hardly credible that she herself didn't know how good she was.

"Shall I drive you home?" Jack was asking her.

"Would you?" She gathered up her coat and script from the bench.

"Which way are you heading?" inquired Marty.

"It's really just around the corner. Maybe I should walk. It might be good for the figure."

"Your figure," Jack assessed it approvingly, "needs no shaping up. Besides, who ever heard of anyone in Los Angeles walking any place? Thanks, Marty, and before I forget, I want to tell you I think you've got just the right attack on Tony's character." He led them toward the front door.

Laura gave Marty a tentative smile. "I hope it's not too much trouble, carting an extra body along. I think you should know I'm a notoriously stingy tipper."

"I don't expect tips. I don't accept them. I'd be glad to drive you home." He found her glibness abrasive.

"It's on Copa de Oro about a quarter of a mile north of Sunset."

"That's easy enough." He settled behind the wheel.

"Where do you live?"

For some reason, he realized, she was slightly uncomfortable and making idle conversation to cover it up.

"Mulholland, near the top of Benedict Canyon."

"A swinging bachelor pad for a swinging bachelor?"

"It's a nice place. I like it."

The conversation ran aground. Laura shifted in her seat and arranged her skirt neatly around her.

Marty grinned. "Do you know you have great legs?"

"No, but hum a few bars of it, and I'll try to pick up the melody."

"That's a tired old joke, Laura."

"So am I." She looked out the side window.

"Can't you accept a compliment? You come off sounding rude, although I don't think that's what you intended. Don't tell me you're fishing."

"Your fatal charm is laying a big egg, Marty." She didn't bother to look at him.

"So? Honesty isn't always charming, I admit. But it's a lot less charming for a beautiful woman to sound hard-boiled. You sounded much more attractive when I first met you, when you were a bright-eyed kid going to her first big party."

"Maybe you just dig teeny-boppers."

Neither of them spoke again until they reached the house. "This is it," she said.

He pulled into the driveway lined with symmetrically-cut topiary trees and, not bothering to turn off the motor, walked to the other side of the car and opened the door for her.

"Thanks for the lift. I'll mail you a check."

He failed to smile. "That's not necessary. I like the company of pretty women. They're good to look at." He waited a fraction of a second and saw her catch herself before replying. She glanced up at him, half annoyed, half sheepish. He smiled, "Big improvement."

"Thank you, Professor Tabor. Nice to know I'm coming along so well." Her shoes crunched on the well-raked gravel.

Impulsively, he bent down and kissed her on the cheek. "So long. See you at Jack's tomorrow evening." He got back into the car. Her fragrance stayed with him. "By the way," he leaned out the window, "I'm glad you're the one who's playing Jennifer. I think you're going to be fantastic."

"Thank you," she said a trifle primly.

He drove away. Glancing into the rear-view mirror, he watched her image gazing after his car. It looked quite small against the large and rambling house that loomed up behind her.

Laura was less flip in Mike's company, Marty noticed. She seemed more subdued during the evening rehearsals when her husband was present. Mike, it appeared, was her security blanket.

At the end of the week, most of the group left for the location work in New York. Lisa stayed behind, as did the writers. Mike flew to Acapulco to oversee the second-unit filming. Ian and Jack caught an eastbound flight late Friday night, while Laura, Marty, and the rest of the cast took a Sunday afternoon plane. Laura settled herself in the seat beside him, ceremoniously marked with a little sticker on which was printed "Miss Curtis." The stewardess took her mink coat and hung it up. Laura kicked off her shoes and leafed idly through a magazine.

When they were airborne, she took out a gold cigaret case. "Have one?"

He thanked her and lit them both.

She pushed at the lid of the ashtray on the arm of her seat. It refused to open. "Damn," she said, "they can't even keep a simple thing like an ashtray working. Makes you wonder how they're doing with the complicated stuff like the motors."

"Don't you like to fly?"

"I'd like it a lot better if my husband were along."

"That's not exactly a compliment."

"You know I didn't mean it like that."

The plane banked out over the Pacific and turned inland. Marty bent to the window next to him. A flotilla of white sails was weaving its way out of the Marina del Rey, past the breakwater and into the broad ocean. They dotted the water like a sprinkling of white confetti. A Sunday afternoon race. He could see the committee boat beneath him now. Beyond, he recognized the hills of Catalina Island, skirted with a wispy fog, rising out of the silver sea like a mirage. Inland, the entire Los Angeles basin lay spread out under them, looking like a miniature created by the special effects department. White office buildings stood out in stark relief against the backdrop of mountains.

Laura glanced over and saw him looking below. "Watch that first step, Marty. You could break your ass."

"It's a hell of a beautiful sight. I never get tired of it." He noticed that she had finished with her magazine. "May I? Here's the newspaper if you want it."

"I'd like to burn the damn paper."

"Why so?"

"Didn't you read Claire Poland today?"

"I prefer nonfiction myself."

"Too bad some people believe that crap she writes."

"Such as?"

"A rather obvious blind item hinting that there's trouble between Mike and me because I'm going to New York and he's going to Mexico." She shoved the paper into the seat pocket in front of her.

"Forget about Claire. One of these days somebody will drive a stake through her heart. You should be used to that junk by now."

Evidently, she did not wish to discuss it further.

It was a pleasant flight. The patterns of snow beneath them gave way to a spectacular sunset and a cloudless night. After a hold over Kennedy they landed and were deposited by limousine at the Sherry Netherland Hotel.

Central Park lay blanketed with snow. The bare trees and gray buildings stood against a colorless sky like objects in an etching.

"Perfect," Ian enthused. "What luck, this paleness. I'm trying for an almost white-on-white look here, something rather ethereal to add to the delicacy of the dialogue." He clapped his heavily gloved hands together impatiently. "How are we coming?" he asked, walking away toward the camera, leaving Marty and Laura standing together in the snow.

Laura jammed her hands deeper into the pockets of her beige mink coat and shifted her weight from foot to foot. She wore long ivory-colored boots which covered her legs entirely. Her blonde hair fell free. Marty saw that her cheeks were scarlet with cold.

"Are you warm enough?" he asked.

"Hell, no. Are you?" She gave him the frozen semblance of a grin.

"Do you want another cup of bouillon?"

"Thanks, but no. I'm floating already, and the damn dressing rooms are too far away to be convenient."

Despite the temperature, the work was going well. It was not unusual to begin shooting with a scene that was far into the script, out of chronological sequence. They were both used to it. This particular love scene demanded great intimacy, preceded as it would be in the film by an affair between the two of them. The actual circumstances hardly lent themselves to intimacy. The weather was bone-chilling. The presence of thirty-odd members of the crew, swathed in scarves and thick coats, breathing steam into the icy air as Laura and Marty kissed tenderly was anything but conducive to love-making.

"Laura, Marty. Ready?" called Ian.

They nodded. Marty seated himself on his marked position at one end of a park bench. Laura stood several feet away.

Ian was speaking to the camera operator. "We pick it up on his rise and pan with him as he goes to her. Then we push in closer, still holding the skyline. Got it?"

The first take was spoiled by a mike shadow across Laura's chin and the second by a plane passing overhead.

"Let's try for a clean one," Ian said. "I'd rather we didn't have to loop this. How many feet have we got in the camera?"

"Not enough. Reloading."

Laura shivered. Marty enveloped her in a bear hug. "Better?"

"Not much. I guess I'm just a cold broad."

He drew away from her. "Do you have to do that?"

"What?"

"Talk so tough."

"Oh, Christ, Marty, drop it, will you?"

"If I cracked that hard shell, what would I find?"

"A limp gray oyster maybe."

"And a pearl?"

"Don't count on it."

"Brittle things usually break easily," Marty said quietly.

Laura looked at him. Then, turning, she moved away toward the others. "Call me when you're ready," she said to no one in particular.

Over lunch, he apologized. "It wasn't my intention to upset you."

"Just exactly what is your intention?"

He glanced up over the edge of his coffee cup.

"It's not your express purpose in life, is it, to improve Laura Curtis?"

"No."

"Then quit picking at me. I don't like it." She directed her attentions to her plate.

"I'm only being honest."

"That's not the point." Without looking up, she demanded, "Why are you staring at me?"

"I'm trying to figure you out."

"Don't." Laura glanced up. "Did anyone ever tell you that your eyes make people uncomfortable? It's that ice-blue color, I expect." She studied his face. "You've got more gray in your hair since I saw you a few years ago. How old are you, forty?"

"Thirty-three." He smiled. "Is it important?" He realized she was trying to provoke him. "Have you got something against blue eyes or gray hair?"

"Not especially. I never thought about it one way or the other." She toyed with the remainder of her éclair.

"In your opinion," he asked with mock earnestness, "do you think I should dye my hair all black?"

"Do what you please. It's not altogether unattractive the way it is."

"What do you suggest we do about the eyes?"

Laura sat back in her chair and laid her napkin on the table. "All right, Marty. You win. Now are you happy?"

"I was thinking of brown contact lenses."

"Shut up." She suppressed a smile.

"Just trying to please."

"Oh, hell," she finally laughed. "You're a rat."

He stood up and helped her on with her coat. "You look much prettier when you're smiling. And softer."

She tossed him a warning glance over her shoulder.

Marty changed the subject. "Nice coat," he commented. "Yours?"

"Wardrobe." They started toward the door. "I don't like it

very much. The color's too pale for me, but Ian wanted it for the scene. You should see the one I got for Christmas." She gave a start as the cold wind outside struck her face. They walked across the sloshy street and entered the park. "Mike gave me a sable coat for Christmas. Actually, I asked him for it. He always gives me exactly what I ask for."

Marty turned up his collar against the breeze.

"Exactly what I ask for," she repeated. "I guess I have everything I've ever wanted."

"Sounds awful."

Laura scanned his face and frowned slightly. "I get the impression you don't like my husband."

The snow muffled the sound of their footsteps. "I won't lie to you. I did like him when we first met. That was here in New York. He could have been a damn fine actor if he hadn't copped out."

"There's more to life than acting. Mike would rather produce."

He dropped the topic. Pointing to a white-mantled statue, he announced "Cesar Romero's grandfather."

"Him?" she laughed incredulously. "Up there?"

"José Marti, the Cuban patriot and poet."

"You're full of surprises, aren't you?" She ducked as a snowball whizzed between them.

"Almost got two birds with one stone," Jack's breath puffed frostily as he caught up with them. "Here are those script changes for tomorrow's stuff. How's it going?" He handed them each a manila envelope.

"Not bad," said Laura, "except for this fellow here. I can't think why you hired him for the part."

"A case of outright nepotism. You two want to join me for dinner tonight?"

"Sure," said Marty.

"On one condition," Laura replied, "that I have time for a hot bath first."

"Fair enough."

The following night, at Marty's invitation, they dined at "21"—Ian, Jack, Laura, and himself. Film companies on location tended to remain close to their own, cemented by a shared endeavor and the long working hours. Their evenings ended too early for partying, and they all endured the same degree of fatigue. It was easier to be with each other than it was to try to keep up with other people.

Conversation was sparse. Marty was bone-tired and assumed the others weren't much better off. The second round of drinks relaxed them sufficiently for small talk. Laura was reading the menu hungrily.

"Hot soup," she decided. "Tomato soup. Then the Dover sole with French fried zuccini and a small green salad."

"Hearty appetite for such a wee person," Ian winked.

"Are you kidding? I've been freezing my tail off all day for you. Got to stock up on fuel for tomorrow. Besides," she added, "those are all my favorite things here. When I was a kid, I used to come to '21' with my manager and one or another of her dyke friends. Christ," she shook her head, "we must have been an interesting threesome to behold. Two gay broads and a skinny little bastard."

Marty winced inwardly and proceeded to give the waiter their orders.

The noise from the bar had swelled to its nightly crescendo. The waiter brought a telephone to Jack and plugged it in. "I hope whoever it is has a strong pair of lungs."

It was Mike, phoning from Mexico, reporting on the second-unit shooting. Everything was going as scheduled. "Laura's here with me," Jack told him. "Want to talk to her?"

She put down her soup spoon and took the receiver. The others continued their table talk.

"I can't think about that now," she was saying, "it's over a month away. Yes, I know we'd planned it, but how can I do it when I'm so busy here?" She paused. "All right, so I should have gotten things rolling before I left, but Mike, there's only one of me. I can't do everything at once." She gave the others an exasperated, slightly embarrassed smile. "Well, how far in advance do we have to book the caterers? Can't it wait until I get back?" She listened. "Then you do it. You'll be home before I will. Tell them it's for me, and they won't mind the short notice. Yes," she said resignedly, "you go ahead with it. I'll leave it all up to you. I'm sorry I didn't get onto it sooner." She fingered the stem of her spoon, nodding at his words. Abruptly, she dropped it back onto the plate. "You what?" her voice rose. "Damn it, Mike, that's not very considerate. You know how involved I am with this picture. You knew we might have to postpone the party. Now you've got us committed. Where in hell am I supposed to find the time? I know you can do it, but that's not the issue. The issue is," she continued irritably, "that if I wanted to tell Claire Poland everything, I'd do it myself. Jesus, it's getting so I'm afraid to talk in my sleep for fear you'll call her up and pass it along."

The others busied themselves with their plates. "Jolly good," Ian remarked, in an effort to ignore Laura's conversation. "How's yours?" he asked Marty and Jack.

"I will, I will," she was nodding. "It'll be a great party, really. I'm sure of it. It's just that I'm too tired right now to think of anything but the picture. Yes, love you too." She hung up the receiver and shook her head. "I goofed," she told them.

"What happened?" asked Jack.

She let out a sigh. "Mike and I had planned to throw our first big party. A black-tie bash with all the stops out. We'd been waiting until the house was entirely furnished, and it looks like that'll coincide with his birthday. We set March eighteenth for the date, and then I sort of let things slip when this location came along. Now he's gone and told Claire that the party's on." She shrugged. "It's his baby from here on in."

"Not to change the subject, troops," Jack interjected, "but it's possible you'll have a day off tomorrow. The weather report said snow. Your morning calls are weather-permitting."

The snow held off. The next day found Laura, Peggy Smart, Marty, and several others making exits and entrances outside one of the town houses on East Sixty-second Street. It was dull, repetitive work. At lunch time, Laura was joined by a reporter from *Paris Match* for an interview. *The Marriage Trade* had already been translated into French, Spanish, German, Portuguese and Swedish and was on its way to becoming a major hit on the Continent. News of the filming had aroused interest from all parts.

"Un succès de scandale," the reporter commented with relish. "You speak French?" he asked Laura.

"I'm afraid not." She motioned to Marty to join them at their table, but he demurred, choosing the booth behind them.

He ate alone, reading first the morning's *Times* and then a tattered copy of *Playboy* someone had left lying in his dressing room. Fragments of Laura's interview drifted over the top of the partition separating them.

"My husband? He's a producer. He's interested in several properties right now, but he took time off to assist Mr. Haller with this picture."

"It is difficult to work with one's husband?"

"Difficult?" she laughed lightly. "Certainly not. We worked together before we were married. It's wonderful."

"You must," he commented, "be very much in love. Not all married people want that much time together."

"We are."

"And how long are you married?"

"Almost two and a half years. I can hardly believe it myself."

"And still so content," he marveled.

"Fantastically," she breathed. "Where I come from, they'd say 'happy as a clam at high tide.' I don't know if you can translate that," she apologized.

"Where is that, the place where you were born?"

Marty returned his attention to the page in front of him. He was halfway through a Ray Bradbury story before he realized that he'd read this issue before. He fanned through the remaining pages and closed the magazine.

"Will you start a family soon?" the reporter was inquiring.

"I doubt it," replied Laura. "I think some people need children, don't you? I mean, their marriages aren't complete for them without a family. But that's not the way with us. We have each other, and that's enough."

"Your husband is with you on this film, you say. Have I met him?"

"No, he's shooting some footage in Acapulco."

"He does not mind leaving his beautiful wife alone?" Marty could hear the smile in the Frenchman's voice.

"Oh, he minds. It's awfully hard on both of us. But that's the way it is. We keep reminding each other that it won't be for long."

"How fortunate that he is not a jealous man. He is not upset to see you make love on the screen to someone else?"

"Heavens, no. He knows it's all a part of the work. We're both very secure in our relationship."

He murmured something, then said, "For Hollywood this is remarkable. One hears so many stories."

"We never listen to gossip. We keep to ourselves a great deal. I suppose that in itself is remarkable for Hollywood, but we're quite happy just to be with each other."

Marty rose and paid the cashier. Ian caught up with him at the door and signaled Laura to come back to the set. The two men walked together up the windy street.

"Who's that chap with Laura?" inquired Ian.

"Fellow from *Paris Match* doing an interview." He shook his head. "I hope the poor s.o.b. isn't a diabetic. He's getting a lot of sugar poured into him."

"Par for the course, old boy."

"She lays it on pretty thick."

"In direct ratio to the necessity," added Ian.

"What does that mean?"

"Our boy Mike has been cutting a bit of a swath. He's been making vague promises to any number of ladies. Sent me quite a roster of sweet young things to use in bit parts. I'm afraid I had to call him up on the carpet about it." Ian wrapped his scarf around his reddened ears.

"Does Laura know?"

"Maybe yes, maybe no." He changed his tone briskly. "This next business is where you carry Peggy down the steps to the ambulance. She'll be screaming all the way, having hysterics. I told her I wanted a lot of fight to the scene. Hope you're up to it."

Marty grimaced. "On a full stomach."

"You'll need the energy. I'm going to shoot the whole thing in a master, then break it into a close two and a pair of head shots."

Halfway through the afternoon, the snow materialized. They kept shooting as long as possible and finally, about three thirty, they wrapped for the day.

Marty was in the shower when Laura phoned.

"Have you gone over tomorrow's stuff?" she wanted to know.

"The argument on the Plaza steps? I've read through it, but that's all." He tossed the damp towel onto the sink.

"It's a bitch of a scene. There are so many interrupted speeches and nonsequiturs. It's going to be hell to play with all those extras milling around us. Do you want to go over it tonight? I'm having dinner in my suite."

"Fine. Jack's going to the theater, and I told Ian I'd join

him and some girl for dinner, but I'm sure they'd rather be alone. What time?"

"Let's make it early. Seven?"

They rehearsed for nearly an hour after dinner. The scene gradually came easier to them both. When they were satisfied, they called it quits. Laura ordered drinks from room service.

"Double Chivas and soda." She handed him the glass.

He raised it to her. "Christ, but it's a pleasure to work with you. This stuff is going to play like gangbusters."

"We're both pretty lucky. Arnold wrote a hell of a script." She curled up in a corner of the sofa and wrapped her hostess gown around her legs. "Why are you looking at me like that?"

"Curious, I guess. I've noticed that it doesn't faze you in the least to accept compliments about your work, but when the compliment is personal you throw it back. Is it possible you're only secure in your work?"

She poked at the ice in her glass with her forefinger. "It's possible." Then, regretting her words, "Don't start this stuff again with me, Marty, not when we were getting along so well."

"What makes you think I'm attacking you? I'm interested, that's all. You're a beautiful girl. You're a movie star. So why are you insecure?"

"Stop it."

"Laura," he said gently, "it's quite attractive, a little insecurity in a woman. Invulnerable ladies don't much interest men. Christ!" he laughed, "you're blushing!"

She was furious. The ring of the telephone interrupted her reply.

"Claire! No, of course you're not intruding. I was just going over my lines." She placed a hand over the mouthpiece. "Guess who," she said to Marty.

"I think I'll leave."

"You don't have to. I won't tell her you're here. Yes, Claire," she told her, "go ahead."

Marty browsed through the pages of his script.

"Lies," Laura was saying. "Ask Jack Haller. Ask anyone. Mike's there because he has work to do. I talk to him every night. How can people be so mean, Claire?"

When she had hung up the phone, she walked slowly back to the sofa. Marty was silent.

"Sorry," she said.

"I'm sorry too. I didn't mean to embarrass you by hearing all of that."

"Rumors again."

"Is she printing them?"

"I don't know. Do you know what she said? She asked me if I was considering a divorce. That's the first time anyone has ever used that word about Mike and me. It's sort of a shock to hear it."

He said nothing.

"Mike is—" she broke off. "Mike is my home. I have his name. That's the only home of my own I've ever had, the only name of my own I've ever had."

"Did you speak to Mike about the gossip?"

She shook her head.

"Maybe you should. Talking it over might help."

Laura said, "I didn't ask. I never have. Maybe I never will. What if," her voice faltered, "it turned out to be true? It's not very smart, is it, to ask a question when you may not want to hear the answer to it?"

Marty took a moment before he spoke. "A lot of marriages," he said carefully, "are saved by silence."

Half in a whisper, she said, "He's all I have."

"That isn't quite true, Laura. You have yourself, and that's a lot."

"No. Without Mike I'm nothing. No home. No name. Nothing."

"Had you thought of giving up the business and just being there with him as his wife?"

"But I can't!"

"Why not?"

"Because—" she frowned in confusion. "That would be impossible."

He saw more of it now. Her work had brought Mike into her life, and without it, who knew what might happen? Looking at Laura, he wondered just how aware she was of the situation. Her success and what she could buy with it were assets she could depend on. It was evident her evaluation of herself went no further. She plainly doubted that her own value was sufficient to make her desirable or wanted.

Laura spoke. "What are you thinking?"

"It's your boat. It's up to you to rock it or coast. You know best."

She gave him a small smile. "I remember the first night you took me out. You treated me as if I was a foreigner who didn't speak the language." He started to protest, but she stopped him, "You were truthful, though. I liked that. You still are."

"As often as I can be."

Laura rose. "You're a nice man, Marty."

He kissed her forehead. "Thanks." He noticed that her hands were shaking visibly and glancing down, added, "You know, you look much more beautiful without makeup."

"Truly? Do I?"

"You do."

She smiled self-consciously. "I'm glad you came."

He retrieved his script from the coffee table and waved it. "See you in the morning," he said from the door.

The picture of her stayed with him as he walked down the hall. Laura, looking very young, standing in her robe in the middle of a vast hotel living room. It was a fragile picture. An insecure girl with trembling hands, clinging to an ambitious husband for stability. And the storm warnings already clear to everyone but her.

"What time is it?" Laura asked him as he stepped into the limousine and lit a cigaret.

"A little after ten."

"Do you think we'll go past midnight?"

"I doubt it. Christ, but it's cold out there."

"Six degrees. I heard it on the radio."

Marty unbuttoned his topcoat and peered through the misted car window. He rubbed a portion of the glass clear.

"What are they doing?" she asked.

"Setting up for your exit from the house." He watched in silence as the lights were rolled into place in front of the ornate entrance to the Italian consulate. "Beautiful building," he commented, taking in its façade.

"It's all beautiful," Laura agreed, contemplating the span of Park Avenue punctuated by streetlights and passing traffic. "But," she added, "Thank God it's Friday."

Outside, a few hardy pedestrians huddled in the cold to

watch the movie makers at work. "They must be crazy," said Laura.

"Without people like them, where do you think we'd be?"

"Someplace warm and cozy."

"They're ready for you. Someone just called your name." Marty opened the car door for her.

"If you don't hear from me in half an hour, send out a Saint Bernard with a full keg."

It was almost two in the morning when they returned to the hotel. Marty waved her a wordless good-night and went to his rooms. After a long hot shower he fell asleep immediately.

The shrill jangling of the telephone awoke him. He glanced at his watch. A quarter to six.

"Marty," she said weakly, "Marty, can you come here? Something's wrong. I'm sick."

He tried to clear the sleep from his mind. "What's the matter?"

"I don't know." She sounded frightened. "It hurts. I called the desk and asked them to send a doctor right away. It hurts so bad I'm doubled over." She paused. "I'm scared, Marty."

"Can you get to the door to open it?"

"I will."

"Hang on. I'll be down in a minute." He pulled on his slacks and a sweater and slid his bare feet into his loafers.

A worried desk clerk waited in the living room of Laura's suite.

"Where is she?" demanded Marty.

"In there," he inclined his head toward the bedroom door. "The doctor is with her. Unfortunately, he's not our regular man, but I didn't want to keep her waiting, Mr. Tabor. I prevailed upon one of our guests, Doctor Foss. He's from Rochester, Minnesota, and he's a very well-known internist. I told him it was Laura Curtis and said it was an emergency. He was most cooperative."

"Thanks." Marty sagged into a chair. The clerk continued to pace the carpet. Several minutes passed before the doctor emerged, slippered and clad in a brown bathrobe.

Marty introduced himself. "How is she?"

"Nothing serious. An acute colonic spasm. Uncomfortable, but she'll be all right. I telephoned a colleague of mine, and he'll have his pharmacy send over a prescription as soon as they open."

Marty offered to pay him for his services. Foss brushed the suggestion aside. "Miss Curtis was most gracious," he produced a scrap of paper from the pocket of his robe. "Her autograph," he smiled, "is quite sufficient. My kids will get a real kick out of this."

When they had left, Marty tapped softly on her door and went in. Laura smiled up at him sheepishly from the bed. "I'm sorry. I guess I scared us all to death."

He dismissed it. "You were frightened. How do you feel?"

"Awful. It hurts like hell. I couldn't imagine what it was. I've had so many things wrong with me these past few years. I guess I panicked."

He seated himself on the edge of the bed.

"Marty," she sounded disheartened, "I am so damn tired of being ill. If it's not one bloody thing it's another. Sometimes I wonder if I wasn't born unlucky."

"Don't be foolish. May I have a drink of your Scotch?" He moved to the bureau and poured an inch of liquor into a glass tumbler.

"With everything I've had, it's a wonder I'm not dead by now," she said morosely.

"You're just depressed because you feel lousy. Come on," he returned to the bed, "cheer up. You're made of rugged stuff. It'd take a lot more than a bad bellyache to do you in."

"I almost did die once. That was when I got peritonitis. We were on a skiing trip."

Marty's glass stopped halfway to his mouth. He brought it down and rested it on one knee. "How did that happen?"

"It was my fault, I guess." She smoothed the blanket around her. "I thought I had one of my usual ailments, but it wasn't that at all. It got worse, and I felt terrible, but I didn't want to ruin our vacation so I didn't say anything. Finally, I made a mess of our whole trip by getting carted off to the hospital. Pretty dumb of me," she winced slightly and held her stomach.

"And?"

"And, well, it was quite a scene. The doctors couldn't figure out what was wrong. It was all very dramatic, the way they'd whisper in a little group and shake their heads. They

ended up taking out my appendix. How's that for an anticli-
max?"

He looked at Laura's face, pale against the pillows.

"I didn't mean to get you depressed too. I shouldn't bore
you with my famous illnesses."

Marty chose his words with deliberate caution. "If I were
you, I wouldn't work so hard. Why don't you take more time
off, pamper yourself?" He proceeded carefully, testing her,
"Maybe take a year off and start a family." He watched her
expression.

"No way."

"What do you mean?"

"Motherhood will have to get along without me."

"Why so?"

"Half the equipment is gone, and my doctor says what's left
won't work correctly. He says something happened somewhere along the line to make it crap out."

"That's too bad." He found he had to clear his throat to
say it.

"It's okay. I'm used to the idea now. At first it upset me. I
almost went to pieces whenever I saw a child. But then I
started thinking how many women are in the same boat, and
it seemed stupid to feel sorry for myself."

"You do a good job. You put up a tough front."

"Don't start that again," she said impatiently.

"This time it was a compliment." Marty drained his glass.
"Do you want me to stay with you until your medicine ar-
rives?"

"I'll be all right. Thanks."

He patted her leg through the bed coverings. "Phone if
you need anything."

Unable to sleep, he stood looking out of his window at the
meager early morning traffic on Fifth Avenue. He had never
been, he reminded himself, the kind to stick his nose into
somebody else's life. It wasn't his style. Yet what she said
dogged his mind. He made another attempt to dismiss it as
coincidence. Still, if it were true, then the hard-talking, stubborn, frightened, and vulnerable girl in the suite down the
hall had been monstrously victimized. The suspicion refused
to budge. He shaved, changed his clothes, and went for a
walk. A cold wind knifing through the air failed to clear his
thoughts. He bought a paper and went to Reuben's for break-

fast. Irritated with himself, he left abruptly, his food half-finished. He walked along Fifth Avenue, staring into store windows. When the Museum of Modern Art opened its doors he was waiting. The first floor was given over to a Calder exhibit. Normally he would have enjoyed it.

Marty was angry now. Angry with himself for wanting to know too much. For being curious about something that was none of his damned business. But in spite of all efforts, he could not shake loose the suggestion that plagued him.

He postponed his return to the hotel as long as he could, finding excuses to stay away. It was after six, and a fresh snow was falling when he turned back. He knew what he was going to do, and felt ashamed. It was a shabby, unpalatable business.

Marty phoned Doctor Eliot Green.

When the call was over, he sat quietly by the telephone. Green, without realizing it, had told him enough to convince him it was not only possible, it was probable that Mike Stanton had knowingly caused Laura to become sterile. He had knowingly watched her grow ill, knowingly kept silent, and knowingly allowed her life to be endangered. For what? For what, Marty kept asking himself. And the answer was always the same. To protect his position. There could be no doubt of it. The thought gagged him.

It was a couple of hours before he felt sufficiently controlled to call her. She sounded as if she felt better.

"I'm watching an old movie on television. I'd have thought you'd go out. It's Saturday night."

"I was out all day. It's started snowing. How are you?"

"The pills did the job. I'm taking it easy today, but I'll be fine tomorrow. You're missing something," she laughed. "I'm watching Joan Crawford being very gallant in her padded shoulders and ankle-strap shoes."

"I'm coming over."

Laura eyed the French toast the waiter had brought. "Bland foods, the doctor said. Do you mind if I have a bit of your dinner?" She glanced hungrily at Marty's steak. He sliced off a piece and placed it on her butter dish.

"If Claire Poland saw us now, she'd make headlines of it." Laura handed him the salt and pepper.

"She knows I never make love to my leading ladies."

"Company policy?"

"Something like that."

"It's so easy to fall in love with someone you're working with. I should know—" she cut short the thought. "Were you ever married?"

"No. Almost. Once."

"What happened?"

"She died."

"What was she like?"

He waited a moment. "She wasn't at all like you, if that's what you're asking. She was," he reflected, "quite different."

"In what way?"

"She was self-reliant. She could take care of herself."

"And I can't?"

"No," he said matter-of-factly, "you need someone."

She cut the toast on her plate into neat squares. They ate in silence.

Sometime later, Laura laid her napkin aside and smiled at him. "That was good."

He stirred his coffee. "Why can't you be this soft all the time?"

"You caught me with my defenses down." She offered him the sugar.

"Are you quiet like this at home?" For some reason that last word intruded into their privacy.

She snapped shut the lid of the coffee pot. "Empty. I doubt it. I'm always too busy. Too much to do."

"Like what?"

"I'm an actress, remember? A commodity. Victory peddles me. So does Obie. Mike too, in a way. And," she went on, "at any given time I have to be ready to be sold. I read the material they send me. I talk business. That's my life. The interviews, the personal appearances. You know it as well as I do. So," she continued, her customary sharpness returning, "if your idea of heaven is some bovine, syrupy stay-at-home, you are definitely in the wrong room."

"It was a mistake for me to ask. You're prettier with your mouth shut."

She got up from the table and walked to the window. "It's still coming down. There must be a couple of inches on the ground already. Do you like the snow?"

"When I can watch it from inside a warm room." He went to the window and looked out over her shoulder. The snow swirled restlessly under the steady glow of a street lamp. He reached out to touch her arm, but suddenly that was not enough.

She met his mouth hungrily. When she broke free, she huddled against his body, her head on his chest. "I'm afraid. What will happen?"

"I don't know." He touched his face to her hair and enjoyed her fragrance. She did not move as he opened her robe and slid her nightgown off of her shoulders. She slid between the sheets of the bed and waited for him silently.

"Laura." His lips caressed her shoulder. He cupped her breast in his hand, fondling it gently.

"Oh God, Marty," she whispered. He kissed her trembling mouth, his hands traveling eagerly over her smooth skin, wanting every part of her at once. She reached between his legs and took him in her hands. She touched him to her. "Please."

She was warm and ready. They rocked together, their bodies straining with their desire. Her legs gripped his waist. He felt her begin to pulsate under him, and together they moaned at the moment of release. Her head jerked convulsively as she shuddered and lay silent. She said his name. "Hold me."

Marty saw all the nights before when in darkness voices had begged him to hold, to kiss, to fuck, to tell them he loved them And there had been the overriding emptiness, the absence of feeling. Now, here, there was warmth that needed and demanded to be shared. He stroked her face, neither one of them caring that her tears flowed down her cheeks and soaked the pillow under their heads.

They awoke tumbled in each other's arms and made love again, as if to reassure themselves that it had really happened.

Afterward, she said softly, "You never get involved with your leading ladies."

"It's too late now." He kissed her, their mouths soft with remembered passion. She lay close to him, her body contoured to his.

"It's not snowing anymore. The sun is out."

He ran his fingers lightly over her hair.

"Can we go for a walk in the snow, Marty? In Central Park?"

He grinned at her enthusiasm. "Is that what you want?"

"Yes. Before it gets all dirty with soot."

He stretched and extracting himself from the tangled sheets, held her hand, making the moment last. "Agreed," he said, "on one condition. Stay the way you are."

She sat up. "Naked?"

"Sweet. No tough talk. If for one moment you go hard on me, I'll walk away and leave you. I don't want a business woman and I don't want a movie star. Just Laura, no make-up, taking a walk in the park."

She frowned. "No makeup? Shit, Marty, now you've gone too far."

His hand traced her body through the sheets. "When you're with me, what you are is enough, Laura. It pleases me. What you pretend to be isn't worth discussing." He stood up.

She stopped him halfway across the room. "Why are you so damned hard on me?"

"Because," he said simply, "it matters. I don't want what the others want. I want what you're most afraid to give. The real Laura."

She looked at him, saying nothing.

"It will be more than enough." He turned and walked out of the room.

In front of the hotel, several taxis waited in a line, a slash of startling yellow against the whiteness around them. The Plaza fountain, its shape softened by the topping of snow, gave the appearance of an ornate ice-cream cake in the process of melting. Laura took Marty's hand as they made their way across the partially cleared street to the park entrance. The hush around them was broken only by the distant rasp of a shovel on a sidewalk. Neither of them spoke for some time. At last, Laura asked quietly, "What was her name, the girl who died?"

"Kathy."

"It must have been hard."

"It was. It taught me to take happiness where you find it; there's always the chance it won't be there the next time you look."

Laura touched his arm and pointed skyward. A bright red balloon floated up through the bare trees and drifted errati-cally higher and higher into the cloudless blue. "I love this park. It's the only thing I miss about New York."

"I miss it all," he said, "but mostly the seasons. Sometimes in California I can't even remember what month we're in."

"Where did you live?" she asked.

"When I was starting out I lived in the west eighties. Then I came back to do a play and sublet an apartment on Fifty-seventh street. There wasn't much difference, except that the roaches ate better at the second place."

She shuddered. "I'd forgotten about the cockroaches."

"It was a sport, surprising them. I'd flick on the kitchen light at three in the morning and watch the whole floor scatter. Jesus," he shook his head wonderingly, "those were crazy times. The first place I lived belonged to an actress I knew. She couldn't make the rent, so she shared it with another guy and myself. She used to get up in the middle of the night to bang on the radiator with a monkey wrench. Drove us nuts. It turned out her ex-husband lived in the apartment upstairs and she couldn't take it that he might be asleep with some other girl."

Laura smiled. "Did she finally stop?"

"Sure. She married the other roommate, and I was put out on the street."

The snow crunched quietly under their feet. Laura eyed a statue of a horse and rider as they walked past. "Poor bastards, they look cold up there."

"Did you know that if the horse has both front hoofs in the air it means the man died in battle?"

She studied the figures. "I'll take your word for it. Suppose," she inquired slyly, "it has both rear hoofs in the air?"

Marty thought for a moment. "That means he got kicked in the ass during a rodeo."

"Crazy man." She hugged his waist.

"Your face is freezing cold. Do you want to go back?"

"I'm warm inside." She tilted her head up for his kiss. "Should we be doing this in public?"

"What public?" he laughed, taking in the vast white expanse around them.

"Well, there are the pigeons," she nodded in the direction of a few small birds huddled at the foot of the statue. "Maybe they carry messages."

"Who's crazy now?"

"Both of us," she decided. She walked on in silence.

At the top of a slope several children had assembled with

sleds and tea trays. They stopped to watch them careening down the fresh crisscrossed tracks.

Laura spoke softly. "That reminds me of when I was a kid in Devon."

"Devon, Massachusetts?"

"You've actually heard of it?"

"It's on the Cape. I played a summer theater near there once. Do you ever go back?"

She shook her head. "There's no reason to. Everyone's gone." Slowly, in bits and pieces, she began to tell him about her family and her life after that.

He glanced sideways. She was gazing down at the snow-covered ground as she walked. Marty listened, putting together the fragments as she recalled them. It became increasingly plain why Laura trusted her value as an actress over her value as an individual. Her success had proved the only dependable element. He really understood now the lack of self-confidence. He also understood why she allowed Mike to manipulate her and why she indulged his whims without complaint. Mike was, as she had pointed out, all she'd ever had. It didn't, to Marty, seem like much. But then, something was better than nothing. With an uncomfortable sense of misgiving, he wondered how Laura would react if her illusions about Mike were irrevocably destroyed.

"He came along when I was alone and needed someone," she told him. "He's been so good to me. I owe him so much."

"You've given him a lot already. Most men would be content with the simple pleasure of your company."

She looked at him as if she was not quite sure she could believe him.

He changed the subject. "Do you miss Devon? That's beautiful country around there."

"Hardly ever. I only remember the special things. Corny stuff. Christmas caroling. The Fourth of July parades. They were the big event in the town. We had a fife-and-drum corps and patriotic floats. The kids with bikes would have them decked out with red, white, and blue streamers." She laughed softly. "The whole town followed the parade to the cemetery. There was a memorial marker under a weeping beech tree, and some soldiers who always wore red neckerchiefs fired off a salute, and everybody stood still while they played taps. Then there would be a mad scramble for the empty rifle shells. We'd hide behind the gravestones, blowing into the shells, making whistles to interrupt the dull speeches that came after." Laura stopped. "Am I a deadly bore?"

"Never." He brushed the snow off the slats of a bench and motioned her to sit beside him. Two elderly gentlemen in black hats and coats trudged by them, each carrying a cumbersome cello. Marty watched them diminish in the pale distance. "They look like figures out of a Magritte painting."

"You're talking to the wrong girl. I don't know about those things. I can tell you how many frames of film make a minute of screening time, but that's about the extent of my formal education."

"Tell you what." He stood. "We'll walk down to the Museum of Modern Art. That's a good, warm place to spend a cold afternoon."

But as they passed the hotel they glanced at each other in wordless agreement. There were warmer places.

It was almost eight in the evening. "I'll be back in half an hour," he had told Laura. "I want to collect my messages and return a few calls. I'll shower and shave while I'm at it."

His phone rang persistently as he removed a clean pair of slacks from one of the hangers in the closet. He reached across to the night table and lifted the receiver.

"Marty?" Static crackled on the line. "Marty? It's Mike Stanton here."

"Yes, Mike." He let the slacks fall on the bed.

"I spoke to Laura just now. She said she'd been ill night before last and that you'd gone over to help her."

"That's right."

"Is she okay now? She says she's feeling great, but you can't be sure with her. She'll drive herself into the ground rather than admit she can't handle a situation."

"It was minor. Nothing to be upset about. A spastic colon, and the medication took care of it."

"Good. And thanks," said Mike. "I wanted to hear it from you. Laura glosses over these things. I think she gets carried away with that stuff about the show must go on."

Marty cut him off. "Anything else I can do for you?"

"Did you hear about the terrific footage we got in Mexico? Not to mention a few choice hangovers. Christ, but if that damn tequila isn't sneaky———"

"You'll have to excuse me, Mike, I have a dinner date waiting."

"Sure. I only wanted to double check on how Laura was feeling. Thanks again for stepping in."

"Don't mention it."

"See you when you get back."

"Right." Good old Mike. Nice guy, nice husband Mike. . . . He dressed, pocketed a pack of cigarets, and walked down the hall to the suite where Laura waited for him.

Marty reported to work Monday morning outside the Seagram building. Wind whipped across the wide plaza, carrying with it stinging particles of fallen snow. Laura had the day off. It was just as well. They would have difficulty enough appearing casual on the set.

His face burned from the icy wind as he shaved and changed for dinner. Ian had discovered a new restaurant in the Village. Five of them—Laura, Marty, Jack, Ian, and a tall dish inappropriately named Alex—dined together. The food wasn't much, but the passing parade of local color was worth the trip downtown.

"I'll walk you to your door," Marty said as he and Laura left the others in the elevator. He followed her into the living room.

"Wait here a minute." She went into the bathroom, and Marty heard the sound of the window being opened. "See?" She returned with a frosty bottle of champagne and a pair of glasses. "I had them on the outside ledge."

He set the open bottle on the bedside table. It pleased him that she was slower to undress than he. He enjoyed watching her reveal her body to him. He remembered watching his grandfather paring an orange with a jackknife, gradually, painstakingly, until its ripeness lay bare and appetizing on the plate before him. Laura slid into the bed and nestled close. He handed her a glass of champagne.

She raised it. "To sin."

"No," he stopped her. "Unfunny. You don't mean that."

After a few minutes, he placed both their glasses on the table and, bending over her, kissed her lingeringly. Marty drew back and looked down at Laura's face. He ran his thumb over the soft contours of her mouth. Reaching into his near-empty glass, he moistened a finger and traced the outline of her nipples with the wine, watching as they grew hard and tight under his touch. He lowered his mouth to her breasts to catch the rivulets. Laura sighed softly and opened her legs to him. He lifted the glass and allowed the remaining droplets of pale liquid to trickle onto the dark triangle between her thighs. He tasted her, probing her softness until her fingers grasped at his hair and she pulled him upward on top of her. He drew her legs onto his shoulders and moved into her. She gripped his forearms. With a gasp she came to him, and he exhausted himself inside her.

They lay without speaking, and Marty, drowsy, felt himself slipping into sleep. The telephone shrilled him awake. Laura reached for it reluctantly.

"Hello?" she paused. "Yes, I just got back about half an hour ago. I had dinner with Jack and Ian."

The obvious omission was his cue. Marty sat up and, reaching for his clothes, walked into the living room.

"You didn't have to do that." She stood in the doorway, tying her robe around her.

"Yes I did. It would have been unpleasant for both of us for me to lie there while you talked to him." He stubbed out his cigaret and went to her. "Laura, you're shaking."

"I'm so—so sorry."

"What happened?"

"Nothing," she said blankly. "Nothing happened."

He led her to the sofa.

"It was too much. All at once I realized I don't know what I think anymore. I'm not sure of who I am or what I'm doing." She looked at Marty. "I don't know what I want."

He took a deep breath. "Would it be easier for you if it never happened again?"

"No!"

"Laura," he told her, "it is not a choice that has to be made now, tonight."

"Marty, I don't know what to do. He's all I've ever had."

"You have me."

"Don't leave. Stay here tonight. I don't want to be alone."

He stayed that night. And all the nights that followed. Her fear had touched him more than he wanted to admit.

Marty circumspectly motioned to Jack to seat himself beside Laura. He pulled out an adjoining chair. They were careful. They measured their moments together on the set, spreading their time and company among the others. He realized he had begun to feel fiercely protective of her safety and serenity. It was harder on Laura. Sometimes when they stood speaking together, straining to appear casual, he caught her eyes flicking warily over his shoulder like a trapped rabbit alert for the hunters.

"It won't be long now," Jack said over coffee. "One more week and then back to the sunshine country. What are your plans for the weekend, Marty?"

"None. Just to take it easy."

"I'm going down to Bucks County to get a breath of country air. I thought you might like to join me." He lit Laura's cigaret.

"Thanks for the offer, but I think I'll stick close to home base."

"Laura, you're invited too."

She looked up sharply.

Jack continued, "Some friends of mine have a house near New Hope. They're in Florida, but the servants stayed behind. Sure you won't come?"

Laura glanced hesitantly at Marty.

"I can't speak for Laura," he said smoothly, "but I'll have to pass it up."

"Suit yourselves." He rose from the table.

Laura looked anxiously at Marty.

"Don't worry." He reached across the table and gave her hand a brief pressure. He noticed her eyes move instantly to Jack's retreating figure.

"He didn't notice anything. You're overly sensitive." Marty held her coat for her.

The weekend passed in privacy, neither of them mentioning the unalterable fact that this was the last such weekend they might have together.

Marty stepped aside while the prop man dimmed the glare of the car window with dulling spray. "I have an idea for that last speech," he said to Laura. "At the point where you stop in mid-sentence and pause to let the words get to me, I'm going to take slightly longer to react. That way you'll have more to play off of. Okay with you?"

"Good. It'll punch up the scene. Did Jack tell you that the Major is very enthusiastic about the footage he's seen?"

"He was congratulating everyone this morning. I think he even congratulated the guy who delivers our coffee."

"I'm glad for him." She moved for a length of cable which was being laid between them.

"We're not out of the woods yet. We haven't even begun the biggest portion of the shooting."

"But it will be good. I know it. Haven't you ever been on a picture that just felt good from the start? That's the way this one feels."

"That," he said quietly, "is because you're so content."

"I am," she murmured.

"Everything looks promising when you're in love."

Laura glanced at him. "Are we?"

"Pretty close to it." With his thumb and forefinger, he flicked his cigaret into the gutter and stepped back into position by the car door.

"What are we going to do, Marty?" She took her place beside him.

"Right now, we're going to shoot this scene." He waited for Ian's last-minute directions.

Laura mixed a drink and set it on the coffee table in front of him. "Did you mean what you said this afternoon?"

"Jesus Christ," Marty chuckled, "why is it that women always ask you if you meant what you said? Why the hell would anyone say anything he didn't mean?"

"Assuming you meant it, then it presents certain problems, doesn't it?" She rubbed her palms together nervously.

"What do you think?"

Laura stared at her hands. "I'm so confused. Will I have to choose?"

Marty leaned forward, his arms folded on his knees. "Sometime you will. Otherwise it becomes a much dirtier business. I don't like the idea of taking turns with another man. And I'm not at all sure you could stand up under it. You're not sophisticated enough to take it lightly."

"But it isn't light, is it? It's serious."

"It is."

Laura shook her head. "I just can't think." She was plainly

relieved when the telephone rang. She covered the mouthpiece. "It's Jack. He asked if you were here."

"Yes, Jack?" said Marty. "We're just going over tomorrow's work. Care to join us?" He paused. "I don't know. Maybe Laura would like to see it. I'll ask her." He turned. "Jack has a pair of tickets to the Pinter play that just opened. He says he's too tired to go."

"He won't think it's odd that you'd take me?"

"It's almost seven. Where would I find someone else on such short notice?" He turned back to the phone. "Sure we can use them. I'll pick them up on the way out."

A fine, granular snow was sifting down when they left the theater, already powdering the streets. They stopped for a moment to sign several autographs. "Let's walk," she suggested. Laura took his arm, and they crossed Broadway in the direction of Fifth Avenue. "I love this kind of storm," she said, "when everything looks so soft." There were few people on the sidewalks. They strolled in virtual seclusion. Here and there steam issued whitely from a manhole, blending into the downfalling flurry in a misty swirl. The blanketing quiet stiffled the sound of their voices.

Marty reached over and brushed the snow from Laura's hair.

"It couldn't be much more beautiful, could it?" she said.

"In a minute someone will say 'Cut,' and they'll turn off the snow machines."

"You're a cynic."

"A realist."

"I guess one of us had to be."

At last, in a small voice, he heard her ask, "Why? Why does everything have to be so damn complicated?

Laura leaned on a railing, looking out over the bright blue river. A pair of red-and-white tugboats glided past looking absurdly dainty, like bathtub toys. Marty watched her from his chair a few feet away. The wind that was whipping choppy waves in the water blew her hair around her face. He wondered what she was thinking about. It wasn't hard to guess. He rose and walked past the camera to where she stood.

"Hi."

She continued to observe the river traffic. A sight-seeing

boat cruised by, and the commentary of the guide over the loudspeaker floated across the water and was gone. A chunk of melting snow fell off the railing and splashed into the current lapping below them. He watched it drift toward the distant bridge.

"I think," Laura said dreamily, "it would be wonderful just to get on a boat and float away. Everything would be so simple."

"Would you go alone?"

She turned. "It was only a fantasy."

"I'll play along. Who would you take with you? You're going to have to decide what you want out of life."

She didn't look at him. "I already have a life."

"And what's known always seems safer." He shook his head. "Even if it's an appalling compromise."

"Are you so sure that's what it is?"

"Laura," he said heavily, "you haven't the vaguest idea how to handle love. You're accustomed to settling for whatever you can buy, and as far as I can see, that's never been much more than companionship."

"Take it easy, Marty. I don't want the others to notice anything."

He glanced over his shoulder. "They're changing the camera setup. Nobody's interested in what we're doing. What it is," he continued, "is a question of value. Your value as an actress is never in doubt. You have every right to it. It's even tangible. All those reassuring dollars and cents. But personal value is something else. It can only be measured by other people's reactions to you."

"Go on."

"I'm not blaming you for anything. It would be impossible for you to place much personal value on yourself when all the people who should have been close to you seemed to have given you up so easily. Christ," he said bitterly, "the only people who ever hung around were on your payroll."

She spoke softly. "I'm not sure I could live without it. I don't know anything else. What would I do? Keeping house bores me. I'm not much for reading. Nothing else interests me. What would I do?"

"For God's sake, people change their lives, develop new resources. All it takes is guts, and you've never lacked those."

She prodded a loose piece of ice with the toe of her shoe, edging it toward the water and watching it fall with a splash.

"Laura, haven't you ever seen a champion tennis player or a great jockey? You can see with your own eyes what makes a winner. You can always spot the champions. They're the ones with the intuition. They know instinctively when to stay cool, to hold back and, other times, when to risk everything in one big push to win."

"What in hell has that got to do with me?"

"You've always had it in you to be a champion. Look at your career. You're successful in a profession where ninety percent of the entries never even make it to the starting gate. Surely you don't believe that Victory Studios manufactured Laura Curtis from scratch. The material was there all the time."

"Get to the punch line. They'll be calling us in a minute."

"Just do me a favor and trust your intuitions, that's all. I seem to have more faith in your instincts than you do."

"I don't suppose it's occurred to you that you could be wrong. That without the makeup department and the publicity office and the rest of it, I might be nothing more than your average dumb cunt."

"Stow it, Laura. It's unbecoming. Unfeminine. But then," he said pointedly, "women who are married to weak men often become ballsy."

She turned on him. "Mike's not weak!"

"He is, Laura, and you know it."

"I need him. If I don't have Mike, I have nothing!"

"Bullshit."

Laura opened her door, "I didn't know if you'd come."

"Why shouldn't I?"

"I thought after what happened you might stay away." She rested her head against his chest.

"You're the one who kept retiring to the dressing room to sulk. I was right there on the set all afternoon."

"Mike and I hardly ever have arguments."

"That's you. You're afraid to rock the boat. Don't worry." He kissed the top of her head. "I still love you even if you are a bitch sometimes. Did you really think I'd let go so easily?"

She hugged him closer.

"Hell, if you find a little happiness, you hang onto it. Even if it means enduring some crap now and then." He tilted her face up to his. He realized that what he saw in her eyes was gratitude. "Oh, Christ," he said bitterly. Before she could question him, he asked, "What's the plan for this evening?"

"Ian wants us to go to a new place he found. I'm beginning to think that's his hobby, scouting restaurants."

"Do you want to go?"

"You know what I want." She kissed him. "But we have to stay visible. If both of us drop out of sight, people will get suspicious."

"I'll call him and tell him to count us in. But tomorrow and the next night you'd better plead a splitting headache. I'll find some excuse to stay home. They're the only two evenings we have left." He reached for the phone.

"Don't talk about it, Marty, please."

He woke in the middle of the night and found Laura crying. Marty held her in his arms. It infuriated him that he felt so damned impotent to relieve her fears. He wondered how much longer she could stand it. She was clinging for dear life to her illusions, but something had to give. Would it be Mike? Or himself? Or, God forbid, Laura? Could the trembling that seized her in these moments finally shake her apart? Before that could happen, he knew he would have to leave her, for her own sake. It would be a feeble compromise. For a while it might console her, but inevitably the sham of her life with Mike would lie exposed. It had to happen sometime. Perhaps when she was alone and had no one to fall back on. What would become of her in that case? Marty had made up his mind to hang on as long as he could safely do so without threatening her equilibrium.

He knocked at the door of her suite.

"Come in. It's open."

He pushed the door back and a snowball smacked him square in the face. "You bitch!" He hopped up and down, shaking loose the bits of ice that had gotten inside his sweater.

Laura shrieked with laughter. "You looked so surprised!"

"Who wouldn't be, for Christ's sake? We're on the nineteenth floor. It's a little high up for guerrilla warfare."

"I got it off the windowsill," she giggled.

"You're a sneaky broad."

"All's fair in love and war."

"I'm not sure which one we're engaged in." With a quick motion, he dove for her.

Laura leaped behind a chair. "Don't you dare!"

He circled her stealthily. "You made up the rules."

She dodged, steaking across the room. Marty followed.

"I'll scream," she threatened, laughing.

"Do that." He reached, and she sprinted out of his grasp. Marty darted after her. As Laura tripped over the ottoman, they collided and fell together to the floor, dissolved in lunatic mirth.

"You never told me you did slapstick," Marty gasped.

Laura caught her breath. "How am I going to explain carpet burns?" She looked at his face and broke into laughter. "Okay, I'll say uncle. You've got me pinned to the mat."

"Winner takes all." He plunged his fingers into her soft hair and kissed her.

When it was over, they lay in quiet dishevelment on the floor. Laura smiled. "Does this constitute rape?"

"No jury in the country would convict me. I was provoked."

"Remind me to provoke you again sometime." She rolled over on her side and kissed his neck. . . .

"I guess Jack's happy," she said over dinner. "We finished location on schedule."

"I guess." The conversation had become fitful, broken by thoughtful pauses. Tomorrow morning they'd be on a plane, heading back. Marty reached across the table and took her hand in his. She studied his face.

"Laura, whatever happens——"

"Don't, Marty. I understand."

She woke him with her hands on his body. Drowsily, he lay with his eyes still shut, feeling her light touch travel over him and come to rest between his thighs. She took him in her mouth and, when he was ready, straddled him. He felt the softness of her breast brushing against his lips and tasted her. Soundlessly, they stirred together. Her body tensed, and she started to throb around him. Holding her buttocks, he pushed into her and together they sighed and fell still. Her head rested on his shoulder.

"I wish," she whispered, "that it could last forever."

"Maybe it will."

She turned and lay on her back, staring at the ceiling.

When there was no more time, Marty got out of bed. He started to speak.

Laura cut him off. "I know. We have to hurry." She didn't move, watching him dress.

He leaned over the bed and kissed her. "See you in the lobby."

"Yes," she said, her face without expression.

"I want to rehearse this for moves only," directed Ian.

Marty stepped into place beside Laura, and they went through the scene slowly, mechanically, for camera cues. When they had finished, Marty asked, "Did you do your scenes with Peggy this morning?"

"Yes. What did you do?"

"Stills in the portrait gallery and some fittings."

"Would you like to run lines?" asked Laura.

"Not unless you want to." He moved toward the group of camp chairs off camera.

"Seventy-one, seventy-two, seventy-three, seventy-four," Peggy Smart was counting the stitches on her knitting needles. "Sit down, you two." She moved a skein of yarn from the seat of Marty's chair. "Glad to be home?" she asked him.

"Sure." He motioned to Laura to sit down.

"No, I think I'll go outside. It's stuffy in here."

"I'll join you. Care for a breath of air, Peggy?"

She shook her head. "Seventy-five, seventy-six . . ."

Marty waited until the heavy door had swung completely shut. "How was your weekend?"

Laura shrugged. She sauntered across the sunbaked alleyway to an open shed where several dozen staircases of every conceivable style stood ranked beside each other down the length of the street. "Don't they look strange, all those steps leading to noplace?"

Marty brushed a fleck of peeling paint from an ancient banister.

"And those," she said, gazing at the hundreds of doors stacked in threes and fours to lean against the rear of the shed. "How many people do you suppose have walked through those doors?"

"Laura, how was the weekend?"

She turned to face him. "It was all right. What did you do?"

"A lot of thinking. A little tennis."

"Mike bought me a present. A dog."

Marty sat on the bottom tread of a rotting antebellum staircase. Laura leaned against its sagging balustrade. "A Lhasa Apso. It's very chic. This year's dog, Mike says."

"Do you like it?"

"He has an ugly face. He can't help that, can he? Mike named him Yeti. That's because——"

"Never mind. I can figure it out for myself."

"I feel sorry for him."

"The dog?"

"He's so unattractive." She picked at a loose splinter of wood. "When am I going to see you?"

"You're sure," he said carefully, "that it's still what you want."

Laura nodded. "It's not—" she hesitated. "It's not so good anymore. Mike and me. I don't——" she halted again, at pains to select a word, "enjoy it as much as I did."

Marty was silent for a moment. "That's not enough reason, Laura. That can happen to anyone, but usually things go back to normal after a time. It could be as good as it ever was."

"I want to be with you."

"Does that mean you've made a choice?"

A flicker of alarm crossed her face. "I can't. Not yet. Give me time, Marty, please. But I have to see you. Can't we go to the dressing room?"

"Don't be a fool, Laura. Mike could walk on the set any minute. The situation is uncomfortable enough without the addition of any shabby dressing-room sex."

Across the alley, the stage door opened. "Principals, please. We're ready to try a rehearsal."

Marty rose and brushed off the dust from the stairs. Dutifully, Laura followed. "What will we do?"

"Work. Say the lines. Shoot the scenes. You say you need time. Take it." He opened the door for her.

By Thursday, he was beinning to wonder if he'd done the right thing. Laura was taut as a bowstring. Once or twice he saw her wardrobe woman, Indigo, glance at her worriedly.

Did the others sense something? He was in no position to ask.

Coming out of his dressing room, he saw the two of them. Mike and Laura. They were sitting with a man he didn't recognize, a reporter, judging from the notes he was taking. Marty stood watching. They smiled and nodded in unison, as if their strings were being manipulated by the same puppeteer. Another pair of nods. More smiles. Mutual beaming at some compliment. Laughter all around. They were performing a duet. Serious talk now. Sober expressions. Two intellectual frowns. Christ, he thought, their marriage might as well be written on cue cards. He turned away and walked over to the coffee wagon in the corner of the stage.

Ian was stirring a paper cup full of strong tea. "Sugar?" He handed Marty the box of cubes. Leaning against the wagon, he idly observed Mike, Laura, and the interviewer. "Laura's under a bit of a strain. Have you noticed?"

"Maybe she's not sleeping well."

"We don't usually have to mess about much with the lights and diffusion on her closeups. The way she's looking lately, we'll have to use a Mitchell C before long." He went on to another thought. "Marty, when you exit the scene, you'll be going camera right. Keep as close to camera as possible, will you?"

"Check." He followed Ian toward the set.

"Mr. Tabor." The reporter extended his hand. "Bill d'Antonio, U. P. I. Could I impose on you for a few minutes?"

Marty seated himself in the group and greeted Mike.

"Miss Curtis here says this is the finest script she's ever had." Bill d'Antonio looked at him expectantly.

"She's right. It's largely the girl's story."

"Does that mean you're not happy with your role?"

"No, but it does mean that Laura has a good crack at an Academy Award." Out of the corner of his eye, Marty saw the two of them assume identically respectful countenances. He returned his attention to d'Antonio's questions. When it seemed he'd satisfied him, the notepad was slapped shut. Bill d'Antonio lit up a cigar.

Mike asked Marty, "Did Laura tell you about the mutt?"

"She did."

"I bought Laura a Lhasa Apso," he explained to the other man. "Champion stock. We haven't decided whether or not to train him for show. Right now it's all we can do to train him to be housebroken. Every time I try to discipline him, he runs upstairs and hides under our bed. The bed is so wide that I can't reach him from either side. The smart little bastard knows it, too."

"Excuse me." Marty stood. "I have a call to make."

It was after six when they wrapped for the day. He changed into Levi's and a sweater, handing his suit to the wardrobe man.

He headed for the stage door. A glow of lights and a small flurry of activity was still going on in an empty corner of the darkened soundstage. He paused, curious, and walked over.

The sleek red Ferrari that Laura drove in the film had been brought onto the stage. It stood against a hastily rigged backdrop of painted countryside. Two green men lugged several potted shrubs into place around it.

"What's going on?" Marty asked.

"It's supposed to look like the Riviera," grunted one of the green men. "Look like the Riviera to you, Frank?"

"Very," said the other.

More lights were being rolled in. "Bring me a baby junior," some called.

"Coming up."

Laura stood beside him. She surveyed the activity, saying nothing. She looked exhausted. Beneath the pancake, the rouge, and the stuff smeared under her eyes to obscure the circles, he knew she would be pale. At the first sign of fatigue, Laura became wan. Suddenly the falseness of the makeup and the fake lashes seemed grotesque on her. They gave her a slightly ruined look. He wondered how much more ruined she might look if the charade continued.

"I thought you'd gone home," he said.

She shook her head. "Mike likes the Ferrari, so he made a deal with the advertising agency. I'm shooting some publicity stills. The car is his birthday present."

"You're tired."

Laura nodded.

"What are you doing Saturday?"

She glanced at him quickly. "I have to get a dress for the party, but that won't take long."

"I'll give you directions to find the place."

When he unlocked the door to the house, there was a telegram lying on the floor. He dropped his script on a chair and ripped open the envelope. "Please join us for dinner and dancing at our home 51 Copa de Oro Road on Saturday March 18 from eight until dawn. Black tie. R.S.V.P. CR3-4025. Laura Curtis and Mike Stanton." Marty crushed the paper in his fist and aimed it into the wastebasket. The wording, he knew, was Mike's. He had pointedly signed it Laura Curtis in case anyone forgot who Mrs. Mike Stanton was.

Marty answered the doorbell. Laura stood hesitantly on the flagstone steps. "Come in."

She looked around the room. "It looks like you," she said softly.

"What does that mean?"

"Warm. Comfortable. Solid."

"I sound dull." He moved to one of the large chairs by the window.

"You have a beautiful view of the hills."

"Is that what we're going to talk about? Or maybe you'd like to discuss the weather. That's pretty exciting too."

She smiled sheepishly. "It's been so long since we were alone like this." She reached out her hand, and he held it. For a few minutes they sat in silence, watching a pair of raucous bluejays strutting across the green lawn outside. "I bought a dress," she said. "Would you like to see it?"

"Not now."

"You will come to the party, won't you?"

"Are you sure you want me to? It won't make it too difficult for you?"

"I never wanted this party. Now it's going to be a sham. I detest it. Please," she insisted, squeezing his hand, "you have to be there. It will help."

"I'll be there, if that's what you want."

"We can get lost in the crowd. Nobody will notice. Mike sent out almost two hundred telegrams. It's going to be a mob scene."

"Sounds like a big deal."

"He's hired one of the studio set designers to decorate the house. Now he's afraid maybe he's going a little overboard with the Mexican theme. After all, it is mostly a French-style house, and——"

"Jesus, Laura!" he exploded. "I don't want to hear what Mike is or is not doing. I don't give a damn about his frigging plans. It's you I care about."

"Take me to bed."

He took her.

He woke and saw that the afternoon sun was casting brassy rays on the white bedroom wall. Laura was still asleep. He studied her face on the pillow next to him. In repose, she looked very childlike. The unlined innocence of her face touched off a protective response in him. She moved drowsily, and a strand of hair fell across her cheek. He brushed it away. Laura opened her eyes and smiled.

"Have a good nap?"

She slid toward him and kissed his cheek.

Marty held her close to him, tracing the blue veins of her breasts with his finger.

"Be careful," she murmured sleepily, "you know what happened the last time you did that."

He kissed her, his tongue probing the pliant warmth of her mouth.

"I don't believe it," she said. "So soon?"

"Try me."

When he had showered and dressed, he found Laura in the living room. He stood in the doorway, observing her as she moved about the room, stopping to examine things that caught her eye. She picked up a crystal paperweight from a table and held it. She laid it down and ran her hand over the contours of his desk. Her fingers traveled over the books on the shelf. It was as if she wanted the touch of his things to cling to her after she had left.

He walked with her to the door and placed both hands on her shoulders. "Laura, I'm not going to let this become something we do on alternate Saturday afternoons. I've seen what's happening to you. It's not getting any easier for me, either."

"I'm trying, Marty. I am. I'm so torn up inside that I can't think clearly. If I could just sort out my feelings." She bent her head to one side and kissed his hand.

"I won't put any more pressure on you, Laura. That would only make it harder on you. On the other hand, things can't continue this way forever. Neither one of us can put up with this indefinitely."

"Be patient with me. I have to be sure."

He opened the door. The pale afterglow of sunset still illuminated the sky. Laura got into her car.

"You were away all day," he said. "There won't be any questions?"

She patted the dress box on the front seat. "I had a dreadful time finding something I liked," she said lightly. "Had to go to I don't know how many stores. Finally I found two that I could wear, but then it took me an hour to make up my mind."

"Don't become too devious, Laura. It's not a talent I want to see in you." He put his head through the car window and gave her a brief kiss. "See you Monday at work."

"Marty?"

"Come on in, Jack." He laid his newspaper aside as Jack stepped into the trailer.

He seated himself next to the makeup table. "The Major was in town earlier this week. He just took off to go back to the yacht."

"What's the verdict?"

"Good. Raves. He even went so far as to okay the new scene Arnold wrote. When the Major commits himself to expending cold cash on a scene with a hundred extras, you better believe he likes the film."

"That's a point for our team. Have you told Laura?"

"Just now. She's outside talking with Mike. You doing anything tonight?"

"No plans. Why?"

"Come over for a drink after work. Lisa's going to one of her lectures on baby care."

Marty flashed a grin. "She's going at this thing full tilt, isn't she?"

"The kid doesn't stand a chance. Well," Jack rose and stretched, "back to the office. I just dropped by to raise the morale of the troops."

Marty waited until he saw Mike leave his chair and walk away from where Laura was sitting. His eyes followed him to the stage door. Marty went to her and took the empty seat. "What was that conference about?"

She gave him a quick, tense smile. "Outdoor heaters. Mike got the weekend weather report, and the temperature is supposed to be around fifty degrees in the evenings. He's thinking of renting a bunch of heating units."

"Are you beginning to look forward to this thing?

"What do you think?"

"Why did you let him do it?"

"He wanted to."

"Will you be able to carry it off?" Marty scanned her face, assessing the strain he saw there.

"Of course," she replied vacantly. "Don't I always? I've never missed a performance yet."

Marty put his hand on her arm. Hastily, she jerked it away, as if his touch had burned her.

"Nothing wrong with that, Laura. It was a very ordinary gesture."

"All the same . . ."

"I don't like the thought of you performing your way through that party like some sort of trained animal. It makes me sick."

"What would you have me do? The damn party is only two days away."

Marty leaned forward toward her. His voice was low. "This thing between us isn't making you happy, Laura. It could get to the point where it'll be no good going on."

"You could do that? Just walk away?"

"I don't want to, but I'm not going to force you to suffer."

She said, "I need you, Marty."

"You also said you need Mike."

"It's not the same!" she whispered. "I believe in you, Marty. I've never trusted anyone so completely before."

"You just admitted what's wrong with your marriage."

"That's different. Mike and I want our life the way it is. We want the same things for each other."

"And what might those be? Fame and fortune?"

She didn't reply.

"That's a wonderful basis for a marriage. Who negotiated the contract? Obie?"

"Is what you want so different?"

"Damn right. I want a woman. Not," he gestured toward the camera, "the darling of millions. Christ, Laura, I've seen the kind of woman you can be."

She frowned. "I couldn't work anymore?"

"I never said that. I simply mean you have to dare to let go, to let it come second or third in your life, after things that are more important. You have to learn to trust my motives and your own worth without it. I know it frightens you. That's what's ripping you apart. That and your obstinate, pigheaded loyalty to a marriage that isn't satisfying you."

"It's hard for me to give things up. I'm afraid."

"You're spoiled rotten, Laura. You're used to getting everything you want. Two of everything, if that's what pleases you. I know," he said, "it's hardly surprising, considering your life. But this time is different. You're going to have to grow up. That involves making choices. Jesus, you're like a barnacle holding onto a rotting piece of driftwood. You're aware of the stuff that Claire Poland and the others have been printing. For all you know, Mike has been betraying you all along. Yet you're so afraid of disturbing your eight-by-ten glossy photograph of rosy domestic life that you won't even broach the subject to him. Do you want to go on like that? Do you call that living?"

Laura's eyes filled with sudden tears. She bolted out of her chair and into the dressing room.

Ian came over to Marty. "What was that all about? We're ready to shoot this number if you are."

Marty stood up. "We were running the lines for the last scene. Laura got to the weeping bit and overdid it. She went to get a handkerchief. I'll go tell her we're on." He strode quickly to her trailer. She sat with her back to the open door, her face hidden in her hands. Marty bent over her. "They want us out there. You okay?"

She wiped her eyes with a tissue. "Marty, don't ever say anything like that to me again. Don't try to use Mike against me. It's a cheap trick. You know how much he's given me. I owe him a lot."

He started to reply, but she cut him off. "I will make a decision, but not now. Not now. There's still time. Don't make me think about it now. Don't spoil everything. Please."

He wanted to put his arms around her. "Take it easy."

"I do love you, Marty."

They walked in silence across the dim stage and into the brightly lighted set.

"First positions, please," Ian requested. "We'll take it from the top."

Jack came back into the study. "How does cold roast beef with coleslaw and potato salad sound to you? Teresa's fixing a couple of trays for us. Let me freshen that drink." He took Marty's glass and went to the bar. "Are you going to Mike and Laura's on Saturday?"

"For a while, I guess."

"From what I hear, the whole town's going to be there." He handed Marty the glass and seated himself in the large chair opposite him. "Who are you taking?"

"To Mike and Laura's? I hadn't thought about it."

"Maybe you should."

Marty glanced across at Jack. "I'm just going to make an appearance. I don't intend to stay long."

"You're worried about her. It shows."

"How long have you known?"

"A couple of weeks."

"Is it common knowledge?"

"I haven't heard any talk, if that's what you're getting at." He added, "I don't know about Mike."

"Let me make it clear, Jack. It's not one of those road-company involvements."

"I see." He leaned back in his chair. "What happens now?"

"That's her decision."

"It's a tough one."

"The hell of it is," Marty said, "Laura may be very self-assured in her work, but outside of that she hasn't a shred of confidence in herself. You've seen how that marriage operates. Christ, she'd have given Mike the key to Fort Knox if he wanted it, just to make sure he'd stick with her."

"Seems to me she already did."

"It's a long story, Jack, but the fact is that she's afraid that's the only way she can hold anyone."

"It doesn't occur to her that he abuses the privilege?"

"She overlooks it. She won't risk calling his bluff. There might be a big blowup if she did, and she doesn't dare chance it."

"Does she think he still loves her?"

"That's what she says, but she's not about to test it by squeezing the purse strings. Shit, once she's away from the bright lights, she's putty for anyone. All her life she's been manipulated by people at their convenience." He took a deep swallow of his Scotch. The alcohol was beginning to reach him. "Jesus, she's a goddamn victim is what she is."

Jack set his glass down on the table. He spoke slowly. "Victimized people have been known to strike back quite suddenly. Laura could be a powder keg. That doesn't disturb you?"

"You think she's turning to me just to get back at Mike?"

"No, that's not what I meant. It is a thought, though."

"Scratch it. I believe she's in love with me."

"And you?"

"Laura's got a shot at being one hell of a woman. That's all I want for her. I'll be damned if I'll see her go on being used by all those bastards who've done exactly what they felt like with her. God knows if she's ever done anything she wasn't pushed into."

"Are you sure," Jack asked cautiously, "that you aren't guilty of pushing her too? She's under a lot of pressure. It's becoming obvious."

He stared morosely into his glass. "I hope to Christ it's not too much for her. She's never had to deal with anything like this before. You don't think she'd crack up or anything?"

"We never know, do we, what the other person's breaking point may be. Everyone has his own threshold of tolerance. I wouldn't pull the rug out from under her, if I were you. She may need that illusion of a happy home more than you know. Take it easy, Marty."

"Is it her or the picture that worries you?"

"Both. Believe me."

Marty shook the water out of his hair and ran a towel over his body. Wrapping it around his waist, he padded barefoot into the kitchen and put some ice cubes in a glass. On the way back to the bathroom, he paused at the bar to add a couple of jiggers of Chivas. He set the glass on the edge of the tub. The bathroom was still steamy from his shower. He slid open the window to air it out. The night was cool and clear. There was no breeze. The tops of the eucalyptus trees were unmoving silhouettes against the inky sky. The phone rang, and he shut the window and walked into the bedroom.

"You are coming," she said softly. "It would look odd if you didn't."

"Yes, but I don't promise to stick it out. I don't know how long I'll stay."

"Please. I told you I need the support. I don't know if I can go through with it. It's all such a lie." Her voice faltered slightly. "It's a pose, a fake. Laura playing the dutiful wife, when all I really want is——"

He interrupted her. "I'm starting to dress. I'll be there soon."

"I can't stop my hands from shaking. I had to go into the other room to put on my lipstick so that Mike wouldn't see."

"Once you're caught up in the party you won't think about it."

"No, Marty, I'm scared. I don't know what I'm going to do. I can't take it anymore. I want to see you." She paused. "I have to go now," she said hurriedly. The phone went dead.

He shaved and dressed. It was just past nine when he left the house. As he drove down the canyon, he noticed that the night was no longer still. A slight, fitful wind had come up, disturbing the leaves of the tall palms bordering the streets. Their arching fronds shifted in the breeze and chaffed against each other, making a restless sibilant sound.

10
Lisa

8:15 P.M.

"What time is dinner?"

"In about half an hour."

"Want a martini? I'm going to have one."

"Thanks."

"I brought the paper home. It's there on the table. Laura made the front page. A picture of her at the funeral."

I never want to read or hear another word about it. But that's not possible yet. Perhaps after the inquest. And I must not snap at Jack for mentioning it. He would only wonder why.

"I spoke to Marty earlier. I asked him to join us for dinner this evening. He said he thought he'd eat alone. You two haven't had a disagreement, have you?"

"Of course not."

"Then why do you suppose he refused? That's not like him."

"I don't know." *But, yes, I do. It's too soon. Too soon for any of us to be together without our thoughts getting in the way and making idle conversation impossible.*

"It's strange. Well, it's not worth thinking about, I guess. I saw the footage on the fire scenes today. Special effects did a hell of a job. Looks like a million bucks."

Dear Jack. The work is to you what our home is to me. You shelter yourself inside it, allowing nothing to intrude.

"You're awfully quiet."

"Am I? Did Marty tell you he saw Ed Montenegro this afternoon?"

"That attorney? No, but he did say he was on his way to an appointment."

"You know how rumors can stir up trouble. I think Marty was concerned because of the talk about him and Laura."

328

"What did Ed say?"

"He's coming with us to the inquest."

"Good. He knows his stuff. I don't imagine it's going to be a pleasant experience for anyone."

"No."

"Lisa, you're not afraid of it, are you?"

"A little."

"Don't be. It's only a matter of answering questions. Try to think of it as just another interview."

"You're being a bit simplistic, aren't you?"

"If I am, it's because you're worrying needlessly."

You make it sound so easy, Jack. But from your point of view, you would. How I envy you that ignorance.

"So don't get yourself all stirred up over nothing."

Over nothing. Could it conceivably be that simple? As if it were nothing but what it appeared to be? Are the old rules so easily disposed of? The old formula, the rights and wrongs, we knew them once. When? Only as children? When did we learn to accommodate ourselves so easily? Somewhere along the way it happened. The old foundations were eroded by time and by other things. And when that night arrived we were already locked into something none of us had recognized. But what is its name? Expediency? Compromise? The new rightness? And we grow accustomed to it, like becoming used to the taste of soured milk. Disagreeable or not, it keeps our lives going. So the inquest will be over, and nothing will be changed. The old rules are dead. Long live the new.

"Excuse me, Mrs. Haller."

"Is dinner ready, Teresa?"

"In a few minutes, Mrs. Haller. I was wondering, did you mean to put this in the wastebasket? I thought it might have fallen in by mistake."

"There's a stain on the hem that won't come off. Put it back in the trash, please."

"What the devil was that all about? The dress looked perfectly good to me."

"You heard me, Jack. There's a stain on the hem."

"Can't you shorten the damn thing so it won't show? Christ Almighty, Lisa, you can't just heave a three-hundred dollar Pucci jersey into the garbage can."

"Jack. Please. No more. I don't want to wear it again."

"Because you wore it to that party?"

"*Yes.*"

"*Don't you think you're being melodramatic?*"

"*Please, just this once, indulge me. I am not going to wear it again, so it might as well not be taking up space in the closet. Let's drop the subject, Jack. Please.*"

"*I think you're behaving like an idiot.*"

"*How were things at the studio today?*"

"*All right, have it your way, but it's still sheer foolishness. Things were fine today, if you mean Laura. Everyone handled her like she was made of glass. She's getting protection from all sides.*"

"*Jack?*"

"*What?*"

"*Nothing.*"

So the new rules hold. There are certain questions which are forbidden. Certain subjects not discussed. I must never demand to know what you mean by this or that remark, and you must never ask why it should interest me. From now on, that is the way it will be. And something changes between us.

Does he know? Is that why he hasn't questioned me? I can't ask him. But is it fair to play a game if only one of us knows the rules? If only one of us knows there is even a game? But even those questions can't be spoken. And something changes between us.

"*Did I tell you Ian and I have decided to trim most of the dialogue from the last scene in the picture? We're going to let the looks sell it. It'll be stronger that way. Here, do you want some of these cheese things with your drink?*"

"*Thank you. That would be nice.*" And something changes between us.

A LINE of cars inched up the driveway to the entrance of the house. Along either side of the gravel drive were rows of flickering candles set on the grass between the topiary trees. The music of an orchestra drifted through the cool night air. From the open pair of front doors came the sound of many voices. Jack stopped as the car valet, wearing a serape over his uniform, opened Lisa's door. He handed Jack a claim check.

On either side of the curving steps to the house stood giant wrought-iron candelabra, perhaps ten feet high, casting fitful illumination over the oleander bushes against the brick façade.

"Recognize those?" asked Jack. "There were about a dozen of them made for the big fiesta scene in *Border Blaze*. Looks like Mike raided the Victory prop department."

Inside, the large foyer revealed the remaining candelabra, placed around the huge hall at regular intervals, providing the only light. The rooms beyond seemed to be lit as usual. In the center of the entrance hall a tiled fountain splashed gracefully. Flowers floated on the surface of the water. A maid wearing a red rose Latin-style in her hair, approached Lisa.

"May I take your coat? It will be in the master bedroom upstairs." She indicated the massive staircase that rose from the first floor to a balcony overhead encircling the foyer. Someone leaned over the balustrade and called out a cheerful obscenity to one of the arriving guests below.

The party was already in full swing. Jack took Lisa's arm, and they made their way through an arch and into the main living room. Music and noise reverberated from the high vaulted ceiling.

"God knows how we'll ever find the host and hostess," Jack all but shouted over the crowd.

At one end of the long room was a dance floor. Several couples, some holding their cocktail glasses precariously, were gyrating frantically. The orchestra came to a halt, and the musicians laid down their instruments.

"That's a little better," commented Lisa. "Now I can hear you. My God, that's a full orchestra they've got. And look." A group of mariachis in *charro* outfits stepped into place to play while the band took its break.

"Do you see Mike and Laura anywhere?" Jack asked.

Lisa glanced around at the throng. Familiar faces, most of them, and the others familiar types. Beautiful young girls with bored expressions, attired in velvet pantsuits, see-through shifts, or low-cut silks. The men, talking loudly, laughing too heartily, wore a variety of costumes, tuxedos mostly, some with white turtleneck jerseys, others with cascades of white lace on ruffled Edwardian shirts. Some had Western-style black string ties. Near her, Lisa saw one guest proudly displaying his cummerbund and matching suspenders on which were embroidered the figures of naked women in erotic poses. "Hong Kong," he explained to those around him.

"Excuse me," she spoke to a vaguely familiar dark-haired woman wearing a fur dress of white mink, "have you seen the Stantons anywhere?"

"Who?" she said.

"Never mind." When she turned back, she had lost Jack. After a moment, she saw him farther across the room. He motioned for her to follow.

She edged past the doors to the dining room where three large tables lay spread with platters of food. Jack waited for her at the far side of the room.

"Christ, but it's some establishment." He inclined his head in the direction of the mariachis. Beyond the bandstand was the conservatory filled with leafy greenery undistinguishable at this distance. "Look at that chandelier." He pointed upward to the glitter of crystal prisms above them. "Beautiful."

"Beautiful," she said, moving toward the terrace outside.

"Hi, Jack, Lisa," someone called. "Get yourselves a drink. There's a bar at either end out here."

The bar was jammed. Behind it, cases of liquor were stacked into a wall of cardboard cartons. Jack managed to extricate their drinks from the press of people without spilling more than a few drops.

At the edge of the bricked terrace a row of glimmering gas lamps on wrought-iron standards dappled the baize lawn beyond. Across the richly green grass lay a turquoise pool, its surface ablaze with dozens of small floating candles. The air was sweet with the scent of flowers.

Lisa accepted an hors d'oeuvre from one of the several waitresses who were weaving their way through the multitude, unconcerned with the celebrity of the guests.

"Let's try the other end," suggested Jack. "Maybe there's more room."

A flow of conversations swirled around them. "Didn't we meet at Sonny's party in Palm Springs? The one with the painted elephants? . . . Love the red hair, darling, much better than that dishwater blonde you had. . . . Isn't that Tony Quinn? No, he's in Paris. Well, it certainly looks like Tony Quinn. . . . And the sonofabitch aced me out of a meal penalty, would you believe it? . . . The last time I saw you, you were in the Piazza San Marco, covered from head to toe with pigeons. . . . It's the goddam unions that are screwing this industry, that's what. . . ."

"Jesus," exclaimed Jack, leaning against a railing, "we made it. Here, sit down." He pulled out a chair from one of the small circular tables that dotted this end of the veranda.

"I see them." Lisa smiled at Laura as she came toward them wearing a strikingly simple white silk jersey sheath that fell in soft folds to a deep décolletage.

"You look smashing," Jack grinned, taking her hand in his.

"Do you really think so?" She kissed Lisa's cheek. "Do you think anyone will notice in this mob?"

"My God, Laura, your hand is ice cold," interrupted Jack.

She withdrew it hastily. "Peggy dear." Laura greeted Peggy Smart and the tall man who stood beside her.

Peggy introduced her husband, "Doctor Sam Cochran."

Lisa shook the doctor's hand. "Of course. We met at the Cedars-Sinai benefit last year. I remember you said you had to duck out early for a house call. I was very impressed to meet a doctor who still made house calls," she laughed.

"Once in a while, just to keep up the image."

Mike appeared with a woman and two men whose names Lisa didn't hear distinctly. After a moment's conversation, he moved on, leaving one of the men behind talking to Laura.

"Who is he?" Lisa whispered to Peggy.

"One of the astronauts. He's retired now."

She glanced at him again. "Which one is he?"

"I don't know," confided Peggy. "I can't tell them apart."

He pulled out a chair and seated himself next to Lisa.

"Do you know all these people?" she inquired politely.

He smiled. "I know everyone here. I just haven't met any of them."

"No matter," Jack broke in. "There's famous and then there's famous. Compared to you, most of these people are small potatoes." The two men fell into a conversation about the problems of extraterrestrial research. Doctor Cochran joined them.

"Have you seen Marty?" Lisa asked Peggy.

"I don't think he's here yet."

After a time, the orchestra switched from fast tunes to slow dinner music. People wandered by with plates piled high with food. Jack and Lisa, returning from the dining room, settled on the brick steps to the lawn, their plates balanced on their laps. Above them, at one of the little tables, a rather quiet bunch was blowing pot. "Viva Acapulco," someone said happily. Lisa shifted position to allow a group to snake its way past them onto the lawn. In the dimness of the garden at one end of the pool, she could make out a couple in an intimate embrace. The mariachis were playing again, this time outside. They sang a plaintive Spanish melody.

"Hello there, you two." Bob and Vickie Mann squeezed onto the steps beside them. "I figured you were somewhere among this cast of characters," said Bob.

"Guess what I've got," Vickie bubbled. "Look." She spread her hand for Lisa to see. "It's to remember the picture by."

Lisa exclaimed over the dazzling emerald and diamond ring.

"Don't look too closely," amended Vickie. "I was making cookies this afternoon and I think I got some shortbread stuck in the prongs."

"Hey, excuse me." Bob dashed up the steps to speak to someone.

Vickie watched after him. "That's whatshisname. The one who won the Los Angeles Open last year. You know, the golf champion. I tell you," she said delightedly, "I've never seen so many famous faces under one roof. Why, half the Rams team is up there in the billiard room, shooting pool."

A hand-holding couple walked by them down to the grass below. "All in black leather," the girl was saying. "And he digs feet the most."

Near the pool, two graying ladies rushed into each other's arms with a chorus of the shrill cooing sounds that women make who have not seen each other in years.

"Spaced out," one of the pot smokers was crooning softly, "so-oo spaced out."

"Duncan, you fool," a starlet came up the steps with a short pudgy man in tow, "you're thinking serious thoughts again. Quit it," she scolded, "and come dance with me."

Someone pitched a glass into the swimming pool. Lisa watched it float gently to the bottom.

Jack laid his plate aside. "Let's see what's happening indoors." He took Lisa's hand and helped her up.

"Lisa." Vic Strong stopped her in the doorway, giving her arm an overmuscular squeeze. "Good to see you. I hear we're both reading the same script. Hope we get to work together.

I just ran into Marty and told him so." Vic gave her that famous, slightly malevolent grin of his.

"Where is Marty?" she raised her voice over the din.

"He was in the library, discussing something with Ian Driscoll."

"Jack," Lisa glanced around her. "Jack?" But he had been absorbed into the crowd.

Mike was introducing Laura to a small knot of people. "This," he gestured expansively, "is the talented part of the family. Not to mention beautiful." He slid an arm around Laura's bare shoulders. "Say something talented to these nice people, honey."

Lisa drifted through the living room, avoiding a couple of energetic dancers who flung their arms in her face.

A dreamy-eyed girl dressed in yards of black fringe and little else blocked her path.

"Excuse me," Lisa said loudly.

The girl's bearded escort laughed. "Hell," he apologized, "she's so high only the birds can talk to her." He moved the girl out of Lisa's way.

The foyer was less jammed. Lisa sat down on the tiled edge of the fountain. The splash of the water drowned out some of the other sounds. A large, perspiring man, a writer she dimly recalled, seated himself near her. In his outstretched palm he held three pastel-colored petits fours which he proceeded to consume with undivided attention.

Arm in arm, a pair dressed in identical caftans and with identical haircuts strolled by. "Marie," the man was saying tiredly, "doesn't anything impress you anymore?" The girl thought for a second. "Circular driveways," she said.

Lisa trailed her hand in the water among the floating blossoms. In the distance, among the horde in the living room, she caught sight of Obie and Ruth. Jack was still nowhere to be seen. She rose and walked across the hall to an open door. It was the billiard room. "You go ahead and rack," someone said, "and I'll get us some coffee."

"Lisa!" From the other end of the foyer Ian hailed her with a wave of his glass and, coming closer, kissed her on the left ear. "Jack with you?"

"Somewhere inside."

"Marty's in the library. I'm afraid I buttonholed him the minute he came through the door. Wanted to talk over the possibility of his doing another picture for me after this one. Come have a dance with me."

"Later. It's a promise." Smiling, she crossed her heart.

"I intend to collect on that."

Marty stood with his back to the door, examining the titles on one of the bookshelves that lined the darkly paneled room.

"Hi." Lisa sat on a brown velvet sofa.

He turned. "The collected works of George Eliot," he announced, "the collected works of William Shakespeare, the collected works of practically everybody."

It was obvious to Lisa that the Scotch in his hand wasn't his first. "Are you smashed?"

"No, but I'm trying."

"Don't complain when you feel lousy tomorrow morning. Why don't you put that down and join the fun? There's a party going on."

"So I've heard." He placed his glass on a shelf. "Is it any good?"

"It's big. Come on."

In the doorway, a flush-faced man stepped directly in front of Marty and stuck out his hand. Marty shook it.

"The party's a regular who's who," Lisa was commenting.

"Whose zoo?" flush-faced queried boozily as he drifted past them.

"Friend of yours?" laughed Lisa.

"He produced my *Caravan* series for a season. One of those types who goes from failure to failure with a raise in pay."

Marty surveyed the crush in the living room. "Lot of fat cats here. Very impressive."

"Christine, darling." It was the unmistakable voice of Claire Poland. She held the elegantly dressed brunette at arm's length, executing a quick appraisal of her turnout. She must have been worth a quarter of a million in sapphires alone. Claire seemed properly impressed. She made small clucking sounds of approval with her tongue. "My," she enthused, "you have come a long way, haven't you?" The woman gazed evenly at her and then, with deliberate languor, flicked the ash from the tip of her cigàret, as if the gesture might reduce Claire to coals also. She walked away with a slim young man, leaving Claire alone. She turned to Lisa and Marty. "Have you ever," she said, undaunted, "seen so many absolutely neon names congregated in one place?"

"Who was that? She's new," said Lisa.

"Correction, dear," Claire replied, "she's old. It's a long story. She used to be married to Ian Driscoll, and now that she's a duchess she's come back to town to ram it down our throats. The boy with her is her decorator." Claire affected a limp wrist. "Didn't you see how he was looking at the furniture as if he was pricing every piece? Christy's remodeling the old Barrymore place."

Lisa, bored by now with the recitation, didn't bother to ask which Barrymore.

The mariachis had launched into *Cielito Lindo* and were joined by a chorus of offkey voices. Claire viewed the room with a professional eye. Marty, Lisa observed, was watching the festivities as if he were less guest than spectator. Groups of people swarmed around them. The increasing noise and movement gave Lisa the sensation of being on a fast-moving merry-go-round. Finally the mariachis stopped, but before the waiting band could resume, Aces Norton vaulted on top of the piano bench and commenced to do a monologue roundly, if amusingly, insulting every big name within earshot.

"That," said Marty, "does it." He turned away.

Lisa caught sight of Jack and Ian inside the entrance to the dining room. Laughter built around her as Aces laid on one of his bluer punch lines. She sighed with mock relief as she reached them. "Remember me?"

Jack put an arm around her waist. "Where did you disappear to?"

"I was with Marty, but he did a quick fade when Aces grabbed the stage."

"Who can blame him? Ian and I were just reviewing the troops on hand."

"In particular," Ian put in, taking a large gulp of his drink, "the miraculous appearance of my last wife. Touchy, what?" Ian smiled somewhat blearily. "Quite an assortment. A bit of fraction——" He shook his head and corrected himself, "Friction. A bit of friction here and there. Several jokes on the guest list. I should say."

A smattering of applause signalled Ace Norton's departure from the floor. The band struck up a Beatles number.

"Dance?" Jack invited.

Close together, they moved in rhythm to the music. "Having a good time?" Lisa asked.

"Fair for one of these things."

Lisa rested her head on his shoulder, enjoying the smooth and polished way he danced. Too soon, Ian cut in on them. The tunes moved faster now, and at last Ian breathlessly suggested they take a break. "Got to refuel, old girl," he pointed to the bar outside.

"I'll wait here." She moved off the floor and stood in the archway to the conservatory. Fragments of shouted conversation bombarded her ears. "He's in transportation," a redhead explained to her mustached companion. "Transportation, bullshit. He sells used cars." An intense-looking man in horn-rimmed glasses was talking to a tall black girl with an Afro hairdo. "Sure I'm involved. I teach six hours a week of acting classes in Watts. What do you want from me?"

Lisa escaped into the comparative quiet of the conservatory. It was a beautiful room, rich with green and glossy plants in various stages of bloom. Here and there a cigaret butt smoldered in a flower pot. From the glass dome of the ceiling hung trailing orchids and air ferns. A pair of parakeets hopped nervously on their perches inside a white cage. Lisa seated herself on a cement garden bench and removed her shoes, flexing her suddenly aching feet. She heard Laura speaking somewhere in the room, obscured from view by a cluster of small palm trees.

"What did you do all day?" she was inquiring.

Marty answered her. "The track. I went to Santa Anita with Obie."

"Did you win?"

"A little. It kept my mind occupied." He paused. "That's not what you wanted to talk to me about. Are you all right?"

There was a silence. "Don't," Laura said weakly.

"Your hands are trembling. Maybe you ought to have a drink."

"No. I can't. I don't want to fall apart."

"You're wound up tighter than a mainspring."

"I don't know if I can stand it another hour. I want to scream. Marty, why am I so afraid? I can't seem to think straight."

Lisa recovered her shoes and put them back on.

Marty's voice came closer now. "I won't go. You'll always know where I am."

At the moment Lisa stood up, they appeared. She faced them across a short interval of waist-high greenery, glancing in helpless embarrassment from one face to the other.

Marty said nothing.

"I shouldn't have left my guests," Laura said lamely.

"At last!" Mike stood smiling in the arch. "Is this where you've been? What are you three plotting?" Without waiting for an answer, he motioned to Laura. "Come on, angel, Claire has a photographer here, and I promised him a few pictures. You'll excuse us?" he said to Marty and Lisa. As an after-thought, he added, "Enjoying yourselves?"

"It's quite a party," Lisa told him.

"What do I know?" he rejoined jovially, taking Laura's hand in his. "I'm only a simple country boy."

She glanced at Marty, waiting.

It was a while before he spoke. "It happened," he said simply. He took a swallow from the glass in his hand. "In New York."

"Don't tell me too much," said Lisa. "Please."

He gave her a long look. "I guess we should join the party."

Mike and Laura sat posed on the terrace railing near one of the bars. Mike raised a glass in a toast in the direction of the camera. "Wait a minute," he interrupted the photographer. "Hand me one of those cans of Fresca instead," he instructed the bartender. He turned the can in his hand, facing the brand name into the lens.

Lisa and Marty, together with Claire, stood observing the photography ritual from the doorway. Changing the pose, Mike drew Laura closer to him and kissed her cheek lovingly. Lisa noticed Claire's eyes flick instantly to Marty's impassive face. Just how many people were privy to this alliance, she wondered. Or were there merely the standard rumors about two attractive stars filming a love story? There was no way to ask without revealing more than was politic.

"Are you tired, darling? How are you holding up?" Mike was inquiring solicitously. "This is our first big party, you know," he added for the benefit of the assembled group.

"The first of many," Claire called out, "we hope."

Several people applauded. Marty disappeared back into the

living room. The photographer, having got his shots, packed up his gear.

"They are," Claire decreed, "a dream couple. Aren't they, Lisa?"

She had been caught off guard. "Yes," she said quickly.

"The beautiful people," persisted Claire. "Looks, talent, success, money, and love. But of course, love's the most important ingredient, isn't it? Where did Marty go?" she asked, as if she had not noticed his absence.

"I've no idea." She could see that Claire was posed to ask another question. Fortunately, Kurt Vogler chose that moment to thrust his bulky form directly in front of Claire and reel off a couple of items he wanted to plant in her column. Vogler had graduated from producing Laura's Nikki films to become the master of the blood-and-gore thrillers, the latest of which, he assured Lisa and Claire and anybody else who was listening, "is going to scare you shitless, babies." A wiry young agent tapped Vogler on the shoulder and introduced him to a voluptuous large-eyed blonde. "Ideal for the picture, Kurt," he urged.

Vogler took a drag of his cigaret and peered judiciously through the smoke, sizing up the goods. "But can it act?" he said finally. "What have you done?" he asked the blonde.

"To whom?" she rallied sweetly.

Vogler guffawed and gave her a genial cuff on the ass.

"The part of Irene," the agent put in. "I know it's small, but Fiona here can really make something if it."

"It's cast," said Vogler. "Gloria French is doing Irene, but call my office Monday anyhow. There may be something." He elbowed his way past them to the bar.

Fiona looked after him. "I hate to see someone like Gloria French playing such a small part."

"Balls," retorted her companion. "You don't hate it a bit. You're just scared that the same thing could happen to you." He took her arm and propelled her inside toward the dance floor in search of a more productive encounter.

"Vogler must be getting old," commented Claire. "His hair, what's left of it, gets blacker every year."

Lisa had no desire to get stranded here with Claire. She glanced around the terrace hoping to sight Jack or Marty. Colin Kirkwood lay stretched out on a garden chaise, apparently asleep.

"Passed out," Claire noted.

A heavy woman in a brocade dress, resembling a slightly overstuffed sofa, perched on the foot of the lounge. She extracted a half-empty glass from Kirkwood's hand, sniffed the contents, and polished off the rest.

With relief, Lisa saw Marty's head among the faces at the far end of the veranda and excused herself.

"I'm missing a husband. Have you seen Jack?"

"He went out front to inspect Ian's new Rolls. It turns my stomach."

"What? The car?" she asked, surprised.

"No, watching him operate." Marty nodded almost imperceptibly toward Mike who was laughing heartily at some witticism just delivered by a portly white-haired man.

"Who's the other one?"

"Mark Fields. Owns a chain of theaters," Marty set his glass down on a table. "Watch Mike. Watch his action. He takes great care to make himself memorable to the right people. He's storing up friendships like a squirrel hoards nuts, for use when the right time comes."

"Marty, be fair. We all do it."

"Christ!" He turned to face her. "Where do you get off defending him, of all people?"

"Stop," she ordered.

Marty exhaled tiredly. "This damn town is a basket of snakes."

"A what?"

"Basket of snakes," he repeated. "You lift off the lid, and there we lie, our lives all twined around each other. It's damn near incestuous."

"Here comes Jack," she silenced him.

"I was just talking to Laura in the dining room. She looks a little feverish. Is she all right?"

Marty frowned. "She's keyed up. She knows she's playing a part, and I think she's beginning to get an idea of what a fake it's been from the start."

"She seemed quite disturbed. You've spoken to her?"

"Excuse us." A stream of guests momentarily separated Lisa from the conversation. "Believe me," said one, "it was the F.B.I. that kept that picture from being made. The word came straight from the top—yes, thanks, a Scotch and water."

Lisa looked at Jack, wondering how long he had known. How typical of him not to have said anything. He despised gossip. Early on, she had learned to drop the habit when he was around.

"Good God!" Marty exclaimed in a low voice. "Will you look who just walked in?"

Hans Deitrick stood smiling in the doorway. Beside him was Tula Jackson, looking very African in a dashiki. They came toward the group.

"Who the hell invited him?" muttered Marty.

Lisa, puzzled, suddenly recalled something about Hans and Laura. A suicide attempt, the stories had said. She looked quickly at Marty.

"Were you invited?" he asked Hans bluntly.

"I'm escorting Miss Jackson."

"Have you seen Laura?"

"Oh, is that it?" laughed Hans. "The past is gone by. We are all adults here. We have our own lives. No, I have not yet seen our charming hostess. You're looking lovely, Lisa," he told her.

She nodded.

"What do you say we get a drink," suggested Tula, leading Hans in the direction of the bar.

"That's all Laura needs," said Marty grimly. "One more thing to shake her up."

There was a shrill outburst of laughter from the lawn below. Three girls had stripped to their panties and were diving into the pool, splashing around among the floating candles. Obie materialized next to Lisa, surveying the frivolity. "Youth," he said a trifle wistfully. "Did you ever see so many great looking young bodies at one party?"

"Where's Ruth?" asked Jack.

"I was looking for her. Who knows," he continued to watch the swimmers, "maybe they arrested her for being over thirty."

"Arrested who?" Ruth demanded, approaching them. "Oscar, Claire Poland was showing me her new chincilla jacket, and——"

"No."

"I thought maybe for our anniversary . . ."

"We'll see."

Ruth rattled on cheerfully. "Isn't it a wonderful party? I've

all but danced the soles off my shoes. It's such a glorious evening, but what on earth is the matter with Laura? I bumped
into her in the library a moment ago and spoke to her, but
she gave me the blankest look. I don't think she heard a word
I said. Just stared at me as if I were speaking some foreign
language and then she went off."

"Where did she go?" demanded Marty, retrieving his glass
from the table.

Ruth gave a bewildered shrug.

Jack broke in, a hand on Marty's arm. "Maybe you'd better lay off the sauce, Mart," he said, taking the glass. "You
may need a cool head."

"Right." Marty exited into the house.

Ruth asked something, but the band was playing too loudly
just then to make out what it was she had said.

In a more subdued moment, Obie asked Jack, "What's up?
Why the sudden vanishing act from Marty?"

Jack gestured toward the steps to the lawn where Hans
and Tula were laughing over some shared joke.

"Shit," he said softly. "Well, let's hope the old wounds are
long since healed. It's been over three years."

"Laura's been under a strain lately," Jack explained.
"We're all a little concerned."

"Pushing herself too hard at work? Damn it, she never
learns." Obie struck a match impatiently and lit a cigaret.
"Who handled the guest list for this party, anyway? From
what I've seen, there are more people here who can't stand
each other than those who can."

Over the talk of the others, Lisa spotted Laura winding her
way from the door to where Mike stood with Mark Fields.
Marty was nowhere to be seen. Midway across the veranda,
Laura froze. Directly in her line of vision was the back of
Hans Deitrick's head. She stood rigid, the crowd jostling
around her. Her eyes were too wide and bright. Lisa tapped
Jack's shoulder and pointed her out, but Laura had begun to
make her way to Mike. She drew him aside from Fields. In a
corner of the terrace, they spoke. Lisa could see that Laura
was upset and not bothering to conceal it. They were talking
in hushed voices. It was impossible to overhear their conversation. Mark Fields finally sauntered over and joined them.

"That's better, darling," Mike announced, kissing her bare
shoulder. He assumed a smile. Laura, her face blank, turned

hesitantly back into the house, threading a path through the dancers inside. Kurt Vogler, with the voluptuous Fiona, thrashed gracelessly around the middle of the floor. Laura passed them, as though not seeing the frenetic activity around her. The orchestra, loud and spirited, was playing a medley of Streisand hits. A man Lisa didn't know stood crooning at the piano. "Everyone knows she's got a——" he hiccuped, "secondhand nose." He was thoroughly drunk.

It struck Lisa that something had happened to the party, something frenzied. The gaiety was out of control. Everything seemed suddenly off-center. She watched the guests around her. Like bright bits of a kaleidoscope they clustered momentarily, broke apart, and were rearranged into other combinations, all this with a maximum of decibels.

Claire was chattering to Obie and Ruth. "Laura's quite high-strung tonight, don't you think? Do you suppose she's on some sort of pills?"

Vickie, Bob, and Ian came through the doorway, talking to Peggy Smart and her husband. They moved onto the terrace.

"Christ, but it's hot in there." Bob mopped his forehead.

Ian drew Jack aside. "I think something's happened," Lisa heard him say. Ian leaned unsteadily against the brick wall of the house.

"What is it?" demanded Jack.

"Damned if I know," he replied fuzzily. "Milt Gibson and I were standing by the fountain in the hall, debating whether or not to piss in it. Milt directed Laura's first film, and everyone knows she's fond of him. She came across the room, and Milt said something to her, some affectionate pleasantry——" Ian waved one hand vaguely. "Laura stared right through him and walked into the library. Now," he paused, "what do you make of that?"

"Lisa," Jack said, "do me a favor and find Laura. See what's troubling her. See what you can do."

Halfway across the living room, a disheveled woman attached herself to Lisa's arm. "I'm staying!" she shouted. "That bastard wants me to leave. The invitation said 'until dawn.' I'm staying," she repeated. "Fuck him."

Lisa pried herself loose. There was no sign of Laura in the foyer. The library door was closed. She knocked gently and opened it.

Laura sat on the sofa. Marty was with her.

"Is there anything I can do?"

"We were just coming out," Marty said.

"No." Laura laid a hand on his arm. "I don't want to. Mike's trying to get me to talk business with that man. Mark Fields. I never met him before. I don't even know half the guests. And the others——" she halted. "They're not friends of mine. What are they doing here? What are they doing in my house? Stay here, Marty. Please stay here with me," she begged.

"You know we can't do that." He helped her up and, putting an arm around her waist, led her past Lisa and into the noisy hall.

"My head aches," Laura said. "I'm going to the powder room to get an aspirin."

"Do you want me to go with you?" asked Lisa.

"No, thanks."

Marty waited in the archway ahead. Coming toward him through the crowd was Mike. Lisa saw them speak briefly. Marty inclined his head in the direction Laura had taken and, breaking off the conversation, walked away. Mike came over to her. "Having a good time? That's what it's all about. . . ."

"There wasn't any aspirin in there," Laura said as she arrived beside them.

"What is it, sweetheart? A headache?" Mike reached out and stroked her cheek.

"There must be some upstairs," she said.

"Look on the second shelf of the medicine cabinet," he called after her.

Lisa brushed past him. She could see Jack with the Manns and Arnold Kramer beside the bandstand. The mariachis had taken over and were playing a theme from one of Jack's pictures, smiling and nodding at him as they did.

"How is Laura?" asked Vickie. "Jack seems to think she's sick or something."

"A headache," explained Lisa. "She went to get some aspirin."

"Oh, is that all?"

Jack glanced at Lisa, but before she could speak, Marty rejoined them.

"Sonofabitch. Where the hell is she, Lisa?"

"There she is," Arnold responded, "coming from the hall."

Marty crossed the room and stopped Laura in the arch-way. He took her arm and maneuvered her out of Lisa's vision.

"Intrigue?" asked Vickie.

"Nothing so dramatic," Jack assured her. "Perhaps a mis-understanding of some kind. Bob, you were right, it's too warm in here. Let's go back outside."

Mike disengaged himself from the Strauses and Claire Po-land. "Where's Laura?" he asked Lisa. "Did she come back down?"

"In the foyer," Vickie said, "talking to Marty."

Jack and Lisa exchanged a look as he left them. The crowd outdoors had begun to thin in the evening chill. They found an empty table, and Jack went to the bar for drinks. Returning, he pulled out a chair and sat down, exhausted. The breeze unsettled the flickering candles in the pool. Lisa shivered.

"Do you want to go in?" Jack asked.

"No. It's too damned noisy. When I finish this," she held up her glass, "I'll go get my coat. I'll be warm enough."

"Get mine too, would you?" requested Vickie. "It's a dark mink with my initials in red on the lining."

The mariachis had come out onto the veranda again, fol-lowed by several tireless, perspiring couples. A petite auburn-haired girl danced alone on the lawn, a man's jacket draped over her shoulders.

"Red initials in the lining?" said Lisa, standing.

"That's right. Dark mink with a Revillon label," Vickie re-plied. "Thanks."

She ran into Mike in the foyer. "I can't locate her," he said. "I thought I saw her and Marty go out the front door, but his car is still there."

"Maybe she's in the kitchen." She wondered if the sugges-tion sounded as ridiculous to him as it did to her.

Upstairs, she found the master suite, its bed littered with fur coats, looking rather like a table at some extravagant rummage sale. She rooted among the soft heap, finally ex-tracting her coat and Vickie's. Tossing them onto a chair, she went into the bathroom. After she had washed her hands, she paused at the mirror to refresh her makeup. From the adjoin-ing bedroom came the sound of muffled conversation. Lisa opened the dressing table drawer in search of a comb and, finding one, repaired the effects of the breeze. The voices were louder now. She realized that it was Marty and Laura again and decided to leave before risking another embarrassment. One of her earrings was loose. She removed it and tried to bend the clasp, but still it failed to hold properly. She took them both off and slipped them into her minaudiere. Replacing the comb, she closed the drawer and opened the door to the bedroom. They glanced up.

"I'm awfully sorry," she said sheepishly. "I guess I've done it again." She moved to the blue velvet chair where she had left the coats.

"Stay," Marty said sharply. They were sitting on the edge of the fur-piled bed.

"What?"

"I want Laura out of this house. I want her out of this stinking charade."

Marty might have had more to drink than she'd thought. He didn't look drunk.

Laura's eyes were fixed straight ahead. Lisa's only thought was that she should get the hell out of the room. "Jack's waiting for me," she said uneasily.

"Jesus Christ! Whose side are you on?"

"Nobody's. I don't want to see anyone hurt."

"The hurt's been done! You know that better than anybody!"

"My God, Marty, don't!" She saw that Laura was looking at her now. Lisa walked quickly to the chair.

"Well, hasn't it? Hasn't it?"

"Leave me out of this, God damn you! I refuse to be dragged into it." She caught Laura's glance to Marty, uncomprehending. "If Laura wants to walk out," she lowered her tone, "she'll go. I will not allow you to involve me in this situation. You talk about using people. What the hell do you think you're trying to do to me?"

For the first time Laura spoke. Her voice came dully. "He's stayed with me. Mike wouldn't leave me. He wouldn't. He's not like the others. He stays. Even when I'm ill, all those times. He stayed with me, taking care of me. He's good to me. Isn't he?" She looked blankly at Lisa.

Lisa wondered if Laura was losing her mind. Laura turned to Marty.

"Don't you know how much I care for you?"

She rested her head on his chest, and he stroked her hair, as if trying to calm a troubled child. "I know. I'm afraid."

Lisa was somewhat reassured. At least Laura was making sense.

"He's been so good," Laura said again. "He's stayed with me."

"Don't make me vomit!" exploded Marty.

Lisa turned to the chair, and as she did so her eyes swept past the doorway where Mike stood.

He stepped into the room and pressed the lock on the doorknob. "No sense inviting everybody in," he said pleasantly.

"I'm leaving," Lisa said.

Mike stood in front of the door. "You might as well stay. You're already here."

She started to protest, but Marty broke in. "Laura's coming with me."

Mike did not look at Laura. "I don't think so."

Laura sat numbly on the bed.

Marty bent his head close to her face. "Come on," he said gently, "time to leave."

She spoke in a small voice. "He needs me," she said weakly and, thought Lisa, without much conviction.

"Damn it, Laura," Marty said, "doesn't it mean anything that he cheats on you at every opportunity? It's the truth, and you know it!"

Laura's head jerked up.

"Face it!"

She waved a hand in front of her face as if to brush away his words.

Marty fixed Mike with a look of undisguised hatred. "Can't you say a goddamn word? I'm in love with your wife."

Mike spread his palms. "Millions are."

"Please," Laura said, "please stop."

"Stop what? Stop loving you?"

She was shaking. "No, Marty," she whispered.

"You were much too obvious, you know," Mike said. "But these things pass. I doubt that yours will outlive the picture by much. Get up, darling," he told Laura.

Bewildered, she stayed seated. "It doesn't matter?" she asked in a puzzled tone. "Don't you care?"

"Sure I care. Get up, sweetheart. You'd better break this up and go downstairs. We have guests, remember?"

"Is that all you care about? Your party?"

"We can talk it over tomorrow. Mark Fields is waiting for an answer."

"Not tomorrow." Marty stood up. "Now."

"All right." Mike moved away from the door. "Take my wife downstairs, Lisa. Marty and I have something to discuss."

Lisa looked at Marty.

"Not behind Laura's back. She's not going to be manipulated. She's had enough of that after what you've done to her."

"What does that mean?"

"This is where she gets off."

Laura got up from the bed and slipped her hand into Marty's.

"What do you have to say?" Mike asked her.

She didn't, or couldn't, answer.

"You see?" said Mike. "She doesn't know what the devil you're talking about. You're a jackass, Marty. These things happen. You win some, you lose some." He moved toward them.

"Christ Almighty! Laura's a woman, not some cheap door prize that goes to the man with the lucky number!"

"She's my wife," Mike said.

"Does that mean you can abuse her?"

Mike stopped short. "I've never laid a hand on Laura."

"You know damn well that isn't what I mean!"

"Laura has what she needs. Me."

"A fucking parasite!"

"Don't push me, Marty."

The thought went through Lisa's mind that she should get Jack. If there was going to be a fight, someone would have to stop it. No one moved.

"I will," said Marty slowly, "damn well push you. You've used Laura. You've used every weakness she——"

Laura dropped his hand. She appeared dazed. Lisa wondered if she even heard what was being said.

"You're acting like a fool," Mike said. "Laura, come with me."

She took a tentative step. Marty put a hand on her shoulder. "Be sure you know what you're doing," he said quietly. Laura stopped. "Leave her alone, Mike," he said wearily. "Haven't you done enough?"

"She won't leave, not just for some quick bang on a picture."

"Jesus God. Is that what you think? Is that the way your cheap goddam mind works? Is that all you think it means to either of us?"

Mike shrugged. "She belongs to me."

"She is not one of your possessions! God knows you've used her like one. You've used her to push your way up without a single thought as to what it's cost her."

"Drop it."

"Like hell I will. Does she know what you've done to her? Does Laura have any idea what you did to her?"

"Marty! Don't!" Lisa said.

Mike spun around and glared at her. Suddenly his expression changed, but it was too late.

"If you won't admit it, Lisa, I will! He was fucking his brains out and he gave both of you gonorrhea. He knew what he'd done because I spoke to him. He stood by and watched her nearly die. You let your beloved wife become sterile because you didn't have the guts to risk what you'd worked so hard to accumulate."

Laura made a small sound, a gasp for breath.

"That's not it——" began Mike.

"Do you deny you made Laura sterile?"

"This isn't the time or the place to discuss it, but for your information Laura has never wanted any children. Have you, Laura?" He didn't wait to hear what she might say.

Lisa could not bring herself to look at Laura's face. Marty, Lisa realized later, had finally panicked him.

"Don't press your luck," Mike said. "Laura's mine. She knows that. Look at her. The hair, the face, the clothes, this house, our friends. . . . Do you think she could have done it on her own? Laura needs me. Without me, she's just another neurotic actress."

"Stop it!" Laura shrieked, covering her ears. "Stop it, both of you! No more! Don't! Don't negotiate for me! I am not a piece of property. You can't divide me or exchange me or give me away."

Mike moved toward her. She pulled away. Her voice dropped, the words spilling out. "You did use me. Like all the others. All of you." She looked around the bedroom as if it were peopled by some invisible crowd. "What," she screamed, dragging out the words, "have you done to me?" Her dark look accused the entire room.

"I'm getting her out of here," Marty said.

"I suppose it makes you happy to see her go over the edge like this! You're the one who pressured her! This is your fault!"

Lisa's attention was on the two of them, confronting each other. But now, out of the corner of her eye, she saw that Laura had moved away from them. She stood at the bedside table. For a second it occurred to Lisa that in her delirium she had chosen a preposterous time to make a telephone call, but she bypassed the phone, slid open the drawer, and without looking, reached inside it. Lisa felt a faint warning, some obscure fragment of a memory. She was trying to recall what it was. Laura's back was to the room.

"Christ! No!" Lisa lunged across the disheveled bed, but at the same time there was another sound, louder, over hers. She saw Mike's hand move upward to touch himself, but where? It rose no higher than his chest. It stopped, fell, and he started to topple sideways. There was no more sound. Below, on the terrace outside, some million miles away, the mariachis could be clearly heard, the music fused with the moment.

Lisa, flat on her belly on top of the bed and the coats, lay still. Her mind refused to accept it.

Marty moved first. He stepped forward a few feet and bent down. He looked at Mike for a long time, saying nothing. Years later, he stood, turned to Laura, and held out his hand. She backed away from him. "Give it to me, Laura," he said, his hand outstretched.

She dropped the thing on the floor and shook her head. Marty took another step toward her, and she made a small coughing noise somewhere in the back of her throat. At the moment he touched her arm she sprang at him, beating him with her fists. Her mouth was open, but she made no sound except for her hoarse, rasping breaths as she hit at him again and again.

"For God's sake, Lisa, move!" There was a long scratch on one side of his chin.

She rolled aside as he threw Laura onto the bed and pinned her there, holding her arms. Lisa pulled herself up. As she stood, she saw Mike plainly, his throat wet and red. The top of his white dress shirt was drenched with red, and a dark stain had seeped onto the blue carpet. She looked away.

"My God." The words were her own.

Laura lay quiet now over the jumbled furs, her eyes closed. Marty relaxed his hold on her.

"What can we do?" Lisa asked dazedly.

"Nothing. It's done."

Lisa made a small gesture, trying not to look at the floor.

"No. There isn't anything that would help now."

She turned and walked in the direction of the bedroom door.

"Where do you think you're going?" Marty said in a tone she had never heard from him.

She found herself looking at his mouth, wondering if it was he who had spoken. "To——" She stopped in confusion. "To tell the others what happened."

He came to her and, taking her forearm, seated her on the bed.

"Lisa, think. Think, damn it, before you make a bad mistake. What are you going to tell them?"

She was trying to follow his words. It was difficult to keep up.

"Don't you see? Nothing can be changed now. Nothing can be undone. Are you so sure you want Jack to know everything? And the others?"

It struck her that what he was saying must be important.

"It's done. Understand that. It's happened, and we have to face that part of it. But we have to go on now. What matters is where we go and how we go. So help me God, if you do anything to hurt Laura, to repeat one word of what took place here, I'll see that Jack knows all the details. The whole story."

She glanced at Laura, immobile beside her.

"Think for a minute. What will happen to Laura? What

will happen to you and Jack? Christ Almighty, you have got
to consider the consequences."

"Marty," she said faintly, "be reasonable——"

"Reasonable! Are you so sure? Are you so damn sure you
want everything tied up so neatly? Is it worth gambling your
marriage? Have you thought of what it will mean to you?
And what about Laura? Hasn't she paid her dues already?
Hasn't enough happened to her? Give her a chance. In God's
name, give her a chance. Do you want to make her suffer
more than she already has? It was an accident. Can you understand that? An accident."

"Everything?"

Someone was knocking on the bedroom door.

"All of it. Look after Laura." He went to the door and
opened it a few inches. "Vickie," his voice was low, "don't
come in. Go downstairs and send up Doctor Cochran.
There's been an accident. And don't say anything to anyone
else. Just get the doctor up here immediately." He closed the
door and locked it.

"Prowlers," Lisa said. "He told me they had prowlers.
Maybe just kids, but he bought it to frighten them off. It was
in the other house."

"You'd better pull yourself together."

Lisa went into the bathroom and threw up.

Doctor Cochran was crouched over Mike. Jack stood with
his back to the closed door. Lisa went to him. He put his
arms around her.

Cochran bent over the bed. "Laura." He tried again.
"Laura?" He reached down and slapped her face lightly
twice. She opened her eyes and her mouth, but no sound
came. In a spasm of movement, she hit out at him. "Hold
her."

Marty seized her arms, and the doctor took a syringe from
his bag. "What are you giving her?" demanded Marty. "Will
she be all right?"

"That remains to be seen. This will calm the hysterics."

Jack spoke. "How did it happen?"

"It was an accident," Marty said quietly. "I'm sure she
didn't know there was a bullet in the chamber." He touched
the cut on his chin. "I tripped in the upstairs hall. Lisa was in
the bathroom fixing her face, and I went in to see if I could
do something about this." Briefly, he glanced at the smear of

blood on his fingers. "When I came out, Laura had that." He nodded toward the black object on the floor. "She was joking with us. She pointed it and cocked it, and then, of course, she started to lower it. But Mike had come into the room behind her. She hadn't heard him, and when he spoke, it startled her. It happened just as she turned around."

"Laura," Doctor Cochran asked her, "did you hear what Marty said? Is what Marty said correct?"

She stared up at him. "Yes." She nodded weakly.

"Dear God," said Jack

Lisa began to cry.

"Have the police been called?" Cochran asked.

"I phoned them before you came upstairs," Marty answered. "They're on their way."

From under the bed came a whining sound. The small white dog emerged out of the draped spread, keening miserably. It looked around, confused, and settled at Laura's feet.

"Get the dog out of here," Jack said. "Give it to the maid, Lisa. I'll go down and get rid of everyone."

She picked up the whimpering dog and followed him.

Calmly, unhurried, Jack moved among the guests. He sent Lisa and the maid upstairs to get the coats. There was no more music. When had it stopped, wondered Lisa. A man and woman were arguing at the foot of the stairs. "Like hell you're going to drive!" he shouted. Arnold Kramer intervened and escorted them to the front doors. The sound of hushed conversation echoed through the foyer as people streamed out, looking upward in curiosity. Gradually the crowd thinned. Lisa stood close to Jack. Obie and Ruth joined them with a polite, soft-spoken young man in uniform. They were asked to go up to the second floor.

"The doctor gave her some kind of tranquilizer," Marty was saying to the officer standing by the bed.

"It was advisable," Cochran put in. "She was quite incoherent."

Peggy Smart sat rigidly on the blue velvet chair, her reddened eyes turned from the policemen bending over the form on the carpet.

"Shall we go into the hall?" the officer suggested to Marty.

They stood in an awkward cluster. The sounds of the last departing guests reached them from the open stairwell.

Marty repeated what he had told the doctor.

Lisa could add little. It had been chilly, she said, and she had gone for her coat. "It was a terrible," she fought back the tears, "accident."

With Cochran's permission, the officer returned to the bedroom to speak to Laura. Lisa stood leaning against the door jamb. He asked Laura several questions, repeating them over and over. "I don't remember," she said, the words indistinct and slurred. Doctor Cochran finally put a stop to it.

"Does she need anything?" Marty asked. But she had fallen back to sleep.

Obie edged into the doorway. "She can't stay here. Ruth and I will take her to our house unless," he looked to Sam Cochran, "you think she should go to a hospital."

The doctor shook his head. "We can make that decision tomorrow. The disturbance may only be temporary, due to shock. She may snap right out of it. It might be better if she came to among friends. Bring your car up to the door. I'll ride with you and give you a hand."

They carried her downstairs. She didn't wake. Past the stragglers, the caterers, the musicians. The mariachis in their *charro* outfits, the bartenders and the parking attendants in their serapes.

In a corner of the hall, Claire Poland broke off the conversation she was having with one of the policemen. She observed the procession silently, then brought out a notepad and began to write on it.

But the thing that Lisa remembered was the look on Marty's face. He stood in the doorway at the top of the steps, the light from the candelabra moving over his features, watching the car drive slowly away. He stared after it as if, she thought, he were trying to draw it back by some superhuman exercise of will.

No one spoke.

THE INCREDIBLE STORY
OF A MAGNIFICENT REBEL
WHO WOULD LIVE FREE...
OR NOT AT ALL!

THE INTERNATIONAL BEST SELLER
NOW A POCKET BOOK

"A tale of adventure such as few of us could ever imagine, far less survive."—Book-of-the-Month Club News

Over 20 weeks on *The New York Times* BEST SELLER LIST

FOR THE FIRST TIME IN PAPERBACK

HAROLD ROBBINS' LATEST BEST SELLER

With all the excitement of *The Carpetbaggers* and all the power of *The Adventurers*, **THE INHERITORS** is the gripping inside story of how the communications empire in America has been forged. Harold Robbins takes readers behind the imposing corporate altars on which careers, reputations, and even lives are sacrificed. Here are the headline-makers who lust after position and world prominence: legendary moguls of movie production; self-made tycoons; hustlers; financiers and bankers—modern-day adventurers who have clawed their way to the glittering top of this colossal industry.

And don't forget the other seven Robbins' blockbusters with sales totaling over 70,000,000 copies!